MESSALA

To Harolyn
Best Wishes!
From Lois Scouten

MESSALA

THE RETURN FROM RUIN

A SEQUEL TO BEN~HUR

LOIS SCOUTEN

BPS books

Toronto and New York
www.bpsbooks.com

Published in 2011 by
BPS Books
Toronto and New York
www.bpsbooks.com
A division of Bastian Publishing Services Ltd.

ISBN 978-1-926645-66-7

Cataloguing-in-Publication Data available from Library
and Archives Canada.

Cover: Gnibel
Text design and typesetting:
Daniel Crack, Kinetics Design, www.kdbooks.com

ACKNOWLEDGMENTS

I very much appreciate the help I received from my publisher Don Bastian and his assistants Richard Hicken and Monica Kanellis in preparing my novel for publication.

CHAPTER ONE

ABOUT twelve years ago I was enjoying my service as a tribune in Antioch, the greatest city in the province of Syria. I had won some military honours, but for more than a year I had had time to practise driving my quadriga, my four-horse chariot. After winning several local races, I'd rewarded myself with a magnificent gold-decorated chariot and a black and white team that almost had wings. Life was great – except for the odd ugly memory of things that weren't my fault.

That August, Antioch was the host city for special summer games presided over by the consul Maxentius, prior to his beginning a campaign against the Parthians and their local allies. There would be contests of amateur athletes as well as professional gladiatorial combats, some of them to the death.

The most publicized event was a chariot race with competitors from different countries, and of course I chose to enter with my four – two black stallions and two white trace mares. I knew a little about my rivals; they were quite good but I really believed I was better.

A last-minute entry was a Jew named Ben-Hur, driving four bay Arabians for a desert sheik named Ilderim, a vocal opponent of

Rome, though he had once signed a peace treaty with us – in a spirit of total insincerity.

I knew Ben-Hur from years before. He had been my best friend and boyhood companion when I was living with my father in Jerusalem. He had cause to hate me as I had given evidence against him after his failed attempt to assassinate Valerius Gratus, the Roman procurator of Judaea. He'd been sent to the galleys without a public trial, and his mother and sister had been imprisoned. More than three years had passed since then, and I had assumed that he'd perished at sea.

Now it was a considerable shock to see him again in the Grove of Daphne and to learn a little later not only that he'd been restored to full liberty but that he'd been adopted by the Roman naval commander Quintus Arrius, whose name he wasn't shy about using when it was convenient.

His object in racing against me was obviously to humiliate and destroy me for revenge and to shame Rome in the eyes of the excit-able eastern world we were trying to subdue. I should have been more vigilant in anticipating his tactics. And I should certainly have been more discreet about my expectations of winning the race.

He approached me through Sanballat, a crafty Samaritan with Roman citizenship who acted as manager of supplies for the consul's army. As a matter of pride, in the presence of fellow officers, I agreed to Sanballat's proposed bet. Six gold talents if I failed to beat Ben-Hur and his splendid Arabians. I accepted his odds of six to one, and I didn't even bother to point out that I would still be obliged to pay even if neither of us won whereas Ben-Hur, Sanballat's employer, would have to pay only if I won – and then only one gold talent.

Six gold talents! Though a silver talent is valued at twenty-five hundred sesterces, one talent of gold is worth about two hundred thousand sesterces. Six of them would amount to one million, two hundred thousand sesterces. More than enough to get a man into the Senate. I had very little more than that although Gratus had given me the customary informer's reward for turning in Ben-Hur. I'd thought of using the money to make a name for myself before leaving military service and following my father and half-brother into the political course of honour.

I saw Ben-Hur in the grove and, though I didn't immediately recognize him, I couldn't help but notice his hostile glare. It was the same day I met Iras for the first time. She was strikingly beautiful, with shining blue-black hair, uncovered, contrary to the customs of the East. She had enormous almond eyes and golden skin with the tones of a peach ripened in the gardens of Persia or India, though I guessed that her homeland was Egypt. I looked at those passionate eyes, the rose-tinted full lips, and said silently, "Girl, you are for me!"

I expressed it more formally when I spoke to her. "Not knowing your country, I don't know to what Gods I may commend you, so by all the Gods I will commend you to – myself!"

Judah Ben-Hur, now my enemy, was politely filling a water cup for her old father. "I am your most willing servant," he said, eager to please. Not that she wanted a willing servant. She was gracious to him and I ignored him.

The attraction between Iras and me was powerful – the call of like to like, the male and female lead wolves recognizing their natural mates. It didn't matter what Balthazar, her old father, might have had in mind for her. We had a few secret days and nights getting to know each other. She was eighteen years old and she'd had some previous experience with a lover in Egypt, whom her father had rejected. Now, she declared, her first love seemed long ago and far away.

I could laugh with Iras while facing the greatest danger of my life. I never lied to her, never misled her about my problems with Ben-Hur, with whom she was also becoming acquainted. I don't know if it's possible to be completely fair to an adversary under such circumstances (or why I want to be fair to him anyway), but I know I never implied that he hated me without cause. She recognized without my telling her that part of our conflict was political, ideological – Roman imperialism versus Jewish nationalism. Being an alert young woman with a talent for eavesdropping on her father's friends, she soon found out that Ben-Hur was a revolutionary, conspiring with the excitable Arab Sheik Ilderim.

Then there was the chariot race. I won't review all the details turn by turn around the long central pillar, the spina. Nor will I report all the gory accidents and dirty tricks which are typical of chariot races. However, I was maintaining a lead to almost the very end, and if Ben-Hur hadn't deliberately taken off my wheel, I'd most certainly have won. He cut me off, catching my outer wheel with his inner one and causing my chariot to crash. I was lucky to escape with my life. Well, perhaps lucky isn't quite the word for it. I was a ruined man with a ruined body. Because of my reckless bet, I owed Sanballat – really Ben-Hur – a vast sum. Once I paid him, I'd be nearly destitute. And I was hopelessly crippled.

Hours after the race Iras came to my bedside with tears flowing and voice trembling.

"My darling, what has that despicable Jew done to you?"

"I can't move my legs. The doctors say I'll never walk again."

From her desperate wailing, she might have been keening over my corpse. But she pulled herself together.

"They must be wrong. Wait and see! Dearest, name it: What can I do for you?"

I held her hand. "You came to me. You didn't run to – congratulate the victor."

"The victor!" she laughed. "The pompous, handsome fool, smug in his crown of leaves! I waved my fan at him – to let him think I favoured him. But all the time I was saying to myself, 'Iras, what a liar you are.' You know, he thinks he's the God of Israel's gift to women, that he can take his pick of me or the mousy little daughter of the merchant Simonides."

Her laughter became almost hysterical. "Wouldn't he be amazed if he knew I was here with you?"

I couldn't laugh with her; I was struggling with a strong wave of pain. The doctor had come back in; he said something about not upsetting the patient.

"It's all right. Let her stay. I can't be – any more upset than I already am. Iras, I wouldn't care if you brought in professional mourners to practise for my funeral."

"Don't say that. You aren't going to have a funeral. Mother Isis, have pity! You mustn't think of dying."

Then she became practical. "I could get very close to Ben-Hur. My father is a good friend of both the Sheik and Simonides. What if I put poison in your enemy's wine? I know a little about poisons."

"No, Iras. Absolutely no! They'd trace it to you – you could wind up nailed to a cross. But I have another idea. What if you made a date with him – and then broke it?"

"Broke a date with him?"

"For me, love! Just arrange to meet him, perhaps at the Palace of Idernee. Say your father is taking a suite there. I can have someone – take care of him."

That didn't work out very well. I gather Ben-Hur bought off the chief assassin, a gladiator named Thord, who later opened a wine shop in Rome with what he had collected from both of us. It must have been his assistant assassin, conveniently Jewish looking, even circumcised, who provided the corpse. I will never know if he died trying to carry out his obligation to me (may the Gods rest his soul) or if Judah and Thord picked him for the body whether he liked the idea or not.

Later my old mentor, Valerius Gratus, the former procurator of Judaea, disgusted at my failure, commented, "Since you couldn't go and identify the remains yourself, why didn't you have the gladiator bring you the Jew's head? That's the best way of making sure an assassination is carried out properly."

No doubt! He would've known. Even if it had crossed my mind, I think I would have said no. I was miserable enough without seeing Judah's bloody dripping head. And what would I have done with it afterwards?

So Ben-Hur went on, still determined to mount an armed rebellion against Rome. Iras and her father met him travelling in the desert. She made a plausible excuse for the broken date and pretended to be delighted to see him. He was completely taken in by her. I don't think her old father had a clue what she was really up to.

After recovering his family home in Jerusalem, which had been confiscated when he'd been arrested and sent to the galleys, Ben-Hur rented it to Balthazar, Iras' father, whose astrological studies had convinced him that a great king of the Jews was about to appear.

And I, meanwhile, left my Roman lawyer in charge of my appeal to Tiberius Caesar against the claims of Judah's wily agent, Sanballat, to collect the large amount I had bet on the race. How could I have been such a fool? I knew I'd lose my case when it came before the Emperor unless I could get my adversary convicted of high treason. His criminal record would be remembered against him even though he'd been freed from the galleys by the commander Quintus Arrius, whose life he'd apparently saved. My idea was to have my lawyer stall the hearing as long as possible while I tried to obtain the necessary evidence against Ben-Hur.

Instead of going home to Rome, I returned to Judaea where I'd spent my boyhood when my father was stationed there as legate to the governor of Syria. I went to work for the new procurator, Pontius Pilate, a decent enough fellow. I ran a propaganda operation from my desk – and ran it very well. Of course I had considerable cooperation from the Jewish High Priest, Caiaphas. I believe that Caiaphas and I saved Rome from a bloody Judaean war. Our agents kept us – and I kept Pilate – informed about everything the rebels were doing. They also did their best to undermine the confidence of Judah's secretly trained troops.

Their job was made easier because Ben-Hur had the crazy idea that a carpenter, Jesus of Nazareth, would fulfill Balthazar's prophecy and become the king of the Jews, leading them to victory and getting rid of the Romans. My agents, supposedly Ben-Hur's loyal soldiers, made a point of telling their mates about all the puzzling things the Nazarene had said and done. For example, he declared that it was proper to pay taxes to Caesar and criticized the priestly leaders of his own people, as though reform of the Jews were his only real concern. In fact, I never knew him to speak out against Rome, though his followers were often a different story. In the end, Pilate wanted to set him free – but didn't.

Finally everything happened at once. I had to go home to Rome to pay off my disastrous bet. My lawyer had been compelled to argue my case without me, and the Emperor was outraged that I hadn't had the courtesy to appear before him. He accepted no excuses. Never mind that Sanballat was also represented by counsel, not in person, as he was in Antioch assisting the merchant, Simonides, Ben-Hur's financial manager. Tiberius Caesar made scathing comments on my conduct, saying I'd disgraced the Roman Empire.

Miserable old hypocrite! He had no idea that all the time I was struggling to *save* the Roman Empire. Judah had three so-called legions in the hills, ready to come down during Passover week and seize Pontius Pilate as hostage. I had warned Pilate and Caiaphas; the military and religious authorities were on defense alert.

Jesus entered Jerusalem in triumph as crowds shouted Hosanna (whatever that is), but no military display at all. He said nothing that could be taken as a call to revolution. Instead, the next day, he attempted to clean up the Temple market, as though the Jews were dishonouring their own God. Most of Judah's glorious troops deserted immediately. He couldn't possibly have carried out his revolution. And much of his failure was due to my hard work. My agents, Jews handpicked by Caiaphas and his trusted associates, were quick to get the news to the revolutionaries of Jesus' peaceful entry into Jerusalem and his behavior in the Temple Court. They heard how Jesus had looked at the cheering crowd in sorrow and lamented over them like a Jewish Cassandra whose inner eye saw something like the flames of Troy.

Caiaphas and the other temple leaders played an active part in what followed. They were obliged to show their loyalty to Rome by dealing with their own, so they pounced on Jesus as a convenient sacrifice. They insisted he was a dangerous troublemaker, and they pushed for the release of a chieftain named Barabbas, a genuine rebel. We didn't stay for the execution. Iras and I left Jerusalem that same day to sail from Caesarea to Rome.

Before leaving, Iras had a nasty scene with Judah Ben-Hur. I had asked her to strike a deal with him – not a bad deal either. Cancellation of the bet in return for our silence about his failed revolution. After all, he had considerable incentive to settle down and be a good Roman citizen; he had even been adopted by Admiral Quintus Arrius, now deceased, and owned an estate at Misenum on the Bay of Neapolis. However, Iras wouldn't share his peaceful life; she told him the truth about her feelings – that she never loved him, she loved me.

We had agreed not to tell him that I was in Jerusalem or that I'd actively worked against him. Our blackmail would be based only on the information she'd picked up herself, much of it through his fatuous boasting to her. Whereas he might pay a reasonable amount to ensure the silence of good old Balthazar's daughter, he'd probably react with murderous fury if he knew how I was involved in the defeat of his rebellion and how easily I could be got at. He'd do his best to keep me from reaching Caesarea alive, especially if he thought I had notes on his revolutionary activities.

I hated the idea of bargaining with him, including the appeal to his imaginary spirit of generosity. As soon as Iras had set out, I wanted to send a servant to call her back and tell her to forget the whole thing – we could manage some other way. No blackmail, no promises to Rome's enemy and mine. Instead we would tell Aelius Sejanus, the Emperor's chief minister, all we knew.

Another idea I considered – but not seriously enough – was telling Iras goodbye and going to Rome without her. My family would've been happier and more willing to help me with Iras out of the picture. In hindsight, it's clear it would've been the best choice.

When Iras told me what she'd said to him, my first thought was, "Are you crazy?" I certainly didn't intend her to infuriate Ben-Hur by ridiculing him and demanding reparation about four times as much as the actual bet.

"I told him the money would be repayment for the kisses that should have been only for you," Iras said.

"Sweet Venus, woman, what would you have charged if you'd gone to bed with him? You didn't, did you?"

I had never felt easy about her pretended love affair with him, but reassured myself that he was busy drilling his volunteers in the desert hideout, and that when he did have free time in Jerusalem, he spent most of it discussing religion with old Balthazar.

"Of course I didn't sleep with him! How can you ask? I've made love only with you. Ben-Hur didn't succeed in taking that away from you."

It had been some comfort to me that not all my functions below the waist were ended when the iron wheels and pounding hoofs turned my back into a sight for a butcher's block. It was just my legs I couldn't move. They gave me only a few tantalizing hints of sensation.

Once Iras had calmed down, she told me what he had said. He went on and on in a fury about all the various wrongs he considered I'd done to him and his family. I wasn't guilty of *every* vicious deed he accused me of, but in all fairness, he did have cause to feel wronged – enemy of Rome though he certainly was. I know how I would've viewed things if I'd been in his shoes – which I suppose I could wear as we are about the same size.

He even threatened Iras that if pushed to the wall, he'd go and work for Rome's long-time foe, Parthia.

I'm not likely to forget his message of defiance. It was a masterpiece of gloating self-righteousness and malice. I hoped never to see his smug face again. I swore I wouldn't accept a cup of water from him even if I were dying of thirst.

Iras wondered if I should accuse him to Pilate. So far I hadn't named him in my reports except for the assumed name he used with his trainees. Having been adopted by a high-ranking Roman, he could have claimed full rights as a Roman citizen, and things could have gone all wrong. Pilate had some concern about civil rights and the problem of reasonable doubt. But if we took the story to Sejanus, he wouldn't burden himself with scruples. Caring only about his own advantage, whether political or financial, he was likely to pounce without warning and convict a rich Jew without due process on scanty or even spurious evidence. He may have done this with a few relatives of Caesar himself. He was willing to scheme his way to more and more power.

Years ago, at seventeen, Ben-Hur had apparently pushed a roof tile down on the head of Valerius Gratus and started a riot. He insisted it was an accident. It's possible, I suppose, though it didn't look like it. Anyway, Gratus had the power to dispense with certain formalities, such as a trial, and sent him to the galleys. His mother and sister went to prison. It seems he attributed his good luck in regaining his freedom, property, and money, and being reunited with his mother and sister to the favour of his God, the one true divinity in the world. In the old stories Gods sometimes took an interest in special individuals, but I don't know why one would bother with him.

There was something he didn't know. I kept a leather case full of information about him and his attempted revolution. It might be sufficient to convict him even without Iras' testimony. Although he had used an assumed name with his troops, two men Caiaphas had planted in his army wrote depositions to the effect that they recognized him as Prince Judah Ben-Hur, the head of a noble house. One of the men had been his neighbour at the time of the tile incident; the other said he had attended Bet Talmud classes with him when they were growing up.

In Rome I showed my report to Aelius Sejanus. He said, "This is most impressive, Messala, but we'd better wait till the fellow slips up and comes back to Italy."

Personally, I suspect that Sejanus was being regularly paid off now that Judah was fabulously wealthy. His affairs were being managed by Simonides, the crippled merchant. The Hur/Simonides organization controlled enormous merchant fleets in both the Mediterranean Sea and the Indian Ocean, as well as large caravans that went practically everywhere. And that wasn't all. He had mines in Spain and Sicily, real estate all over the civilized world, and who knew what else.

As it turned out, Sejanus did not have many more days of power before his whole world crashed completely and finally.

CHAPTER TWO

AFTER a brief informal marriage ceremony in Caesarea, Iras and I sailed to Rome. Though we had good weather, I didn't enjoy the voyage. On land I'd been capable of some activity. I could swim at the baths, though I hated displaying my scars. I could also ride a horse, if a couple of slaves helped me mount. Once in place, my legs stayed put, secured by foot-rests attached to a harness.* I'd even begun to try out a pair of crutches which functioned as extensions of my arms. My legs dragged along; I couldn't do anything with them. On the boat, I was absolutely dependent on Iras and my slaves. I had to be pushed in a chair or carried in a litter.

Moreover, although I'd saved my country, I was returning to Rome in dishonour. I could imagine the disappointment of my family and the disgust of my peers. I was the Roman who had not only lost a chariot race to a Jew but had made matters worse by resisting payment of a bet and by failing to commit suicide. And I was a poor man.

We were at my family home, my father's house, for less than a month. Before leaving Judaea I'd paid off my bet, sending a money

---

*The Romans didn't have stirrups, but apparently Messala devised something along the same lines.

draft to Sanballat in Antioch, thankful not to have to see his trium-phant sneer. Next I tried to work out an arrangement with my elderly father whereby I could receive an advance on my inheritance as a younger son. The greater share of my father's estate would go to my elder half-brother, Barbatus.

Father, never demonstrative, was cordial but displeased. The whole business of the chariot race was bad enough, but I'd also been a fool not to come home right away and get the bet paid off. And had married Iras, an Egyptian who looked and behaved like the popular image of Cleopatra.

My brother was coldly polite, and his wife, Domitia Lepida, was resentful of Iras. Though told that Iras was the daughter of a well-born Egyptian, Lepida persisted in intimating that I'd picked up my bride in an Antioch bordello.

My father was willing to give me an allowance and let me use a rural villa. He would've done more than that for me if I'd divorced Iras and sent her back to Egypt. He planned to give her a settlement of ten thousand sesterces. I seriously considered this; it really would have been better for Iras as well as for me. Even she was almost ready to see the wisdom of our parting, since I couldn't give her the social advantages that a wealthy patrician's wife would expect. The best she could hope for was a quiet life of rural retirement with enough money to live on. Iras still seemed to love me, but she was torn by her natural ambition.

Unfortunately, the green silk bag containing her best jewellery disappeared from the drawer where she had put it. Iras accused Lepida of taking it, and the two women got into a screaming match which deteriorated into a brawl. From my chair, I tried to pull Iras away from Lepida, while my brother and a couple of slaves did what they could to separate them. By that time the women had scratched each other, and Iras was holding a handful of Lepida's blonde hair.

As a result, Barbatus protested to our father, who was forced to give me an ultimatum: Either divorce Iras and send her away, or leave the house with her and fend for myself with no help from my people. We no longer had the jewellery, except for a box of coin necklaces and pretty ornaments of small value, and the money Father offered her was now only five thousand, not ten. Not much of a dowry if she wanted to remarry.

Despite a mind well-trained in the philosophy of self-interest, I wasn't prepared to abandon her like that. She had continued to love me when the world in general had turned against me. So we left together and got a fairly decent apartment that accommodated us along with Iras' maid and two male slaves for my chair litter. I had some money, but it wouldn't keep us long. I had to find another source of income.

Sejanus came to our rescue. He may have been bribed by the enemy, as Judah had hinted he would be, but it was his nature to work both sides. He gave me a modest government job at a desk, nothing very important, but it paid me a living wage. So we lived for a year. Then suddenly Sejanus was convicted of treason – a conspiracy against the Emperor, no less – and put to death; his young children were also killed. His excessive ambition had catapulted him to destruction. In the midst of the chaos, I managed to retrieve my report on Ben-Hur's revolution, then cleaned out my own desk and left my job. I couldn't have kept it after Sejanus' fall.

I was, in a way, almost fortunate to be poor. Over the next two years, many men of wealth and influence known to have been close to Sejanus were arrested and convicted of complicity in his conspiracy. It's true that those who informed on them received rewards from their confiscated estates. But I didn't have anything that anyone wanted, and no one stood to gain from bringing me down any further. Already I'd lost my rank in the equestrian order because my income and total assets had shrunk well below the required four hundred thousand sesterces.

At that point a senator approached me with an offer. He knew I could write well and do research. He had been governor in part of Spain and wanted to write a book about it without doing any of the actual work. A benefit of this assignment was the use of his beautiful villa on Lake Benacus* in northern Italy, a comforting distance from

---

* Now Lake Garda

the Sejanus investigation. He had stacks of notes on his Spanish province and he had kept a diary; he also had a fair library. He just lacked the ability to organize it all into book form. I did my best for him, and he received high praise for a good book.

Those months by Lake Benacus were the happiest of my marriage. Iras and I swam in the lake or went riding along the local trails. The servants treated us like the master and mistress. Even so, we weren't invited to the villas of the neighbours.

Finally my work was finished. We had to go back to Rome, and I had to find employment. Besides being a good writer and researcher (when I have use of a library) I can do accounts. In fact I'm better than most people at keeping track of numerals in my head. Some of my best-paid work in this field has been, you might say, creative. Some businessmen employed me to go through their books in prep- aration for tax audits and to give advice to investors, some of it clipping close to the boundary of what is legal. Unfortunately, there are plenty of slaves and freedmen who can do that sort of thing very well, and they have permanent positions as private secretaries.

There was another way I could have made some money. Iras' beauty attracted attention. Several people approached me, offering to pay me for her sexual favours. I'd been willing for Iras to be friendly and charming to men who might give me remunerative work, but I balked at becoming her pimp. It would mean the final and irrevocable disgrace; it could bar me legally from a status even just above the lowest rank. My family would be completely shamed. It's ironic that, for the rich and secure, sexual license is common- place; most husbands have their mistresses, slave or free, or else they go for pretty boys. Sometimes they delight in both sexes, together or separately. And their wives have their lovers too.

Save myself from beggary by prostituting my foreign wife? I'd have become an object of even more contempt than I already was. Don't think the money wasn't tempting, though. Especially when some people had trouble believing that my no meant no. We received invitations rarely, fewer and fewer as time went on, and I came to expect that whenever someone did ask us to dinner, it was probably in hope that Iras would stay the night. Well before dessert, they would hint broadly at their expectations. Iras and I quarrelled about the behaviour of a hearty but crude tribune named Calvus. She denied encouraging him, but I couldn't help but wonder.

I'd been told that Sanballat, now back in Rome, liked to recount the details of the chariot race when he could collect an interested audience in Thord's bar. He predicted that I'd recover part of my fortune from all the men lusting for Iras. When I heard that, I said, "No, you bastard, never, never, never! I'll find a better way."

My former guide, my first military commander, ex-procurator Valerius Gratus, had managed to go on a long yacht cruise to Greece just before the fall of Sejanus. He stayed away about two years, returning only when he felt safe enough. At first I was pleased that he called on me and seemed concerned about my future.

What a fool I was!

He invited us both to dine at his house, and while Iras was out of the room and we were finishing our wine, he put his proposal plainly.

"I'd be willing to give you a permanent position as my secretary. I'd make an immediate gift to you of fifty thousand sesterces. In return, let me say that I'm strongly attracted to your pretty Egyptian."

"You too, Gratus?" Revolted, I adapted the words of Julius Caesar to Brutus. Seeing Gratus again, I'd been shocked by his increased bulk. His whole body seemed tilted by the pull of his huge belly toward Mother Earth. And his face was so much redder, laced with purple veins all the way to his receding hairline.

Before I could recover my breath, it turned out that he wanted even more.

"This seems like a good time, to be quite frank, Messala. I've always liked you, if you know what I mean. When you were serving with me, I knew you were a ladies' man. I'd seen that, even at all-male parties, you drew the line at certain intimacies. You were too proud to – turn over for any man. I never harassed you; I was content with your work as one of my best officers, and in those days I was more interested in skilled eastern whores. But now – in your condition – you really should consider a more passive role. Actually

I was thinking the three of us could begin a new life tonight – in my steam bath!"

I blurted out the first thing that came into my head.

"What – share your crab lice?"

I knew he'd always been interested in both sexes, but as he said, he'd once seemed to prefer women of the sort that would gladly do whatever a customer could pay for. Now he thought my reversal of fortune would make me more accessible.

He leaned toward me, his sour breath in my face. I backed away, pushing myself with my hands. He couldn't help seeing my revulsion.

Just then Iras came back, and I told her I was tired. With stiff courtesy I thanked Gratus for his hospitality and sent for our litter. Gratus was brusque in his farewell.

Iras and I had drawn apart. She had quite a lot to say about how depressing she found our life. She was convinced her gifts of song and story telling and her conversational powers were given her by the Goddess Isis that she might adorn the highest circles. She believed she belonged in the rare world of princes and great statesmen. She felt herself wasted, particularly when I was inattentive and irritable, as was increasingly the case.

Still, I should have confided in her, told her exactly what I'd refused. But it was so humiliating – to be solicited, doubly solicited, by a former commander and friend whom I'd admired for his hard-headed pursuit of success and his clever cynical speeches. Now he was a physical monstrosity as well as an opportunistic old lecher.

I received a note from him the next day: "Do reconsider your position regarding our conversation of last night."

My position! He'd have taken pleasure in humbling my patrician pride. He was of the Valerian clan, as I am, but the Gratus branch is neither ancient nor distinguished.

My response was simple: "Never!"

And what did the filthy bastard – may he rot in Tartarus – do then? He approached Iras and told her *I* wanted her to pleasure him for one afternoon; he said I was embarrassed and didn't want her to speak of it to me – just to do it. And she did it!

If only she'd told me. The thought of her with that foul body of his! The perfumed oils with which his slaves rubbed him down before the banquet hadn't masked a sickly body odour.

Though she denied it, Gratus probably gave her some money for herself. She may have opened a bank account* that I don't know about, perhaps with a previous contribution from Calvus. Gratus sent me a money draft for two thousand sesterces with a mocking explanatory note to the effect that he was paying more than the value of what he had received: two hours with a not very enthusiastic or innovative female whose charms were fading.

The money would have been useful but I couldn't keep it. I'd be throwing away what remained of my reputation. I could imagine him telling everyone triumphantly, of course saying that I'd consented. Maybe he'd even pretend he'd enjoyed both of us. How my greatest foe would exult if he knew to what level I'd been reduced. I'd go down in the general memory as the crippled pimp. Or even the crippled catamite.

Riding in my chair litter, carried by my two slaves, I went down to the Forum around noon when people would be gathered to read the newest Acta Diurna.† As I expected, there was Gratus in his senatorial toga with the magisterial stripe of purple around the border. Laughing, he declared loudly to a small audience, "Certainly he agreed. He needed the money badly, you see. But I overpaid. The Egyptian isn't half as good as a professional whore."

I controlled my fury, though I was thinking what a pleasure it would be to personally crucify him. I had my bearers approach him. Then I leaned out of the curtains and said, "I have something for you, Gratus."

I handed him a rolled paper, tied with a black string.

In a puzzled tone he said, "What's this?"

"Just unroll it. You'll see."

Stupidly he opened it up in front of everyone and saw his own money draft of two thousand sesterces made out to me. On it I'd

---

*The Romans had a banking system.
†The Acta Diurna was a daily record of political and social events posted in the Forum.

scrawled in large letters with very thick black ink, CULUS*. I'd
considered mixing ink with liquid excrement but didn't – I was too
fastidious, and it would've ruined my pen.

Several people were close enough to read it over his shoulder.
They repeated my message and laughed uproariously.

Calvus guffawed and then sneered, "So Messala doesn't want
your money, Gratus! Are you sure he gave consent? Maybe you
should have paid the woman directly."

Had Calvus done that?

Gratus turned beet red, streaked with purple lines, and scowled
at me. "You'll be sorry for this, Messala! Very sorry!"

I ordered my bearers to take me to my family mansion. I was
ready to divorce Iras for adultery. However, everyone, Father
included, had gone on a cruise to our property in Sicily. So I went
back to our apartment. Back to Iras.

When I confronted her, she was surprised that there'd been no
deal with Gratus. She'd been angrier with me than with him.

"I always said I'd do anything for you. I was trying to keep my
promise, but believe me, I hated it. The smell of his discharge made
me want to vomit."

Maybe I should've sympathized with her, but I couldn't. I'd
always suspected her tendency to keep one step ahead of me, so
much easier with me in a wheelchair. Even the spying on Judah and
the artificial romance with him was something she started before
saying anything to me about it. I knew then I might have a problem
with her eagerness for intrigue and her inclination to lead even the
man she supposedly loved.

I accused her of perverse lust for ugliness combined with wealth
and power. I suggested that she was bored and curious, craving an
excuse for a new experience after nearly three years of marriage to a
man with immobile legs. I poured out my disgust at the thought of
her with that poisonous slug. She had shamed me unforgivably in
front of my peers.

She repeated her apology, then exploded in anger, telling me all

*The anal opening

she had sacrificed for me, all she could have enjoyed if she'd married a whole man, a man with undamaged reputation. A rich, handsome man. And she knew just the man. Judah Ben-Hur!

After that quarrel I couldn't bring myself to make any kind of love to her even though she tried repeatedly to patch things up. Calvus' name came up. She denied that she had had intercourse with him, but she wasn't convincing. When I mentioned to her that Calvus was about to marry a young girl, Iras frowned and said, "I know who she is; I've seen her – an insipid creature."

A few days after the incident in the Forum I lost my accounting position. I was told my services were no longer needed. Then people stopped asking me to collaborate on books or write speeches for them. I was sure Gratus was behind this, though I couldn't figure out how. Surely not everyone would listen to him.

Iras contributed two golden coin necklaces to our financial relief, and in gratitude I tried to be pleasanter to her, though I still didn't want to be her lover. Then suddenly my two male servants and Iras' Syrian maid, whom she had slapped several times, took all the money and jewellery they could get their hands on and ran. I had a small bank account at the Temple of Mercury, not enough to keep up the rent in our modest apartment. So, hiring a litter for my transportation and a cart for our few possessions, we moved to a wretched room on the sixth floor of a ramshackle building in the worst part of the Subura district. It was full of cockroaches, bedbugs and – except in winter – mosquitoes. Not to mention rodents.

I hoped that our home there would be temporary. I composed a letter to my father, who was home again. I apologized for my errors and offered to divorce Iras, provided that she was given a sufficient sum to return to Egypt and live respectably. I don't know why my letter wasn't answered.

Fortunately, some old acquaintances, having left military service, looked me up and gave me work. In the spring, not long after our move, I'd made three hundred sesterces at once doing accounts for a former soldier, who had turned to importing Greek wines. He happened to be breaking a silly restriction in connection with a monopoly held by the Jewish merchant Simonides of Antioch, but with my help was able to get around it.

Then, during the summer, an old classmate, Quintus Metellus Caprarius, who was always awkward with words, decided to quit the army and try for a quaestorship, the lowest rung on the ladder of political honour. He needed help composing three speeches to be delivered in the fall. Although we no longer have real elections, because appointments come from Caesar, candidates still make speeches to demonstrate their ability. Not only did I write his speeches, but I also drilled him on his delivery. He paid me six hundred sesterces.

Moreover, recommended by Caprarius, I received a visit from Sextus Manlius Quadratus, who had finished his military service and was trying to become a lawyer; he also needed help with his maiden speech to a jury. So I wrote it for him and listened to him practising it. For that I got another two hundred sesterces.

My successful labours took care of the rent and food for a time, and I even had a bank balance left over. However, soon it was November, and the thought of winter in our present quarters was oppressive. Summer had been bad enough, with the sweltering heat, the smells, and the noise of the most overcrowded run-down part of Rome. And there was the problem of getting down five flights of stairs, which I had to do almost every day.

Once again I wrote to my father and found someone to deliver the letter – at least he said he did. But no answer ever came. I looked at Iras, her face thinner and lined with bitterness and depression; her beauty was disappearing fast. I looked at my filthy surroundings and asked myself, "Is this the very end of the road? Will I be here until I die?"

CHAPTER THREE

THERE were a few times during the years of my poverty when someone approached me with a proposal to be part of something crooked. My role would've been planning or maybe forging documents, and Iras might have helped trick the victim of the plot. She took to the idea every time and urged me to get involved. It wasn't due to my superior moral principles that I didn't go for these schemes; rather it was that I could see too many flaws, too many unacceptable risks. As for forgery, the penalty is having one's hands cut off. Merciful Gods, if indeed you are sometimes merciful, not my hands too!

In fact, I wasn't offered many supposedly brilliant money-making schemes. Though it might surprise Judah and a few other people, the truth is that my capacity for devious thinking was neither well-known nor sought after. Iras found my attitude frustrating; she wanted me to take risks, to be more daring in pursuit of the fortune she felt I deserved by right of high birth and natural merit.

We lived in a community where, in the midst of squalor, small businesses flourished. Our building was supervised by a ground-floor tenant, a Jew named Reuben, who collected our rent. He had a bakeshop with the chimney detached from our tumbledown nine-storey structure, thus avoiding the fire regulations for the area. None of the tenants had the right to cook; in fact, we could've been evicted for using a charcoal brazier in winter. But we didn't resent the special privilege of Reuben's outdoor establishment which projected into the plaza at the intersection. Instead we bought quite a few cheap meals from him – mostly bread rolls with a filling of vegetables or cheese.

I needed a regular income, even a small one, which could cover basic needs. So I set myself up as a public letter writer, serving people who couldn't write and didn't have educated slaves to do it for them. This is a correct description of quite a few Suburan residents, though not Reuben. Like most Jews, he was literate.

My money came in sesterce by sesterce, or as by as*, several almost every day. Out of it I had to keep buying writing supplies: paper, pen and ink, and sand for blotting, as well as wax tablets and a stylus. I had a workplace on the street corner next to the bakeshop, for which I paid protection money to a local fraternity of thugs. It was outrageous – and they collected frequently.

Crawling down five floors was horribly humiliating. Iras carried a folding chair for me at first – not my wheelchair because it was too heavy. Then I learned to drag the light chair along with me. Sometimes an amiable drunk named Ruso helped, if I could get him in the morning before he was staggering all over the place.

As I mentioned, I could use crutches, moving them with my arms and shoulders, letting my feet drag. I suppose this looked extremely undignified, and it wasn't a safe way to come down a staircase (I know this, having tried a couple of times), but on the ground it gave me some mobility. I could sit outside on my folding chair and write, and if I needed to relieve myself, I could raise myself on my crutches and go down the street a short distance to the public latrine. I got better and better at walking with my arms. My only hope at the time was never to meet anyone from my past – except Caprarius and Quadratus, who were sympathetic.

---

* An as = less than half a sesterce, and four sesterces (or sestertii) = one denarius, an average worker's daily pay.

The trouble is, on the street one is more vulnerable to thieves, who see a cripple as a natural victim. I kept exercising my arms by lifting weights and have surprised more than one thief by my strength. Ruso the drunk liked to get into fights on my side – I don't quite see why, but he did. Still it was dangerous on the streets of the Subura. In a way I was lucky not to have much money on me – not enough for a group of thieves to divide.

Iras helped me for a while, and we got on better when we were sharing a project. But there was no proper outlet for her gifts of singing and dramatic story telling. She thought of teaching and applied to a small select school for little girls but was turned down. She worked for a short time in a small factory where they made straw hats, bags, and other articles. However, she wasn't fast enough at it, and it hurt her hands – so well cared for when I first knew her. I don't know if she quit or was discharged.

She considered telling fortunes, but here it's illegal, though not unheard of. When she did try it, a local witch attacked her for intruding on her territory.

I first realized she'd found a new source of income when I questioned her frequent trips to the public baths, the ones that had mixed bathing. Prostitutes went there to pick up business. We had a furious quarrel, both of us raising our voices. I said, "I'll divorce you. I can manage without you. Just get out of my life – you can whore your way back to Egypt!"

She screamed at me, "It shouldn't matter to you; you don't want me in bed. You've probably become completely impotent now."

I felt like strangling her. Was it true? I didn't want Iras, but I'd felt a stirring within myself (and even in my organ of manhood) for attractive women such as the curvaceous girl who sometimes came down the street selling fruit. Of course, for an act of genital sex I would need help from caressing hands stimulating and guiding me into her most intimate opening.

Iras continued her complaint. "I want nice clothes and jewellery. One way and another, I lost all my jewellery because of you. I hate this life."

"I hate it too! If only I could hear from my people. When I write, they don't answer me. It's as if Father and Barbatus want me to be dead and forgotten."

She gave me a strange look. I thought of renting a litter and going to the family mansion, but what if they turned me away at the door? Unless I could go home to my father's house, it would be difficult to get rid of Iras.

With the coming of winter I sometimes worked in our room, letting people come to me if they would. The room that had been like a furnace in summer was damp and cold in winter and had an evil smell in all seasons. In our previous apartment, there'd been a daily service for collecting everyone's chamber pots and taking them to the public latrine. It cost only a few sesterces each eight-day market interval. Here there was nothing like that, and Iras naturally put off such disgusting tasks. Sometimes I paid a sesterce to a neighbour woman to take care of an otherwise impossible buildup of filth. There were also the smells of stale, greasy food from the street stands (Reuben's was the best).

Business was certainly poorer when I couldn't force myself downstairs into the cold rain and sleet. During January, no one came to see me about any large projects such as speeches. We were falling back on our diminishing savings, which would cover the rent through February but not leave us quite enough for March if we didn't do better. Iras, who'd promised to refrain from whoring, offered to go back to it, and I hoped she wasn't already doing it.

"No, Iras, it wouldn't help us as much as you think – and you'd be exposing yourself to disease. Also, what if people of our own class found out? Consider the shame! No, I have another idea."

Two years before when I helped the senator write his book, I'd met his publisher, Sosius. I had Ruso push my rickety wheelchair through the streets to Sosius' establishment and asked him if there was anything I could write for him – for modest pay.

He replied, "You know the Greek novels that I publish in sections, each one leaving the reader in suspense until the next one comes out? They sell really well. You could give it a try. I'd pay you ten denarii per installment if I like it."

Write a wild, far-fetched romantic adventure? Why not, I thought. It might take my mind off reality for a while. But it certainly wasn't the sort of thing people would expect a Messala to write, considering the dignified literary tradition of my family.

Then Sosius said, "I wish someone would attempt a novel in Latin. It would reach a lot of middle-class readers that don't read Greek well. There are even educated people that would rather read Latin."

We agreed that we wouldn't use my true name because it might embarrass my family. In refusing to divorce Iras, I'd rejected my father's authority as pater familias*. I wondered if I would ever be forgiven. How could I have been so stupid, so stubborn? It would be of little use to divorce her unless I could see that she had money enough to return to Egypt. Without it, she wouldn't go very far away from me.

She'd been so proud of marrying a Roman patrician, even a bankrupt one. Now she was shamed by grim reality. My work as a public letter writer was certainly a comedown; I felt it even more than she did. It would have been all right for me to write history or poetry like my grandfather. But a scribbler of sensational tales? There were many such writers in her native Alexandria, and she could dramatically recite their best stories, but she had small respect for them.

"I could do worse," I said.

Though I hated to do it, I got enrolled with the Head Count citizens of Rome, the poorest people, who collected the welfare grain dole and traded it to the baker for bread and coins. Thus we could count on loaves of bread and augmented them with salad vegetables and sour wine, which we watered down, as most people do.

In March Quadratus came to me, in need of another speech for a court case. He really needed me to work with him on the evidence too so that I was kept busy advising him about leads to follow, as well as writing the speech for him. He won his case and came through with three hundred sesterces for me – it was well-deserved.

At that time I was recovering from the worst cold of my life. It had gone to my chest, and for a while I was afraid of coughing up

---

*Head of the family, a position of high respect in Roman society

some vital organ. I could imagine myself dying of lung rot. I also thought reluctantly of two women – one of them an eloquent patriotic Jewish lady, the other a young girl who had been a shy child. Judah's mother and sister, both of whom had been imprisoned in a concealed lower cell of the Fortress of Antonia in Jerusalem. I'd expected them to die quickly of fever as others had before them; I never intended them to contract leprosy in that cell, as people say they did. But I did expect them to die. Every time I had a coughing fit, I asked myself, "Is this retribution?"

During my sickness I realized that Iras was absent most afternoons and evenings. One day I found a coarse yellow wig, such as prostitutes wear, hidden under the bed in our one-room flat. It must have been very unbecoming to her. I accused her. She admitted it; moreover, she was beginning to think she could be pregnant – she had no idea by whom, but it certainly wasn't by me.

"I thought you were going to die. Anyway, you wanted to get rid of me and make your peace with your family. I was trying to save money to go home."

"You idiot! I would have tried to get my father to give you a settlement – not much, perhaps, but more than you would make on the streets or wherever it is you conduct your business."

At least she hadn't brought anyone back to our place.

"Your father might never answer you. You defied him, and he's hard and unforgiving. A typical Roman! So I made up my mind to get some money for myself."

"Were you very successful? Or did you share your earnings with a pimp?"

She was silent. I snapped at her, "Answer me!"

"Yes, yes!" She began to sob loudly. When she lifted her arm, I saw bruises. Then she defiantly stripped away the upper part of her gown and showed me the black and blue spots on her breasts.

"There's more!" She stepped out of her gown. Her buttocks, belly, and upper thighs also had purple marks.

"It's too bad, Iras, but you brought it on yourself."

"You don't care at all, do you? I wish I had enough to go back to

Egypt. But I've been robbed several times in addition to paying off Sporus. Don't think I've enjoyed it. I've hated it all. I think I hate all Roman men, including you. And now what am I going to do?"

"Iras, I warn you – I won't acknowledge your brat as mine."

"I know that. There's an herb woman who makes potions. It may be early enough to get rid of it that way. Oh, it's such a miserable piece of irony. I used to want *your* child, but we couldn't afford it, so we were careful."

Maybe there was no need to be careful, but we'd paid attention to her lunar cycle and had got into the habit of cutting short some of our mutual satisfaction so the seed couldn't be implanted. The wonder was that the sexual act was possible at all. One doctor found it encouraging; maybe my legs would regain life too. But now it seemed my manhood had failed. For a long time, since she had lain with Gratus, there had been nothing between us. I felt no urge toward Iras.

She was afraid of an abortion, and part of her wanted to bear the child no matter who the father was. She reverted to a favourite theme – if only she had married Ben-Hur!

"If only – I would have had everything: a beautiful home, servants, plenty of money – and we would have had children."

"I wish you *had* married him. It would've served him right."

I remembered something else. "He wouldn't accept another man's child. In fact the Jews stone adulteresses to death; I've seen it done."

She screamed several obscene epithets at me – she had picked up the street vocabulary fast. The remnants of her beauty had vanished over the winter. She was constantly tired, with circles under her eyes, and she was careless of her appearance at home, whatever she may have done to brighten herself up for her customers. I almost told her, "Just go now, Iras! Get back to Egypt any way you can." It would be no use if she didn't have money, not just boat passage but something to live on after she got there. She'd be ashamed to become a prostitute in her native city.

I was considering promising her half of what Quadratus had paid me. But just then she said, "I'll see the herb woman."

That wasn't the end of the topic. She was upset when I began a letter to my father. She pleaded, "Don't shame me before your people. Lepida will mock me and tell her friends."

Indeed I realized that if I explained things to Father, he wouldn't want to give her money to go to Egypt and produce a child she might insist was really mine.

Iras said, "If I did wait and have the baby after all, you wouldn't have Ruso take it to the garbage dump, would you?"

Unwanted babies are often taken there. It's legal. But Ruso is sentimental about babies – and puppies and kittens, and I admit to some qualms myself, though for years I've tried to rise above softer feelings, signs of weakness.

"No, I'd send you away before you ever gave birth; somehow I'd send you to Egypt."

I didn't know how I could accomplish that. But I hated the idea of her giving birth in our small room. I could imagine the screams and the blood.

"You could tell your relatives it was my child – and hope it at least looked Italian, not like a straw-haired barbarian or a black African. Were you at all particular about your sexual partners?"

"You unfeeling brute! You know I can't go back to Egypt pregnant and poor. My father must be dead by now, and my cousins would despise me. You remember, once I wrote to them but they never answered. I have nowhere to go. I have no choice."

She began to cry again. "Father probably died disowning me."

I didn't know the medicine would make her so deathly sick. She bled heavily and could hardly stir from the bed (which I didn't share, preferring my chair and a footstool), and she retched and had prolonged diarrhea. Understandably I crawled downstairs whenever I could, dragging a folding chair with me.

I paid the rent and put some money in my bank – not the Temple of Mercury anymore but a nearby mercantile firm that caters to small accounts. Every market interval I completed an installment of my romantic adventure serial in Latin. Iras wasn't fit for anything; I had to get Ruso to push my chair to the street called the Argiletum, where Sosius has his office and his big room where slaves make copies of manuscripts. He liked my story and gave me ten denarii every time. I always tipped Ruso a couple of sesterces. The last time I went, I couldn't get hold of him, so I made the trip on my crutches, resting on benches a couple of times. I'd never before gone so far with the crutches.

There was another brief crisis involving Iras: the matter of the cat. She had brought in a black female cat that appeared pregnant. Cats were always sacred to her ancestors, Iras said, and now she wanted this particular cat. I wasn't enthusiastic but I agreed. The cat snuggled up to Iras but avoided me – perhaps instinctively.

Then the creature began defecating and urinating all over the room, although Iras took it outside with her twice each day. In the excrement I could see little white pieces and then longer white strips that wriggled. Tapeworms!

Ruso came by, and I asked him to put the cat outside. He had to chase it around the room, but when it stopped for another bowel movement, he caught it and carried it down to the street. Then he told Rebecca, Reuben's wife, of my problem, and she kindly sent a slave to help me clean the room up. I gave the girl a decent tip.

A little later Iras came in, crying and screaming, "You Roman bastard! You cruel brute! You killed my cat!"

"I did not. I had Ruso put it out because it was full of diarrhea." I was hoping she wouldn't find it and bring it back.

"The dogs on the street got Nefertiti and tore her to pieces. I found part of her." She held up a dark-furred object with one leg and a torn head.

"She couldn't have run away fast enough; she was heavy with the kittens inside her. How could you be so cruel?"

"Those weren't kittens. She had tapeworms, which would have killed her. I didn't plan for the dogs to get her."

"You're a typical brutal Roman. If it weren't for your pride, you'd get yourself carried to the Games and use your citizen's pass to watch animals and criminals kill each other. You'd probably laugh while victims were dismembered and devoured."

Actually I've always been rather squeamish about that sort of thing, though, owing to my upbringing, I've been trained to conceal my weakness. There was no use arguing with Iras. She continued to mourn her cat, and we didn't speak to each other.

June came. I'd managed to keep the rent paid, and had been lucky enough to get a couple of windfalls. Quadratus required another speech of summation for a jury, which I dashed off for two hundred sesterces. Then Caprarius came by, wanting help with a report he had to put together and deliver in the Senate. It was to be his first long speech there since his attaining a quaestorship, a minor magistracy. I helped him for another two hundred sesterces. How grateful I have become for anything I can get.

Iras often sat brooding in our room. Her hair, unwashed since she stopped going to the baths, looked lusterless and greasy. Her complexion was sallow and she had a perpetually bitter expression.

When I collected my money from Caprarius, I asked him to take a letter to my father. I wonder if my other letters, entrusted to local messengers, ever reached him. I couldn't believe he didn't care.

One day Iras took a walk to the Forum where she read the daily bulletin, the Acta Diurna. She came home with interesting news which, all things considered, she would have been wiser not to tell me. One of Misenum's leading citizens, Quintus Arrius, the adopted son of the late great admiral, had returned from the East to his seaside villa, next to the Emperor's own residence. At last he was within my grasp! I knew Iras wouldn't help me. Once she would have been my star witness against Ben-Hur, but things had changed. She had come to hate me. In her heart she had gone over to the enemy.

I needed to find someone to take my portfolio on Judah to Macro, who had succeeded Sejanus as Prefect of the Praetorian Guard. I thought of asking Ruso to help, supposing he could keep sober long enough. Revenge was beginning to look possible after all. Not a reward – Macro wasn't a generous man. But he could be counted on to use my information.

But what would life hold for me after that? What would I have to live for if I destroyed him? Nothing. I couldn't walk, I was poor

– every wretched day was a humiliation. My family didn't care. They continued to ignore my letters. It was as if I didn't exist.

On occasion I imagined strange sensations in my legs, a change in the usual semi-numbness. But there was nothing I could be sure of. Nothing that responded to my will. When I told Iras, she laughed – how I've learned to hate her laugh – and said I was having delusions, perhaps even losing my mind! When she said that, I shouted at her to go away out of my sight and leave me alone. She went out for about an hour but returned just as I was beginning to hope she had left me for good.

How I longed to fall asleep for the last time, knowing I'd never have to crawl or slide down five flights of dirty stairs again, never have to sit on a street corner hoping someone might pay me a sesterce to write a long letter, never have to be grateful when an old classmate came to the slums and generously paid me two hundred sesterces for composing a speech or report for which he would get the credit.

I decided that once my revenge was sure, I'd use my dagger on myself. Iras could take everything of value and try to get back home. She should have done it long ago. Instead, our marriage, even before the incident with Gratus, had been full of cloying declarations of unselfish love demanding unflagging gratitude, mixed with the inevitable belittling comments about what a failure I was. How I ruined all her dreams. I admit, I was not at my best then either. I'd lost all my feeling for her. Not just sexual feeling but sympathy, liking. In fact I couldn't stand her.

I wondered if she intercepted any of my letters to my father. The men of the Subura who specialize in taking letters and messages were all greedy for an extra sesterce or two; they might well have taken my pay and then handed over the letter to Iras for just a little more. She might have even offered them quick sex. Now, if I'd asked Ruso, he would have been loyal to me, but he might have turned up at my family mansion dead drunk – or he might not have got there at all. Ruso had his good and bad days.

She would hardly have been able to prevent Caprarius from delivering my letter. What if my sweet sister-in-law, Domitia Lepida, had got hold of it and destroyed it?

I knew, whatever happened, I would like things to be neat and rounded off properly. So I had to first finish the final chapter of the story I'd been writing for Sosius, *Strephon and Dynamene*, a tale of romance and adventure by Incognitus.

After that the problem would be getting the portfolio to Macro, which was as difficult as getting in touch with my family. But, assuming my family still cared about me, would they want me to approach Macro? His attention was dangerous. It would be wisest to defer my revenge for a while. If I could have found some real help, I wouldn't have minded.

I knew I couldn't rely on hearing from my family. I decided that, when I committed suicide, I'd leave a note for them and hope they cared enough to arrange my funeral. My immediate problem was Iras. She knew I was thinking about Quintus Arrius (alias Ben-Hur) in his fine villa by the sea in Misenum.

What if she tried to warn him?

CHAPTER FOUR

THE day I will never forget, I'd awakened early to June sunshine coming in our narrow window. It promised to be a very hot day. I'd slept, as was my custom, on my chair with my feet on a stool. Next to me a bowl of tepid water sat on a small table. I washed, put some oil on my jaw, and then shaved clumsily, looking into the little metal mirror on the wall.

How thin I had become, my cheekbones like ridges, my eyes sunken into deep caverns under straight, slightly slanting brows. Shaving revealed the lines around my mouth, the hollows above my jaw, and the pallid weariness of my whole face.

Just bathing my face and hands in water from the basin didn't satisfy me. I thought about getting Ruso to push my chair to the free public baths, then to Sosius' publishing office, and finally my bank. Every now and then I reached the point where I couldn't stand just washing from a basin – I wanted to get really clean all over.

At the baths, instead of tipping a bath slave, we helped each other, rubbing on the oil and scraping it off with a metal strigil. Ruso helped me in and out of the warm and cold pools. I hated exposing my scars to public view, I still do, but with Ruso it was different. He apparently thought I'd faced a charge of British war chariots brought across the Channel to assist rebel tribesmen in Northern Gaul.

The problem was – really there were two problems. One was that my chair was getting more rickety every trip. If it had been a chariot I wouldn't have driven it; I'd have sold it for kindling wood and scrap metal.

The other problem was Ruso. In the morning he wasn't bad, though hardly the sort of companion I would have had in my days of prosperity, but if he had a chance to drink – and refreshments were always on sale at the baths – he'd be confused on the way home. All my patience and alertness from my days of driving would be called on to keep him on course. "Slower, Ruso. Slow up as you come to the corner, then make a left. Don't get the wheel caught between those blocks at the pedestrian crossing."

I have never in my life tried to drive a drunken horse – but the closest thing was steering Ruso home. I could only hope no old acquaintance saw us.

If he drank *too* much, we wouldn't get home at all before the next morning; we'd have to spend the night on the street, despite all its nocturnal dangers. Once Ruso imagined we were in the Teutoberger Forest, separated from our legion, watching out for German snipers behind phantom trees. At times like that I could feel myself slipping over the edge into Ruso's fantasy world. Someone listening to us might have thought we were both out of our minds.

I sat and viewed my wretched dirty room. That June day in the Subura I had no prospects of anything better. It was my only reality, and I had to live with it – damn it!

I shook off my self-pity and got my crutches, carefully positioned them upright, and pulled myself up so that I had one under each armpit and could drag my body across to the shelves to get some dry bread and sour wine. I thought of buying a fresh loaf from Reuben, but I had no appetite.

There was no sign of Iras that morning. The wooden bed hadn't been slept in; the covers were bunched the same way they had been the day before. The bed once had a straw tick, but we threw it out because of the bedbugs.

Maybe that was the reason I'd been able to sleep so long. No hoarse breathing to waken me.

The previous day I'd given her a little money and said, "Go to the baths, Iras. The place with morning hours just for women."

She was indignant. "Do you think anyone would want me now? The prostitutes at the mixed baths are all fine-looking. I'd be laughed at, for sure."

"Well, go to the women's session, as I said, and see if there's anything they can do for your hair and skin. I can't stand looking at you the way you are."

She could get in free but having a beauty treatment while she was there cost money.

She looked better when she came home. Her skin was cleaner, her hair had been washed, trimmed, and styled, and her nails had been manicured so that they were no longer jagged and grey-black. But the lines on her face were still visible, dragging down her mouth and furrowing her brow. Worse, she must have got the wrong idea.

She'd been drinking and was in her sexy, sentimental mood, not her cynical, complaining mood. She suggested that we get together on the bed and try to revive old feelings. She seemed to think I must have had sex in mind when I gave her the money for the baths, though it was certainly not the first time I'd given her the money to get cleaned up decently.

"Are you crazy? It's been more than two years. I can't make love to you."

"Maybe you don't know yourself. Remember that first autumn, after the chariot race – how we lay together and I used my hands and lips to restore your manhood?"

She slipped off her gown and posed provocatively with one hip thrust forward, her legs somewhat apart. She still had a good figure, though it was thinner than it used to be. Slim-hipped, and with good breasts.

It had been a thrill that day in Antioch when I found I could … rise to the occasion sufficiently to penetrate her a little.

But this time I couldn't respond. She came over to me and started touching me, slurring her endearments. She smelled like sour wine mixed with terrible cheap perfume. Close up, her skin was coarse-pored under thick paint, and the black eye-shadow was grotesque. I said, "Don't!" and pushed her hands away.

I'd be risking what remained of my health, entering where the Gods knew what filthy scum had gone before me. Moreover, I knew I couldn't.

She pleaded, "Can't we try?"

"Iras, it's too late for us. Go to bed – alone! I don't want you."

She broke into loud weeping, then went to the shelves and found a thin red dress slit up the side. I said, "Are you going out on the streets again? You promised to give that up!"

She put on a yellow wig, the badge of prostitutes.

"You don't want me; you make me feel ugly and worthless. I've been depressed for a long time. Yes, I'm going out!"

"Then go! I'm going to divorce you. I should have done it before." As I spoke, I wondered how I could actually get rid of her – it didn't look as if there'd be any help from my family.

Looking around the room the next day, I wondered if she was gone for good. I was afraid to get my hopes up.

I didn't want any wine. I decided to get myself downstairs, work for a while, and see if Ruso turned up. If he didn't, I'd try to make my own way to Sosius' establishment.

I wore dark tunics because they don't show the dirt as much. For the trip downstairs, crawling and sliding, with my work materials in a bag around my neck, I wore my over tunic, letting it pick up dust. I dragged the crutches with one hand. At the bottom of the five flights, I removed my dusty over tunic and put it into the bag. Really the under tunic wasn't very clean either.

I hadn't brought my folding stool, so I sat on the curb and got out my writing supplies. I had a good hour of letter-writing and made four sesterces, which made up for what I'd handed to Iras yesterday. Ruso didn't appear, so I had to go to see Sosius on my own.

I got up on the crutches, wishing as usual that I could better feel the cobblestones under my feet, even under the tops of them as they dragged along. Uphill, rest, downhill, rest, and on to the Argiletum and Sosius' offices.

Sosius welcomed the final manuscript with its absurdly happy ending. He paid me the ten denarii, equal to forty sesterces, and then said, "Listen, this story of yours has been a great success, more than I dared hope. People have been asking me if I intend to bring out a complete edition with the chapters all together, several scrolls in a book bucket.* I think it would sell very well. Only I'd like to use your correct name. People realize there's no one named Incognitus; they've been asking about the author."

"My correct name? All of it? Marcus Valerius Messala Secundus? Maybe even adding Corvinus like my grandfather? I think, considering my reputation, that I'd better not seem pretentious. Maybe just Messala."

"But you should make it clear that the novel wasn't written by a relative. How about Messala Secundus?"

"As you wish, Sosius. By the way, do I get paid extra for my name?"

"I was thinking about another hundred denarii. You know, some people are beginning to ask what happened to you. I was at a banquet recently where a young lawyer, Sextus Quadratus, was saying what a pity it was, and how gifted you are – besides being a really good fellow."

Bless Quadratus!

"I don't think your family would be embarrassed if your novel proves popular under your true name. I'd really like you to agree."

Of course I consented. A hundred denarii is the same thing as four hundred sesterces.

My next step was my bank, which serves small depositors. Just before entering, I encountered an unwelcome face. Sanballat, the slick contractor, Judah's agent in the matter of that miserable bet. As usual he was dressed in a fine white toga that proclaimed his Roman citizenship, if not his true loyalty. He looked at me with his typical supercilious smirk.

"Well, well! For a moment, Messala, I thought you were actually walking on your own feet."

---

* A leather container of several scrolls

Sanballat has a cat's instinct for playful torture. I turned my face away from him.

He didn't give up. "Going to withdraw a few denarii for betting?"

Thinking of several obscene expressions, I controlled myself and said slowly with what I hoped was Stoic dignity, "Sanballat, I can't recall any anatomical epithets quite gross enough for you."

I went inside before he could come up with a clever retort, and I added the hundred denarii to my account, which already contained what I'd received from Caprarius. The ten denarii for the last manuscript I changed into sesterces for daily use.

The public baths were my next step. Actually, they were on the way home. Not the most lavish baths in the city but good enough – and admission is free. One can meet anyone there, but most of the clientele are working people, including slaves.

I checked my clothes and draped myself in a large towel. I would have paid for the services of a bath slave, but just then a voice spoke my name. It was Caprarius. I was relieved that it was a friend.

Caprarius and I decided to stay together and help each other. First there was the steam room. Sitting around in the warm vapour and making conversation, Caprarius told me he'd come to this particular bath facility because he was hot and tired after walking around the Forum. It wasn't a day when the Senate met, but he had had business affairs to settle.

On to the massage area, where we spread olive oil on each other, scraped it off with a metal strigil – in my case removing a lot of grime, and gave each other a rub-down. I tried not to think about Caprarius' view of my scars. In any case, he said nothing.

We soaked in the hot pool, then worked some more with the oil and the strigil, then went to the pool that was merely warm and restful. We finished up in the large cold pool, where it is possible to swim – something I can do without using my legs. My strong arms were a comfort to me, and the sense of mobility I had in the water made me feel like not committing suicide after all.

Out of the water I tried to keep the large towel around me, especially covering my back. I was thankful that Sanballat probably wouldn't go to a public bath because he wouldn't want to expose his circumcision in front of a lot of naked uncircumcised men. Most strict Jews disapprove of activities, such as nude wrestling and public bathing, where men get a view of each other's genitals.

Dressing ourselves, we went to the colonnade, rested, and watched an exercise class. It had been a good day, so far.

I asked Caprarius about the letter he'd delivered for me.

"What was your impression? Do you think I'll get an answer?"

"Yes, for sure. Your brother was pleased you'd written. He said it was the first time they'd heard from you."

"Really? I wonder why."

"I don't know. But lately your father's been very ill. It's his heart. When he thought he might die, he asked for you. Barbatus told me. He's recovering now and still wants to see you. They'll send someone to you soon if you don't go home on your own. Only – they still don't want your Egyptian wife. Barbatus said he wouldn't mind giving her enough to get her back to Egypt and have something to live on when she got there – if she would just go."

That was good news. I decided I'd divorce Iras and send her off with a better settlement than she'd ever have if we went on struggling hand to mouth in the Subura. And I'd go home again.

We had a little lunch together. A vendor came around with bread pockets stuffed with a mixture of chickpeas, some kind of ground meat, and I'm not sure what else. There was also fairly good wine.

As there was a barber in the colonnade, I got a haircut and a shave. I'd shaved at home, but I knew I hadn't done it very well.

Caprarius and I parted, and I slowly made my way home. It had become extremely hot. Perspiration was soon streaming down my face and soaking my armpits as I struggled awkwardly on my crutches. I almost ordered a litter to take me to my family home as I had enough money now, but there were a few things I wanted to take with me, particularly my portfolio on the Hur rebellion.

Although I was very tired, I was happy. I'd more money than usual and I hadn't had to part with a tip to Ruso. My family did care. And Sosius wanted to publish my book with my name on it. I was glad I'd postponed my suicide.

As I stopped to rest on a shaded bench, I began to scratch my left leg, wondering where I'd picked up an itch. The right leg also felt itchy. Then I gasped as I realized what this might mean. My legs normally felt numb, in some ways almost dead. Sometimes there seemed to be a little sensation, but it was elusive.

The doctors who first attended me at Antioch all said I wouldn't walk again; they wanted to amputate my legs. Later, when I recovered some control of embarrassing necessary functions, I consulted another doctor, who said that evidently my spinal cord wasn't completely severed, just injured. He thought it was encouraging that, although I couldn't will my legs to move, I had a slight degree of feeling at times. He advised me that the muscles had weakened during the period following the race, and perhaps I couldn't make myself believe I would ever be able to move them. He said I should keep massaging my legs and moving them by hand to keep the muscles from deteriorating beyond hope.

I recalled a Jewish story in which a prophet had a vision of a valley of dry bones, probably of soldiers who had perished on the battlefield. The prophet, who was in the habit of speaking personally to the Jewish God, asked, "Lord, can these bones live?" And miraculously the bones reconnected with each other, flesh came upon them, and finally they were living, breathing men.

Often I'd gazed heavenward toward whatever unknown Power or Powers might hear me – though naturally the Jewish God wouldn't care – and asked if my legs might indeed live again.

The kindly doctor, whose name was Luke, said that a prickling feeling, like flesh gone to sleep, could be the signal of recovery. An irritating prickling sensation was just what I felt that day.

I tried moving my feet but couldn't even move a toe and wondered if it was only sensation I was recovering and not movement.

I came back to our building. Reuben, the Jewish baker who acted as our superintendant and collected our rents, greeted me, his face long and sad.

"It's Ruso! He's dead."

"Whatever happened?"

"He got into a fight in Thord's bar. Thord personally threw him out on the pavement. Ruso staggered home with his head bleeding. He was able to tell me about it in a confused way. He said something about a burial plan – that you would understand."

Ruso seldom had more than a few sesterces from doing odd jobs, yet his funeral was all paid for. The army had regularly deducted money from his pay to provide for his pension and his membership in a soldiers' burial society. He spent all his pension money soon after he got it in a lump sum, but the money in the burial fund was intact. He had told me this several times.

It is a pious duty to bury the dead properly, if one can. Ruso had befriended me and helped me in his way. So I wrote a polite note to Ruso's burial society explaining where they could have the body picked up and taken to the undertaker near the Temple of Venus Libitina, who presides over death. There would be a military funeral, rather simple, and the ashes would be placed in a niche in the monument owned by his burial society.

I signed my name simply Messala. If they thought the writer was my father or brother, they might suppose that Ruso had a distinguished patron taking an interest in his funeral and would be careful to do their best.

Reuben found a reliable fellow to take the message. He and I together shared the cost of paying the messenger. Reuben's a good man; it isn't his fault he's the superintendant of a dilapidated building which should be torn down.

Having done what I could to ease Ruso's entry into the next world, where I hoped Bacchus would provide the best wine for his faithful servant, I took my dingy outer tunic out of the bag, put it on, and prepared to struggle up the stairs. Ruso would never again be there to help me.

I'd dragged myself up to the fourth landing – crutches, workbag, and all – when someone coming down stumbled against me, swearing at me for being there. As I pulled myself to the next set of steps, I felt a sharp pain in my right knee, which the fellow's heavy sandal must have bruised.

Oh, joy! I was definitely registering feeling in my paralysed legs. A step – metaphorically speaking – in the right direction!

I crawled up the rest of the way, then painstakingly got myself back up on the crutches (a trick that had taken a lot of practice), and went down the dim corridor to our room. Inside, I looked around. Still no Iras. But the light from the window illuminated a strip of floor on which I saw tiny scraps of paper with writing on them. I came in farther. There were more tiny scraps on the narrow window ledge. I picked one up and confirmed my growing fear.

It was what was left of my file on the revolutionary career of Judah Ben-Hur. The miserable woman had ripped it up and thrown most of the pieces out the window to be carried away with the wind that incessantly blows trash all over the Subura. My life's achievement, the proof that I'd saved my country! She'd deliberately left some bits on the floor so I'd know what she'd done.

Why hadn't I thought of this possibility? I knew she was angry and bitter and that she felt protective toward Ben-Hur. Ironically, I'd been thinking twice about using the material as my family would likely want me to avoid attracting Macro's attention. They might be worried by the fact that, for a short time, I'd worked for Sejanus in a very minor position. The insignificance of my job, as well as my poverty, likely saved my life at a time when many people of wealth and reputation were being accused and convicted of complicity in Sejanus' plot and their estates doled out to their accusers.

I got out my writing materials. I was going to write out a divorce certificate as well as a scathing personal note of farewell. Then I planned to get my things together and leave. Once away from the slum area, I could probably get a litter home.

Suddenly the door opened. Iras was coming toward me, smiling nastily. Ye Gods! She was holding a dagger in her hand. My own dagger!

CHAPTER FIVE

S HE was still in her tawdry red dress, though she'd removed her yellow wig. She came close enough for me to see her bloodshot eyes.

"So you got yourself all cleaned up. How nice."

She laughed as if she would never stop.

"Iras, shut up. Put that damned dagger down on the table. Now!"

Then I noticed the stains on her flimsy skirt, dark red against the scarlet. Her dagger hand was also smeared.

"What have you done, Iras?"

"Settled an old score. Oh, I may as well tell you. I ran into Sporus, the pimp. He grabbed hold of me – and I stabbed him in the chest. Then, as he lay dying, I decided to be thorough. First I took his money pouch, which I kept – see? And then I cut off his testicles and threw them to some dogs to fight over. Quite a productive morning, wasn't it?"

"Ye Gods, have you gone mad? Now you'll have to get away before they track you down. Put on something decent and try to get on a barge at the Tiber docks. If you can't, you'll have to try the road to Ostia harbour."

Not that the vigiles* were likely to go after a mere whore who'd killed her pimp. But he'd have underworld friends to avenge him. What if they came to our apartment? I could be killed or mutilated! I had to leave for home soon.

For that moment I'd forgotten my anger over the documents. I was prepared to give her some money in addition to what she'd taken from Sporus, though for all I knew he could have been carrying around more than I had with me. I didn't want to write her a money draft; she might be caught with it.

Iras took off her bloody dress, kicking it into a corner. She went to the basin and washed her hands. She found a dull grey dress and put it on. It displayed her figure to some advantage, but the colour wasn't becoming.

Turning back to me, she said mockingly, "I'm sure you've noticed what else I did. Where is your precious set of notes on Ben-Hur? Just little bits and pieces blowing in the dusty wind out there. You'll never be able to use them."

"You faithless slut! You had no right to touch *my* papers. But of course you know nothing of loyalty or respect for property."

"Nor do you! You weren't a loyal friend to him, were you? And you accepted an informer's share of his property when Gratus condemned him."

"Shut up! Don't say another word! I'm going to write you a certificate of divorce. You can take it and go. Anywhere well away from me. To Ben-Hur if you think he would welcome you – and maybe protect you against Sporus' thugs."

"No, I won't ask him to do that. If only I'd married him when I had the chance! Now he has a wife, I think. The Acta Diurna mentioned his family. Probably that insipid little Jewess, Esther."

Esther is the daughter of the rich merchant, Simonides, who was once the steward of the Hur family and now is Judah's partner. I'd never seen her. She sounded as though she'd be much more Judah's type than mine.

"My beauty is destroyed. To think that once I outshone that little

---

*Watchmen

mouse completely! But I lost everything for you. My jewellery is gone, my health is poor – I feel sick most of the time. I have no children, and perhaps never will because I took that terrible stuff. You won my love and lured me away from my poor old father – to a life of miserable degradation. I kept on loving you for a long time, too. But you don't know the meaning of gratitude, much less love."

"No, I don't understand your kind of love. In fact, Iras, I detest your occasional nauseous outpourings of passion. I'm sick of your drinking and whoring, your lies about sacrificing yourself for me. Thank the Gods, I've never touched any of your money!"

I was conveniently forgetting about the two coin necklaces we'd turned to cash.

I added, "*I* have paid our rent here, you take coins from *my* wallet for food and other needs. It's *my* enrollment in the Head Count that gets us the grain dole, not that it's much. And now you and I have come to the end."

"So you think you're casting me out!"

"Don't be stupid! You can't stay here and wait to be attacked by Sporus' helpers."

"What about you? Are you planning to throw yourself on the mercy of your family? How do you know they want to see you? You disgraced them and then defied your father. They haven't answered your letters. Maybe they wish you would die quietly."

Her smile was incredibly ugly, the sort one might see on a gorgon or harpy.

"Iras, did you intercept any of my letters?"

"Yes, yes, I certainly did. I watched every time and got the messenger to hand the letter over to me." She laughed wildly, ending in a screech. I wished I need never hear her again.

"It was so funny, the way you kept offering to give me up if they would just let me have a little money to get back to Egypt, far from you. I can see myself facing my female cousins – with a few sesterces in my purse, poor and shamed, a divorced woman who has lost her beauty."

Would she never stop laughing? "No, my dear!" she said at last.

"You and I are going down together to the end. You notice I have your dagger."

"Put it down! You're talking nonsense." Was she thinking of a suicide pact? Or did she just want to kill me?

"I've been thinking. Destroying your notes wasn't enough; you could find some other way to get Ben-Hur, especially if your family helped you so that you had some money again. You are a cruel, evil man. You tried in every way to destroy a finer man than yourself. Judah Ben-Hur is the noblest man I ever met, and I'm going to save him from you."

My enemy – who couldn't even stay in his own damned country. He had to come back to Italy, to stroll around on the grass and earth of my homeland, where I could only drag myself. Although there was now some hope that could change. I thought, "Gods, don't get carried away by your sense of irony. Don't let me die at the hands of this night hag, just when Hope is at last fluttering out of Pandora's box of horrors."

"Can't you ever shut up about that Jew? Once you thought his patriotism and intense religious fervour a deadly bore."

"Yes, I think I've said enough. It's time to *do* something."

She sprang toward me with the dagger. I'd already sat down on the edge of the bed, putting aside the crutches so my hands would be free. Now I braced myself to withstand her lunge, to catch hold of her dagger hand.

I seized both of her wrists and began bending them back. She screamed with pain. "You – you bastard! You're breaking my hands!"

"Let go of my dagger or I'll break your wrist and your fingers – one at a time."

I could've done it; I have the strength in my hands.

She spat at me. It's very disagreeable getting a gob of saliva on one's face. I wanted to wipe it off, but my hands weren't free. I said, "You disgusting hag!"

She tried to bite me, but I evaded her teeth, and twisted her dagger hand behind her while still gripping her other hand hard. She was screeching as if I were killing her. I wished someone would come and see what the matter was, but people in the Subura don't bother much about other people's fights. Many of our neighbours had loud domestic battles all the time.

I kept my head down so that she couldn't spit in my face again or try to bite me. I twisted her hand until, with a scream of pain, she dropped the dagger to the floor.

It would have been so much easier if I'd been able to cover it with my foot. Instead, Iras and I both reached for it and found ourselves on the floor together. Soon I had it, however, in my right hand, and was on top of her with all my weight. She stared up at me with wide angry eyes, and I had the thought that, if I'd pushed up her skirt a little and penetrated her with my man's natural weapon, she would, for the time being, have forgotten about saving Ben-Hur from me. Her legs started to encircle my thighs – merciful Gods, I could feel them! But I couldn't oblige her; my manhood didn't stir at all. I hadn't the slightest desire for her – just revulsion.

"No, Iras, no! Forget it! Or fantasize about your precious Jew but not me. You revolt me!"

Suddenly her hand struck at my face, her nails raking across my cheek. Then she was sinking her teeth into my neck. It was a painful bite, and she hung on like a vampire.

I made my free left hand into a fist and struck her hard between the jaw and cheekbone – the first time I ever struck her! Her head fell back, and her eyes closed for a moment. My neck felt as if it were bleeding, as did my cheek where she had scratched it. But I'd won. She was dazed, breathing huskily, as she tried to focus her eyes.

I rolled off her and attached my dagger to my belt. I said, "Get up and get out!"

She stood up shakily, and I pulled myself up till I was sitting on the bed. She said, "Please let me get my other clothes."

Thoughtlessly I said, "All right."

She went to the drawer of the wall cupboard and took out a few things, probably her other sleazy dresses, breast bands, and cloths for her loins. She tucked them into a bag.

Then suddenly she picked up a stool by one leg and came at me.

I was too late to parry her attack with a crutch. My head seemed to explode as the heavy wood struck my brow. I was fumbling for the crutch when she swung the stool again and connected with the top of my head. I think she managed to strike a third time.

She must have sprung on me while I was still dizzy from the blows. She didn't have my dagger but she had another knife, perhaps one taken from Sporus' dead body. I felt it slicing across my throat. The cut burned and I could feel warm blood flowing across my skin.

"Has that infernal gorgon struck a major blood vessel? Am I going to die? What if she got my windpipe?" I realized that I'd fallen to the floor again, and she was standing over me, just a little out of reach.

Soon I knew it wasn't my windpipe, but the blood was flowing fast. I'd heard that when certain throat veins are cut, the blood spurts forth in a fountain-like arc. It apparently wasn't doing that, just pouring out of what felt like a long cut.

Iras said, "You're going to die. And I'll go to Ben-Hur and tell him what I've done – that I killed you for the great misery you brought me. I'll tell him he's safe from you and that, for the harm I tried to do him, I've been punished until even he would pity me."

"He may – reward you – with his protection. But you're a murderess. Twice – if I die! Don't be – too sure – you won't be caught." When I spoke, it made the blood flow more.

"You don't understand. I won't stay for Judah's pity and protection. I've nothing to live for, even if he were to give me money and help me escape to a far country. No, I will be coming after you very soon."

The thought made my flesh crawl. "Making sure my – afterlife is torment too!"

She laughed again. "You'll never be free of me! Why don't you hand me your wallet now? That will save me the trouble of taking it off your corpse."

The light was getting dimmer. I could barely make out Iras now. She looked like a hazy monster out of a legend. But she wasn't going to fleece me for my wallet while I had breath to fight her off.

Mockingly she said, "Remember Judah's message to you through me – that instead of a curse in words, he was sending you someone who would prove the sum of all curses? That's just what I am."

I closed my eyes to shut her out. I was lying on my side; my dagger and wallet were attached to my belt. Both of them under me. I could hear her moving around the room, probably choosing more things to take with her.

"I can see your lifeblood like a crimson river, all down your tunic, dripping on the floor. If someone comes and finds you, maybe he or she will put a coin between your lips so that Charon* will take you across the river. But if not, you can spend forever wandering around on the wrong side."

If I can wander on my feet, I don't care which side of the Styx I'm on, I thought. And, Pluto help me, the living will know that I wander.

Half opening my eyes, I saw that she was near the door, hesitating. "I wonder if he's gone yet," she said, and came closer. I prayed silently, "Gods, can't some of you make her leave now – and send someone to help me?"

I thought I could hear a sound besides the raucous street noises. Was it the creaking of steps?

"I can't wait for your final heartbeat." She must've picked up the stool again. I could feel heavy blows to my skull, and I think a sharp edge cut the side of my head. I probably fainted briefly – which may have saved me since I would have seemed dead.

I wasn't aware of her touching me, though she may have done so. If she did, she must have missed my pulse, thank the Gods. Perhaps it was too weak or she was too upset to detect it. When I came round, she was still there.

"If I don't take your dagger, it will look like suicide. You really are dead, aren't you? Soon you'll be cold. I've no time to try to get your money; I think there's someone coming up the stairs."

I kept still; my head was throbbing, and I could feel the blood coming out of my throat.

She spoke again. "I truly loved you. What a fool I was!" Then she must have gone out and closed the door behind her.

---

*The ferryman who took the dead across the Styx

I opened my eyes and felt blood dripping into them. I tried to wipe it away, smearing it on my face. The cut on my neck was less painful than the cuts and bruises from her fingernails and the stool.

I needed something to use as a bandage. I grabbed Iras' dingy blanket from the bed.

Her footsteps had retreated toward the nearer stairs, but then there was another sound in the corridor. I tried to call "Help!" How weak my voice was!

I tried to crawl toward the door. My hands and the floor were sticky with blood.

There *was* someone coming. I called again, not sure if I could be heard.

I was suddenly aware that my left foot moved to my will. I moved it again. Surely it was a sign from the Gods. Unless they were playing a cruel trick on me.

Iras hadn't locked the door. It was opening. I whispered "Help," hoping it wasn't Iras. I couldn't see; I think I fainted again.

The next thing I knew, someone was holding a cloth against my neck. I recognized the voice of Reuben's wife, Rebecca. There seemed to be other people present.

She held a spoon to my lips, and I could taste sour wine on my tongue. Good kind Rebecca! She had twice brought me soup when I had that miserable cold. Iras hadn't been very appreciative. In fact, she resented every kind gesture from my female neighbours. She never made friends with other women.

There were black rain clouds in front of my eyes. When they cleared, I was on the bed, and a large dark-skinned man was applying wine to my cuts while Rebecca held a cloth to my neck wound until it was time to pour more wine into it. It burned, but I knew something was being done for me.

He was stitching my neck up with something. It should have been painful but really didn't make me feel any worse. I couldn't see clearly, but I could feel someone wrapping a bandage around my head.

The black man had finished stitching my neck; he put more wine on it. Then he applied a bandage.

A man spoke: "Messala, I'm Philip, one of your father's freedmen. My companion is Africanus. Your brother sent us to you. We have a litter waiting downstairs."

A litter would have been quite an unusual sight on our crowded slum street.

I kept drifting off but was aware of my facial and scalp cuts being bathed again. I suppose their first covering had become blood-soaked. I think they must have put a very thick bandage on my stitched-up neck. The black man said something about salve for my bruises when we got home.

Reuben was there; I could hear his voice. Philip said to him, "If that woman comes back here, send for the vigiles."

In fact, I don't think the vigiles bother with criminals in the Subura. They get sent to more respectable crime scenes. Here anarchy reigns. Perhaps Sporus' death would concern only his fellow thugs.

I whispered, "I can move my feet a little."

They didn't understand. Philip said, "No, you must rest. We have a litter for you."

The black man called Africanus picked me up easily. I don't know much about what happened after that. He must have carried me down the five flights of stairs, but I wasn't aware of it. I was sleepy, and everything was so dark.

CHAPTER SIX

I opened my eyes to darkness. To my right, was a soft light. I wondered where I was. If it was Hades, then which section? My neck was very sore. But it didn't feel like a sore throat. The raw spot felt as if it were mostly outside.

No, not Hades. A small room with hangings on the walls. In daylight I'd be able to make out what was depicted on the hangings. There was a lamp beside me on a stand. Also a pitcher and a cup. I realized I was very thirsty.

By the door there was a woman with straw-coloured hair and heavy features, not very young, and not at all pretty. Maybe she was a slave from one of the barbarian tribes.

She must have seen that I was awake, for she came over to me and, raising my head, held a cup of water to my lips. With a cloth she wiped away the drops that had missed my mouth.

"Can I get anything for you, sir?"

"No, thanks." I felt so tired, and my head hurt. It was sore and tender. I closed my eyes again.

Where was I? Certainly not in my dingy room in the Subura. It smelled too clean. Then I remembered. Philip, my father's man, had come for me – just in time.

Iras had tried to kill me. She had hit me with a stool and then cut my throat. I remembered the floor, blood all over, and – was there a leg broken off the stool? My wheelchair had been by the window. Was it still there?

I must have revived for a moment when we got outside. I could picture a litter with red curtains. A crowd of people were talking excitedly, but I couldn't make out what they were saying, except for one shrill female voice proclaiming, "She came down the back stairs – and she had a bloody knife!"

The back stairs! Rebecca and the others must have been coming up the main stairs at the same time. They'd come soon after Iras left.

I remember Africanus placing me in the litter. Although the June sun was bright and I should have felt hot, I was cold and shivering. I had covers around me, one of them the old toga that I'd kept in a drawer. It was discoloured and moth-eaten but useful as a blanket. They'd probably wrapped me up so well to keep my blood from staining the litter cushions, as well as to keep me warm.

Africanus gave me more wine, then closed the curtain. I'm leaving here forever, I thought. I heard Reuben say "Shalom," which means "Peace to you."

I felt a sick feeling as the bearers started out and the litter began swaying. The street sounds seemed far off and muted. I must have passed out then.

I can't remember arriving at my family mansion, though I seem to recall seeing my brother's anxious face. There were people around me, and someone was touching me, gently examining my head.

They placed damp cloths on my face and gave me a swallow of some kind of broth. Perhaps there was a doctor who examined my wounds and changed the dressings, but I can't remember that at all.

My feet. Was that a dream? Please not a dream. Let it be real!

I tried the toes on my left foot. Yes, yes, they moved a little. The other foot? At first nothing, but then – joy! – I drew in the small toe.

I felt like Archimedes discovering the principle of water displacement. So excited, he jumped out of his tub crying 'Eureka!' Well, I couldn't do that.

What would the Jews exclaim? Hallelujah? No, I'd better not say anything to attract the attention of their unseen God. He must still have it in for me.

For a while I just lay there drowsily as I practised wiggling my toes and saying to myself, "It's all real, all real! The Gods have given me my life back."

The slave woman gave me more water. It was more painful when I swallowed, but I kept getting thirsty. I remembered that there were stitches in the burning cut on my neck.

The next thing I knew, it was morning. I'd a better idea of where I was then – a ground floor room off the peristylum*. The sun was coming in through the latticework in the top of the door; I could see green leaves through it. I could hear a fountain – and a bird singing. The only birds in the Subura were the little sparrows in the square – and the pigeons, making sick noises and relieving themselves all over the windows and roofs.

The slave woman of the night had gone. Soon a manservant came in, bathed my face and fed me breakfast, which consisted of bits of bread softened in broth. I realized I wouldn't be able to eat anything very solid while my throat was so sore.

I told the fellow I could serve myself if he just helped me sit up, but he said he was following orders.

"The doctor will be coming to you later, sir."

My head throbbed when I moved it. It was easier to close my eyes and just feel the breeze from the garden on my face. However, I sometimes opened my eyes and looked around the room, noticing the hangings with their bright pictures, one of fruit and flowers, another of a pair of lovers on a green hillside. I observed that there was usually someone in the room, ready to tend to me. The slaves probably covered the assignment in shifts.

I think it was late morning when my brother came. Marcus Valerius Messala Barbatus. His cognomen Barbatus means bearded, but in fact he wasn't. He tried wearing a beard for a while in his late twenties. I think the name has stuck because he was very dignified;

---

*A formal garden surrounded by a colonnade and a wall

everyone says he was born that way. I never had the opportunity to know him well. He was the son of Father's first marriage and was a fifteen-year-old student in Rome when my parents were married. I was born in the East, where I stayed until I was fourteen. Then, when I came to Rome for my higher education, my brother was away on military service or other government assignments, so that I saw him only twice during my student days. And naturally we met when I returned to Rome in dishonour.

He was well into his forties at this time, and his hair was mixed with grey. He had a serious face that often looked worried. Coming to my bedside, he greeted me kindly.

"Secundus, I'm glad to see you again. You're welcome here. I wish you had got in touch with us sooner. Caprarius told me you had written before, but we didn't receive the letters."

I started to tell him, "Iras intercepted –", but he didn't let me continue.

"Don't try to speak out. Just whisper or nod. You must be careful of the stitches in your neck. And you shouldn't move your head much until the swelling goes down."

He continued, "The doctor is coming in now. He'll see how you are doing. I'll wait to talk to you."

I whispered, "Father?"

"Father knows you are here. He's been recovering from a heart attack. We've been worried about him, but we think your return may have helped him. He's very much relieved. Will you divorce that woman now?"

"Yes – gladly!"

"We'll see about it later. I'll send the doctor in."

Xenophon, the doctor, had seen me the day before, but I'd been unconscious, or at least unaware of his ministrations.

He changed the dressings and cleansed my wounds gently, especially around the stitches. I discovered that he had put a few stitches in one cut on my forehead. He applied wine and ointment to the cuts before covering them and also wrapped up the swollen bruised areas, which felt quite large and were probably dark purple by now.

He didn't want me to speak, but I managed to say, "I can move my toes a little. Please – do all you can – to help me walk again."

He looked at my feet and observed that I really could wiggle a few toes, just as I said.

"I'll inform your brother and I'll recommend an expert to help you with the right exercises. I've heard of cases where paralysed men and women have made amazing recoveries. But now you must rest and take whatever light nourishment you can get down. It's important to restore your strength and at the same time keep your injuries from getting infected. It must feel good to be at home with your own people."

"It certainly does," I whispered, thinking of Barbatus' kindness and also of the comfort of a clean bed. I could feel the freshness of the sheets on my legs. They had cut away the bloody garments from me and dressed me in a soft cotton robe.

"You are safe now from the evil person that attacked you. So just rest. However, you might practise flexing your toes when you feel like it." He also said I must avoid everything distressing, such as thoughts of past troubles.

He left me, and I closed my eyes. It was late afternoon when I woke to be served more broth with bread bits. Later in the evening, Barbatus came in for a brief visit. He said he was delighted by Xenophon's news about my ability to move my toes. He promised to do all he could to see me restored to health and to some place of honour in my world, where I could be a credit to my family. He would discuss divorce when I was able to speak more easily.

Left alone, I thought about family life. I'd had rather less of it than most people I knew. My mother had left us suddenly when I was four, and I'd rarely seen her since. My father had always been good to me when I was a child growing up in Jerusalem, but I'd had little contact with him after I went to Rome for my education because he returned to Italy about the same time I went back to Judaea to serve under Valerius Gratus. It had, for many years, seemed natural to feel far from him in every way.

If I were writing my thoughts in a serious journal for posterity to read and wonder at, I might – out of consideration for readers in a distant time with changed customs – explain about names. My father, my half-brother, and I have the praenomen Marcus, the nomen or clan name Valerius, and the cognomen Messala, which was received by an ancestor who relieved the siege of Messana* in Sicily during the conflict with Carthage. When I was born in Antioch, my brother was living in Rome. My mother, Lollia Velleia, thought I should be Marcus too, though the name was usually reserved for the eldest son in our family.

My father had been stationed as a legate to the governor of Syria. We lived in Antioch until I was two and then went to Jerusalem so that my father, assisting the procurator of Judaea with the tax system, could study the problem of understanding the Jews. Not that anyone can. While there, he was still reporting to the governor of Syria, for although the Jews hated the situation, their land was officially part of the large province of Syria.

My parents both called me Marcus or, if they wanted to be formal, Marcus Valerius. Later on, companions of my own age often called me by my family cognomen, Messala.

After I came in contact with my relatives in Rome, who were well-acquainted with my brother, I became Messala Secundus[†], which doesn't make me feel much like a natural leader but is preferable to Ultimus[‡].

As far as I know, I don't have an extra cognomen. Such names come as a result of achievements or striking personal characteristics. If my contemporaries, viewing my unfortunate career, have thought of referring to me as Messala Infelix[§] or something equally embarrassing, no one has had the heart or the audacity to tell me.

Incidentally most other cultures have a very different system of names. Take the Jews, for example. There is only one personal name, followed by Ben Whatever, the name of the father. Occasionally it is Ben plus the name of a distinguished ancestor; for example, my enemy, once my playmate, was named Judah and could have been known as Ben Ithamar after his immediate father but is more often

*Modern Messina   †Second   ‡Last   §Unlucky

addressed as Ben-Hur, after an ancestor who once upheld one of the great leader Moses' arms in prayer during a battle. I don't know what other claim to fame he had; surely there was something.

When darkness fell, two slaves came in, one of them with a lamp. They had more soup to feed me, and then they helped me into a fresh garment. The same woman who had watched over me in the night settled into her chair again. Probably she would be relieved at some point. As the shadows deepened, I fell asleep.

CHAPTER SEVEN

FOR the next three days I remained in bed, asleep much of the time. The doctor said this was the best way of helping my wounds to heal. I gather he was especially concerned about further swelling and internal bleeding from either the throat or the puffy purple area on my forehead. So my visits from Barbatus were short because the doctor thought I should refrain even from any kind of mental exertion.

However, I did hear things, little by little. For instance, Barbatus said that two years ago my father had written to me twice; the messenger had taken the letters to the modest middle-class apartment where we were living then. Iras had accepted the letters both times. Obviously she had read them and destroyed them; she couldn't bear the idea of being divorced and sent back to Egypt with only five, or at most ten thousand sesterces, while I was given a steady income and a country villa without her.

"Father even spoke of calling on you in person, and I'm afraid I discouraged him, even urged him not to plead with you. I didn't realize what that woman was capable of."

I didn't blame Barbatus. During my short stay with Iras at my family home, I'd been proud and defiant, sensitive to every critical word. Iras had flaunted her exotic beauty and wit, deliberately provoking my sister-in-law. Naturally Barbatus had dreaded further disturbance of his family peace.

Now he told me that his wife was truly sorry for me and wished to get along with me. I knew Lepida could be hot-tempered and haughty. She was like all members of her family, the Ahenobarbi. She saw Iras as greatly her inferior. Even so, I thought that conflict might have been averted by a little self-control on Iras' part. She had never mastered the art of being coldly superior to the slurs of the ignorant. She always descended to the level of the attacker.

I said in my still-weak voice, "I'll be pleasant to Lepida, but please ask her not to speak about Iras to me."

He agreed to caution her on that point.

Another time Barbatus spoke of his only child, his daughter, Valeria Messalina.

"She's so pretty and intelligent. I know I spoil her – her mother says so – but she's the delight of my life." I wondered if Barbatus still hoped for a son. I remembered hearing that Lepida had had a difficult time giving birth to Messalina, who'd been a small child when I first returned from the East. Perhaps Lepida didn't want to go through child-bearing again.

During other visits my brother reported matters of some interest. Philip and a couple of other servants had gone back to the Subura to make enquiries. They had talked to Reuben, who said that Iras had been seen later the same day of the attack. The undertaker's black litter had arrived for Ruso's body, which had been laid out inside Reuben's quarters. Unlike many Jews, Reuben doesn't worry about ritual pollution from a dead body, especially when it's a matter of doing a kindness to a neighbour, even a neighbour of a different religion.

Reuben and Rebecca both saw Iras come down the street and gaze in apparent astonishment at the black-curtained litter and black-garbed bearers. Then she turned and ran, her gown caught up in her hand so that she could make all haste. She must have thought the litter was for my corpse, that someone had found me, that my people had been informed, and that I was to have a proper funeral and burial instead of being thrown into the lime pits beside Rome's major cemetery where only the reasonably affluent had mausoleums full of urns for their ashes.

Philip had brought money to reward those who had helped save my life. At first Reuben had declined, saying that his effort had cost him nothing, but Philip persuaded him to take it. Reuben and Rebecca were planning to leave the Subura and open a bakeshop in the port town of Ostia where the Tiber enters the sea. There the apartment buildings are newer and better built. There is a substantial Jewish community in Ostia. So perhaps I have seen Reuben and his wife for the last time. I certainly wish them well.

The undertaker who had received my letter about Ruso called at our house. I wasn't able to see him personally, but Barbatus acted for me, realizing that I'd been Ruso's patron (which was rather absurd in view of the fact that we were both so poor). Barbatus gave the undertaker money to pay for drinks for the mourners after the final ceremonies. It was expected that some veterans of the Rhine legions would be present for the cremation.

"Which tavern, Barbatus?" I asked. "Not Thord's?"

"No, I heard from Philip that Thord was really responsible for the poor fellow's death. He couldn't just put a drunk out of his establishment quietly but firmly – he had to show off the fact that he'd been a champion gladiator. So I picked out Androcles' tavern, which is about a block down the street on the other side."

So Ruso had a send-off party in a rival bar!

On the fourth day the doctor said I could sit in a chair for a while outside in the sunshine of the garden. After my daily bed-bath, two servants helped me into a robe and slippers and lifted me into a new wheelchair. I could have done more for myself, but they had been given clear instructions about me; they were not to let me exert myself too soon.

They took me to a shady spot and wrapped a cloak around me although the day was warm. Under my feet, they placed a footstool.

I was happy – such a contrast to the street corner where I had my small sign and my folding chair, surrounded by bustle, discordant noises and an odd assortment of smells: spicy food cooking in rancid grease, garbage decomposing where it had been flung down from above, urine and feces, mostly animal, but not all, even though the public latrine wasn't far.

Here I was in a colonnaded garden, sheltered from the outside world, with green grass, stone walks, and scented flowering shrubs and a bubbling fountain in the middle.

Lepida came to speak to me. She is a pretty woman of about thirty, with the reddish blonde hair typical of the Ahenobarbi. She brought Valeria Messalina with her. She is a lovely girl, ten years old, physically rather mature for her age, with black curls, sparkling dark eyes, and a fair complexion. She politely called me 'Uncle Secundus.'

They were brief in their visit; they just wanted to convey their best wishes for my recovery and comfort. Lepida said hesitantly that there was another small matter of which she would speak another time. She hushed Messalina, who had begun, "It's about the –" Naturally I'm curious to know what she wanted to tell me.

In a little while the slaves brought out a cushioned chair for Father, who followed slowly, leaning on a cane. He looked very old and thin, and his face, with the high cheekbones (which I have to some degree inherited) was deathly grey. He hadn't been very young when he took my mother Lollia Velleia as his second wife. Now he was over seventy, and I could see he wouldn't be here much longer.

He held out his blue-veined hand to me. The slaves left us together.

"Is it true? Can you really move your feet now?"

I assured him it was true, and wiggled several toes to demonstrate.

I couldn't talk very much, and he was still weak from his heart attack, so we couldn't get into a long conversation. Father said he would send a special offering of thanks to the Temple of Aesculapius the Healer, the son of Apollo. He was horrified to see my forehead and the one side of my face so patched with purple. The actual cuts on my head and neck were still bandaged.

Barbatus came to join us. He brought Philip along to take a few notes while we discussed my divorce.

"Do you have any idea where that woman has gone? I presume you don't want the embarrassment of charging her with assault, but she should be formally presented with her divorce paper."

"She could have gone – to Quintus Arrius, as he is called – in Misenum. But I wouldn't want to send her divorce paper there before I knew for sure."

"I was thinking," said Barbatus, "that since her whereabouts are uncertain, you might just announce your divorce in the Acta Diurna."

Father smiled. "If they – that is, Iras and her kind friend – see a copy of the Acta Diurna, they'll be puzzled. They'll wonder if you are really alive or if it's some kind of trick."

Judah probably has slaves or employees in Rome who send him copies of whatever seems important on the public bulletin board.

We considered what to say in the notice of divorce. All of us agreed that we didn't want to mention attempted lethal assault or physical abuse; that would be too humiliating.

Barbatus suggested desertion, but I said, "She knew I wanted to divorce her, that I wished she would leave me."

I could still have said she deserted me, but I really prefer to be truthful if it isn't extremely inconvenient.

Was she unfaithful? Yes, yes! Forgiven repeatedly, she had gone back to whoring like a sow to the mire. That isn't an original comparison; I believe a Jewish writer used it first. But did I want to tell the world of her adultery and have people gossiping about it? Not that they wouldn't anyway.

The announcement which Barbatus sent to the Acta Diurna was as follows: Marcus Valerius Messala Secundus divorces Iras, daughter of Balthazar of Alexandria, for unchastity and infidelity.

Romans have occasionally announced their divorces from the public platform in the Forum, especially when they felt the occasion called for a speech about the woman's gross misconduct. But I didn't want to do that. If I learned where Iras had gone, I would have a divorce document delivered to her, as is the usual procedure.

Since we hadn't been married in the confarreatio* form, which is for patrician couples of pure Roman bloodlines, divorce was a simple matter of declaration with no reason necessary. Iras could have divorced me if she'd wanted to.

Barbatus also asked if Arrius was Iras' lover. I shook my head rather than irritate my throat with a speech about it. Finally I whispered that he had been her father's friend and my enemy.

"I've heard of the fellow. Adopted by the old admiral, wasn't he? They say he's really a Jew."

Father said, "I think I know who he is. Sometime we should talk about him, Secundus."

Father had still been in Jerusalem at the time of Judah's arrest for dropping a roof tile on Gratus. We'd never really discussed the case. I wondered how much of the story he had figured out.

Father was tired, and my throat was still painful. Barbatus left us sitting quietly until the servants brought our early dinner trays of very light food – for me, mainly soup. Father wasn't well enough yet to dine with the family.

When we had finished eating, it was still only late afternoon. Although the June sun was bright, we were both tired enough to go back to our beds. Father used his cane, followed anxiously by slaves. I was pushed in my wheelchair; it would be a while before I could go back to crutches, and I would need new ones for the old ones had been left behind in the Subura.

I dropped off to sleep soon after returning to my bed. There would be serious conversations – about the future and the past – when Father and I both felt up to it.

---

*The strictest, most ceremonious form of a Roman marriage

CHAPTER EIGHT

IT was several more days before I had my serious talk with Father. The doctor called every day, and soon he brought an expert in massage and special exercises for recovering paralytics. The black man, Africanus, who was Father's special attendant, observed the expert so that he could assist me in the future. Some of the exercises I'd done fairly regularly anyway – for example, sit-ups which strengthen the back. The new exercises were mainly persistent efforts to move my feet and legs, and to bend my knees without using my hands to put them in the proper position.

Barbatus got me new crutches, and soon I was able to use them. I was still dependent on my arm power and couldn't control my feet yet, although now I could distinguish the sensation of wearing shoes from that of standing directly on the tiled floor or grass. Every day I spent most of the time in the garden. I gained a companion, Father's big dog, Tarquinius Superbus, Tarquin for short. Named for the last king of Rome, he is a fierce-looking mastiff of gentle disposition, though I'm told he's had attack training. He lies beside me in the shade or comes over and rests his head against my legs.

Inevitably it made me think of my childhood in Jerusalem. When

I was four, my mother went back to Rome, and my father divorced her. I was bewildered, wondering what I'd done wrong. I hadn't met Judah then, and anyway he wouldn't have been as much comfort as Argus, my big dog, who went with me nearly everywhere.

Argus died when I was eight. I wanted his ashes buried in the garden, but we were living in part of a palace owned by the royal Herod family and supervised by the Jewish High Priest, who said it would be a terrible defilement. So Father found a place for Argus' grave in a grove outside the city wall, and he gave me a block of marble into which I scratched with a knife as deeply as I could the inscription 'Argus Semper Fidelis.' Even now, Argus ever faithful, I miss you.

My niece Messalina was usually busy with her governess or with companions of her own age, but some days she played board games with me, cheating as much as she could. Sometimes I would let her get away with it, and sometimes not.

Messalina and her mother both liked reading novels, and I discovered that their favourite at that time was *Strephon and Dynamene*! I knew I would enjoy telling them who wrote it.

Quintus Caprarius called to see me, and we talked a little in the garden. My voice was still weak, but he was happy to do most of the talking, telling me about Senate business and social events in the aristocratic world that was once mine. He was very sympathetic about my brush with death, and glad that he had been the one to take my message to my family so that Philip and Africanus arrived in time to save me, as from the claws and teeth of a tigress.

Father sat out with me for a while each day. A slave had made a copy of the Acta Diurna in which my divorce notice was proclaimed and we read it together.

He asked, "Suppose Quintus Arrius has lost no time in getting Iras out of the country? What if she's on a ship bound for Egypt, still thinking herself a widow?"

"It's possible. Arrius owns a fleet of merchant ships, so it would be easy for him to arrange."

Strictly speaking, I believe Judah and Simonides own them

together. Simonides was the steward of the Hurs, and he kept control of the ships and caravans when Ben-Hur's property was confiscated by Valerius Gratus. I'm not sure how they have finally worked out who owns what.

I remembered that Iras had mentioned suicide. But would she really want to die if she had any hope at all for a better future?

Father asked, "Is Quintus Arrius also known as Judah Ben-Hur?"

It took me a moment to recover. "Yes, he is. How did you figure that out?"

"I knew that Arrius' adopted son had been in the clothes of a galley slave when he and the admiral were rescued after the battle with the pirates. Nothing was said of his background then, and I didn't see him, or I might have recognized him. But later I put things together. I knew that your rival in that wretched chariot race was called Ben-Hur, so it appears your childhood companion got out of the galleys. I know that Arrius is a Jew, who always holds himself aloof from the fashionable set of his own age and has only lately returned from the East after a number of years. As soon as you said Iras might have gone to him, I felt sure my suspicions were correct. Tell me, were you and Ben-Hur ever rivals for her?"

"Yes, we were. I won that contest – but it could be called a Pyrrhic victory*."

"Amazing! She still preferred you even when you were crippled and bankrupt. I would have thought her more ambitious and self-serving."

"Essentially she was. It pained her greatly to give up so much, and she kept talking about her great sacrifice. On the other hand, she could imagine what would happen if he went on fighting Rome – and lost. She knew what would happen to his wife and family."

"So he was – and perhaps still is – an enemy of Rome. And what of Iras' father? Is he living?"

"I doubt it. He had a weak heart and he was very old. By the way, he genuinely liked Ben-Hur and wanted him for a son-in-law."

"Indeed! Yet Ben-Hur knocked that tile down on Gratus. It

---

*A victory in which the winner loses more than he gains

certainly looked deliberate to me and evidently to you, since you helped with his arrest. Tell me this: was he into any revolutionary activities in the East as far as you knew for certain?"

"Of that I'm absolutely sure, though I don't have proof." I told him what I'd learned from Iras and from other spies who had infiltrated the rebel ranks. I spoke of his alliances with the Sheik and with Simonides, who had resisted Gratus' torture – twice – and, at the cost of his ability to walk, had kept his grip on the Hur financial projects entrusted to him.

I explained that the chariot race was more than just vengeance on me personally. From my agents, I knew that he had gone to the trouble of getting the exact measurements of my chariot and had told one of his associates that something was going to happen on the sixth turn of the spina*. His victory was meant to encourage the mobs of Eastern dissidents by demonstrating that Rome could be defeated.

I described my subsequent activities to prevent Ben-Hur from leading a successful Judaean revolution, and told Father about my secret work with Pontius Pilate and Caiaphas to save my country.

"Iras destroyed all my files on that subject. So I have no real evidence against Ben-Hur."

"I can see you must feel disappointed after all the work you had put into the project. But I would be worried if you were to take anything to Macro. He doesn't do any favours for members of Rome's old families. He uses people and then destroys them. I'd stay away from him."

I couldn't help seeing that Father was right. Maybe I should put vengeance aside for the time being and try to make something of my new life.

We spoke a little of my childhood and of the quarrel I had with Judah when I came home to Jerusalem from Rome after five years of study. At nineteen, I was assigned to service as a contubernalis† under Valerius Gratus. I'd tried to get Judah to compromise a little

---

*The divider down the centre of the race track
†A young cadet in training

with his strict Jewish code, to get the same fine education and thorough military training that I had, and to plan a wonderful career. Judah had taken offense. He kept telling me that my comments on his culture and religion were out of line, but I couldn't stop trying to make my case – for his own good, I told myself.

When I told Father about this, he said, "Mind you, the shoe was once on the other foot. He and his gracious mother could say anything they liked about non-Jews wallowing in error, worshipping false Gods, and so on, and you just listened politely, then came home and asked me what I thought. At that point, I had a private talk with the lady. I told her she was doing you no good, trying to alienate you from your heritage."

This was a new insight into my childhood. I remembered a time when Judah and his mother became more reserved in talking to me about religion.

Father said, "I was trying to protect you, and she was trying to protect her children from foreign influence. You know, don't you, that if it had been left up to her in the beginning, young Judah wouldn't have had a Roman playmate at all?"

Father had understood more than I realized. I remember how I'd felt when I discovered that this great lady – whom I admired – was counting the days until I went to Rome for my education and would be out of her children's lives. What a pity I hadn't shared my feelings with Father.

"It was Prince Ithamar who introduced us; he wanted Judah to practise his Latin with a native speaker."

"I remember him well. He wasn't such a keen nationalist as his wife. He liked to travel and do business in far-off places and meet all kinds of people. I gathered he thought Rome had been a positive help in enlarging his business empire."

"He was full of stories about the places he'd seen. I thought he was like Odysseus."

Prince Ithamar had drowned when Judah was seven and I nine. I'd been very sorry. If I see him again in the afterlife, I don't know how I will explain things to him.

"Do you think Lady Miriam encouraged Judah to dream of the coming of the Messiah to deliver Judaea?"

"I'm sure of it. There were things she said when she forgot I was within hearing."

The evening after Judah and I had quarrelled, I'd sensed how strongly her personality was deliberately opposed to mine. She must have been rejoicing that my brief reunion with her son had ended in estrangement. I knew she wanted to be rid of me.

"Would she have wanted him to throw the tile at Gratus? It seems such a stupid, suicidal way of starting a revolution – so disorganized. Though it wouldn't be the first time a revolution had started with something stupid."

"I don't suppose she told him to throw the tile. I expect she was horrified that her motherly eloquence had produced such a result. No, she would more likely have wanted him to work cautiously with an underground movement – until the time seemed right."

"And the young girl – what was her name?"

"Tirzah. She would have been fifteen. Probably absorbing her mother's ideas, but she would have been more passive. Lady Miriam and Judah were the chief speakers of the family. Tirzah mostly just agreed to everything."

"And the mother and daughter were imprisoned in the Fortress after the assassination attempt. The property was confiscated, and your ex-friend was sentenced to the galleys. No trial because of emergency measures."

"Can you imagine how it would've been, Father? Protesters screaming all the while the court was in session – some of them the same rioters that threw whatever they could at the Roman troops after the tile started things moving."

"Yes, I appreciate the problem. I thought Gratus had his hands full, and I wished you hadn't been assigned to him. Tell me, did you ever have any doubts about Ben-Hur's throwing the tile? Could it have been an accident – even though in his heart he hated Rome?"

I was honest with my father, more than I would have been with most other people.

"At the time I was convinced of his guilt. I'd lain awake thinking about our quarrel, and there, the very next day, was this act of defiance. I felt he had rejected my friendship, even ignoring my hand, because he was a revolutionary. I couldn't help suspecting that his welcoming visit had been just to pump me for information about the time of Gratus' parade."

"Did you have doubts afterwards?"

"Yes, I often thought about it for the first year or two. Although I believe he was dreaming of himself as a soldier of the Lord marching to victory and expelling all the heathen, it's possible that when he leaned on the miserable tile it just slipped."

"It seems just possible. But even if you had wanted to, you could hardly have gone to Gratus and said, 'Maybe we made a mistake.' He'd have said, 'No mistake! I made enough money out of this affair to cover all my political expenses, everything it cost me to get this procuratorship!'"

"That would be Gratus all right."

"He gave you a reward as well – which was legal. You had given evidence – in camera – to convict an assassin."

"Yes, it felt strange to have some of Judah's money. I never quite got used to it, though I'd accepted it very willingly. And now, of course, I haven't got it. He recovered it with interest."

I'd tried to be flippant in my thoughts about the reward from Judah's estate. Some of that flippancy had got into a comment in a letter I'd written to Gratus when I first discovered that Judah was alive, free, and plotting my ruin. Unfortunately, one copy of my letter (the one sent by land) was intercepted by an agent of Sheik Ilderim who saw fit to rob a government mail courier. This, despite the fact that the Sheik had agreed to help protect our routes. Subsequently, Judah got to read the letter and it confirmed his opinion of me and reinforced his hate.

Father said, "It seems the Fates or the Gods, or just his God was working for him. Imagine a galley slave saving a Roman admiral during a naval battle and being freed and adopted as a result."

"Extraordinary!"

"I imagine he used Admiral Arrius' help to get training so that, in time, he could drill zealot legions. That seems like the logical step for a dedicated revolutionary."

"Yes, I believe he gave it his total concentration. He always had a way of focusing intensely on an objective. It was often an advantage, except sometimes in a board game when he would get caught up in his grand strategy and forget about his peripheral vision – and then I could surprise him."

"As you evidently did in the matter of Iras. How very embarrassing that must have been for him!"

"By now it may be that Iras has told him how desperately she regrets her poor judgement."

"I feel sorry for the admiral. Probably thinking he had the perfect son and heir, the perfect Roman warrior, in his grateful adopted son. I trust he died undeceived."

"That I don't know. It was after his death that Judah came to Antioch, apparently to serve with the legions of the consul Maxentius. And there we met again."

It was by the Fountain of Castalia in the Grove of Daphne. The same place and time we had both met Iras.

"I suppose you don't want to talk about the race."

"Not much. I should never have let myself be pressured into that crazy bet. It was probably the stupidest thing I ever did in my life. And I shouldn't have struck his beautiful Arabian horses. Normally I don't hurt animals. But I was sure he would aim for my wheel when he got the chance."

Sometimes I have wondered what would have happened if the race had been scheduled for the Jewish Sabbath. Would Judah still have participated?

"It's too bad the public has got hold of exaggerated accounts of what happened. For example, the story that you drove a Greek chariot with spikes on your axle points for drilling your rival's wheels."

"Mother of the Gods, I had *tigers'* heads carved on my axle points! They couldn't have damaged anyone else's wheel. They were just a foolish showy extravagance on my part."

"We had heard they were lions' heads."

I had to smile a little. "I told the artist I wanted tigers. I would hardly choose the Lion of Judah as my personal symbol, would I? But the artist forgot or misunderstood. I didn't want him to start over from scratch, so I told him to reduce the manes as much as he could, paint stripes on, and make the faces as tigerish as possible. The result was a unique hybrid. Of course, after the race, it would have been hard to determine what sort of animals they were."

My chariot had been badly smashed – beyond repair – but I'd been able to salvage some of the gold ornamentation.

"Well, what's done is done," said Father. "You're going to live all that down, with your family and the Gods helping you. But I think you should consider a compromise."

"What compromise? I will never try to conciliate Judah. He has enough without that. He told Iras that he'd recovered his mother and sister. He even said that the Nazarene prophet whom Pilate later executed had healed them of leprosy, allegedly contracted in prison. I don't see how they could have got it; contrary to what Judah assumes, I never arranged for them to be exposed to it, and if they were actually healed, surely that proves they never really had it."

"It would seem so. The East is full of miracle stories, for most of which there are natural explanations. All things considered, I'm glad the women are well and safe, aren't you?"

"Yes, especially Tirzah. She was probably blameless."

I hadn't let myself look at her properly when the arrest was made, though I'd glanced hastily and said, "That's his sister."

"I'm thinking now," said Father, "that it might be a good time to let well enough alone – not to go after revenge but to concentrate on rebuilding your own life."

I could see that he might be right. Yet, less than a month before, revenge had been so much in my thoughts. To turn in my enemy – Rome's enemy, not just mine! My second last act on earth. And then, when I knew he was gone, to take my own leave.

Father said, "As far as we know, Ben-Hur isn't involved in another revolutionary plot. If we thought he was, that would make a difference."

"I don't know. The fact that he's living here means that at least he's not personally drilling zealots in his homeland. Of course, he could be funding revolutionaries."

"As long as we don't know for sure, maybe you could promise the Gods – conditionally – to live and let live. We don't know what the Fates have in store for any of us, but what if you simply aren't destined to destroy the Jew – and he isn't meant to destroy you either? He got out of the galleys – and now *you* are literally setting foot on the road back. The Egyptian didn't succeed in robbing you of life to protect him. Suppose the Immortals want you both to survive?"

Judah had told Iras he thought my physical affliction a just punishment from God, accomplished with his invaluable help. He had thought the whole universe inexorably turned against me, the very stars in their courses driven by a relentless God to trample forever on my hopes.

What if I lived to prove him wrong? Wouldn't it be too bad if I recovered my strength and went on to honour and good fortune but Judah didn't live to see it! Then he'd never know that his pronouncement of doom wasn't divinely inspired after all.

But I would certainly want him to know. And I wouldn't want to go to a Jewish cemetery to tell him. But would I ever be able to walk upright easily without tiring? Would I ever live down that damned race in the memory of my countrymen? Would I ever be able to win their respect?

"Father, I don't promise that I'll never try to get even in some way. But I won't go with accusations to Macro. You are right – it wouldn't be wise."

"I'm so glad you see that." He looked weary. Our conversation had taken a lot out of him.

"I won't try to have him assassinated. If the Gods don't want him killed, I'm not going to waste the effort or the expense."

"That is a relief to me, since I intend to help you all I can financially. You've been in my will all along, and I'm going to transfer some money and property to you during my life. I expect my lawyer and business adviser to call tomorrow."

"Father, I'm going to concentrate on getting back on my feet. Nothing else for now. I'm not going to waste energy on hate, or think about Ben-Hur or Iras at all if I can help it."

"Good! Your recovery should be your first priority."

"It helps that you understand. I promise to do my very best to satisfy you and bring honour to our family. Whatever you ask."

"Thank you, Marcus!" He sounded so tired and relieved. I was touched that he had used my praenomen as he had when I was a child with him in Jerusalem.

CHAPTER NINE

WHILE my father was with his lawyer the next morning, the doctor came and removed my stitches. He advised me against immersing myself in a bath too soon. I could continue having sponge baths from a basin, or I could use the sort of small bath that I could sit in while a slave poured warm water over me. Two of the female slaves, both middle-aged and good-natured, were assigned to attend me and rub me down with oil and then scrape it off very gently with the strigil. It was pleasant having this sort of comfort on a daily basis.

Then Sosius came to tell me about his plans for my book in an edition acknowledging my authorship. He wanted to be sure my family had no objection. Barbatus joined our discussion.

"The same story Messalina was reading yesterday?"

"Yes, that's the one."

"Lepida says all the ladies are reading it. I trust there aren't any disgraceful indecent things in it."

Barbatus has high moral standards.

"Barbatus, I wrote nothing you could object to your daughter's reading. I aimed my story at the public in general, not the fans of pornography."

If Sosius had asked for a pornographic novel, I might have given it a try – though I would never have wanted my name on it.

"It's really a fine work," said Sosius. "Very imaginative, full of action and excitement. And, unlike so many novels of similar type, this one has wit. You can be proud of your brother, sir."

"I'm pleased to hear you say so," said Barbatus. To me he added, "Almost everyone who knows you would probably read it, just to find out if he's in it. Did you caricature anyone?"

"Not so that anyone could sue."

I had created a nasty entrepreneur with some resemblance to Sanballat. However, I had made sure he didn't have a Jewish or Samaritan name; in fact I named him Haman, after the arch-enemy of the Jews, whose downfall they celebrate every year at the Feast of Purim.

I also created a sketch of Gratus – by another name. I called him Holofernes, after a Babylonian general in a Jewish tale.

My novel had helped save my sanity. When I was spinning adventures for Strephon and his fair Dynamene or composing excessively romantic dialogue for them, I could leave harsh reality, including Iras, behind for a little while and enter a world in which two star-crossed lovers fled from ocean to ocean, visiting lands unknown, sometimes clinging together against a perverse and hostile world, sometimes searching for each other because a cruel fate had driven them apart.

I drew freely on mythology – Strephon had an encounter with Circe while he was trying to find his beloved, who had been kidnapped by pirates. Strephon was very courteous to the great sorceress, and she rewarded him by enticing the pirates to her beach and then turning them into small crabs. Meantime Dynamene was rescued from the pirate ship by her lover.

Another time Strephon was shipwrecked and nearly drawn underwater to become the husband of a gorgeous sea-nymph, who yearned for him and could have given him the power to breathe like the sea-people.

Outrageous balderdash – and yet I enjoyed it! Strephon did so much that I would have liked to do. He fought duels, he drove a chariot, he even had a ride on a flying horse that was provided by the Gods to help save Dynamene from a band of British Druids bent on sacrificing her. Installments always ended with the characters in appalling situations from which it seemed impossible to escape. But of course they did.

Father was pleased about my novel. Our family has a tradition of writing both poetry and prose, and of sponsoring writers, who can't make a very good living on the small amounts which publishers will pay them – if they agree to pay them anything. It is mainly the publishers themselves who make the money, employing many slaves to copy manuscripts, then selling the copies to the public. A writer needs a patron who will see that his needs are provided for so that he can be without worries as he devotes himself to his calling. For example, Maecenas, the friend of Augustus Caesar, bought a farm for the poet Horace – the kind of farm where slaves did the work and Horace could relax and entertain his patron and friends in a beautiful rural setting.

My grandfather, Marcus Valerius Messala Corvinus, wrote history, poetry, and a textbook on grammar, which is still used by students. He also sponsored Ovid and Tibullus, who were both very grateful for his financial assistance and his steady encouragement. He did his best to bring their work to the attention of important people.

Now I too had patrons: my father and my brother.

After meeting with his lawyer and his banker, Father told me that I now had a million sesterces in an account with the reliable bank of Granius, and some farmland and real estate here and in Sicily. There were vineyards and orchards, and sheep and cattle grazed on the hilly slopes. There were also rental buildings in small towns located partly on my land. I would have enough money to qualify for the equestrian order. This requires at least four hundred thousand sesterces, partly in annual income, and the rest in net worth, including land and slaves. However, to be in the Senate I would have to have an income of a million sesterces, and even then I wouldn't have money to throw around, buying political support and putting on showy public games to impress everyone. Father said that I would ultimately inherit enough to get into the Senate in a modest way, even if I couldn't buy my way to high office.

Barbatus, as the older son, must receive the greater share of what Father will leave. He is already rich, having inherited a fortune from his mother and been given a generous advance from Father; in addition, he married a rich lady, though Lepida has kept control of her own money and Calabrian estates. He has no son, and believes he will never have one now. He doesn't want to divorce Lepida and try for a son with another woman, nor does he wish to adopt a boy. The fact that I have a chance of getting back on my feet and living a more normal life means that perhaps I will be the one to carry on our male line. He told Father that he didn't grudge me anything; on the contrary, he will try to help me be a success.

Of course Father would have to leave a sizable legacy to the Emperor, as he was known to overturn wills that left him little or nothing on the grounds that to be so ungrateful the testator must not have been of sound mind.

"There may be a problem about my admittance to the equestrian order, Father. The Emperor doesn't regard me kindly – at least he didn't five years ago, and he isn't famous for his forgiving spirit."

"If only you had made it home in time to be present when your case came up."

"I thought I'd make it in time. It's just that suddenly there was a court opening, and my lawyer couldn't postpone things. Meanwhile I was struggling to get the last bit of evidence against my enemy and stop his Judaean rebellion. I was trying to save Rome, if Tiberius only knew it."

"Unfortunately, he doesn't. But there may be some opportunities to improve your reputation. Even now you have some friends of standing, such as Caprarius and Quadratus, both of whom are doing so well."

Caprarius and Quadratus had come together to visit me. I was glad that in my school days I'd never belittled them, though I could and did vanquish rival wits who were out to demolish me.

Caprarius and Quadratus were natural engineers, the sort who could be depended on to plan and organize the construction of a good aqueduct or road. They could also express themselves plainly and strongly when motivated, but they didn't have a lot of confidence in their fluency. To my credit, as I remember it, I encouraged them. And now they were my true well-wishers. And I needed as many as I could find.

Caprarius wondered if I'd have time to check over a speech he'd been writing. I said I'd be glad to, at no charge, since my situation had improved so much. Quadratus wanted my opinion on a case he was working on, and I listened to him willingly.

June was passing. Each day I woke early and was helped to the garden, where I had a light breakfast as the sun was rising. Aurora with her flaming chariot leaving a pink streak in the sky.

I stretched out my toes and enjoyed the coolness of the smooth colonnade floor. Then I did my leg exercises, still basic, with just a little movement repeated again and again. Wiggling the feet, rotating the ankle, extending and bending the knee, stretching the sinews. A stranger who didn't understand might have laughed at so much effort for so little.

Several times a day two servants – or just Africanus – would lift me up and support me while I tried to put my weight on my legs and feet. I knew that I would collapse if they let go of me. When I used my new crutches, I still couldn't manage to coordinate my feet properly. It was just that my feet had much more feeling as they dragged along, and sometimes I could get them turned the right way for a baby step or two.

We were making plans for a summer at our villa near Baiae. I imagined myself swimming off our dock, even taking out a rowboat and building up my arms and my back muscles as, at the same time, I braced my legs.

Although I'd felt severe back pain for some time after the race, I had none now and hoped I would have none when I was able to walk. For the first time in years I was happy and looking forward to good times.

Really the only thing wrong with Baiae was that it was very close to Misenum, where my enemy had his villa. He might be sheltering Iras. There would probably be no occasion to see either of them if I stayed at our own place, swimming close to our private dock and beach, or taking short rides in the laneways behind our villa. But we might meet if I took the main road or went to the town of Baiae or out in a fishing boat. All right, so what? As the Gods will.

A couple of days after my father had arranged the liberal advance on my inheritance, Messalina came to me gleefully.

"There was a man asking about you; his name was Sanballat. My father told him to get out. He wouldn't let the man see you; he said he'd deliver any message if necessary. But there wasn't any message."

She found the spectacle of her father's indignation quite entertaining.

Was Barbatus furious on my behalf or was there something else? Why had Sanballat come to our house? Had he and Ben-Hur read my divorce announcement? Perhaps Iras had told them I was dead. They would want to find out for sure before breaking out the kosher wine and toasting my arrival in Sheol, which is the Jewish shadow world of spirits.

My brother came in red-faced and frowning. "That Sanballat fellow, the one you had the stupid bet with. He came to ask how you were, if you were here; he wanted to see you. I told him to go away, since I was sure you wouldn't want him bothering you. He didn't leave any message for you. Actually, if he comes back, I may set the guard dogs on him."

We have a couple of ferocious guard dogs that, unlike Tarquin, aren't pets at all. They have a handler who controls them and exercises them, and they are taken around on patrol at night when the household has gone to bed.

"Have you a personal reason for disliking him so much?"

"Yes, I have. I've been told on good authority that he's repeated, perhaps even started, rumours about my wife. Apparently he's made innuendoes about Lepida's friendship with Appius Silanus. Just because the man has visited us a few times! And that's not all.

He asked someone if it was true that Lepida had taken Messalina
to certain ceremonies in the Temple of Priapus, to teach her about
sexual matters. How dare he? The filthy – abominable – piece of
excrement!"

"I don't blame you for being outraged. You have to understand
how Sanballat thinks of us – and all Romans. He and his good
friends have utter contempt for us; they consider us all immoral,
debauched and rather stupid – compared to themselves. Add to that
the fact that Sanballat likes to tell stories of the rich and infamous
whenever he can collect an audience, whether it's in a bar or on a
ship's deck, where the passengers can't go very far from the sound of
his voice even if they want to. To do him justice, I'm told he can be
fairly entertaining."

"If I had enough proof that he slandered my family, I'd sue him.
Even though a court case would be embarrassing for all of us."

"Barbatus, wait a little. Sooner or later that smirking hyena will
go too far. Meantime I'd like to think I've finally done something
that he can't get me for – something he won't like at all."

Then I told him about my portrait of Haman, the slick conniving
entrepreneur, grain dealer, slave trader, money lender, and gambler.
I'd also included examples of his fondness for telling scandalous tales
which were sometimes, but not necessarily, true.

"If he tried to sue me, he would have to admit that there is a
resemblance between him and Haman. There's no way he would
want to do that."

Thank the Gods, I hadn't had to see Sanballat or endure even
a few moments of his overdone politeness and undisguised sneers.
How dare Judah try to inflict him on me! Unless Sanballat acted on
his own.

Poor Barbatus! One of the most correct and scrupulous men in
Rome. I don't believe Lepida would take her child to the Temple of
Priapus or have her initiated into the sort of behaviour one might
expect of a child prostitute. My niece and her young friends talk
a lot about their romantic fancies, but she is probably a virgin.
However, Lepida might have had a secret love affair with a handsome

distinguished man such as Appius Silanus. It is quite possible that she finds my brother not exciting enough.

I was glad the slaves were packing up the things we would take with us to Baiae. Some things would be sent by road, but we ourselves would, in a few days, be boarding our yacht, the Nereid, from Ostia.

CHAPTER TEN

FATHER remarked that Sanballat's name was Samaritan, not Jewish. He might have converted to orthodox Jewish practices and tried to be accepted, but to many Jews of unstained ancestry, he would still be considered a Samaritan, a mongrel of mixed blood, whose people worshipped at hilltop shrines rather than at the great Temple in Jerusalem. You would think this might have given Sanballat a sense of inferiority to overcome, but he never showed it. He derived a lot of pleasure from outsmarting us Romans in business and holding us up to ridicule in gossipy monologues whenever he could find willing listeners.

When in Antioch he had sailed up the Orontes River, keeping his fellow passengers entertained with the story of how Valerius Gratus had been hit on the head with a tile but subsequently made a fortune from the seized estate of his attacker, and how he had unsuccessfully tortured Simonides, the Hur steward, who had refused to give him access to his employer's ships and caravans. And, of course, how Simonides, though permanently crippled from the torture, had greatly enlarged the wealth of the Hur family, on which he had kept the unbreakable death grip of a fighting mastiff. Incidentally I never met Simonides and wasn't involved in his torture.

Valerius Gratus had heard about Sanballat's story telling and wished he could lay hands on him, but Sanballat was well out of his reach and could afford to laugh at Gratus. He was protected both by his Roman citizenship and his status as praefectus fabrum* for the army. He also enjoyed the trust and friendship of Simonides and Ben-Hur. I wondered if Ben-Hur was aware how Sanballat scrounged for malicious bits of gossip. He went after those choice items with the zeal of a starving dog scavenging for garbage.

Twice we had my cousins for dinner guests. Father was well enough to take his place on a dinner couch, though he retired early, turning the duties of host over to Barbatus. My cousins said things like, "Nice to see you again, Secundus" and "I'm so glad you're on the road to recovery." They seemed to mean it.

They talked of the latest news of the Forum and the Senate and particularly the gossip from Capri, where our elderly Emperor usually stays. He is old, and by temperament, grumpy. While sometimes very witty and perceptive, he can be capricious and unfair and is always on the lookout for treachery. On occasion, he crosses over to his villa at Misenum, where he can get a good look at the assembled western fleet in the harbour. The Misenum establishment is for receiving respected guests, but Capri is for private pleasures, and the source of many scandalous tales. Maybe the Emperor is a maligned man, but no one in my family would want his child invited to spend a holiday with the ruler of Rome. And yet he was a man who passionately loved his first wife, Vipsania, and hated being forced to divorce her and marry the Emperor Augustus' widowed daughter, Julia. How love can change and people with it.

The servants were cleaning out attics and odd corners as well as packing for our trip to our seaside villa. They brought me a leather chest with my name on it. It had been in storage for five years. Fortunately I still had the key; Philip brought it along with a few books and other small items from the Subura apartment.

I had a good time looking through my old souvenirs. There was an ivory elephant from an Antioch bazaar and some childhood toys:

---

* A civilian in charge of military supplies

a ball for playing trigon (a three-cornered game which I usually played with Judah and Tirzah, since I seldom had other playmates except when the Herod families brought their children to Jerusalem for Passover and other holidays), a knife, an old bow, and some arrows. There were several scrolls of stories I wrote when I was twelve. The ink was faded; I couldn't read them clearly.

There were also some wooden animals, some of which had been given to me by Father, and some I'd carved myself. They weren't completely realistic but had expression and personality. There were two ridiculous donkeys, a double-humped camel, several dogs and sheep, and a tiger that had surely a suggestion of feline grace and ferocity. I'd wanted to give some of them to Judah, but his mother would have objected, as they were graven images.

On one side of the box, rolled in soft leather, I had my military decorations, such as they were. I hadn't seen much major action, just some border fighting. I'd won two gold armillae, wide arm bracelets, for exceptional bravery. I had stored them with my childhood keepsakes. Did I sense that I might need to sell them one day? Long ago I had sold my sword and other military equipment I would never use again. I mentioned the armillae in a couple of the letters Father never received. I would have hardened myself to sell these special trophies. But the Gods be praised, I've still got them.

Lepida came to me holding a green bag of oriental silk embroidered with gold thread, a jewel bag with pockets for different items. It was rolled up and tied with green ribbon.

"By the girdle of Venus! Where did you find it, Lepida?"

"Before you came back here, the maids were going through the drawers of the garment chest in the room where you and Iras slept five years ago. The bag had dropped down behind the drawers. The maids found it because the bottom drawer wasn't pulling out as it should. I presume this is the missing bag that Iras made such a fuss over. I meant to tell you sooner."

Somewhat embarrassed, she watched me as I checked the contents. No doubt she had already taken a look. In one pocket was a thin gold necklace with a matching bracelet in the form of a coil, both with snake faces and green jade eyes. There were jade earrings to match. Another set took up two pockets: a gold headband, long earrings, two bracelets, and a necklace, all decorated with small and medium-sized rubies. The necklace had one very large pendant ruby, which must have been very valuable by itself. Iras had inherited these from her dead mother and treasured them.

Here also was a ruby ring that I remembered well. Sheik Ilderim had sent it to Iras after the race as a victory souvenir. Actually he had handed it to the messenger who had come from Iras to invite Ben-Hur to a rendezvous – a fatal rendezvous according to our plans. I had always said it ought to be the very first thing we would sell to meet expenses.

"Quite ostentatious, don't you think?" said Lepida.

She should talk. With her, ostentation takes the form of very elaborate hairstyles achieved by a couple of artistic Greeks who come several days in a market interval* to produce stunning effects beyond the skill of her maid. She and Barbatus often get invitations or invite guests to their home, and she likes to display ever-new masterpieces towering above her forehead: piles of shining red-gold waves on which a tiny ship might sail or golden flowers and coloured birds float gloriously. She also uses costly perfume.

She said, "These jewels ought to bring you a lot of money, even though the dealers probably wouldn't give you anything like what they would sell the pieces for."

It was rather nice of her not to sell the jewellery herself, though perhaps Barbatus would have questioned her. He had seen both the ruby necklace and the gold and jade set on Iras. Also, Iras had described her lost treasure to a few people.

I hated the thought of haggling with some slimy fellow of Sanballat's type, who would snicker to himself over the way he was taking advantage of me. I could have Philip do the bargaining, but he might not do much better than I against an expert. And I thought of a further problem.

"Lepida, Iras accused you of stealing the jewels. She'll go on saying

---

*The Romans had eight-day market intervals instead of seven-day weeks.

that as long as she can. She may have gone to some people I know in Misenum. Unless you want her accusation to become more widely publicized, maybe I should see that she gets these wretched baubles back – with a clear explanation. And I would demand a receipt."

Her initial response was a near-screech. "Give them back to that bitch after what she did to you? She doesn't deserve anything!"

Then she frowned as a new thought came to her. "You said *Misenum*. We know so many people there. Some of them, like my brother's wife, would enjoy a nasty story about me."

Now she was worried. Her brother's wife, Agrippina, is the great-niece of the Emperor. The two women have apparently treated each other with perfectly courteous malice since the day Gnaeus Domitius Ahenobarbus had the great honour of marrying Agrippina.

"When we get to Baiae," I said, "we must find out for sure if Iras is the guest of Quintus Arrius, and if so, we can have one of our people deliver the jewels with an appropriate note – and her divorce paper at the same time. And then we'll all be finished with Iras for good."

"What a detestable creature! But I'm glad you want to protect my reputation. When the two of you left here, she evidently told some people that I'd robbed her. Certainly there were a few catty women who made pointed remarks. They'd pretend to admire a necklace Barbatus had given me, but say, 'I don't suppose it's part of the Egyptian's lost collection? Just a joke, of course, dear!'"

She mimicked the other woman's sweetly affected voice.

Then she reminded herself – and me – that I wouldn't need the money the jewels might have brought me because Barbatus was being so good-natured about Father's generosity to me. I said I was very grateful to him.

I hated Iras' jewellery – it was too much like her, showy and foreign. I especially hated Ilderim's garish ring. If I'd been poor, naturally I would have sold the jewellery and banked the money, likely a paltry sum compared with what Iras had claimed the real value to be. I would then feel uncomfortable that I still retained some part of Iras. This way, I would be free, owing her nothing.

CHAPTER ELEVEN

I T was the beginning of July, time for our trip to Ostia where we would take Barbatus' yacht, the Nereid, and sail to Baiae. We rose very early to get on the road with our vehicles before sunrise because they were forbidden on the city streets during daylight hours. This is one reason Rome's business streets are so noisy at night when all the delivery carts go into action.

Father and I, with Tarquin beside us, rode in a large carriage driven by Africanus. Barbatus, Lepida, and Messalina had another carriage, and the servants who were coming with us occupied a third vehicle. Some items had been sent on by road the day before.

We had a good road, but a two-wheeled travelling carriage or carpentum is not particularly comfortable. Even though we had cushioned seats, we felt every jolt. As we went on, and the morning light grew, we could see crowds of travellers, many on foot or riding horses and donkeys. There were also many litters carried by strong slaves. It was time for the vacationers' exit from Rome.

When we reached the waterfront, Father and I transferred to a hired litter to take us all the way to the ship. Barbatus, Lepida, and Messalina felt able to walk from the carriage stop to the gangplank.

One of the carriages was to continue by land to Baiae, possibly arriving after we did. The other two would be taken back to the rental establishment on the edge of Rome.

It had been five years since I had gazed out over the sea and I drank in the blue water, the white froth on the waves near the shore, and the brilliant sky above the harbour. If only I didn't have to be carried to the ship.

The wind was with us, so we spent only two nights at sea. The women, Father, and Barbatus all had small cabins inside the ship, and the slaves had an area below the deck near the sailors. Philip, Father's best secretary, had gone on by land a day earlier to see that everything was ready for us. The Baiae villa was staffed with servants all year round.

I had a pavilion on deck, a scarlet tent partly open at the sides, where I slept attended by Africanus and Tarquin. It was pleasant to fall asleep there, feeling the breeze and listening to the waves.

Before dozing off, I thought uneasily about the prospect of meeting Judah. I hoped it could be avoided. I didn't care about him, but I would have liked to know how his mother and sister were. I could never ask him. Maybe Tirzah was married. I wondered about their disease, what it could have been. I'd heard that Pilate had released a couple of Jewish women with symptoms of leprosy, but I didn't know what that meant, whether it was like eczema or boils or something else. I wondered if Judah had actually seen the healing take place. How had it been done? Surely Jesus didn't do it with just a word and a wave of his hand! He was said to be a healer – maybe he gave them special poultices, or told them to go and bathe in the Jordan. There was a story about how someone had done that long ago in the days of the Jewish prophets.

Judah would be beside himself with wrath if I asked for details. The fact is, we absolutely can't talk to each other.

By late afternoon of the third day we sailed into the blue bay of Neapolis*. We could see the white sails of the main fleet gathered at Misenum and, high on a promontory, the majestic residence of

* Naples

the Emperor. The villa next to it, partly sheltered by trees, would be that built by the famous admiral Quintus Arrius, now the home of his adopted son.

We passed Misenum on our left and proceeded to our own villa at Baiae, now a popular resort, though once it was mainly an area for fish farming. At that time, Cumae, on the other side of the peninsula facing the open sea, was the more fashionable resort. But Baiae was now built up. Many villas were constructed close to the water which was deep enough for yachts to be tied up right at their owners' back doors.

At our place, there is a high platform above the shoreline. The dock itself is raised above the water; some stairs and a ramp lead up to a more elevated platform surrounded by a low wall. Inside there is a formal garden with a colonnade on three sides; it's a bigger garden than the one at our house in Rome.

On one side, our property extends for some distance with no neighbours. There is a beach a little way from the dock; waves come in just below the sand and rocks. Farther back there is a grove, and Barbatus says that behind the sheltering pines are the orange trees and grape arbours.

In no time, slaves were unloading our baggage and the villa servants welcomed us to our summer home. Africanus quickly pushed my chair up the ramp from the dock to the garden platform, while Messalina skipped up the steps singing. I went to my new room which is close to the garden and even has a window opening on the colonnade. The ladies took immediate possession of the baths, so I had slaves bring hot and cold water and washed in my room. In an hour dinner would be served and I would be able to relax on my dinner couch with the sea wind blowing in lightly from the garden. Maybe tomorrow I could bathe in the sea. The doctor had said it would be safe to immerse my neck.

I'd never been to this family property before. During my student years, I lived in the city mansion of an inattentive uncle, now deceased. He wanted me to excel in my studies and in manly sports, which I obligingly did. In other matters he gave me little guidance.

The next morning after a light breakfast, I worked on my exercises. I read for a while to Father, whose eyes have become weak. Then, when he was ready for a nap, I changed into my new swimming garment, which covers my loins and comes up over one shoulder. I didn't like to expose the scars on my back, but there would be no one but the servants to see. I could have gone into the water naked, but there is always the risk of the unexpected.

Africanus wheeled me down the ramp to the lower platform, and from there I simply let myself fall into the water, plunging down beneath the surface, then rising up to the air again. The sun was so bright I had to shut my eyes. The water holding me up was warm. Even if I didn't move my legs at all, I could swim with my arms. There was so much more space here than in the big pool at the public baths. I wouldn't have to reverse course every few strokes. My legs, still so feeble and heavy on land, became comparatively light. I could wiggle my feet and even my knees, though my arms did most of the work.

"I'll have to practise treading water," I said, and tried it but found it difficult to maintain an upright position.

Africanus stayed near and watched me. If I'd chosen to swim out farther, he would have followed me in a rowboat. However, I didn't go far that first day, nor did I stay in long enough to get a sunburn. My complexion is dark, but I haven't been exposed to the strong force of the sun much lately. During the years in Judaea and Syria I was more used to it.

Later in the day I badgered my brother until he arranged for me to take a short ride on a dark mare called Sheba, distinguished for her smooth gait. Africanus helped me get up on Sheba's back, and a groom named Nestor rode beside me on the trail through the grape arbour and the small orange grove. Just as in Antioch and Jerusalem, I can sit up and hold myself straight, and now I can also let my knees grip the sides of my mount, which is a satisfying sensation.

As I promised Barbatus, we stayed off the public roads. Another day we could try the poorly kept-up road across the neck of the peninsula. It's rocky country with unexpected streams and pools, some of them fresh water, some with warm mineral water from which a vapour rises smelling of salt and sulphur.

When we returned from our ride, all the family except Father and Messalina were in the peristylum with guests. Lepida's glum brother, Domitius Ahenobarbus, and his wife, the Emperor's great-niece Agrippina, were making a courtesy call. Lepida cares for her brother, unprepossessing as he is, but she detests Agrippina, who evidently doesn't like her either. Barbatus introduced me to the company. I'd met Ahenobarbus before, and had won his dislike without half trying. He acknowledged the introduction with a grunt. Agrippina was pleasanter, in fact, rather friendly and obviously curious.

As I settled into a chair from which I could look at both the ocean and the guests, I observed Messalina strolling along the beach. Her head was lifted haughtily, and she was scowling. I afterwards learned that Agrippina had bluntly told her she was a spoiled brat who broke in on adults and tried to focus attention on herself – which is sometimes true enough.

Lepida was icily hostile to her sister-in-law. Barbatus was distressed by this and determined to be polite. While Ahenobarbus held out his cup to be refilled by a hovering slave, Agrippina took the opportunity to survey us all with cool amusement. She is in her early twenties, still childless, with an excellent figure. She has lively dark eyes and thick black hair pulled back into a large bun – a contrast to Lepida's elaborate hairstyles.

Aside from bits of unpleasantness – or at times because of them – it was an interesting conversation, especially when Agrippina told us about a strange woman who had been washed up on the Emperor's private beach. She and Ahenobarbus were staying at the imperial villa, though the Emperor was on Capri. Being thus in charge, Agrippina had given orders for the woman to be confined in a dungeon.

"Maybe she was just a poor creature who'd made a wreck of her life," said Agrippina. "She certainly looked like a rag mop: long tangled black hair wet from the sea, torn clothes falling to pieces, a yellowish complexion. The Emperor has the greatest distrust of interlopers. He's had reason to fear assassins, and if he'd been there, he'd probably have taken stern measures. I thought I should lock her up and later question her closely. But I imagine you'll be amazed at what happened."

Barbatus and Lepida were listening apprehensively; they must have been glad Messalina was far down the beach, picking up shells. If present, she might have blurted out something about Uncle Secundus' divorced wife.

"That upstart Jew, Quintus Arrius, from the villa near the palace, came over," growled Ahenobarbus. "He'd heard about the woman, and he thought she might be someone he knew, the daughter of an old client, or something like that."

Agrippina took up the story. "Arrius is a very courteous man. He said he believed she had tried to reach him but missed him, that he was the executor of her father's will. So I obliged him and had the guards bring her out. But first I had them give her a clean dress, a slave's grey gown. I'd already had her head treated for lice with a strong lotion that reddens the scalp, and after that they'd cut off her hair very close. She did look a fright, and I suppose she was quite embarrassed to have him see her. Maybe she'd been somewhat good-looking at one time, if you admire the dark Egyptian type."

Poor Iras! I could picture her glaring bitterly at Agrippina.

"He recognized her and insisted that she come home with him in his carriage. He said her father had died about five years ago and had left her an inheritance. He was being kind and soothing to her. I felt sure it was safe to let him take her away."

"Women!" muttered Ahenobarbus. "You all take too much notice of Arrius' good looks and fine manners. If you ask me, he's just another smooth Jew who weaseled his way into the trust of the old admiral. We ought to watch out for his kind. Who knows what the real story is?"

I hoped they didn't find out. So Balthazar was dead and had left Iras something after all. He had long ago given away the greater part of his fortune to the poor but had retained enough for his own needs, perhaps invested it with the merchant Simonides, who might also have taken care of his will and other documents.

Barbatus asked Agrippina if the woman was still in the care of Arrius. From what the servants had reported, she remained at the Arrius villa. Palace staff occasionally had conversations with the staff of the Arrius establishment, which was just across a wooded ravine through which the Emperor's property line ran.

Agrippina chose her moment to linger beside my chair while Barbatus and Lepida were showing a bored Ahenobarbus a new statue of Bacchus near the grape arbour.

"I'm coming in a moment," she assured them. "Don't wait for me. I'll catch up to you."

To me she said quietly, "You were married to an Egyptian, weren't you, Messala Secundus? A dark beauty, I was told. And according to the Acta Diurna, you've just divorced her."

"I had ample cause, Lady Agrippina. But I'd rather not speak about her."

"Of course. I heard that she tried to murder you. Obviously a very violent woman. A dangerous creature. I trust Quintus Arrius won't come to regret his hospitality."

"I don't care what he regrets as long as he doesn't bother me about her. And frankly, I would rather no one else connected me with the pathetic refugee you handed over to him."

"I do understand. Your brother says you have some hope of being able to walk again. Naturally you would like to start a new life, untroubled by ugly echoes from the past. I won't say anything more about that miserable female. I truly wish you well."

I thanked her, and she joined the others by the statue of the Wine God. Soon after that, they went home.

I was left wondering what I should do about the damned jewellery.

CHAPTER TWELVE

ALL evening I thought about what I should do. So Iras wasn't absolutely destitute, dependent on the charity of Ben-Hur. In fact, he'd had her inheritance for five years, during which time he probably hadn't wanted to find her – certainly not if it meant finding me too. It occurred to me that some interest should have accumulated. Would Simonides have given her a decent rate of interest? I was inclined to be cynical about that.

I thought again of getting cash for Iras' jewellery; after all, she had tried to kill me, and I would have lasting scars. But for the sake of my family's reputation, it was probably a good idea to give the jewellery back. With communications taking place between the Hur servants and those of the Emperor – and Agrippina's staff too, as long as she and Ahenobarbus lived at the imperial villa, people in the highest circles would soon be learning more and more interesting details about the sad female Quintus Arrius was trying to rehabilitate. My name would come up and things would be said about my family.

The next morning, after breakfast, I had the jewel bag taken from my strong box, and I wrote a description of each item so that the list could be properly receipted. I was thinking of having one of the freedmen take the jewellery, the list, and the divorce paper to the villa of Quintus Arrius, and asking for a receipt. I was prepared to give my man a generous gratuity to make up for the awkwardness he would likely experience.

Having finished with the bag, I was sitting in the garden facing the blue water. My chair and table were shaded by a couple of small flowering trees. I had a footstool under my feet, against which Tarquin was resting his large head. Philip came up to me and announced that I had a caller: Quintus Arrius! Would I be willing to see him?

"Yes," I said unenthusiastically. "But first get my divorce paper from my box. Also, I'd like Africanus to be present, at a short distance." I gave him the key to the box.

I decided to keep Tarquin too. He looked capable of ferocity, despite his loving behaviour to me and Father – and his docility with everyone in the house.

I hadn't seen Ben-Hur since the race. I imagined he wouldn't be greatly changed – just more smug and triumphant. He would still be handsome and healthy, for he would have kept exercising religiously – really religiously.

I, on the other hand, had been battered by time, misfortune, and finally my harpy wife. My hair was as thick as ever, but there was a grey streak above the left temple. The swelling of my bruises had gone down; the purple patches had changed to dull yellow. The bandages had long since been taken off my face and neck, revealing conspicuous dark red gashes, most notably the jagged line on my throat. I was wearing a long dark brown tunic which concealed the thinness of my once-muscular legs.

Ye Gods, there he was, advancing into the garden in a white tunic with the single vertical purple stripe permitted to the noble equestrian order. It probably wouldn't have been visible if he had worn a toga over it. Characteristically, his informal attire flaunted the fact that, because of his wealth, he now outranked me in my own world.

In the moments before Ben-Hur's entrance, Philip had brought a copy of the divorce document, and another servant had placed a chair across the table from me, so that my guest could sit within speaking distance but not too near me. Now Ben-Hur was close enough to see my damaged face and slashed neck in the sunlight. He appeared briefly startled, but then said very politely, "How are you, Messala?"

"Very well – thank you." My tone was ironic. "Please take a seat – right over there."

He went to the chair with a cautious glance at Tarquin, who stayed at my feet but turned his large head a little to follow his movements. Tarquin growled quietly, sensing his unease – and mine. As far as I know, dogs have never been a part of Ben-Hur's life.

He said, "You don't need a guard dog to protect yourself against me, Messala."

"That's reassuring! I'd rather not order Tarquin to attack you; he's my father's pet."

"How is your father?"

"He had a heart attack at the end of May, shortly before I came home. Now he's recovering, and we're company for each other."

I took the initiative. "I'm sure you didn't come here just to ask about my health or my father's. I assume your visit concerns Iras."

"Yes, it does. Let me tell you."

"Proceed."

"Early in June, Iras came to my house and talked to my wife. She was in obvious distress; she said she was sorry for ever having tried to harm me and that God had punished her till even I would pity her."

As usual he had emotion in his voice.

"She also said – that you had died." He hesitated before going on. "In fact, that she had killed you because of the great misery you brought her."

"She came close," I said. "I believe you once told her she would prove to me the sum of all curses – I don't know whether that was a wish or a psychic prediction. However, since I have survived, I must say that your forecast wasn't perfectly accurate, thank the Gods."

As might be expected, he seemed uneasy at hearing praise of Gods he firmly believed to be false. He said, "I didn't wish you dead, though you could be a danger to me and my family. Iras said you had had a file on me – which she destroyed."

"True. It's now in minute fragments scattered in the garbage that drifts around Rome's poorer streets. I'd be a fool to take an accusation to Macro without evidence to back it up. Did your wife offer Iras the refuge of your home as a reward?"

I imagined his wife would more willingly have paid Iras to go away, far and fast.

"Esther offered to help Iras out of pity, but she wasn't glad of your death. However, Iras said she didn't want pity or tears, that everything would soon be over. She evidently intended to take her own life. Esther couldn't stop her from leaving.

"When I came home, I searched for Iras, but without success. I feared the worst. That night I dreamed that only the blue waves knew her tragic fate."

That last poetic touch was so like him!

"The next day I heard that a sick woman had been washed ashore on the Emperor's beach and taken into custody as a trespasser. I went to the palace and talked to Agrippina, the Emperor's great-niece."

"I know Agrippina. Her husband, Domitius Ahenobarbus, is the brother of my sister-in-law, Domitia Lepida. In fact, I've already heard the next part of your story. Agrippina and Ahenobarbus called on us yesterday; they told us all about how you came to the rescue of the prisoner, declaring that you were the executor of her late father's estate."

It was too much – his presuming to tell me who Agrippina was, as though I didn't know, by name, if not by face, all the members of the Emperor's family.

He looked mildly irked. "I hadn't realized Agrippina was connected with your family. Does she know that the woman she imprisoned was your wife – your divorced wife, according to the Acta Diurna?"

"Yes, she knows; she figured it out and spoke to me about it. She said she wouldn't mention it to anyone else – and that may include Ahenobarbus, but I'm not sure."

"I hope Iras won't be an object of gossip. She's been very ill, feverish, even delirious, raving and saying strange things. She's now beginning to recover. Your divorce announcement came as a shock; she couldn't believe it."

"I trust it didn't bring on a relapse, finding out that she isn't a widow after all, just a divorcee."

What had she divulged in her ravings? I didn't think she would be staying long with the Hurs. She'd be eaten alive with jealousy of Ben-Hur's wife. She should return to Egypt.

"Right here I have a divorce document which I was going to send to her. Perhaps you won't mind delivering it." I pointed to the paper near him on the table.

He took it and said, "It's traditional, isn't it, for a Roman to return some portion of his divorced wife's dowry?"

"Dowry? What dowry?"

He must have expected me to be outraged at the idea of giving money to Iras, my would-be murderess. Indeed it took a fair amount of gall for him to raise the subject, considering the fact that he was Balthazar's executor and perhaps for some considerable time had been holding a legacy for Iras. Her dowry, indeed!

Getting no immediate reaction beyond a raised eyebrow, he continued to make his point.

"I know she brought you no money to speak of when she ran off from her aged father, but she had some valuable jewels, all of which were in some way disposed of during her years with you. Indeed her best jewels, left her by her mother, disappeared while she was in your family home. Even if you aren't a rich man, a court might rule that you should at least make a token effort to reimburse her. Possibly your family might assist you, considering the way the jewels disappeared under their own roof."

Now he was waiting for an explosion of Roman wrath. He wanted to humiliate me with his patronizing references to my limited means and the possibility of help from my family. In view of Iras' attempt on my life, which I could prove with the testimony of Reuben and Rebecca, no Roman judge would expect me to pay Iras anything – unless, of course, Ben-Hur bribed him to render a biased verdict.

I touched the green bag. "Might this contain the jewels you have in mind?"

"Are they – surely you haven't had them all along?"

"Naturally not, or I would've tried to sell them, probably for a lot less than their real value. Haggling isn't one of my strong points. No, they've just lately been recovered. Five years ago Iras took for granted that someone had stolen them. She made rash accusations, mainly directed at Lepida, my brother's wife. Really the bag had slipped behind the drawers of a clothes chest. If everyone had remained calm and reasonable, it might have been found sooner. A short time ago, it came to light, and Lepida brought it to me. You may check it out, along with the inventory I've made."

I handed him the list and the jewel bag. I wondered if he had observed that my feet shifted slightly as I leaned forward to give him the items.

"I would like a receipt, and it would be very nice if you saw fit to add that you see no reason to doubt my explanation – that it *wasn't* stolen but simply mislaid and finally found."

He started to examine the pieces, comparing them with my list. "I admit I'm surprised that you're giving up the jewellery so readily."

"Oh, don't misunderstand! It's not out of goodness of heart or tenderness for Iras, whom I hope never to see again. But thanks to the generosity of my father, who's given me an advance on my inheritance, I don't need what I might get for the pieces, and so I have the satisfaction of freeing myself completely from that woman. Also the receipt which you're going to write may benefit my brother and his wife. Lepida has been hurt by Iras' well-circulated accusation of theft."

Then I said, "You told Agrippina you were Balthazar's executor. How long ago did he die?"

"Five years ago. The very day after Iras left him. His will was unchanged. He had given most of his fortune to the poor of

Alexandria, but Iras was to have all that he had kept to live on. It was mainly invested with Simonides, who is now my father-in-law as well as my fellow executor. With liberal interest, her legacy of two hundred thousand sesterces has almost doubled. In addition, there is a small house in Alexandria, which Balthazar had sold but which Simonides repossessed for the estate after the buyer defaulted on payments. So Iras isn't a poor woman. Does all this make you consider reconciling?"

He was being clumsily sarcastic. Taking my silence for encouragement, he went on. "Alexandria is a great cultural centre. You might like it, and the warm dry climate would be good for you. Iras might be willing. She keeps saying that her marriage would have been saved if I'd found her and given her the legacy several years ago."

"No way in Hades! You can't possibly think I'd be stupid enough to trust myself into her bloody hands, far away from my family, far from all help. She'd soon find a way to make herself a widow, acting on the principle that what was left over from lunch must be finished at supper. No, here I stay."

"Maybe you should think longer before refusing."

"You seem convinced I'd do any fool thing out of sheer blind greed. Understand this: I don't want any of Iras' fortune or anything that might bind me to her. Maybe her money will help her find another husband – if she gets back into the habit of washing her hair and cleaning her fingernails.

"By the way, were you diligently searching for Iras during the whole five years?"

His face flushed, whether from embarrassment or anger. Perhaps a mixture.

"I had people search in Alexandria and talk to Iras' cousins, who said they had heard nothing from her. I know now that she wrote to them and they didn't answer. I also had someone make enquiries in Antioch. And when Sanballat went back to Rome, he was supposed to find out if she had gone there with you. He wrote back that he couldn't find either of you."

"Oh, he did? The duplicitous old weasel! He saw me a number

of times; in fact he was – I would say frequently underfoot, but that does sound a little absurd. However, he was almost as ubiquitous as he was malicious – and all the time I supposed he was carrying out your directions."

"No, I never asked him to insult you or to make himself obnoxious – though of course he would respond suitably to any discourtesy from you."

In other words, if Sanballat was impolite to me, I must have invited it. True I'd long ago called Sanballat "redemptor of the flesh of swine," but I had had provocation, and besides I'd had an irresistible vision of grateful pigs lifting up thankful trotters for Sanballat's abstinence from pork.

Ben-Hur said thoughtfully, "Iras also told us she had noticed Sanballat in Rome. He may have imagined he was serving my true wish and protecting Balthazar's money from you. But I don't like being made a careless executor. I shouldn't have trusted him in this matter – and I'll tell him so, despite my past obligation to him."

"A commendable resolve. In future don't send Sanballat to me. I don't want to see him. If you must make use of his dubious diplomatic ability, you might send him to negotiate for the mineral rights of a savage tribe that roasts human victims."

While he was digesting that revolting suggestion and examining the jewellery, I asked, "Will Iras be returning to Egypt soon?"

"It may take her a while to recover her health enough for the sea voyage. She has mixed feelings. She's full of anger and yet partly she wants you even now."

"Then she's at least half out of her mind. She wants to control. At the last she turned into a night hag slavering like a vampire bitch for my blood."

Clearly disgusted by the simile, he took a deep breath.

"I can't blame you for wanting to stay alive. But I pity her. She must have loved you passionately to go away with you in the first place. And now it will be hard for her to live as a divorced woman, especially as she's lost her beauty. I can't imagine the sort of man who would marry her."

"Don't let her hear you say that. Leave her some hope. As it is, living in your house, she'll feel as if she's wearing sackcloth and eating ashes."

I was surprised at my own pity since I still didn't want her.

"She should be thankful; we're all making an effort to be kind to her." He didn't see that his deliberate kindness could end up making things worse.

"Since you so emphatically don't want Iras, perhaps you won't mind signing a statement that you make no claim whatever on her inheritance. I've written a list of her assets in money and real estate. Could you state in writing that you don't want any of it, now or ever?"

"Yes, I could do that. And of course you will write my receipt for the jewellery."

I had writing material on the table, so that we were both able to write what was required. Each of us signed our statements and sealed them with our signet rings, dipped in the hot wax which had been melted over a small lamp and then poured on the paper.

He held up the necklace of rubies and gold with the large pendant ruby.

"This alone must be worth thousands, a small fortune."

"So Iras always said. I wouldn't know; I'm not an expert on precious stones."

Then he picked up the ruby ring that had been sent to her by Sheik Ilderim. To me it looked like a blob of congealed blood.

"This isn't part of the set, is it?"

"No, it was given to her on another occasion." I chose not to be specific. "She may wish to wear it in place of her wedding band."

Long ago iron rings were worn by Roman brides; later they became more attractive. I'd given Iras a copper ring covered with gold that was soon tarnished like our marriage. It had our initials cut on it, but no other decoration.

Ben-Hur said, "That reminds me – she sent her wedding ring back to you. But perhaps you don't want it."

He produced it from the pouch in his leather belt and placed it on the table.

I took it between two fingers. "Now what shall I do with this useless bauble?"

"Africanus!" He came to me immediately. "Dispose of this thing." I handed it to him. "Do whatever you like with it. Sell it, give it to the next beggar you see, or throw it into the waves down there. But I don't want to see it ever again."

"Very good, sir," said Africanus. He had received many gifts from my father and a few from other relatives who had experienced his healing skills. Accordingly, the ring didn't appeal to him; he may have shared my aversion to it – a ring that had come from her bloody, knife-wielding hand. He walked swiftly to the stone parapet and dropped the ring into the blue depths. Then he returned to his post.

Ben-Hur said, "Well, that's certainly final. But no doubt the sight of her jewels will lift Iras' spirits. What about you, Messala? Are you happy now – or at least content at last?"

No doubt he would've preferred to see me pathetic and grovelling. I answered him slowly, determined to seem relaxed and untroubled by his condescension.

"Yes, I'm quite pleased with my life. It has much more to offer than it had a month ago. Iras' departure is a particular joy. Now I'm home; my family has welcomed me kindly. I'm financially secure, though not extremely rich. And this is an agreeable place, isn't it?"

Judah looked round at the flowering garden with its fountain and the bright blue sea below the stone wall. At a distance, one could see a few orange trees and part of the grape arbour.

"It's very attractive. So you're content to be here – or on some other family estate, I suppose. Though wherever you are, your activities must be quite restricted. It's the same with Simonides, my father-in-law, who was tortured at Gratus' orders."

He may have come with the intention of being restrained and almost kind, but he couldn't help twisting the knife.

"Not completely restricted. Actually I'm planning to go swimming and riding after you leave. But don't let me rush you."

He looked at me in disbelief. "Surely you can't swim or ride in your condition. Iras says you have no use of your legs."

I was thinking of correcting this information, but then I had another idea.

"Just think about the water down there. It's full of fish, and you may have observed that they don't have legs at all. Believe me, I can swim very well; in fact I went swimming just yesterday."

"Indeed! And how do you manage to ride – if you really do?"

"I need some help getting on and off a horse, but everything is fine when I'm in position. I've heard of Scythian chiefs – dead chiefs – being strapped sitting up on their horses, which are then made to gallop into battle with the cavalry. It's easier for me – I'm alive."

He frowned. "It's too bad Iras doesn't have your resourcefulness. She sees no joy ahead of her. And you feel no pity."

"Ye Gods, why should I?"

"Because she was a foolish romantic girl, deluded into abandoning her poor old father. You made her your accomplice, your spy, who pretended friendship and more for me, yet plotted betrayal – in my own house! All because you charmed her. You actually managed to become her lover even though you were – and still are – a cripple."

So! Now that the legal statements had been signed and he had his hands on Iras' jewels, he allowed his righteous anger to surge to the surface and come pouring out.

Slowly, in my best irritating drawl, I said, "Yes, in those days, Iras preferred half – no, it was more like two thirds – of me – to all of you."

Glowering, he rose and took a step forward but halted when Tarquin gave a warning snarl. Africanus, who had been over by a pillar of the portico, moved closer.

"Simonides was tortured twice. I don't know for certain you were personally involved, but I'm sure you would have been if Gratus had ordered you. All his bones were broken, and many of his joints dislocated. He's been confined to his bed or cushioned chair ever since. When the slaves move him or bathe him, they must be very careful. But you – you boast that you can swim and ride. If you ask me, you've got off easily."

"I didn't ask you. Your opinion of what I deserve is unimportant to me."

"You helped Gratus send me to the galleys and my mother and sister to a prison cell to get leprosy. All to get your rapacious Roman hands on my fortune!"

"I didn't torture Simonides. I've never even seen him. And I never planned for anyone to get leprosy. Moreover, if – as Iras reported to me – you recovered your mother and sister, healed by Jesus the Nazarene, it seems self-evident that they never had leprosy at all."

Was his blood pressure rising dangerously? Considerately I said, "I really think you should leave now. Africanus will show you out."

Immediately Africanus was right there, saying, "Follow me, sir."

"Don't forget Iras' jewellery," I reminded him.

There was a moment's hesitation as if he thought of saying goodbye but choked on the words. *Vale* is a Latin word of well-wishing; the Hebrew *shalom* means peace.

Only when his footsteps had died away on the marble floor of the inside corridor could I relax. He hadn't learned that I was regaining the use of my feet. I was glad I'd kept it from him. He might have prayed, "Lord, stop him in his tracks. Make him at least limp for the rest of his miserable life. Afflict him with severe arthritis. Amen!"

CHAPTER THIRTEEN

IN the warm sunny days that followed, I tried not to think about my encounter with Judah Ben-Hur, though I felt that I'd conducted myself well. He was the one who lost his temper. There'd been a moment when I felt I was facing a furious bull elephant about to charge. I was glad to have had Tarquin and Africanus near me.

I filled my days with activities. Accompanied by Nestor the groom, I went riding regularly. We never went far from home, but each day I felt more at ease riding Sheba.

I did a lot of swimming and diving down into the deep water near our dock. Under the direction of a trainer, I practised lifting weights: heavy ones for my arms, lighter ones attached to my legs. Sometimes I tried rowing a small boat, not just as exercise for my arms but because it requires bracing my legs and thus retraining calf and thigh muscles. Africanus went with me in the boat. I handled the oars while he sat back quietly, likely confusing onlookers who must have thought I was his servant.

We'd been going out in a sailboat too. I'd found I could do a lot of useful things without standing up or walking. I could work the ropes while sitting on the thwart or even the edge of the boat, and I could stretch or twist my body to reach things. Africanus was comfortable on the water. He used to sail boats off the African coast near Cyrene; it was family debt that made him a slave, he wasn't born to it. He'd be freed when Father died as a provision of his will.

Of course I still could not stand alone. Being completely vertical on my own was beyond me. When the slaves held me on my feet, I feared that, if they let go of me, my legs would buckle. With their help, or with the crutches, I could shuffle my feet a step or two. I offered regularly to the Gods, praying for more mobility.

After a day of exercise I used our rather small private bath, with the heated water kept warm to steamy hot, depending on the hypocaust system under the floor. After an oil treatment and massage, I finished off in our small cool pool. It isn't cold at this time of year, but it doesn't have hot air pipes under it.

Father usually sat in the garden in the late afternoon, so we would talk or play a board game. He also introduced me to a couple of the property stewards who would bring us reports on our lands, including the Sicilian estates. I wanted to learn all I could about our possessions.

We had some family meals all together, but Barbatus and Lepida dined out a lot. They entertained a little on a very small scale, not at all as lavishly as Lepida would have liked. She would have preferred having many guests and hiring musicians and dancers to perform in the centre of the dining room, but Barbatus felt that the noise and bustle would be bad for Father, even if he didn't stay all the way through a long meal. When we fulfilled our obligation and had Ahenobarbus and Agrippina for dinner, Father excused himself early and so did I, both of us because of our health. Thus we missed the worst of Ahenobarbus' bad temper and heavy drinking, as well as the catty exchanges between the two women. Actually, I wouldn't have minded conversing longer with Agrippina, who was quite friendly – to the point of irritating her husband.

I gather that my hopes of recovery would have been much poorer if I hadn't kept up the massage and manipulation of my seemingly lifeless legs, including toes and knees, during the years when it seemed hopeless. Certainly Iras thought I was wasting my time. But the one doctor who had given me a word of encouragement – his name was Luke – had said it would do some good, that it might prevent the total shrivelling of muscle tissue. Even so, I needed to build leg muscles and strengthen my bones all I could. The poor diet of that year in the Subura must have been bad for them.

In August came Caligula's wedding day. He was marrying Junia Claudilla Silana, the daughter of a consul chosen for him by the Emperor, then in residence in Misenum. Caligula himself may not have been very keen on marrying anyone. There were rumours that he enjoyed plenty of sexual variety and that his strongest attachment was to his sister Drusilla, even though she had a husband.

Caligula had developed a passion for chariot-racing, and although Tiberius Caesar had criticized me for entering a contest in which I was competing with persons of inferior birth, he seemed to encourage Caligula. With the Emperor's blessing, Caligula would compete in the September Games.

Barbatus and Lepida went to the wedding feast. Messalina thought she should have been invited instead of having to stay home with her grandfather and me. Petulantly she complained, "Nobody asks a girl of nearly eleven – even a very mature, intelligent girl like me – to adult events. It's too bad! Tiberius Gemellus will probably be there, although he isn't old enough to put on the toga of manhood."

"Don't fix your silly imagination on Gemellus," said Lepida. "He isn't very promising even if he is Caesar's grandson. And I'm not bringing you into society yet."

Young Tiberius Gemellus was the son of the Emperor's dead son Drusus and his cousin Livilla, who was privately executed for her affair with Aelius Sejanus. He was not often seen in public and was said to be sickly, the victim of frequent severe colds. His cousin, Gaius Caligula, the grandnephew of the Emperor and brother of Agrippina and two other sisters, was more likely to become the next Emperor.

Caligula was considered ambitious and crafty. Whereas his mother and two older brothers provoked Tiberius Caesar's suspicions and were imprisoned and put to death, Gaius Caligula had been the soul of attentive servility to the old man and had been his frequent guest at Capri. I disliked Caligula. I remember too well his coming into Sejanus' office, looking down at me at my desk, and exclaiming to Sejanus, "So you've given employment to the crippled ex-charioteer! How kind of you!"

While I didn't like to feel like a social pariah, I didn't mind missing the wedding. I made good use of my time. After Father had gone to bed, I worked on an idea for another book. Sosius had released the complete edition of my novel and was offering me ten percent of the profits if I wrote another one. He suggested *The Treasure of Dido* as a title. Queen Dido of Carthage was rumoured to have hidden many bags and boxes of gold and jewels in deep mountain caves somewhere in North Africa. For background material, I'd procured a copy of Claudius Caesar's *History of Carthage*, the most extensive work available on Carthaginian times. Claudius, the crippled, reclusive uncle of Caligula and Agrippina and their siblings – as well as young Gemellus – had devoted much of his life to scholarly research into subjects that the average Roman doesn't know or care about. I don't know if he was invited to the wedding banquet. The Emperor didn't like having him around; he found Claudius, who stuttered and drooled, quite disgusting.

Claudius' mother, the great Lady Antonia, widow of the Emperor's long-dead brother, was an important wedding guest. Tiberius had great respect for her as a model Roman wife and mother. Also, she was the one who discovered and exposed the scheme of Aelius Sejanus and her own daughter Livilla to get rid of the Emperor and take power for themselves.

I occasionally took brief trips to one of our nearer farms, returning the same day. I would have stayed longer had it been convenient. Barbatus didn't visit his rural estates, as he found that many of the countryside plants made him sneeze, especially at haying time. Also, Lepida found it boring to live away from fashionable life. Messalina enjoyed it at first, romping happily in the fields with the overseer's children, but then she would become imperious and even tyrannical with them, ready to order them beaten for imaginary offences to her exalted rank. Really she could be a bad-tempered little beast, especially when she didn't have enough to do. So Barbatus and his wife had been leaving everything to the efficiency of their farm stewards.

While I was thinking about my share of the family estates and how I could spend more time there, Barbatus and Lepida came home from the wedding. They said it was very lavish, with singers, dancers, and acrobats performing throughout a long feast. There was a generous display of food, a lot of it wasted, as is usual at such events, but since the Emperor, not Caligula, was paying for it, there weren't many exotic delicacies. Just larks' tongues, huge snails, and roasted dormice, in addition to the more common fish and meats. However, the pastries were decorated fantastically to look like peacocks, saffron-coloured lions, and pink and green elephants, among other creatures.

Barbatus said, "There were some surprise guests from the East. Maybe you know them."

"Not unless – I've met some members of the royal Herod family, though not lately."

"You guess correctly. Prince Herod Agrippa and his wife, Princess Cypros, and their four children. Actually they're guests of Lady Antonia and Claudius, who was Herod Agrippa's schoolfellow in Rome."

"I've met Herod Agrippa, but I don't know him well except by reputation. But Cypros – she and her family came to Jerusalem for the major religious holidays, and they stayed in the Herodian palace where Father and I had our apartments. She was my playmate at such times; she wasn't as restricted as most Jewish girls. She played ball games and climbed trees; we even put together a tree house in the garden."

Cypros hadn't wanted me to tell Judah about our tree house. Since she knew the Hurs weren't supportive of the Herod monarchy, she was a little critical of my friendship with him. But I was a loyal friend in those days; I insisted on bringing Judah to the tree house and tried to keep peace and goodwill between him and Cypros.

Lepida said, "I think Prince Herod Agrippa has got himself into some kind of trouble – maybe financial. So Rome is his refuge because he isn't welcome – maybe not even safe – anywhere else."

I'd heard that Herod Agrippa (named for Marcus Vipsanius Agrippa, our great general and statesman in the days of Emperor Augustus) was reckless and extravagant, and inclined to live well beyond the income of a prince of the Herod family of Israel, a prince with no clear prospect of a throne. His grandfather, Herod the Great, had ruled a lot of territory with help from Rome. He was considered to bring stability to the region. However, Augustus, and later, Tiberius, hadn't the same confidence in his sons; accordingly, Judaea itself is now under a Roman administrator, and some compliant members of the Herod family preside over the tetrarchies, which are little kingdoms. At this time, two of Herod Agrippa's uncles, Herod Antipas and Herod Philip, were childless, and Herod Agrippa had hopes of succeeding them, though aware that Uncle Herod Philip and his young niece-bride, Salome, might produce an heir. By the way, it's legal among those people for an uncle to marry his niece.

I sympathized with Herod Agrippa's delight in showiness and intrigue and could well imagine that he might have overspent his income and then schemed his way out of favour and into trouble with many of his kin and acquaintances.

I wondered if Herod Agrippa and Cypros would look me up after so long. Don't be absurd, Messala, I told myself. Why would they be interested? Whatever would they hope to get from me?

CHAPTER FOURTEEN

A T one time Barbatus would have headed back to Rome at
the end of August along with most other Roman senators.
In those days Senate business used to be of great importance. But
things changed. Under Tiberius, the Emperor let the Senate know
what legislation he wanted, and they passed it. Of course it was still
an honour to be a senator of Rome, especially if one had attained
magisterial office at least once and could therefore wear a purple
border on one's toga. But if no significant business was before the
Senate, there was an increasing tendency to linger in vacation resorts.
True, there was a legal obstacle to cluttering the roads with a lot of
heavily loaded carts once the usual summer vacation had ended, but
those with yachts, like Barbatus, could risk sailing home well into
the fall season if they stayed near the coast in case of storms. Many
people kept complete wardrobes at every one of their residences so
that they could travel lightly from one home to another.

After some discussion, Barbatus and Lepida decided to wait
until after the Ludi Romani* celebrations which begin on the thir-
teenth of September and continue for ten days. They could have

---

*The Roman Games, in honour of Jupiter Optimus Maximus, the best and the greatest celebrated in Rome, of course, but most of Lepida's social circle were still at Misenum. The games feature chariot races, boxing, wrestling, gladiatorial combats, and animal shows, as well as performances of classical Greek plays in the local amphitheatre.

In a way I would have liked showing myself and seeing if there were any old friends to encourage me on my way to full recovery. If there were, I could have endured seeing a few enemies, whom I could probably ignore as if they were distasteful graffiti on a wall. But I wasn't willing to struggle on crutches to a seat in the stands, even though I was getting better at coordinating my feet. Also, I knew Barbatus and Lepida would want to sit in the special section reserved for senators of magisterial rank and their families. I would have had to sit alone.

Not that I cared about seeing Caligula win a chariot race. Of course he would win. No one was fool enough to try to beat him, though conceivably a driver who wished to flatter him could make it look like a fairly close contest and then pull his team back in order to let Caligula forge ahead to the finish.

I could never have done that.

On the second of September I received a letter brought by a private messenger. It was from Iras, brought by one of Judah's servants, I suppose.

"Tonight I sail for Egypt. Ben-Hur is sending some people who will help me get settled in my father's house again. If you have a message for me, you may give it to the carrier of this letter."

Did she actually hope I would want to travel with her?

I told the man I had no letter or spoken message to send back either to Ben-Hur or to Iras.

She had plenty of time to reach Egypt before the autumn storms. South to the coast of Africa and then east, but not too close to shore, for there are rocky shoals and treacherous sands. I hoped the sea wind would agree with her, invigorate her.

Her cousins hadn't answered her letter, but I expected they would be more courteous once she returned with her inheritance to give her some status. I thought of her as evening came on, imagining the farewells and then the ship actually sailing on the darkening waters with Iras on board. Going out of my life.

Africanus and I decided that our sailboat could do with fresh paint. So we painted it red – I helped him for something to do. I had him buy new sails, scarlet sails, and brass letters spelling out the name I'd chosen – Flammifer. I couldn't help thinking of my racing colours, scarlet and gold.

When it was ready we took it out to sea, going farther from home than usual. Since the day was sunny and mild, we sailed out to the end of the peninsula where we could see the Emperor's villa on the rocky heights among the pines. We dropped anchor and fished for a while, catching several decent-sized fish, enough to feed the servants as well as the family.

I longed to be able to stand upright with a hand on the mast, keeping my balance with the roll of the boat – like standing in a chariot. We stayed well off shore from the Arrian villa and dock. Even if someone noticed the Flammifer's red sails, we'd be too distant to be identified.

On the opening day of the Games, I was sitting with Tarquin leaning against my leg while I read Lucretius' *On the Nature of Things** to Father, who was usually too weary to do much reading himself. I'd got to the harmful results of popular religious thinking, which led to such atrocities as the sacrifice of the maiden Iphigenia to secure a favourable wind to speed the Achaeans to the shores of Troy. Father was looking drowsy; I wondered if I should stop.

Out on the water, I could hear revellers singing and yahooing, shouting Caligula's name – probably a drunken party in a boat. Maybe they'd left the Games early after their hero won. Their asinine braying and caterwauling continued. Tarquin put his paws on the top of the waist-high stone wall beside us and began barking, a very loud deep bark that usually terrified intruders. The asses in the boat evidently heard him, for they made mocking cat noises, infuriating him. I was afraid he might spring over the parapet in rage.

Father had awakened, as if from a brief dream. He called to

De Rerum Natura

the dog, but Tarquin was barking too hard to hear his weak voice. Without thinking what I was doing, I put my hand on the top of the wall and drew myself up, putting my other hand on Tarquin's collar. Then I realized that I was standing up, without anyone holding me, just resting my hand on the parapet for support.

"Father!" I said.

He blinked as if he thought he might be dreaming. Tarquin seemed to know that something important had happened, for he stopped barking and sat down at my side, looking up at me with a puzzled expression.

"Marcus, this is wonderful! This is what I'd prayed to the Gods for, but I didn't think you could do it so soon. It's been a little over three months since you came back to me."

He rang, and Africanus was there in no time. He understood, without being told, that I didn't want to sit down again right away but felt insecure about attempting steps alone. He came to my side and stayed near me. I hung on to the wall, walked a short distance, then managed to turn around and retraced my hesitant steps. Africanus helped me when I let go of the wall and took a few more steps to Father. I could feel his supporting arm as I stood by Father and took his hand in mine.

It was an emotional moment. We both had tears in our eyes. In fact, since coming home, I have felt close to tears a number of times, though my eyes were dry all those days in the Subura.

A little later Barbatus, Lepida, and Messalina returned from the Games, which hadn't been very exciting. Caligula had been victorious in his much-publicized race, and he had looked quite handsome in his bright green tunic, his fair hair waving in the breeze.

Lepida had picked up some gossip. She was glad I was getting back on my feet, but she was mainly interested in her own news.

"They say Herod Agrippa has come through a lot of trouble – which he really brought on himself. It must have been very distressing for his poor wife."

"I presume you know some interesting details, Lepida."

"Well, he had a position as an adviser to Flaccus, our governor in Syria. The trouble was he was caught taking bribes from *both* sides in a case coming up before the governor. Taking a bribe from one party would be bad enough, but it does happen all the time. But playing both sides – utter perfidy! Flaccus was furious; he gave Herod his dismissal without listening to his defence, which would probably have been clever and eloquent."

"Probably, from all I've heard of Herod Agrippa. So then what did he do?"

"He and his family visited some of his relatives but wore out their welcome. I believe Herod's kin are difficult to get on with."

I didn't know about his Arab relatives, but I could imagine that his pseudo-Jewish* uncles and their wives might be easily stirred to jealousy of Herod Agrippa's brilliance and Cypros' beauty. Wherever they went they would outshine their hosts whether they tried or not – and they weren't naturally inclined to downplay themselves.

"Everywhere Herod's creditors kept following him and dunning him while the interest on his debts kept mounting," said Lepida.

"Then he obviously didn't borrow from his fellow Jews, who aren't supposed to charge their own people interest. But maybe they doubted that Herod Agrippa would ever manage to pay them back."

"It seems he did finally borrow from one of the Jewish leaders in Alexandria, after he was nearly imprisoned for debt there. He had been so desperate, he almost committed suicide, but his wife talked him out of it."

"Good for Cypros! But what will they do now? They still need an income. I suppose maybe Claudius and Antonia could help them for a while."

"I believe they're trying to find some kind of paying post for Herod. Meanwhile the Herods are living at the imperial villa. Everyone is talking about them because they're very spectacular people. He's so handsome and wears such magnificent clothes. Not being a Roman, he can wear robes and jewels that would seem excessive on one of our men. Even the Emperor, in his formal purple toga, would appear plainly dressed beside Herod."

*Many Jews didn't consider the Herods truly Jewish because of their mixed ancestry and their casual attitude toward traditional observances.

"I haven't seen Cypros for many years, but I imagine she's also very striking."

"So they say. I've never admired Eastern women that much, as you know."

A few days later Barbatus said, "A package has just come for you, Secundus. I think it's the canes you ordered."

It was. Two canes of good dark wood. Both had the initial *M* carved on them, inlaid with gold, but the cane for formal wear had extra golden flourishes. Barbatus remarked that I was being a little extravagant as well as premature, since I was only beginning to stand by myself and trying a few experimental steps, mostly with a hand holding on to something or someone. However, Father supported my choice. If I had to carry the memory of my errors in the form of a lingering physical impediment, I wouldn't slink in shame but would think of my showy canes – which I was sure I'd be using soon – as honourable ornaments, like the gold armillae I'd received for bravery.

We were still talking when a messenger arrived. It was a brief, friendly note for me from Herod Agrippa asking if he and Cypros might call on me the next day.

This was certainly more welcome than the letter from Iras. I quickly wrote a reply for the messenger to take back. I would be very happy to see Herod and Cypros.

"I shouldn't think they'd want to borrow money from you," said Lepida with her typical tact. "Do you think it's just a matter of friendship?"

"I hope it's friendship," I said. "Well, we'll see."

CHAPTER FIFTEEN

T HEY came in the late morning. Barbatus and Lepida had gone out, taking Messalina, leaving only Father and me. Deliberately I rose to greet the guests, holding on to a chair arm and a table.

Cypros said, "So you are recovering! I'm so glad for you."

Herod Agrippa said, "This is splendid news. We'd been led to believe that your paralysis was permanent. On my way here, frankly, I was searching for the right words to express sympathy tactfully, but now it seems we can just rejoice with you."

Then they turned to greet my father. We conversed over light wine. They asked questions about my recovery and my current activities.

"You've written a book, haven't you?" asked Cypros. "Lady Antonia has been reading it; she's highly amused."

I knew my novel was available in its complete form, and I had my own copy from Sosius. But I hadn't thought of Lady Antonia's reading it or liking it. She was the most respected matron in Rome, reputed to be serious and dignified, a pattern of correctness. But it seems she had a sense of humour.

I told them about the story I was working on. Herod said his friend Claudius would be pleased that I was making use of his *History of Carthage*, which undeservedly lacked avid readers. It struck me that the Gods must have been watching over me in those past days when I was perhaps too ready with witticisms at the expense of ridiculous people. I am sure I never got around to mimicking Claudius' stammer, or his lisp, or his pathetic gastric attacks which often followed a hearty meal of his favourite dishes. I don't recall ever saying anything disparaging about him, though he was certainly the butt of other people's humour. In fact, perhaps that was why. I preferred a more challenging topic for the exercise of my wit.

Changing the subject from myself, I asked them about their own plans. Were they thinking of wintering in Italy? I hoped so.

Cypros said, "We've had some very encouraging news. As you may know, Lady Antonia and Claudius have both taken us to their hearts and done everything for our comfort. Claudius doesn't have much influence on the Emperor, who finds him rather irritating, unfortunately, but Lady Antonia certainly has the Emperor's respect. She went to him and asked him if he couldn't find some kind of position for Herod, something which would put his gifts to good use. It's been so frustrating for him to have nothing worthwhile to do. There's nothing for him in our homeland; he feels absolutely wasted there."

"My country doesn't need me," said Herod ruefully. "But it seems Rome has a place for me. The Emperor has agreed that I should become the official tutor of young Tiberius Gemellus. I'd be supervising his training by the various subordinate tutors and sports instructors, befriending the boy, and helping him to understand the international scene. In a way I'll be repaying Rome for the superior education I received here myself."

Just as I expected, he was lavish in his praise of Rome's goodness, both in the past, when he had spent years here being educated with his friend Claudius, and again now that Claudius and his noble mother had exerted themselves to make the Herod family feel loved and appreciated. As for the Emperor, Tiberius Caesar, Herod said that people sometimes misjudged him, perhaps because of his deep reserve, but his generous spirit and his intelligence ought to be more generally recognized.

Herod Agrippa told me he would be given a good salary and a spacious house of his own, really part of the palace complex but separated from the main villa by a courtyard and garden. He would also have an apartment in the palace in Rome. Tiberius Caesar hadn't been in it for years but it had sometimes been used by his surviving relatives.

I was sure that Herod intended to flatter the Emperor whenever they met; he hoped to be eventually rewarded with the tetrarchy of one of his uncles. What a pity it was for him that they were both fairly young and in good health. Though, of course, he didn't say that to me!

Herod Agrippa was tall and handsome; in fact he looked like the kind of king the Jews would be lucky to get. Dark, with classically Semitic features (by which I mean that the curved nose looked noble and full of strength), he wore a tunic with a loose over-robe of crimson linen embroidered with gold thread. Richness became him.

Cypros had grown up into a tall beauty with a touch of natural copper in her dark curls. She had enormous dark eyes, tastefully made up.

Father was interested in the latest news from the East, where he had served for many years, and Herod had interesting stories to tell.

Cypros and I revived old memories. For instance, the leopard cub I'd adopted after a hunting expedition with Judah (but we didn't speak of him). I'd shot the mother leopard with my bow and then realized she was nursing. We'd found the den, and I'd brought the single cub home. Father had said that I must care for it myself, feed it, keep it quiet, clean its cage, not burden the servants – and I'd faithfully carried out my responsibilities, though I came to wonder when I would find time to do much else. Still I'd enjoyed my pet, and unknown to the others in the house, had taken little Jezebel under the covers at night, which kept her from yowling out of loneliness.

"Why did you call her Jezebel?" asked Herod. "She wasn't a national heroine, in fact quite the opposite."

"I know. I was warned that I might give offense if I called her, for example, Miriam or Rachel. Then I found out that once there was a ferocious queen named Jezebel. I thought she might like to come back as a leopardess."

When I went away to Rome, I gave Jezebel to Cypros, who was in Jerusalem at the time. That way my pet would never be killed in the arena; she would be kindly treated by the Herods, who had other exotic animals, including panthers and cheetahs. She'd have a cage at their estate, Herodium, a magnificent place. Cypros or a servant trained in handling big cats would take her walking on a lead, just as she and I already did.

"Jezebel lived for twelve years; she was always friendly and well-behaved. But finally she picked up some kind of sickness and was suddenly dead. Maybe she'd have lived longer in the wild," said Cypros sadly.

"Or she could have died violently," said Herod.

They admired our terrace with its walks circling beds of bright autumn flowers and the fountains, one with a statue of Venus and Cupid. They also saw the new statue of Bacchus in the open space just before the grape arbour. I strolled with them – if my slow hesitant walk on crutches can be called strolling. They were encouraging about my progress.

"By the way," said Herod, "I had a surprise recently when I saw an old acquaintance, Prince Judah Ben-Hur. He lives right next door to the palace. He's known here as Quintus Arrius, having been adopted by a Roman of high standing."

"I'm well aware of it."

"I doubt that many people in the East know he is Arrius, and probably he doesn't call himself Ben-Hur among his Roman friends. Or does he have any?"

"I know nothing about his friendships."

"I see the topic is disagreeable – I'm sorry."

Cypros said, "You see, we've been piecing together something of the story of your broken friendship and the conflict between you. Even though we ourselves are Jewish, you have our sympathy."

From almost any other Jew, this would have sounded insincere.

I said, "To most people in the East, particularly to his fellow Jews, Ben-Hur is a hero: the greatest Jewish charioteer since – what was his name – Jehu?"

I remembered Lady Miriam's story about Jehu driving his chariot furiously as he carried out his coup to wipe out the royal house of Ahab and take over the throne of the Northern Kingdom. When Queen Jezebel, the virago for whom I named my leopardess, was thrown from a palace window by eunuchs collaborating with the rebel leader, Jehu cheerfully drove his chariot over her and then let the street dogs clean up what was left of her.

Seeing Herod's amused smile at the comparison, I asked, "Might I ask how he has failed to win your complete admiration?"

I could have made guesses. The Hurs were always cordial to the Herod family, but it was known that they didn't consider them the rightful rulers of Israel; perhaps they didn't even acknowledge them to be Jews. Another idea – what if Herod Agrippa had tried to borrow money from Ben-Hur or Simonides – and been turned down?

Herod said, "I know that he was sentenced to the galleys for a foolish act which he says he didn't commit, and he has since been given the benefit of the doubt. But many people suspect he was deeply into revolutionary schemes a few years ago. His loyalty to Rome is more than questionable, from what I've heard."

Then Cypros spoke. "I've told my husband about what we both overheard that last day before you went away to Rome."

She was referring to an incident that had shaken both of us and then festered silently in my thoughts during the five years of my schooling in Rome.

"Oh, yes! Lady Miriam's little inspiring talk with her children!"

Father was looking at us inquiringly, aware that there was an incident we hadn't discussed but perhaps should have.

Herod Agrippa laughed. "She was a protective Jewish mother,

with a low opinion of the Herod family. I do wish fewer Jews thought about us as she did – and presumably still does. I can imagine how you must have reacted to her comments on Rome and on you personally. Had you assumed she liked you?"

"I don't think it was all pretence in the beginning. I think that when I was younger she did like me quite well. She seemed to enjoy talking to me along with Judah. But there was a growing coldness in her during the last year. I knew she wished I'd go away soon and that her son would become closer to his Jewish classmates. I just hadn't realized she was so intense about it – or about the Messiah."

"Perhaps we could talk about this another time," said Herod thoughtfully. "We didn't come here to remind you of unpleasant things – though unfortunately life is full of them. Pleasures deserve more attention! Right now we are wondering when you can visit us – both of you."

"I never go out," said Father. "I haven't recovered my strength since my heart attack. But it would be good for Marcus – or Secundus, as we call him when his brother is present – to go visiting. But won't you be occupied with all the celebrations of the Ludi Romani festival? Doubtless you will be dining with members of Caesar's family."

"We are booked for dinners for most of the festival – not just with Claudius and Antonia but with Caligula and Caesar himself," said Cypros. "But it would be delightful, Messala Secundus, as I must call you now, if you could come to dinner tomorrow afternoon and spend the evening with us. The guards will be told to give you directions to our quarters. We aren't expecting anyone else, and it would give us a real chance to talk about – a lot of things."

The prospect appealed to me. I decided I could have Nestor drive the carriage and Africanus come along as my attendant, in case I needed assistance as I walked with my crutches in the unfamiliar paths, up steps, and through Herod's atrium and corridors.

The next afternoon I bathed and then got ready to go out to dinner – the first time in a long while.

No one wears a toga to recline all evening on a dinner couch.

Most people choose an evening tunic or robe instead of the shorter tunic which is standard for daytime. This meant I needn't worry about my not having the thin purple stripe of the equestrian order. Evening garments are more elaborate than street wear but not indicative of one's rank except for the obvious fact that one can afford to dress well.

I planned to wear a new dark-red robe and my gold armillae, which wouldn't seem at all ostentatious beside Herod's jewellery. I would have preferred using the cane with the ornate gold initial instead of the awkward crutches, but was not yet ready for it even with the help of Africanus.

CHAPTER SIXTEEN

BEFORE leaving, I told Father of the incident which had taken place the day before I was to leave Jerusalem for Rome. Judah had invited Cypros and me to his house. His mother was out.

We played a childish game, hiding while one member of our group tried to find the others. Judah was the searcher; he found Tirzah quickly, but was still looking for Cypros and me. We were behind a large couch with cushions and long draperies which helped conceal us.

Lady Miriam came home unexpectedly, and it seemed that something had agitated her. Unaware that Cypros and I were in the house, she sat down on the couch, telling Judah and Tirzah to listen because what she had to tell them was important, and came from her heart.

She was very emotional. She was very ashamed of Judaea's domination by a foreign power, a nation of proud, idolatrous conquerors (her words), who were rapidly losing whatever morals their ancestors had possessed. And now she feared that her children would slowly absorb the standards of their pleasant heathen friends and lose their sense of their religious and cultural heritage.

She got into personal comments. "Messala is quite a nice boy — so far. But wolf cubs do grow up to be wolves."

"Mother!" Judah protested, ready to defend me.

"I know you find him fascinating. But I've always wished you would be drawn more to some of your schoolmates, Jewish boys brought up to honour the Lord. Messala is proud, he will never give up his false religion, and he has a tendency to mockery. These faults may increase. What if he came back feeling superior to you and to all of us, ridiculing what we believe in? Would you follow him — or would you take a stand for the Lord?"

I was hurt, though I'd known a little of her feelings before.

She said that Cypros was a pretty girl with agreeable manners, from the little she had seen. "But rather boyish. I wouldn't want you, Tirzah, to climb trees and romp with boys."

Then she described the Herod family. Cruel, ambitious, half Idumaean, not pure Jewish. Notorious for murder, incest, and other abominations. "Judah," she said, "I would hate to see you marry into that family."

At that I had to cover Cypros' mouth or she would have shouted her indignation. Afterwards she said, "As if I wanted to marry her precious little boy! I'll probably marry one of my cousins or uncles. But I'd rather have you than Judah."

Lady Miriam didn't want her son to get into useless revolutionary activities. No joining up with zealots who raided travellers or got into skirmishes with the legionaries. But one day soon the Messiah was coming. It was prophesied. Wise men had seen signs in the stars; there were rumours that he had been born in Bethlehem a few years before Judah. The Messiah could overcome all opposition with a decisive stroke of divine lightning, liberate Israel, and take control of the whole erring world. It might be a time for a brave man, of the quality of King David or the hero Judas Maccabaeus, to strike a few telling blows in the Messiah's service.

"I would be proud of you if you were just like your dear father, Judah. But I would be proudest of all if you were chosen to do something significant for the Messiah. Judah, just put the Lord first and be ready for him to lead you."

Cypros and I waited until Lady Miriam and her children went into the garden, Judah having remembered to tell her we were on the premises.

"Oh, I wish you had told me. What if they overheard me?"

"I didn't like to interrupt you, Mother."

Soon we walked casually into the garden, greeting everyone politely and asking why Judah had stopped looking for us. The iciness in Cypros' tone may have caused suspicion; I don't know.

Cypros was furious at the insult to her family. Actually, Lady Miriam's attitude was typical of many old Jewish families who didn't welcome Idumaean upstarts as rulers.

I said to Cypros, "She hopes I won't come back from Rome. Maybe I should do my service on the Rhine. Then if Judah ever takes a motherly lecture too much to heart and aims a slingshot at a Roman, I won't know about it."

I never told Judah. On my last day in Jerusalem, he came over early to say goodbye. It was a sentimental parting; there were tears in his eyes (close to the surface in mine too). We hugged each other, and I said, "The Gods keep you." He replied, "The God of our fathers be with you." So whose prayers were answered?

Now, thanks to Cypros, I'd reopened a chest of memories. Street preachers with high voices, ranting on about how the Messiah would trample the heathen oppressors causing rivers of blood to run in the streets and how eventually the Jews would be masters of everything under the righteous Messiah. Everyone would have to keep the Sabbath, no one would ever eat pork again – lucky pigs! No one would carve images anymore, the whole world would learn to write from right to left instead of the wrong way, and the calendar used worldwide would be lunar, not solar. It was an absolutely revolting picture of a nightmare future.

Although the idea of the Messiah is widespread, I don't know that all Jews have such a grandiose concept of world domination. Certainly the ideal of liberty must appeal to them. Long ago Rome helped them obtain their freedom from the Seleucid rulers who had succeeded Alexander the Great. Some generations later, a

peace-keeping force led by Pompey went in by request and settled
a dispute about the throne by rival members of the Hasmonean
dynasty, and there was a brief peace.

Incidentally, Pompey wasn't much appreciated as a benefactor
of Judaea. Being accustomed to unrestricted sight-seeing wherever
he went, Pompey assumed it was his right to walk into the sacred
Temple and inspect everything, even the Holy of Holies, normally
entered only once a year and only by the High Priest. The Jews never
forgot that desecration.

Later, after an ambitious Hasmonean claimant actually brought
in the Parthians to depose his uncle and put himself on the throne,
Rome took full control, supporting a relative newcomer, Herod the
Great, and since then we have never risked losing power. We think
quite well of the Herod family, but we keep an eye on them.

On one occasion in my boyhood I managed to find a centurion
and tell him about a self-proclaimed street prophet. The centurion
and a few of his men came up behind the orator and seized him. I
don't know what became of him. I turned him in not only because
his speech was seditious but also because of the spit which he sprayed
like a fountain on everyone within a certain radius of his eloquence.
I loathe other people's spit, and there seems to be a lot of it in the
East. I didn't tell Judah what I'd done.

I felt better for reviewing the past with Father. We agreed that
Cypros and I had let our dramatic sense run away with us, that Lady
Miriam wouldn't have wanted her son to take foolish risks even for
a great cause.

"Mind you," said Father, "Gratus had enraged the Jewish people
by replacing the High Priest, which was considered sacrilege. It
wouldn't have surprised me if Lady Miriam had encouraged her boy
to get some kind of military training, even secret lessons from an old
revolutionary."

I resolved not to think about the past anymore if I could avoid
it. Could I just have a cheerful evening with Herod and Cypros?
Or would they insist on talking about Ben-Hur? And why was he
important to them?

CHAPTER SEVENTEEN

I started out with Africanus beside me in the carriage, driven by Nestor. It was a beautiful warm September afternoon. I'd thought about driving myself, but it seemed better to leave the management of the team to Nestor while I talked with Africanus and enjoyed the beauty around me, especially the shining blue of the sea below the road.

Turning inland from the sea cliffs, we had to pass the entrance to the Arrius estate, sheltered by a pine grove. I'd been told the gardens were spectacular, enhanced by the wide view of the sea and the distant hills, depending which way you looked. But I didn't wish to linger looking for a glimpse of flowering shrubs and fountains with the sun making rainbows of the spray. I said to myself, "That is a place I never desire to visit."

The road now swung back closer to the cliff, and I could see a little of the Arrius dock. Probably there was a private road from the dock to the villa, which we had passed but not seen because of the thick trees. We saw no one, and all we could hear were the waves breaking and the light wind in the pines. We continued to the Emperor's gates and were admitted by the guards. Dropping

Africanus and me off at the entrance to the villa, Nestor took the carriage and horses to the imperial stable.

A servant escorted us to Herod's residence. Herod met us at the vestibule and personally accompanied me through the atrium to their garden. Africanus could now join the servants but be ready in case I needed him.

They had an attractive garden full of late-blooming roses. Behind it was a grove of pines, and their scent overpowered the roses, which didn't have a very strong perfume.

Herod and Cypros presented their four children before sending them off with their nurse for supper. The older ones, Herod Agrippa Junior and Berenice, were seven and six, respectively. Mariamne and Drusilla were still babies.

"At first we had no children," said Cypros. "Maybe I wasn't mature enough, though many girls marry younger than I did. We had a little boy, Herod Drusus, but we lost him. And now at last we have our family."

She and Herod were affectionate parents; they could make almost anyone feel that having children would be pleasant.

Before dinner we had wine in the colonnade of the garden. Cypros hesitantly said, "I didn't like to ask you this when we met yesterday. But I'm told you were recently divorced. To be honest, our Jewish servants, who talk to the Hur servants, say that your former wife was the guest of Ben-Hur. How did that ever happen?"

I didn't resent her curiosity, and I wasn't surprised that the servants had gossiped. Perhaps Ben-Hur would be told of my visit to Herod and Cypros. Briefly I told my hosts about my disastrous marriage and explained Ben-Hur's role as an executor of the departed Balthazar.

"She went back to Egypt at the beginning of this month."

"She should reach Alexandria soon," said Cypros. "They tell me she wasn't a very contented guest, though she kept telling Ben-Hur how grateful she was. She liked his two little children and told them exciting stories, but she tried to monopolize them and sway them into loving her best, or at least better than their Aunt Tirzah."

"She would! Isn't Tirzah married yet?"

"No, she isn't. Partly because she clings to her family and isn't eager to leave them for an establishment of her own. But she's certainly beautiful, and looks a lot younger than she really is. I saw her and her mother the other day in a bazaar in Misenum."

Tirzah was always a shy, home-loving girl, not very assertive. If, as Cypros said, she was now a beautiful woman in her late twenties, Iras would be envious. To accept the fact that she couldn't outshine Tirzah and looked years older than Judah's maiden sister, even though she wasn't, would be very painful for her.

"I'm sure Ben-Hur will find his sister a suitable husband, maybe a Jew living in Italy," said Cypros. "By the way, he politely turned down Sanballat, who has lately become a widower. Maybe sometime there'll be a new woman for you – though not Tirzah, of course. Someone who'll make you a good Roman wife."

"First I'll have to regain some honourable status. Right now only a plain woman who has abandoned all hope would want me."

They raised their eyebrows as if they couldn't believe my estimate of my undesirability.

I amplified my statement with an imaginative touch. "Perhaps a woman with a fair dowry but terrible breath and a face full of inoperable warts."

"Surely you underrate yourself," said Herod.

"Agrippina remarked that you were quite attractive," said Cypros.

"That's flattering, but of course Agrippina wasn't thinking of me as a possible husband, however tiresome she may find Ahenobarbus," I said. "You see, even though I'm no longer poor, I'm still barred from the equestrian rank that should be mine, and I haven't achieved any distinction that I want people to remember."

A seat in the Senate seemed like a far-off star.

"You've written a very clever novel, which is winning admirers," said Herod. "I started reading it this afternoon, and really – I don't think our worthy neighbour across the ravine could have written it if his life depended on it."

"Perhaps not. Though he might write quite interesting memoirs – if he dared."

Changing the subject, we entered the dining-room, where we took our places on couches. I was at right angles to the central couch where Herod Agrippa and Cypros reclined. Slaves took my sandals and bathed my feet, then gave me socks in case my feet should be cold as the evening came on.

A musician played the lyre and sang during part of our dinner, but not all the time; we were able to enjoy lively conversation as well as excellent Jewish food. Herod mockingly apologized for the lack of pork and shellfish, but I told him I got them quite often at home and really fancied a kosher menu. I didn't say that everyone knew the Herods didn't always observe the dietary rules of their religion. If we had been at Tiberius' table, and the Emperor had offered Herod a slice of roast pork, he would have taken it and praised it as his favourite thing.

A witty man, with a fund of entertaining anecdotes, Herod kept us listening and laughing often. Some of his best stories concerned his uncles, especially Herod Antipas, tetrarch of Galilee, who was married to Herod Agrippa's sister Herodias. Herod Agrippa and his family had visited them briefly but not got along with them. Herodias and Cypros detested each other, the former being malicious and jealous of the latter's beauty and four healthy children.

The conversation turned to the late Galilean prophet and healer, Jesus. There were stories that he had healed people of incurable diseases, driven out demons, and even raised the dead.

"The tale is that, after he was crucified, he rose from his tomb and went visiting for about forty days with his friends, appearing here and there at will, finally ascending into Heaven."

"Mother of the Gods!"

"Not a common event even by Jewish standards," said Herod. "Though now that I think of it, the prophet Elijah was supposedly carried off in a chariot of fire. But as for Jesus, a cult has been growing up. The Nazarene cult. Caiaphas and Uncle Antipas are concerned. The cultists believe he is the true Messiah and will return some day to fulfill the rest of the prophecies. In the meantime they are trying to convert as many as possible to his teachings."

About fifty days after Jesus' execution, the cult burst out into the streets, preaching that Jesus had risen from the dead, that he had died for the sins of the world, and that he was now with his Father in Heaven, being actually, in some mysterious way, the Son of God. According to rumour, some of the cultists became endowed with the power to speak foreign languages. Or at least foreign speakers, Jews from other countries – and some converts – understood them in their own tongues. A former fisherman named Peter was especially articulate; in addition, he and some others went in for healings – like Jesus himself.

It sounded like a hysterical buildup of fantastical stories and wishful thinking by those who had longed for Jesus to be their Messiah. But a man I knew by sight had apparently been healed by Peter. He was a beggar at the Beautiful Gate of the Jewish Temple who had been there when Judah and I were boys. He'd never walked in his life; he wasn't paralysed, but there was no strength in his feet and ankles.

Peter had taken his hand and raised him up, and all at once the beggar was leaping around and praising God for his healing.

So unlike my own experience! The first stirrings of hope and joy, then waking each day to hard work, knowing that the rest of my recovery depended largely on my own effort – which was how I preferred it.

"Could the beggar have had a secret identical twin brother, who took his place?" It didn't sound very probable, but it was an idea.

Then Herod said, "Ben-Hur is in this cult."

"Really? I wonder if he's feeding his military dreams with the hope of Jesus' return."

"The cult is supposed to be peaceful – though one must wonder," said Herod thoughtfully. "Ben-Hur believes in Jesus as the Son of God because he's convinced that Jesus healed his mother and sister of leprosy. Do you think it's possible?"

I said, "It's incredible that Jesus could have cured genuine lepers or raised the dead or any of the other amazing things people said he did. Maybe the Hur ladies suffered from a temporary skin condition, not leprosy at all."

"That may be so. Messala, you helped Valerius Gratus deal with the Hurs after the attempt on his life. When they were imprisoned, did you have the smallest suspicion that they might contract leprosy? I have heard that Ben-Hur thinks you and Gratus planned for them to become lepers, so that if they were ever released from prison, they would be unable to give evidence."

With his frank questioning, he was risking infuriating me.

Was he trying to extract some kind of confession, which he could later hold over my head? Well, as in my conversation with my ex-friend, there were some charges, open or implied, to which I could honestly say "Not guilty." I think Herod counted on my self-control, and I didn't disappoint him.

"No, I didn't plan anything of the kind. If I had, how could I have been sure they would get it? I've heard that in places where lepers aren't strictly isolated, the families of lepers may go for years without a sign of the disease – or they may develop it quickly. One just doesn't know. Also, I've heard of depositions being taken from lepers. If Gratus and I had wanted to keep those women safely silent, we should have arranged a swifter, surer way of death."

I didn't have to be specific. Herod possibly knew more about subtle poisons than I did.

"So you maintain that you never knowingly placed them in danger of leprosy?"

"By all the Gods! By all my hope of full recovery and happiness."

"I believe you, Messala," said Herod. "You wouldn't take risks with that oath."

It was like saying, "May the Gods strike me dead!" or, "May I not live to finish this morsel!"

A Jew might say, "The Lord do so to me and more also if I lie."

Herod remarked, "I understand one centurion said that Gratus had warned him the cells at one end were leprous; however, that's a fairly common story to keep curious employees away from a maximum security section. In fact, my grandfather, who built the fortress in the first place, occasionally used that story to terrify guards and slaves."

That would have been like Herod the Great. On the other hand, Herod the Great would have been perfectly willing to expose his enemies to leprosy if he could. But I'd looked at the records concerning other occupants of the section where the Hur women were incarcerated. None of them had lived long, and it seemed they had died of fevers and lung infections. We were, in fact, killing Lady Miriam and Tirzah by natural means, and I couldn't feel very happy thinking about it, so I tried not to. I told Gratus not to inform me when they actually died.

Changing the subject, I asked, "Tell me, why would your God let the Messiah be crucified? The most degrading death of all."

"They explain it through the symbolism of the perfect sacrificial lamb. John the Baptist – you remember that desert prophet Uncle Antipas beheaded for presuming to criticize his domestic life? John had talked about the 'Lamb of God that takes away the sin of the world.' They have cast Jesus as the Lamb of God."

Herod told me about the mixed attitudes of the prominent Jews. Gamaliel, the famous scholar, took a tolerant 'wait and see' position. Caiaphas was disgusted but was thinking of retiring and letting it be someone else's problem. There was also a group that believed in violent measures against the cult. A brilliant young scholar named Saul of Tarsus was a leader in this movement and had helped organize the stoning of a notable Nazarene speaker named Stephen. Now he had permission from Pilate to arrest Jews he considered blasphemers; he could even go to places outside Judaea but still in the Roman province of Syria: places as far as Damascus.

I still had suspicions about the military hopes of the people called Nazarenes or followers of the Way. Were they secretly mobilizing for the time when Jesus would come back to earth in power and glory – or someone would impersonate him? Was Judah really here to sabotage the Empire at its heart?

Herod said, "By the way, the cultists in Antioch are becoming known as Christians, from *Christos*, the Greek term similar to *Messiah*."

He said that apparently the Christians or Nazarenes were intent on a spiritual kingdom beyond this world. Like Iras' father. They said they wanted to convey to the human race the teachings of Jesus concerning love and forgiveness and repentance of sins. After this message had been taken to the world, their Lord could return.

"The whole world?" I said. "That might take them a long time."

"Of course they may have a secret agenda," Herod said.

"Love and forgiveness. Within reasonable limits, I presume."

"Well, it is reported that Jesus said one should forgive others as one expects to be forgiven by God himself."

"Do you want reconciliation with Judah – each of you forgiving the other?" asked Cypros.

"No, I'd hate it. I will never, never crawl to him."

It was obvious to me that Judah hadn't managed to forgive me though he had forgiven Iras, considering her a weak-minded woman.

Herod began to talk about how the new faith had complicated Ben-Hur's life. As he was a member of an important Jewish family, his example was significant. For that reason, the opponents of the Christians were displeased with him.

"With Saul of Tarsus clamouring for strong measures, Ben-Hur must think he and his loved ones are safer in Italy right now," said Herod. "And why let that beautiful villa go to waste?"

"We've met Judah briefly in the past couple of years," said Cypros.

"A noble-looking fellow, I must say," remarked Herod. "Impeccably moral without being too boring about it. Not an easy man to amuse with light conversation, though he's still perfectly agreeable as long as one doesn't get into deep issues with him. I got the feeling he could be very intense."

There I completely agreed with Herod.

He continued, "I don't like to think of his using his influence to promote the Christian cult in Judaea or any other territory where a Herod might rule with the help of Rome.

"My grandfather Herod the Great liberated Judaea from the invading Parthians with Rome behind him. He worked endlessly to serve his country; he built the Temple we're so proud of. And yet people sneered at him as a mere Idumaean convert, not the true king in the sight of God. Spreading rumours of the Messiah all over the place. I can see why Grandfather became an angry bitter man. I would feel the same if I were a ruler and had to put up with continual ingratitude."

Of course I knew that Herod the Great hadn't worshipped the God of Israel to the exclusion of all others. He had paid homage to various deities, including our own Jupiter. To the true Jews this was the terrible sin of idolatry.

"You would very much like a throne, wouldn't you, Herod?"

"Yes, and if I were a king of the Jews, I'd do my best to protect our religion the way it's always been: faith in one God, loyalty to the law given to us by Moses, though I don't think it need be interpreted in a ridiculous hair-splitting way. But I wouldn't offend my subjects, even if it meant some sacrifice of personal tastes."

He warmed up to his theme. "If prominent Jews, not just ignorant riff-raff smelling of their fishnets and sheep, insisted on giving God a son, and went around promising that any day soon the Divine Son was going to reappear, take over completely and depose me from the office to which I'd given myself heart and soul, believe me, I would be *tough*. I'd do whatever I had to do. For example, *you* might not be Ben-Hur's worst enemy anymore."

"Would you actually replace me, Herod? You're very welcome."

Then he came to what he was leading up to all along.

"When I last saw Caiaphas, he said you had extensive notes on the revolutionary movement that looked to Jesus as the great liberator. Notes that might even implicate Ben-Hur in seditious activities. Do you still have them?"

I wondered what I would have done had he asked just a few months earlier.

"Herod, I'm very sorry. In June just before our breakup, my former wife, in one of her infrequent attempts to houseclean, threw out all my papers. I have nothing."

"What a pity! I would have liked to take a look at what you had."

"I won't risk accusing him without proof."

"Of course not! But, just out of curiosity, what if someone from

Jerusalem contacted you and asked you to work with an undercover organization? For proper remuneration, naturally."

Was he testing me or actively recruiting for the anti-Christian anti-Ben-Hur party?

"Herod, a few months ago I was desperate. I would have worked against Judah Ben-Hur with my last breath of life. And I certainly needed money. But now I ask myself why a group in Jerusalem would want me to work with them. They might have been able to use some of my material, but why would they want *me*?"

"They know how intelligent you are – and how very well-motivated."

"Especially the latter. That's what gives me pause."

"I don't follow you, Messala."

"Don't you? Think about it. Caiaphas and his party must already have a network in Italy; I'm sure they have people placed fairly close to the Emperor. Why would they want me – except to take the blame if things go wrong?"

Just for a moment, from Herod's rueful expression, I knew I'd struck the truth.

I continued. "Too many people know me as Ben-Hur's mortal foe. If someone attacked him – by anonymous accusation or by violence – here in Italy, on whom would suspicion fall? Messala!"

Judah himself would certainly think I was involved. I really should keep an eye on him.

"I just wondered what you would say," said Herod blandly.

"It's like this. Ben-Hur and I can never be friends again, and we can't even maintain a courteous conversation. Two or three consecutive civil words each – maybe. And further contact with him would probably arouse my destructive feelings. He takes such self-righteous pleasure in my degradation."

"That must make you feel miserable. I'm so sorry. We both are," said Cypros gently.

"Thank you, Cypros. However, I've been feeling much better lately. And I've been thinking – what if Ben-Hur and I aren't destined to destroy each other? Or one of us to destroy the other? At least not right now." I'd watch him but not get into Herod's secret plots. I remembered my father's advice.

"You may never know what you *could* do if you don't try," said Herod, as if my courage was in question.

"Herod, in the last three months I've been regaining the use of my legs. Ben-Hur probably doesn't know that yet. Doubtless he would ill-wish me if he knew. He does know that my family has taken me in sympathetically and my father has helped me generously – I didn't tell Ben-Hur how much, but my total assets in money and property come to more than the talents I lost on that damned race.

"Now there's the matter of my reputation – so far resting on one well-received novel. But just suppose – years from now – I attained certain honours. What if I even – far into the future – made it to the consulship? Judah would be welcome to stand and watch my inaugural parade. Now go ahead, laugh!"

"You'd better hope he isn't up on a roof with his hand on another tile," said Herod with a smile.

I liked him, but I knew I mustn't trust him. His ambition would lead him to try to satisfy the leaders of the Temple and the Jewish high court, the Sanhedrin. To achieve his purpose he would use me and, if necessary, sacrifice me. Cypros cared somewhat about me as her childhood friend, but she would put Herod first.

I thanked them for a pleasant evening; they said they hoped to see me again soon. Africanus joined me and accompanied me out.

Twilight had fallen and darkness was taking over the sky, which was a very deep evening blue. The carriage had been sent for, and it was waiting at the front. It would be a fairly long drive. Part of the way there would be cliffs on one side and beyond them the dark sea.

CHAPTER EIGHTEEN

I had no contact with Herod and Cypros for a while. The end of our September festival was followed by a holy period (I think I'm saying that correctly) in the Jewish calendar ending in their Day of Atonement, when they fast. Actually, the special period may have begun during our own festivities. Since the Jewish calendar is based on the moon cycles, the dates are not the same in our calendar from year to year, so I'm not sure when they celebrated their New Year that year. In any case, I doubt if Herod let it cramp his lifestyle here in Italy. Barbatus and Lepida heard that, in addition to mentoring young Tiberius Gemellus, Herod was cultivating the friendship of Caligula, admiring his team of horses, and complimenting him on his skill and splendid appearance.

Barbatus and Lepida waited until the equinoctial rains were over, and then took advantage of some calm sunny days to sail the Nereid back to Ostia, where carriages were waiting to carry them home to Rome. Naturally, Messalina went with them. Father and I elected to stay in Baiae. Philip had remained with us, as Barbatus was promoting another secretary to handle his work in Rome. Africanus was Father's personal servant and Nestor was our chief man in the

Baiae stables. The house had a small permanent staff of servants all year round. So we were really very comfortable and peaceful there.

I worked on my new novel, drawing some ideas from Claudius Caesar's book. Every day I continued with a vigorous exercise program. It was still warm enough to swim most days, and we sometimes sailed around the harbour and did a bit of fishing. I rode Sheba almost every day with Nestor riding beside me.

One morning we rode to the top of a small hill where several spreading pines stood beside a low stone wall where the hill dropped off steeply. It overlooked a small local road that connected with Cumae on the other side of the peninsula, and we could watch the people travelling below us. They would probably not be aware of us even if they looked up – so long as our horses kept quiet.

Then we saw two riders coming from Cumae. Soon after they had passed us, they would come to a junction of roads, where they could either go east to the ports of Puteoli and Neapolis and even farther to Pompeii and Stabiae, or they could turn south to Baiae and Misenum. As the riders came nearer, I recognized them both and wondered if they would go all the way together. They were Judah Ben-Hur and Sanballat, the former on a fine bay stallion – maybe the same one that the Sheik had given him – and the latter on a submissive-looking mule.

They pulled over to the grassy area directly below us.

"Don't look up!" I mentally urged them, though I have no assurance that such attempts at telepathy are of any use.

They didn't look up because they were very much absorbed in their animated conversation. Animated, did I say? Sanballat was angry and frustrated; Judah was exasperated.

"Why can't you even let me show her the house?" demanded Sanballat. "It's really magnificent, and the view of the sea is just as breathtaking as the one from your own terrace. I believe she might feel that it made all the difference."

Who was he talking about? A client interested in a seaside villa?

"Sanballat, I've told you more than once that Tirzah doesn't want to marry you. No matter what kind of fine residence you can provide her. She has said she wants you to stop pressing her. She said to me, 'Judah, please tell him to leave me alone.'"

So Sanballat aspired to marry Tirzah, just as Herod and Cypros had told me. He, a slick Jew of Samaritan ancestry, thought himself a fit match for a lady from a noble and ancient Jewish family going all the way back to Moses and his intimate circle.

"Why should she object to me? I practise the Jewish religion as consistently as if I'd been born to it. I'm well-respected both in the East and here in Italy. Except, of course, for the fools who've been comparing me to a character in Messala's disgraceful novel. I'm thinking about suing him.

"I'm in good physical condition; in fact I've never had a real illness in my life – which, may I remind you, is more than you can say for Tirzah."

"How dare you! How dare you imply that Tirzah is – damaged – because she once had a horrible disease – from which Jesus healed her completely." Judah was furious.

Some people have remarked on *my* cynical sneer. But I don't think I ever surpassed Sanballat – the knowing tilt of his head, the lift of one eyebrow and the twist of the mouth, the mocking tone – all of which I described in the portrait of Haman, the villain of my novel. I couldn't see his facial movements well on this occasion but I was familiar with them, and I could appreciate Judah's irritation, followed by shock at the man's boldness.

"I trust that your precious Nazarene *did* heal her completely. Some men might wonder. They might fear that leprosy still lurked in the darkness of her womb. She didn't have many eligible offers in Judaea, did she?"

Judah exercised self-control as he began his answer, though of course he was offended and became more so as he thought about it.

"There aren't many men who would presume to offer marriage to my sister, as you have done with unjustified confidence, and there are even fewer men I would accept on her behalf."

He was reminding Sanballat that he was the justly proud Prince of Hur, the head of one of Judaea's greatest noble families.

"Tirzah is gentle and sensitive. I would give her only to a man of superior understanding and kindness, a man who knew how to value her refinement – and her tender heart."

"And I don't fit your requirements?"

"No, Sanballat, you don't! I see that you desire the prestige of an alliance with the house of Hur, you're attracted as well to her large dowry, but you don't come anywhere near to understanding Tirzah's feelings. Your words today convince me further that you would make her miserable."

"In what way, Ben-Hur, in what way? Tell me! I was a good husband to Sarah, my late wife, and my two sons are devoted to me, as they should be. I'd give your sister every material comfort that she has now; I could give her splendid jewels, bargains from my trading with Far Eastern merchants. And I could satisfy her in bed, I'm sure! Indeed with my maturity and experience, I think I could serve her better than a young man."

Did Judah wince at the thought of Sanballat bedding Tirzah?

He replied, "And when she displeased you, would you fling at her your extremely offensive suggestion that she might still be carrying leprosy internally? If you *really* feared it, you would never have asked for her hand, but you would still – if you married her – be sure to tell her you took a risk. It would be a way to humiliate a wife and subjugate her, wouldn't it?"

Judah paused for breath – and it was about time. As he reflected on Sanballat's remarks, his sense of absolute outrage had grown. His voice had been getting louder all the time, and his face was probably somewhat red.

"Why do you insist on imagining such things of me? What have I done to deserve this?" Now Sanballat was a much injured man.

"You boast of being a good husband to Sarah. That's not what my mother heard from your wife's cousins in Joppa. They said you belittled her intelligence and ridiculed everything about her from her middle-aged figure to her facial hair. Maybe the poor woman was glad enough to die."

Sanballat was disagreeably surprised; he scowled and then rallied his powers of defence. "Women's gossip! My wife's family were always malicious. They tried to make trouble all the time."

When Judah didn't respond sympathetically, Sanballat continued bitterly. "It seems that your noble and fastidious mother, the great Lady Miriam, is against me. She thinks I'm not good enough."

"Don't say a word against my mother. I warn you, Sanballat!"

Sanballat backed the mule up a step, so that Judah had to turn a little to speak to him. Changing his line of attack, Sanballat asked, "Do your objections have anything to do with that dead Nazarene?"

Jesus of Nazareth! Herod had said that Ben-Hur was still his follower, whatever that might involve. Did Judah remember him regretfully as part of a futile military dream – or gratefully because of a remarkable healing?

"Sanballat, to you Jesus is just a dead Nazarene. But all of us in our family honour him as our teacher – and worship him as our Lord and Saviour."

Saviour? What did he mean? From what could Jesus have saved them? Maybe the disease the women apparently had. Herod had said something about the sins of the world, but that didn't make sense. Jesus had reportedly cured various ailments, but, according to Iras' reports, in the days when Judah was mobilizing his army, he was invariably the picture of robust health, needing no physician. Roman legionaries might get dysentery and other disorders while roughing it in desert camps, but not Judah.

Sanballat spoke resolutely, perhaps feeling he had nothing to lose by taking a stand for correct Jewish beliefs. Previously perhaps he had been careful to say what Ben-Hur wanted to hear.

"I'll be plain with you, Ben-Hur. My future wife, even if she were your sister, would have to keep the religious customs of our people – and respect me, not you, as the spiritual head of the family. There would be no dabbling with strange cults. All of you, even my good friend Simonides, have gone too far with this idolizing of Jesus, calling him the Messiah and even the Son of God. Even I, born a Samaritan, know blasphemy when I hear it. Actually, when you first came back to Italy, I'd no idea your obsession had gone so far."

"You think we're committing blasphemy in worshipping Jesus? Then you ought to find a respectable Jewish or Samaritan woman – maybe a widow near Sarah's age – who thinks as you do. Tirzah wouldn't make you happy; she could never become the woman you really want."

"You are setting up your opinion against the greatest rabbis. You must know that. Why do you think you know more than the expert scholars of the Torah and the Prophets? Oh, never mind, don't answer me; I'm just a convert from Samaria; I don't have a line of ancestors stretching back to Moses. Never mind that I befriended Simonides and helped him get safely home after he'd been tortured by Valerius Gratus. Never mind that I helped you win the chariot race!"

"You *what?*" The words were Judah's but they might have been mine. Sanballat's delusions were unbelievable.

"Now just a moment!" said Ben-Hur. "I acknowledge your goodness to Simonides, and I've tried to show my gratitude. But you did *not* help me win the chariot race! I don't know when I've heard a more ridiculous assertion. If Messala were here, even he might be amused. While I'm on the subject, let me warn you – if you sue him over that novel (which I haven't bothered to read), people will think you yourself admit a resemblance to the villain."

"I'll get him one way or another. As for the race, you must know what I mean. I took care of the bet on the night before the race, and I don't see how Messala could have got a good night's sleep knowing he'd been a proud fool to hazard so much."

"He may not have felt completely rested and relaxed, I grant you, but I don't think his skill was impaired."

"That's right – praise your worst enemy at the expense of your true friend! You blamed me because I didn't make it easy for you to give old Balthazar's money to the worthless slut who'd deserted him for Messala. Maybe you wish you could convert *him* to your foolish Nazarene cult – and then you could bury the past and renew your childhood friendship."

"You're talking nonsense. I've simply refused to give you my sister. Or to change my religious beliefs! And now I want to end this conversation. I've found some of your comments intolerable and I don't want to hear any more. I'm going on home, and your journey is to Puteoli. I wish you well, but I don't want to discuss this matter ever again. Shalom."

Sanballat didn't answer. He struck the mule with his heels and said something unintelligible to me, though perhaps not to the mule. Judah was already ahead of him on his Arabian horse.

I watched them turn in different directions, Ben-Hur toward Misenum, Sanballat toward Puteoli.

What an enlightening scene! Two old allies quarreling in a way that would surely not be forgotten by either of them. Sanballat was certainly going to hold a grudge; he must have built up a dream of becoming related by marriage to the Prince of Hur, and despite his disparaging reference to Tirzah's health, he probably found her desirable. I hadn't seen her since the day of her arrest, and then I hadn't let myself look properly but merely said to the centurion, "That's his sister." The Hurs were a good-looking family, and Tirzah had been a very pretty child, with black curls, large dark eyes and a fine complexion.

As her brother said, very few Jewish men would presume to offer marriage to a young lady of such a noble and wealthy family. Perhaps the rumour that she had had a terrible disease from which she now seemed to be cured would frighten some suitors. Moreover if the Hurs had religious views at variance with most of their fellow Jews, this would make it harder to find the right husband for Tirzah.

She was never a forward child. Musically talented, domestically inclined, rather ignorant of the world outside her own circle – and likely to remain so as a woman in the shelter of her home. She had been timid and retiring, afraid of change, and I didn't expect her to be any different as an adult. She had been restored to her brother after a long separation, and now she might feel safer if she didn't have to leave him or her mother. Certainly I could see why Sanballat didn't appeal to her.

I felt truly sorry about Tirzah, though I'd no desire to seek reconciliation with her brother. Sanballat didn't have to worry about that development.

CHAPTER NINETEEN

IN the middle of October the Capitoline Games took place. I didn't attend. Barbatus wrote about them from Rome. This was the occasion for the annual ceremonial race in which the right-hand lead horse of a two-horse team – the winner of the race – was sacrificed. This race took place in the Campus Martius*, not in any of the regular circuses. Barbatus had an upset stomach, so he stayed home, letting Lepida and Messalina go with friends.

The next day, feeling better, he escorted his family to the ordinary chariot races, at which no horse was deliberately sacrificed, though it was quite likely that some of the animals would die by accident – as my own two black stallions did. The ivory trace mares lived, somewhat scarred and badly spooked at the very sight of a chariot. I managed to sell them as brood mares.

Barbatus said that Caligula was again victorious. No one gave him any serious competition. He was much applauded; the sun shone on his golden hair – one would have to be close to him to notice that it was getting thin although he was only in his early twenties. As usual, he wore bright green for the race. There are four parties in Rome, each sporting ribbons with the colours of their favourite team. With

---

*Field of Mars

Caligula's successes, the green teams had become more popular than the whites, blues, and scarlets.

It was different when I competed in Antioch and a couple of other places, winning on each occasion but the last. We chose our colours without any affiliation with a racing club. My colours were mixed gold and scarlet; Ben-Hur appeared in unrelieved white, possibly symbolic of his purity of character.

Caligula had never had any serious competition; so his races were rather peaceful, bloodless affairs. No one would try to injure a rival to achieve nothing better than second place. But Barbatus said some of the other contests were violent enough to please those who like that sort of thing. Ahenobarbus sat in the stands drinking heavily and shouting applause whenever a chariot turned over or a driver was dragged along the sand by the reins from which he had been unable to cut himself free.

The most interesting race was the one in which a driverless team actually galloped first across the finish line despite the fact that their chariot had lost a wheel and their driver was lying on the track fatally injured. He breathed his last just as it was announced that his team had won. The rules say that it's always the *team* that wins, driver or not.

Barbatus' next paragraph was as follows: "To my surprise, I met your mother, Lollia Velleia, with her brother Velleius and his wife Lavinia. It seems she and Gaius Bibulus are divorced. I always thought that marriage was a mistake.

"She asked about you; she said she had read your book with great amusement and would like to see you sometime. I don't suppose you have seen her very often since you were a child, but it might be a good idea for you to cultivate her."

Mother! I could count on one hand the number of times I've seen her since my early childhood. When Iras and I called on her, she was courteous but clearly uncomfortable. She hinted that Bibulus wouldn't like to find me in his house. I hadn't had any communication with her since then.

Lepida filled Barbatus in on the details of Mother's marriage breakup. That summer Bibulus had taken her on a cruise to Cyprus, especially to visit the shrine of Venus where she is rumoured to have arisen fully formed from the sea waves. This was supposed to rekindle their love. In reality, it seems that Bibulus wanted to get away from his creditors for a while.

The trouble was that Mother still lacked enthusiasm, as had been the case for some time. She was forty-eight, she had three husbands before Gaius Bibulus (two of them had died), and she had three children after me; they were delicate and didn't live long. She had two miscarriages in the five years of her life with Bibulus, and it might now be assumed that her childbearing years were at an end. To Bibulus' annoyance she didn't compensate for her infertility by being a passionate or even a compliant lover. She made it clear that she preferred to be let alone.

She and Bibulus quarrelled loudly, in public and in private. Their turbulent married life became gossip wherever they went. He had a querulous, penetrating voice that carried from the ship to the dock-side of the harbour, exciting laughter and some concern.

Finally, screaming, "You cold barren bitch," he attempted to throw her overboard. She was rescued by a couple of servants: her loyal maid and a seaman who didn't belong to Bibulus but had been rented for the trip. She and the maid were taken ashore to the governor of Cyprus, who arranged for their transport home on another ship. She reached home in September, ahead of Bibulus, and sent him a divorce certificate. Bibulus then went to Rome and proclaimed his own divorce. Property settlements were worked out. Bibulus still had a debt problem, which Barbatus said he hoped to solve by marrying a younger woman of undistinguished ancestry but a very good dowry, though he gave out that he was looking for a healthy bride who could give him a son.

My proper brother was apparently embarrassed to be writing these details to me, but he couldn't keep them to himself after Lepida told him. He felt that Father and I would wish to know the scandalous story of the once beautiful but unstable woman my father never should have married.

I was pleased that Mother liked my novel. I'd been sure she would if she found the time to read it. I have memories of her telling me amazing tales when I was a very young child. Maybe I get my taste for fantasy from her. I've always relished the wealth of stories of heroes and Gods that are part of our culture and Greek culture. I even liked Lady Miriam's stories of the divinely guided people of Israel, though I preferred to hear about the Trojan War.

As for reaching out to my mother, I thought it a bad idea. I decided that if she actually wrote to me, I'd reply in a brief friendly letter. But I wasn't going to solicit her maternal affection by writing to her first, and I'd no immediate plans to go to Rome, so there was no question of calling on her. And I didn't expect she would come to our house to see me; she had never done so before.

When I first came to Rome as a student she sent me an invitation to her third wedding. I hadn't seen her for ten years. She was still very pretty, with dark curls and beautiful eyes. She introduced me to my young half-sister Cornelia, of whom I'd never been told till then. I liked Cornelia very much and wanted to be her big brother and protector, to have something like Judah's role with Tirzah. Unfortunately Cornelia died that winter; they said she had pneumonia. I saw Mother a couple more times during my school years in Rome, but she was quite busy and so was I – making new friends, working hard at both sports and studies, playing dice for money as all my friends did, and getting to know various females intimately – some of them well-born married ladies, some of them professional courtesans. At that time I was proud of being attractive to more mature women.

In the second half of October I received a note from Herod, asking me to join him for a yacht cruise to a small local island, where lunch would be served in a pavilion. Capri, where the Emperor Tiberius had twelve fine villas, would have been too far; fortunately he had erected a small summer house on a much closer islet which has practically no population. The party would include young Tiberius Gemellus and his paedagogus*, Cypros and her two older

---

* A guardian attendant, usually a slave, to watch over a child

children, Lady Antonia and her young namesake granddaughter, the only surviving offspring of Claudius – and Claudius himself. Herod thought that in view of my latest writing plans, I might like to talk with Claudius personally.

Tiberius Caesar himself wouldn't be present, but he was lending Herod his yacht while he stayed at his Misenum residence to attend to business. Apparently several lucky citizens were to have their cases heard by Caesar in person.

By this time, I'd made fair progress in my mobility. I had to walk slowly and carefully with my cane, but I didn't need the crutches. On the yacht I would have to take extra care; in fact I should stay seated as much as I could. Herod's note mentioned that there would be slaves to assist me as well as Claudius, who has weak legs and is naturally awkward.

Early the next morning I had Nestor drive me to the palace, where Herod welcomed me and invited me inside. Cypros was getting Herod Junior and Berenice ready. Two nursemaids were checking the bags containing extra clothes and food, and two more were in the nursery with the two baby girls.

Herod said, "You might like to hear some news. First, a ship has just brought the Hurs two guests: Simonides the father of Ben-Hur's wife, and a young man named Phineas Ben Zebulon. He's distantly related to the Hurs."

"Indeed," I said politely, but not as if I cared.

"Simonides couldn't bear to be away from his only child any longer, so he endured the discomforts of the sea voyage, especially as he could bring with him a possibly suitable husband for Tirzah."

"I question if Phineas *is* suitable," said Cypros, as she tied a bright blue ribbon around Berenice's shining curls. "We've heard things about him that Simonides may have missed. Phineas has been extravagant, gaming and drinking without restraint. He was married three years ago, and his wife died soon after. We don't know the circumstances, and it's been rumoured there was a cover up. After that, he became notorious for his wild parties and riotous living."

"But he's supposed to be reformed," said Herod. "His uncle sent him on several camel caravan trips, on which he was supervised by trustworthy people. After that Phineas appeared more reliable; he declared that he had become a follower of Jesus, and was baptised in the name of Jesus. And finally he has been sent with Simonides to the family office in Misenum and instructed to court Tirzah. A beautiful Jewish bride, a follower of Jesus, a maiden of excellent character, and a large dowry! He *should* be well-pleased."

"Isn't he pleased enough?" I'd picked up a note of doubt in Herod's speech.

"I suspect he isn't ready to settle down with a nice girl, no matter what her qualifications might be," said Cypros. "He may resent his uncle's authority and the virtuous examples of his Hur cousins as well as the well-meant patronage of Simonides and Judah Ben-Hur. Which is too bad. I hear Judah has tried to be very kind and brotherly. No doubt he would have liked to find a real friend in Tirzah's future husband."

"Did you learn all this through servants?" I asked.

"A lot of it," said Herod. "But some things come to us through Jewish friends here and there."

I surmised that he had contact with agents who kept an eye on the Hurs here and in the East.

Cypros explained further. "One day recently I was shopping in the town when I met Tirzah with her mother and Ben-Hur's wife, Esther. Tirzah was friendly, her mother was graciously aloof; they introduced Ben-Hur's wife to me. She's a gentle, pretty creature; I imagine she suits him very well. They mentioned that there might be a betrothal ceremony soon, and a wedding in the spring. They won't wait a whole year between the two ceremonies, although it's customary. I believe Tirzah thought of inviting me, but her mother gave her a warning look. And then Tirzah said, rather nervously, that it would be a very small private wedding, not at all like the sort of celebration they would have had in Jerusalem."

There they would have invited friends and relatives from all over Judaea and turned several rooms and the inner courtyard into areas for feasting which would have lasted several days. There it would have been a definite insult not to have invited those of the Herod family who were in or near Jerusalem at the time.

Cypros said, "We were visiting our Arab kinsfolk at the time of dear Judah's wedding, but I'm sure they wouldn't have asked us even if we'd been right next door – as we are now. But I wasn't distressed at being left out."

"Well," I remarked wryly, "I wasn't invited either."

I was back in Rome by then, but I would have been less welcome than a scruffy street dog – or a poisonous snake.

"That reminds me," said Cypros, "Simonides has been talking to Sanballat, who seems to have a strained relationship with Ben-Hur but is still on good terms with his old friend the merchant. They were heard talking about you. Sanballat is naturally offended by your book. He exclaimed, 'Imagine a character named Haman – Haman, of all names – modelled on me so that my business acquaintances joke about it! Not that I'm really like the fellow, of course – it's a cruel caricature.'"

"Sanballat can't take you to court over the portrayal; that would be laying himself open to more humiliation," said Herod. "So instead he's urging Simonides to use his contacts, whatever they are, to keep you from regaining a prominent place in society. Like your restoration to the equestrian order, I suppose."

This was nasty news. Barbatus had written that he had approached the censors about getting me back on the equestrian list, since I now had the income requirement. The two censors were willing enough, but he reminded me that the Emperor would have the final say. I knew Tiberius might look at the list and cross my name off, even if there were no agent of Simonides at his elbow to remind him of his disapproval of me.

I had felt pity for Simonides; after all, he had been cruelly tortured rather than give up what he controlled of the Hur wealth into the eager hands of Valerius Gratus, whom I now detested. Nevertheless, when I imagined the cunning merchant working against me, I half wished Gratus had finished him off when he had the chance.

"It's time for us to go to the boat," said Herod, looking out of the window that gave a view of the imperial dock.

So we set out from the house that was really a wing of the palace. Lady Antonia boarded with her little grandchild, Claudius awkwardly following. And there was the servant tutor with Tiberius Gemellus, a pale lad, rather small for his age, in his early teens. We joined them and introductions were made. Lady Antonia complimented me on what she called my "very amusing story."

Just then a voice called, "Surely you aren't going without me?"

It was Caligula! What a shame we hadn't boarded and set sail just a little sooner.

"My dear friend!" said Herod. "If I'd known you would be free to join us! But you said you had to see Quintus Arrius about a pair of Arabian colts. Of course, come with us! You're just in time."

CHAPTER TWENTY

CONCERNED about keeping my footing on deck, I quickly made my way to the nearest bench, walking slowly and carefully to avoid slips. Claudius sat down beside me, sighing a little as he watched his old friend Herod arm in arm with Caligula, who was excitedly telling him about some Arabian colts he had tried to buy but had not finished bargaining for.

"So far I can't meet Arrius' price. Being a Jew, not a patriotic Roman, he doesn't feel like giving me a special price, though he ought to. Maybe I can get the Emperor to make me a present of them. Too bad my birthday was back in August."

I told Claudius how interesting and helpful I found his *History of Carthage*, and asked him a number of questions I'd prepared in advance. Thus we were able to have quite a satisfying conversation. Claudius can speak very well when he's relaxed and in command of his subject.

Cypros and Lady Antonia sat on the sunniest part of the deck and kept an eye on the children. Claudius' little Antonia was very close in age to Herod's two children, Herod Junior and Berenice. Tiberius Gemellus was too old to play with them. A pale boy, he sat beside his middle-aged Greek tutor and looked at a book.

The sky and waves were a serene blue. It was the sort of golden, summery day that reappears briefly near the end of October between bouts of autumn rains. I was quite comfortable, and tried to focus my mind on the conversation about ancient Carthage, rather than that vindictive pair, Sanballat and Simonides, working out ways to keep me down. I'd learned, years ago, that Simonides had certain well-placed agents, some of them enterprising freedmen and even an influential Roman or two, working for his business interests in administrative offices that reported directly to the Emperor. Ordinary senators, no matter how excellent their lineage, didn't have such easy access to Tiberius Caesar.

Before noon we reached the harbour of the island. We had brought litters with slaves, one a wide chair litter for Claudius and me, the other – full-sized – for the little girls and their nursemaid, to take us up the steep, curving path to the pavilion.

The more able-bodied walked up. Cypros, and even Lady Antonia, insisted that they wanted the exercise. The two boys followed Herod and Caligula up the slope, and the servants who were carrying the litters made the trip last of all.

When we got there several other servants dressed in imperial livery brought us warmed linen napkins and basins of scented water for washing our hands. Once we had taken our places on the dinner couches, they removed our sandals and bathed our feet. Then the refreshments were brought: platters of celery, olives, and chewy vegetables for a start, as well as fresh bread and light wine, mixed with water for the children.

The central couch was occupied by Herod Agrippa, Caligula, and Tiberius Gemellus. The young boy didn't have much opportunity to talk to his princely guardian because Caligula monopolized Herod's attention. Cypros and Lady Antonia shared a couch with the three younger children, though Herod Agrippa Junior was heard to say that he really wanted to be beside his father.

Perhaps he would have been if Caligula hadn't imposed his presence on the party.

Claudius and I were on the other side of the central couch. We discussed Carthaginian ruins, which he wished he could have visited in person. He was proving easier to talk to than people might expect if they knew of his tendency to stammer and twitch. His weakness decreased as he warmed to the interests of his heart and sensed that he had a genuinely interested listener. I'd resolved to give Claudius my best, with no mockery or sign of boredom, and I didn't find it difficult at all.

Gaius Caligula gets his cognomen from a childhood spent partly in his father Germanicus' military camp. One of the soldiers made little Gaius a pair of miniature soldier's boots, which we call *caligae*. At that time he had been – so they tell me – a delightful little golden-haired boy, the pet of the legions. Now he was much less attractive, especially up close where one could see his pimples.

At first he took no notice of me; then, while the main course of chicken, fish and vegetables was being brought around, he looked at me as if not sure who I was. I think he's slightly near-sighted.

Herod said, "Do you remember Valerius Messala, the brother of Barbatus?"

"Oh, yes, I think I've met you once or twice, Messala. You used to like driving a chariot – winning races – until you took on a Jew. And yet here you are, a friend of Herod."

His tone was mocking; he was delighted to have found someone to ridicule.

I kept my composure. "I value Herod's friendship, as apparently you do also."

He smirked and then turned back to Herod. During and after the meal, he continued to hang around Herod, eager for his praise and his witty comments. Accordingly he didn't bother me. I continued talking to Claudius, who may have been relieved that Caligula directed his sneer at me instead of him, for he was often the butt of jokes in the imperial family.

After the dessert course of fruit and pastries filled with apples and honey, we strolled around the grounds: a small rock-bound park. We had some conversation with Cypros and Lady Antonia. The latter expressed interest in my new project. After a while Tiberius

Gemellus, followed by his anxious paedagogus, approached us hesitantly. We had sat down on a bench near a fountain, neither of us sure of our footing on the uneven cobbled paths. We invited Gemellus to sit with us and tried to draw him into conversation. I did this better than Claudius; he and Gemellus stammered at each other and then ran out of things to say.

Gemellus talked to me a little about sports, but he hated to admit that so far he wasn't very good at anything. He had more trouble than most boys throwing things straight at a target. He was embarrassed when his grandfather watched him. He preferred reading, and became fairly animated talking about the *Iliad*. He wished the Trojans had won, though it was some consolation that, according to our legends, Aeneas had led a large party of Trojans to Italy, where their descendants had founded Rome. I concluded that he was a nice sensitive boy, not at all precocious, either physically or mentally. I wondered then what the future might hold if he became Emperor. But I didn't hold out much hope for it.

I remarked on the absence of Caligula's bride, Junia Claudilla, whereupon Claudius said, "It was a political marriage, the girl's father is one of the consuls. The Emperor thought it time Caligula took a wife from one of the best families. I understand Caligula does his marital duty, but likes his freedom in the daytime."

Presumably Junia Claudilla was moping around the palace. Of course she might have a discreet life of her own.

Herod had certainly impressed Caligula with his dramatic personality, his genial wit, and his natural princely grace. Although he acted as if he were the descendant of many generations of Jewish monarchs, this wasn't the case.

I have no reason to believe they were lovers. Herod was known for his strong attachment to Cypros. Some of his kin might be avid womanizers – and perhaps bisexual – but Herod Agrippa was, I am convinced, the ideal Jewish husband, truly in love with his beautiful, intelligent wife, even though his lavish spending and his scheming must sometimes have made her frantic.

I don't know about Caligula's feelings. Most Romans of the upper classes are educated to share the Greek admiration of male good looks. As a boy, I admired my Jewish friend's striking beauty. I'd like to forget that now. At least I don't have the unwelcome memory of ever being his lover.

Few boys get through their smooth-faced adolescent period without being at least fondled and groped by some older male. I managed to resist some things, especially penetration, which is probably a great way for the passive participant to get hemorrhoids. If the tales of the Emperor's frolics on Capri are true, Caligula, a frequent guest, has tried everything. According to Lepida, his favourite scandalous sexual amusement was incest with his three sisters, but she was merely repeating sensational gossip and had no first-hand knowledge.

We could see Herod and Caligula coming along a hedged path; at another time of year these bushes would be thick with bright flowers. That day the leaves had taken on an autumn colour – pale gold replacing the dull green. Another good rain or two, accompanied by wind, and there would be nothing but bare twigs.

Gemellus was resentful that Caligula had intruded and spoiled his chance to get better acquainted with Herod. He grumbled, "That stupid cousin of mine always gets in the way. That's what he likes to do!"

Claudius said soothingly, "It's just common sense for Herod to keep friendly with Caligula."

The servants packed up the items our party had brought. They had already cleared away the food and dishes from the luncheon. The sky had started clouding up and the wind was rising. The litters came to take us down the winding hill to our boat. We skimmed over the waves, hoping to reach the mainland before the rain started.

Claudius had gone into the cabin for an afternoon nap and I was sitting alone on the deck. The women and children were on the other side of the boat. Gemellus was leaning against the stern rail; I don't know where his quiet Greek paedagogus was.

Caligula appeared around the side. I don't think he saw me; we were both looking at the large white-capped waves. He walked over to Gemellus, and it seemed to me that he said something. I couldn't see if he touched Gemellus or not. At that moment the ship lurched sideways with a huge wave, which swept over the rear of the deck.

Ye Gods! Gemellus! Caligula had stepped back as far as the cabin wall, but Gemellus was suddenly gone. Not even a scream that could be heard against the rush of the waves and the wind in the sails.

I yelled, "Get help!" slipping off my sandals at the same time. Then I plunged over the rail and down into the depths.

My daily practice, which included deep dives, was useful now. I swam underwater in the direction I thought Gemellus might be and soon spotted a white human shape with flailing arms and legs. I surfaced the same moment as Gemellus, who screamed, "Help!" and flung up his arms, after which, naturally, he went under again.

I soon got to him, and took hold of him by the hair, making him turn so that he was floating on his back. I managed a few reassuring words such as "Relax! Don't struggle." In touching his body, I was careful to keep out of his reach, knowing that a drowning person's natural urge is to wrap himself around his would-be rescuer, ironically dragging both of them down to a watery death. As it was, several large waves rolled over us, temporarily pushing us under, then lifting us up.

I wondered if the ship was going away from us. Would no one help us? If no one came to help, what was I going to do if the waves kept hitting us in force and sweeping over us? How long before I let go of Gemellus and just struggled desperately for myself? Fighting for our lives kept me too busy to think much. It wasn't until the danger was over that I let my imagination work on what my obituary might have been.

Then I heard shouts. We'd been seen, and a boat was being lowered to pick us up. Soon it was beside us, and I was helping the two sailors load Gemellus into it. He was conscious but pale and silent, though soon afterwards he became noisily nauseous.

In the lifeboat beside him, I helped him hold his head over the side. The sailors had given each of us a flimsy blanket. One of them pressed on Gemellus' rib cage to help him regurgitate the sea water, mixed with fragments of his lunch.

They had done something to slow the ship down; we were able to pull up beside it, and Tiberius Gemellus was handed up by the sailors. Then we three, the two sailors and I, scrambled up a rope ladder (something I hadn't practised, and the Gods must have helped me), and finally the small boat was pulled up to its place on deck.

Everyone was on hand. Lady Antonia had slaves wrap her grandson in more blankets and take him inside the cabin. Before he went in, he glared at Caligula and said, "You pushed me in."

Caligula exclaimed indignantly, "I did nothing of the sort. You're imagining it. I wouldn't harm a hair of your head. Grandmother, you know me better than that."

"I hope I do," she said severely. "But why didn't you try to save him? You didn't even raise the alarm. Princess Cypros first saw what had happened and screamed at us all. She saw Messala with Gemellus in the water."

I said, "Thank you, Cypros." I wondered how Caligula would get out of this predicament.

"Don't you remember, Grandmother? I can't swim a stroke. Once I nearly drowned in the large pool at the baths. I can't help my fear of water."

He sounded grieved and misunderstood. He didn't attempt to excuse his failure to summon help, though he had been right there when Gemellus went overboard.

Herod took me inside the cabin to a separate compartment where he had put changes of clothing for himself and his family just in case they were needed. Cypros had already dressed her little son and daughter in clean tunics after a romp in the grass.

I dried myself on thick towels and changed to the costume of a wealthy Jewish nobleman: wool tunic, dark-blue robe trimmed with black fox fur, and a matching dark-blue turban.

"Too bad you shave regularly," Herod said. "A neat beard would complete the picture."

"So would circumcision, but I'd rather not go that far."

A servant wrapped up my wet things and put them into a bag. My sandals, which I had kicked off, were handed to me. Although the air was getting chilly, I didn't put on my cloak, as it would have looked strange with Herod's furred robe.

I remained in the cabin for a while. Gemellus was, I knew, recuperating in the other room, attended by his anxious grandmother and the paedagogus. I could hear them talking a little. Lady Antonia was giving sensible advice. I heard her tell the boy not to accuse Caligula unless he was absolutely sure.

Then I heard bits of conversation on the other side of my room. The voices would have been inaudible to those in the room where Gemellus was. Herod and Caligula were talking outside, not far from the wall.

"Herod, I swear to you that I didn't push that silly brat. Even if I'd wanted to get rid of him, I wouldn't have put *your* position in jeopardy."

"It may be in jeopardy nevertheless. Just my usual cursed luck! To gain an honourable well-paid position and then lose it in less than a month."

"Maybe we can avoid telling the Emperor about this."

"Don't count on it. Gemellus will tell. Or the servants and sailors. Or Lady Antonia. She won't want to hurt me, but she may feel it her duty to inform the Emperor that her grandson, *his* grandson, was in danger."

"I'll do my best to convince Grandmother of my innocence," said Caligula. "I suppose Messala must get credit for his heroic rescue. I'd no idea he could do that – a man crippled from a racing accident."

"He says he's always been able to swim," said Herod. "And he's been swimming every day this summer, rebuilding his strength – with very good results. Maybe the Emperor will be glad I invited a superior swimmer on our excursion, since I failed to watch Gemellus every moment as I should have done."

"No one could watch that foolish lad all the time. But it's too bad he's blaming me for his own clumsiness. I think the boy takes after Uncle Claudius."

By the time we neared the dock, a conference had been called. It was clear that the Emperor, himself, flanked by attendants, was about to meet us. The robed white-haired figure, tall and dignified despite his seventy-five years, was easy to recognize if only by his escort of Praetorian Guards.

Gemellus, now dressed in a dry tunic, was still proclaiming that he was sure Caligula had come up behind him and pushed him. I made my way outside and, to my relief, Herod handed me the cane I'd dropped when I dived after Gemellus.

Caligula asked me point-blank, "Messala, did you see me – or anyone else – push Tiberius Gemellus?"

I answered truthfully, "No, I didn't see you touch Gemellus. You were near him for a moment; you may have spoken to him, though I couldn't hear you. Then the great wave hit us, and the next thing I knew, Gemellus had been swept away."

Caligula looked relieved; I wondered if he *had* touched Gemellus, but it seemed likely enough that the accident had been due to the overwhelming force of the sudden wave.

"There, you see, Gemellus? Even your brave rescuer doesn't accuse me. You really should be careful with your flights of imagination. It's a sign of mental illness to think everyone is out to get you."

"Not everyone, Caligula. Just you! I *felt* you touch me on the back – and then I fell into the waves."

The discussion continued, with Lady Antonia urging Gemellus not to say anything he could not prove. Claudius wisely kept out of it. Herod and Cypros were clearly worried lest he be discharged from his new office.

We came down the gangplank and faced Tiberius Caesar, robed in white over an embroidered tunic. He radiated a severe dignity which could terrify many normally brave people.

He didn't know me; probably he thought I was one of Herod's Jewish entourage. Ironically Herod himself was wearing a Roman tunic and cloak.

From my station in the background, I could watch the Emperor greeting his sister-in-law and his grandson, then Caligula. He ignored Claudius but spoke politely to Herod and Cypros, asking if they had had a good day with no mishaps. At that point Gemellus squeakily blurted out, "I fell overboard and nearly drowned."

"I thought you looked sick. You'd better get inside at once," said the Emperor in his deep growl.

Herod Agrippa began to explain how Gemellus had been leaning on the stern rail when a freak wave had swept up over the back of the deck and carried poor Gemellus into the water before he knew what was happening.

Tiberius Caesar frowned and said, "I assume someone was prompt to save my grandson – or he wouldn't be here now. Was it one of the sailors? He should be suitably rewarded."

Herod said, "As a matter of fact it was a friend I invited: Valerius Messala Secundus, the brother of Barbatus. He saw Gemellus fall into the sea, and immediately jumped in after him before anyone else was aware of what had happened. I deeply regret that I was distracted by conversation at the crucial moment when I ought to have been observing the boy. I feel that I have failed you."

He stood there noble and very sad, with just the right dramatic inflections in his voice – contrite and prepared to face the consequences with the regal demeanour of a prince of Israel.

The Emperor's gaze fell on me. He didn't address me directly but said loudly, "I thought he couldn't walk. Did he swim after Gemellus and save him all by himself?"

"Yes, he did. Of course we had the sailors pick them up in the lifeboat, but they might not have got to Gemellus in time if it hadn't been for Messala."

I thought, "The God of Israel bless you, Herod!"

Tiberius Caesar finally spoke to me, "We are grateful, Messala. Are those Herod's garments you are wearing, or have you adopted the Jewish religion?"

Some thanks!

I was polite, however. "Herod lent me his own extra clothing since mine was wet."

One of Herod's servants had all the wet laundry, both Gemellus' and mine, in a canvas bag.

"You did right, Herod," said the Emperor. "We wouldn't wish the man who saved our grandson to catch cold."

This sounded encouraging; maybe he wouldn't strike my name off the equestrian list when it was brought to his attention.

Changing from the regal plural to the more personal singular, he said to the company, "I have some further questions. Shall we go inside the palace now?"

Then he made himself clearer. "I don't require everyone's presence. Princess Cypros, no doubt you wish to take your young children home. And there is no reason for Messala to linger."

So he wasn't going to question me. Had he asked me if Caligula or anyone else was present when Gemellus fell overboard, I suppose I would have had to say yes; Gemellus could have contradicted me if I'd tried to shield Caligula. The next question would have been why had Caligula then done nothing, not even raised the alarm. Maybe Tiberius Caesar did wonder about foul play; maybe he didn't want an outsider to be privy to his close questioning of family members.

If I'd been a common sailor, he would have given me a small reward, but for a man of aristocratic family, a word of thanks was considered sufficient. I'd merely done my duty, and it was everyone's good fortune that I could swim well.

Seeing the yacht arriving, Nestor, who had spent the day visiting in the palace stables, had brought my carriage close to the dock. Herod and the imperial family members followed the Emperor and his guards to the main entrance of the palace.

I offered Cypros and her children a ride home. It was only a short distance but a rather tiresome walk uphill and then across a couple of wide courtyards to the Herod quarters. The two maids walked carrying the bags. There wasn't room for us all.

Cypros was concerned about Herod. Would the Emperor allow him to keep his position?

I could only trust that Herod's wit and charm would stand him in good stead, along with Lady Antonia's kindly support. Claudius was his friend, but Claudius had no influence.

I said to Cypros, "Gemellus lost his nerve when it came to accusing Caligula in front of the Emperor. Do you think he'll dare to tell Caesar that he thinks Caligula pushed him overboard?"

"Perhaps not. He's a very timid boy. High-strung. Herod says he gets upset easily and then he isn't very coherent. He's probably realizing that no one wants Caligula to be found guilty, whatever the truth is. And I do think it was all an accident."

CHAPTER TWENTY-ONE

few days later Herod and Cypros called to talk it all over. They were accompanied by a slave who carried my clean laundry and took charge of Herod's garments which I returned.

"I've been lucky," Herod said. "The Emperor merely warned me to look after Gemellus more attentively. I promised him that I would guard the boy as carefully as my own son."

Cypros commented, "The Emperor also urged Caligula to watch over the boy like a big brother. But I don't think Caligula and Gemellus like each other at all. I hope Caligula won't be present too much when Herod is giving attention to Gemellus."

Herod looked amused but slightly worried. "It's a challenge trying to give them both my sincere interest at the same time. I absolutely can't ask Caligula to stop talking, and if I tell Gemellus he should be seen and not heard, he may tattle to his grandfather, or Lady Antonia."

"I'm glad Caesar didn't discharge Herod and offer *you* his job," Cypros said to me. "You got on very well with the lad."

I told her I valued my secluded life as a companion to my father with sufficient spare time for a program of regular exercise.

In truth, I would have hated living at the palace, the object of sarcastic comments from those who came and went at the imperial residences. I would particularly have wished to avoid Caligula and Ahenobarbus.

Cypros told me that the betrothal of Tirzah and Phineas was expected in early December. It would be a modest party with a few friends from the Bay area: Jews who shared Ben-Hur's belief in the Nazarene as the resurrected Son of the Supreme God. There would also be a Greek couple who followed the Nazarene religion.

"We'll be able to hear the music from our balcony," Cypros said. "I don't suppose you'd care to join us. We could drink our own toast to the radiant couple. That is, if Tirzah and Judah don't change their minds about wanting Phineas in the family."

"Why would they?"

Herod answered, "According to the servants' report, Phineas wants to please his uncle and his kin on the Hur side – and he certainly wants Tirzah's liberal dowry. But he grumbles to his manservant that Tirzah is naïve and not very responsive. He thinks that she should be pleading with her brother for an immediate wedding. Since he must wait to consummate his marriage, he and his servant are trying to make a secret arrangement with a woman of the town to relieve him. But he wants to be sure that Ben-Hur or Lady Miriam don't find out."

"He's a pompous hypocrite," said Cypros. "He makes speeches about the importance of a maiden's purity, calling it the priceless pearl that she brings to her husband's bed. And at the same time he's looking to have a good time with a woman who isn't pure. I don't think Ben-Hur quite trusts him. The fellow belabours the subject of sexual morals every day."

So Ben-Hur could decide to cancel the agreement before the actual betrothal took place. He would think seriously before letting Tirzah become trapped in a dismal marriage. It would be too bad if Phineas turned out to be a lecherous hound running after slaves and harlots, indifferent to Tirzah's feelings. Her ideal man was probably someone exactly like her brother – if possible.

Before Herod and Cypros left, a messenger brought me a letter from Barbatus. He was pleased to tell me that the censors had added my name to the equestrian list. Of course it could be removed by the Emperor at any time, so we must just hope for the best. I hoped the Emperor would take into consideration the fact that I'd saved Gemellus from drowning.

"You should start wearing tunics with the narrow vertical stripe," said Herod. "Ostentation can backfire; on the other hand, it isn't good to show a lack of confidence in your rights. I think you should appear in public more often. Be seen walking – with your natural dignity and self-respect."

My father approved of Herod's advice. He told me he had made over several more pieces of property to me with my brother's ready consent. There were rental houses as well as some undeveloped land close to the sea, in case I wanted to build my own house.

My brother had also agreed that, when I moved into a house of my own, I could help myself to various old but perfectly good pieces of furniture and works of art that had been put into storage because they didn't suit Lepida's taste for the ornate.

At the beginning of November Barbatus wrote again to tell us that my mother was coming to the Baiae area. Part of her dowry included a modest villa near Misenum. She had left the house in Rome, and Bibulus was courting a young bride of a rich middle-class family. He was anxious for the new marriage as he was in considerable debt.

Mother's brother, my Uncle Velleius, whom I barely knew, was arranging for his granddaughter, Sergia Carina, to keep her company for a while. He had a large villa nearby, but he and his wife were planning to visit their estates in Spain. They thought the climate of Baiae would be better for Mother, who had had a lingering cough ever since her disastrous sea voyage with Bibulus. Or maybe she had had the cough longer than that.

Barbatus strongly hinted that I should pay my filial respect to my mother. I remembered when Iras and I had called on her. She had averted her eyes from my body as if my crippled state repelled her – as it did me. Even now that I had a cane, she might still see me as deformed. No matter. I didn't want to see her either. I didn't need my mother.

The month progressed with a lot of rainy days. I couldn't sail the Flammifer very often, and it was now too cold for swimming in the sea. However, I went riding frequently and sometimes drove a carriage, but not the sort of chariot in which the driver stands up. I wasn't sure enough of my balance.

Then at the end of November I received a letter brought by my mother's servant. It was from Sergia Carina, my maternal cousin of the next generation.

"Sergia Carina to Marcus Valerius Messala, Greetings. For the past month I've been living with my great-aunt Lollia Velleia, your mother, in her villa at Misenum. It has been part of Aunt Velleia's dowry from the time she married her first husband, your father. Now suddenly we have been confronted by a very disagreeable person named Sanballat, who declares that Gaius Bibulus, from whom she has recently been divorced, gave him the deed to her villa in payment of a large debt. He wants to show it immediately to a young couple. Indeed, he proposes to bring them this very afternoon.

"I question Sanballat's claim to the deed. Aunt Velleia can't believe it now belongs to him. She says she never gave it to Bibulus and he had no automatic claim to it because they were married coemptio* and also had a contract allowing her to keep certain property and money. This contract should be in the care of my grandfather, Lollius Velleius, who is in Spain for the winter. However, Sanballat is waving in our faces what certainly looks like the deed. He is a very aggressive and supercilious man. If only Grandfather were here, I'm sure he would know what to do.

"I hope you can help us. Aunt Velleia is hesitant about asking you for assistance even though you are her only son because she left you when you were small and hasn't paid much attention to you over the years. Bibulus didn't want her to receive you.

---

* Coemptio marriage was a brief ceremony from which divorce was easy. The bride could retain her own property if she spent one night a year away from her husband's house.

"I have read your novel with pleasure; so has Aunt Velleia. You have great imagination and humour. I have admired you, and I can't believe that you would be unfeeling toward your mother, who gave you life. She has been an affectionate and often amusing aunt to me; I love her dearly. Perhaps there is no way you or anyone else can save her home from the rapacious clutches of Sanballat, but please, please come to our aid if you can. I dread confronting Sanballat's serpentine smirk this afternoon, and no doubt his pair of clients are just like him, mean and gloating. Sincerely – and very anxiously, Sergia Carina."

However I might have reacted otherwise, the mention of Sanballat was like a red flag to a bull. I showed Father the letter, and he agreed that I should go to my mother's villa immediately.

"If Bibulus has given Sanballat a genuine deed to the house, you may not be able to save it," he said. "If Velleius could produce the property contract, it would help. A letter should be sent to him immediately. I hope Velleia wasn't coerced or deceived into signing consent. She isn't stupid, but she doesn't know much about business, and she could be confused by someone persuasive and domineering – which I can believe Bibulus would be. Poor woman!"

"Couldn't we get a court order prohibiting Sanballat from possession until we've had a chance to contact Velleius?"

"I'll send an urgent letter to my friend Judge Antistius; he's in Misenum right now."

"Good! And I'll write to my friend Quadratus, who's doing well with his law career in Rome. Sanballat shouldn't be able to turn Mother and Sergia out, not without adequate notice at least. If they must go, I might offer them one of my houses that could quickly be made ready."

"A couple of them – very good houses – are unoccupied at the moment. Also the ladies would be welcome here as my guests."

I prepared to accompany Sergia's messenger to my mother's house. I certainly didn't want it to become Sanballat's house – and then the residence of Phineas and Tirzah, if they were the young couple he called his clients. The Gods forbid!

CHAPTER TWENTY-TWO

THERON, Mother's servant, had been given another letter from Sergia to her grandfather Lollius Velleius; he would take it to a local business that sent out couriers who carried letters in relays. No postal service is totally reliable; I remember my letter to Valerius Gratus, sent by military post, was intercepted by Sheik Ilderim's band of robbers.

I didn't need to ask Theron for directions to Mother's villa. Father knew very well where it was – just a hilltop away from the mansion that once belonged to the admiral Quintus Arrius. This news confirmed my suspicion that the unwelcome couple Sanballat was bringing were Phineas and Tirzah.

I decided to drive the carriage with its matched pair of greys; Nestor could come with me. If it seemed desirable, I could bring Mother and Sergia back.

As usual, I took the reins in my hands with the thought that it would be really nice if I could stand up and drive like a true charioteer. Soon we reached the driveway to Mother's residence. An open gate, a stand of tall pines, and then the villa; it had the name *Velleia* painted on a large stone beside the gate. Yes, her place was indeed within sight of the Hur place, which could be partly seen on a nearby hill.

Mother's villa was pretty and would be more so in the summer when the vines and bushes blossomed. There was a fountain near the entrance but it had been shut down. Seeing a carriage and a team of mules tended by a groom, I surmised that Sanballat and his clients had arrived.

Leaving Nestor to talk to the other groom, I knocked on the door, and a maidservant answered. I could hear sounds from inside, in particular an angry male voice, somewhat high-pitched. Then there was a bark, the kind of bark that would come from a small dog. Probably my mother had a lapdog. The maid looked worried, and I told her, "I am Messala, Lollia Velleia's son."

"Oh, come in, sir. My lady needs you!"

She led me through the small atrium to a sitting-room behind the office. It looked out on a portico and another garden.

The scene in the room wasn't as peaceful as the deserted garden. A young man in a white robe that wasn't a toga was yowling and trying to kick a tiny white Maltese dog that scurried behind a tall young lady. Sanballat was standing close by with an amused expression. My mother was seated, trying to saying something but unable to make herself heard. And facing me, her eyes wide and shocked, was – probably – Tirzah!

"That vicious little beast bit my leg," the young fellow screamed. "I want him killed!"

"It isn't *him*, it's *her*," snapped the tall girl, whom I guessed to be my cousin Sergia. "Flora was being a good dog, protecting her mistress. It was your own fault, yelling at Aunt Velleia and shoving your fingers in her face. Did no one ever teach you good manners?"

Tirzah spoke then. I think she recognized me, but she turned her face sideways toward the girl. "Please keep that dog away from me. I'm afraid of dogs."

"Then just sit down, but not too near my aunt," instructed the young beauty impatiently. To the dog she said sharply, "Sit."

Then she walked swiftly toward me.

"You are Messala?" She sounded hopeful. I don't know whether she identified me by a family resemblance or by the fact that I had a cane with my initial.

"Yes, I am. And I presume you are my cousin Sergia Carina. Thank you for your eloquent letter. I'll do all I can to help."

An audible sniff from Sanballat. The other two were silent.

Looking past the astonished faces of Tirzah and her suitor or betrothed, whichever he was, I went straight to the divan where my mother was sitting, apparently in a state of shock. There were tears on her face. She was more haggard than I'd ever seen her.

"Messala! My own Marcus. You can walk? Oh, I'm so glad! Thank Apollo and his healer son Aesculapius. But please do help me. That horrible man over there says my house is now his, that Bibulus gave him the deed. And now he's selling it to that other disgusting man who insults me and wants to kill my poor little dog."

Meanwhile Sergia was telling Phineas disdainfully, "Please *try* to stop dripping blood on the carpet."

It was a very fine carpet, a blend of scarlet, green, and gold, probably from Persia or maybe India. Sanballat reached inside his toga and handed Phineas a white cloth, saying, "Tie this around your leg. And don't keep staring at the touching family reunion."

I kissed Mother's cheek and told her that Father was already contacting a lawyer and petitioning a magistrate for a restraining order against Sanballat.

Once more he sniffed. Maybe it was an expression of contempt, or perhaps he was allergic to dog hair.

I took a chair and sat beside my mother. Sergia, on her other side, had picked up the little dog and was gently whispering, "Good doggie." Though my attention was mainly directed to my distressed mother, I did notice that Sergia had beautiful dark-blue eyes with long lashes.

"Mother, Sergia tells me that Uncle Velleius has papers which guarantee you the right to this property in case you are divorced or widowed. Therefore Bibulus shouldn't have been able to use your home to pay off his debt to Sanballat. I suppose the papers are with Velleius' files?"

"Yes, that's where they must be – my original marriage contract and also my divorce settlement. If we could just get word to him, he'd either come back or send permission for us to get the papers. They must be in his office – or maybe he placed them with the Vestal Virgins where they'd be safe."

"How do you think Bibulus got the deed – if that *is* the correct deed – to give to Sanballat?"

She sighed, "Bibulus' secretary took care of business for both of us before the divorce. He could have given the deed to Bibulus – or maybe he made a copy of it. He would've had to fake my father's seal on it – but perhaps he was clever enough to do it. I can see I haven't managed things at all well."

Sergia said, "I've sent a letter to my grandfather in Spain. But it will take a while before we hear from him – and this – this obnoxious man – wants us to clear out of the house within two days. Not only that, he thinks the furniture belongs to him as well."

"He can have all the ugly pieces Bibulus bought," said Mother. "Like the dining tables and couches with Egyptian crocodiles carved in the wood. I was going to sell them anyway. But there are things I don't want to lose, things that even go back to my marriage with your father – like the painting of Hector and Andromache over there."

She indicated a large painting behind Tirzah. "I never should have left him. He was the very best man I ever had."

"Tirzah and I wouldn't want a painting of a couple of adulterous so-called Gods," said Phineas, who had now finished bandaging his bitten leg. "And we wouldn't dream of having couches and tables with crocodile faces. Sanballat can sell them at auction – to heathen idol-worshippers."

I had to react to his ignorance. "Hector and Andromache weren't Gods, nor were they adulterous – they were a married couple like Abraham and Sarah. But I forget – you wouldn't want a painting of *them* either."

My expression may have shown that I considered him culturally impoverished.

Sanballat said, "If the painting, along with the rest of the contents of this house, becomes mine, I'm willing to sell it to you or your father at a reasonable price. But I should introduce my clients to you, Messala. This young man is Phineas Ben Zebulon, a cousin of Ben-Hur. And perhaps you remember Tirzah; I believe you were acquainted long ago."

I bowed very slightly but didn't try to say I was pleased to encounter either of them. Tirzah was silent and motionless, but Phineas frowned and then spat at me. He missed, thank whatever Divine Being concerns himself or herself with the disposal of saliva!

Sergia rang a small bell, and the maid came at once.

"Clean that up immediately." She pointed to the spot on the wide golden border of the carpet.

The maid may have been keeping an eye on things. She already had damp-looking cleaning cloths in her hand and went to work right away.

Tirzah looked embarrassed. Was she reflecting on how she would endure years of marriage to the sort of partner who spits on other people's floors?

"I trust the dog gives you less trouble, Mother," I said thoughtfully.

Mother smiled. "Flora is well-trained."

Sanballat said, "I was about to give Tirzah and Phineas a proper tour of the house, including the sleeping quarters. But the ladies strongly object."

"We certainly don't want them parading through our bedrooms," said Sergia. "And I've told – Phiny – whatever his name is – to keep his sticky hands off our things. He picked up a little bud vase. For all I know, he might have tucked it away inside his robe if I hadn't checked him."

"I'd no intention of stealing anything," Phineas protested.

"Of course you hadn't," Tiirzah assured him sympathetically. "Phineas is completely honest. You insulted him." She faced Sergia indignantly.

Phineas lifted his rather handsome head proudly. His chin was his weakest feature. Aside from that, he had something of the dark-curled, dark-eyed good looks of Judah Ben-Hur, which would naturally appeal to Tirzah.

"Perhaps you don't realize that one of my uncles is simply the richest man in the whole East. The trinkets you guard so carefully look cheap and tawdry beside the treasures in the various dwellings of my ancestors. Really I've seen nothing here that I'd want to waste money on."

"That's my point," said Sergia. "It struck me that you had no intention of paying for souvenirs. Not if you could quietly conceal them in your robe."

"Do I have to listen to the insults of a –?"

I cut in before he could say whatever he intended.

"Don't call my cousin or my mother whatever you've thought of. They are honourable Roman ladies, and you can be charged with slander. Sanballat, I believe Judge Antistius will grant my father's request for time to check this out with Lollius Velleius. That means you should take your clients away, at least for now. You and they have no rights at all in this house until a judge can consider the evidence of Lollius Velleius, both documentary and verbal. He may come to testify in person."

"We'll leave for the moment," said Sanballat. "But unless I see a court order to the contrary, I'll take possession of the house the day after tomorrow, just as I've said. Bibulus contracted his debt some months ago – before his divorce – and offered this house as security. In October he told me he couldn't pay back my money – he was still negotiating a new marriage to a girl of large dowry but inferior rank. He said I could take the house; he handed me the deed which I have right here. I assumed Velleia knew of the arrangement. It seems to me that I gave her plenty of time to see about moving to a new dwelling."

I'd been calm up to this point, but now there was a fury in my voice. The smug suave bastard!

"You gave her *plenty of time* by saying nothing to her at all. You waited till her brother, her natural protector, had left for Spain. Tell me this, Sanballat – is this scurvy enterprise all your own or were you encouraged by your friend Judah Ben-Hur? Does he feel that the glory of his past revenge would be enhanced by a base and petty anti-climax – an attack on my mother?"

"He might consider it appropriate – in the light of certain former events," said Sanballat, smiling enigmatically, as if he'd be happy to tell my mother and cousin about the arrest of the Hurs and the temporary confiscation of their house in Jerusalem – and the imprisonment of the Hur women.

"No!" said Tirzah, determined to defend her brother. "Judah doesn't know about it. He's in Rome right now, settling a problem with the tenant of his house by the Tiber. And he took our mother with him to see a special physician about her heart. He thinks Phineas and I should wait at least until spring before getting married. But yesterday Sanballat came and said this house was available, and we could have it soon. Simonides thought it would be a good idea. We were hoping Judah would agree to an immediate wedding instead of a betrothal with months to wait before the proper marriage ceremony."

Having started to explain her position, Tirzah was inspired to go on. "I didn't know whose house this was. Indeed, Messala, I thought your mother had died long ago. I never heard you speak of her. Did you ever talk to Judah about her?"

She was gazing directly at me with reproachful eyes, as if she thought I'd failed in an obligation to bare my childish soul.

"No, I'm practically sure I didn't. But I thought your family already knew that my parents were divorced. Other people knew; the High Priest's wife was fond of asking me if I ever heard from my mother – and I wished the damned woman would shut up."

Mother whispered, "Dear, I'm so sorry!"

Tirzah may have been shocked at the way I referred to the High Priest's wife. Generally the Jews speak of their High Priest and his spouse with something like reverence.

She wasn't ready to stop talking. "I don't want to take this house if we have no right to it – if your mother has truly been cheated. But I'd rather set my heart on it. We can see it very well from our garden on top of the hill. I used to look down across the valley and then to this lower hill – and admire the flowers and the fountain, and think what a pity there were only servants to appreciate it all because the lady wasn't there then. I kept thinking of what I might do with the garden if it were mine. I'd prune back a lot of those bushes that obstruct the view, and I'd transplant some of Judah's roses. I'm sure he'd let me have them."

Evidently she hadn't grasped the legal issue very well. She said, "Couldn't you just take your mother to live with you, Messala? *My* mother doesn't have a separate house; she lives with my brother and his family. That way she can enjoy her grandchildren."

I answered with somewhat overdone patience. "This is my mother's house, Tirzah. It was part of her dowry when she married my father, and my parents lived here for a few months until he was posted to Syria. In fact I was probably conceived in this house."

I hoped this information would give the happy couple the feeling that their chosen dream house was ill-omened.

At the time of my parents' marriage, my grandfather was still alive and occupying the Baiae mansion. Mother's dower house provided more privacy.

"Actually I have several houses of my own, some currently rented, but one could be made available, and I would be very pleased if Mother and Sergia decided to live in it. I'm still with my father, but I could divide my time between my parents. However, I won't stand back and allow my mother to be forced from the house to which she has a just claim."

Tirzah still had a disappointed expression in her huge sad eyes.

I said, "Your brother could easily build you a palace; there are some excellent locations not very far away."

Phineas rose from the chair on which he had been sitting, glaring in turn at the dog and at me. "Tirzah, I think we should definitely look for another house. But I don't want your brother to build us a palace. There should be something right in Misenum or Baiae – or even as far as Pompeii. Really we don't have to live right under your brother's nose, do we?"

She had the Hur reluctance to give up without a fight, despite her reputation for gentleness. "I see nothing wrong with staying close to Judah and Mother. I think it would be better. In fact, Phineas,

I don't see why you want us to move away from my brother. He would be such a good friend to you – always willing to help you."

"In his special patronizing way! He never lets me forget his exalted position – the head of a famous family, the heroic chari-oteer – who thinks I don't have enough experience to handle his wonderful horses!"

What a lot of bitterness! I wondered if he'd resented Judah even before meeting him. He had been sent by his family to court a daughter of Hur, and presumably he had the approval of Simonides, who had travelled with him. Evidently he had concealed his true feelings up to now.

Tirzah exclaimed, "Judah's Arabians are special; they're bred from Aldebaran, the stallion the Sheik gave him. Of course he won't let just anyone drive them. He could see you were awkward with the pair you bought from that horse dealer."

"Oh, I'm awkward, am I? You don't sound much like an admiring future wife. I took for granted you'd be more supportive."

"I'm only speaking the truth." Her voice trembled as if she were close to tears. "You don't have much experience with high-bred horses. Judah says it takes training. He didn't learn everything overnight."

"Judah says! Judah says! I'm telling you now, Tirzah, I don't want to hear you say that after we're married – not ever!"

She looked bewildered and angry. I couldn't resist making a contribution to their quarrel.

"Maybe you and Tirzah shouldn't marry each other. It begins to sound like a mistake for both of you. Actually I'm surprised that Ben-Hur would even consider giving his sister to such a total creep."

Tirzah gasped, and Sanballat smirked mockingly. His sale was probably spoiled, but if Bibulus' arrangement with him proved valid, he could find another buyer for the house, and it may have amused him that Phineas Ben Zebulon wasn't proving any more desirable than he himself was.

Phineas' face reddened as he clenched his fists and stood erect, stepping forward. "You – you – Roman dog! How dare you insult *me*? I've heard about your evil deeds. You should be ashamed to look me in the face – or to speak to Tirzah! If you weren't a cripple, I'd strike you."

I drawled slowly, "Are you quite sure you could? Have you taken any training?"

If he had swung his fist at me, I think I could have sidestepped the blow and maybe tripped him with the cane. However, Sanballat intervened. He took Phineas firmly by the arm.

"Come, come, let's not have a brawl in a room with ladies. I think for the time being we'd better go home. I'll drop you both off at the Arrius villa – or I *could* show you a couple of other houses if you feel like it."

"I don't feel like it," said Tirzah decidedly. "I want to go straight home. You can look at other houses if you like, Phineas, but maybe you should find a different wife to share whatever house you choose. You clearly don't like my brother – and I must say that he means a lot more to me than you do. So I don't think I truly love you – or esteem you enough!"

He broke away from Sanballat and stamped back and forth, scowling with wrath and humiliation. "You were willing to marry me before – before this – Roman wolf came and interfered. Supposedly for a worthless whore who's had four husbands. A mother of shame!"

Mother looked ready to faint, and Sergia put her arm around her. I stood up and stepped in front of her, facing Phineas.

I didn't exactly intend to hit him – perhaps. But as he advanced, my arm swung forward of its own accord. Just then Sergia extended her dainty sandalled foot and tripped him. He stumbled toward me, and my hand connected quite hard with his prominent nose. He didn't fall completely, but he staggered. Sanballat rescued him and took him by the arms.

"Come on, Phineas, ignore these people. We're leaving. I assume you're coming with us, Tirzah. Unless you hope Messala will drive you home."

She appeared embarrassed at that suggestion.

I said, "I could tell my groom to drive you home while I stay here with my family."

She looked at sarcastic Sanballat and furious Phineas holding a bleeding nose with his hand. He was muttering something about wishing he'd brought his dagger. The thought of their company even for a short drive clearly gave her pause, but she said hesitantly, "No, thank you, Messala. I'll ride home in Sanballat's carriage. But I'm warning you, Sanballat and Phineas both, if either one of you pesters me with another offensive remark, I'll jump out and walk. It isn't so very far."

I thought, "Bravo, girl, you have some spirit!"

"Don't think of doing such a thing!" said Sanballat. "We'll keep silent. It's better we say nothing until we're all calmer."

She walked out the door through the corridor toward the atrium and the exit. The two men followed. Phineas looked back and glared at us – at me, the evil Roman wolf; at Mother, who was wiping away tears; and at Sergia, beautiful and haughty.

He snarled at me, "You'll pay for this, Messala. And as for that insolent young harlot – if I get a chance, I'll have that miserable little mutt destroyed."

Sanballat said, "I haven't given up. Remember that."

And then they were gone. Thank the Gods!

CHAPTER TWENTY-THREE

THREE days later, in the evening, I reached Rome by carriage, with Nestor at my side. We'd changed horses at several inns, spending nights at two of them, one of them in Terracina. It was mild for early December, and I rather enjoyed the journey along the Appian Way.

Judge Antistius had speedily granted Father's request for a court order prohibiting Sanballat from taking possession of Mother's house until we could investigate the matter – finding out if Lollius Velleius indeed had a document affirming his sister's right to the property. If I called in person on his lawyer and his secretary, showing them a letter from my mother, one or both of them might give me the evidence I needed. I could also try to find out how Bibulus had obtained the deed – whether with the help of a secretary he had taken it while still living with Mother, or whether it had been filed away with Uncle Velleius' other papers or perhaps deposited with the Vestal Virgins, who take care of wills and other valuable papers – in which case he would have had to resort to illegal methods: glib trickery, stealing, or forgery.

I'd written to Barbatus and to my old friend Quadratus. Both were at the house to welcome me when I arrived on the evening of the third day. Quadratus had already called on Velleius' secretary, who assured him that the papers concerned with Mother's property and her divorce agreement were in the care of the Temple of Vesta. This should include the deed. Velleius had a copy of the divorce settlement in his own files.

Accordingly, next morning, armed with a written declaration Quadratus had obtained from Velleius' secretary, I went with my lawyer and my supportive brother Barbatus to the Temple of Vesta and asked for an interview with the Chief Vestal. She was a tall dignified woman in the white gown of all Vestals, her hair tucked inside a white rolled headdress. At first she declared that of course the deed was there with all the other relevant papers. But when we said that Bibulus had given what appeared to be the deed to Sanballat, she was shocked and left us to check out the situation for herself. Returning, she was downcast.

"I can't believe such a thing could happen here," she said. "The deed isn't with the papers Velleius deposited, and now I find that the Vestal who was looking after the files – she's been here long enough to have known better – she actually confesses that she handed the deed over to Gaius Bibulus when he came here and said he was the husband of Lollia Velleia. He didn't even have a paper of consent from his wife or from Lollius Velleius. Was he still married to her at that time? It was the Ides of October.*"

"No, the divorce was complete by that time. Mother divorced Bibulus in September, as soon as she returned from the sea voyage in which Bibulus tried to drown her. Velleius' papers would show this – I gather you still have them. Bibulus sent her a divorce paper early in October after arguing with Velleius about the return of her dowry, which he had wanted to keep."

"We don't always know what's going on in the world outside. We don't hear all the gossip."

It is true that the Vestals are sheltered during the thirty years of their service at the shrine of our Goddess of the Home. They have

---

* October 15

an escort of lictors when they go to the public games and chariot races, where they have excellent seats. They have some authority; a prisoner or an abused slave might ask them for protection – this is sometimes, though not always, successful. But they can't go just where they like. They are brought to the Temple of Vesta when they are still children and they end their service when they are in their late thirties. After leaving Vesta's service, they may legally marry, but usually they don't; they are content to live in respectable retirement with a sufficient income.

I gathered there would be some kind of punishment for the woman who made the mistake; however, it wouldn't be the supreme penalty, which is imposed only in instances of unchastity. Then the erring woman – virgin no more – is supposed to be beaten and then buried alive. This hasn't happened for many years.

The Chief Vestal apologized repeatedly, then gave me a written and sealed statement to the effect that Gaius Bibulus had been given the deed by mistake and that he had had no right to it and that the divorce agreement, still in Vestal files, stated that the house in Misenum was Lollia Velleia's and that her divorced spouse had no claim to it.

We thanked her and left. I was grateful that I'd gone to the Temple with the support of both my lawyer, Quadratus, and my distinguished senatorial brother, Barbatus. I had the feeling this may have made a difference in the Chief Vestal's cooperation.

I didn't waste time socializing in Rome after that. I thought I should get back home as soon as possible. Who knew what Sanballat and his allies might be up to? Mother and Sergia had agreed to contact Father if there was any trouble, and he would make them welcome if they came to him. He seemed to have an undying tenderness for my mother – something I hadn't realized until recently.

Arriving back in the evening two-and-a-half days later, I found Mother and Sergia with Father, conferring anxiously. Sanballat had managed to get a court date set for the day after next, and there was a change of judge; Rabirius was to replace our friend Antistius. I wondered if Rabirius had been offered a bribe. Sanballat wouldn't hesitate for a moment to bribe a judge, I was sure. If he had the support of Simonides, he might be able to offer a huge bribe. I asked Father about Rabirius' character and he said sadly, "Yes, I understand that Rabirius is very corruptible; he's known for it."

On the other hand, it would be hard for any official on the bench to ignore a declaration from the Chief Vestal, the revered guardian of Rome's honour and old-fashioned values.

Mother and Sergia had come to stay with us for the present, and fortunately the little dog Flora had become friends with big old Tarquin. I was relieved that there would be no canine blood on the floor tiles, no resultant tears from the ladies.

"We accepted your father's invitation after we'd had a simply horrible night," said Mother. "There was a loud voice in the dark, shouting very bad names at us. And someone threw rocks at the shutters for a long time – at least it seemed long."

That sort of harassment might have come from Sanballat, though it didn't seem his usual style, and certainly Ben-Hur would have had no part in it – he had been brought up to be a gentleman, the son of the gracious Prince Ithamar. However, Phineas Ben Zebulon was different – probably different from his uncle, who was well-reputed among both Romans and Jews, a man of dignity and moderation.

"I hired a couple of trainers with the kind of big fighting dogs your brother keeps at the house in Rome," said Father. "They're patrolling Velleia's house every night."

Barbatus had thought we should have the big dogs at our seaside villa too, but Father hadn't wanted them. He didn't like to restrict Tarquin from roaming around as he pleased, though when in Rome he had kept his dog inside his own room at night.

Mother seemed happy to be with us. She chatted a lot with Father, who was definitely cheered to have her company.

They reminisced about long ago, and I learned how much Mother had disliked Jerusalem. She might have been fairly happy in a place like Caesarea, a coastal port with an ethnically mixed population and a strong Greek cultural influence. In Caesarea the Gods of Greece had temples, resented by the Jews, who were impotent to get rid of them. But Jerusalem had only one great Temple, the splendid shrine of their one God – built mostly by Herod the Great, whom the Jews nevertheless detested as an interloper. No other Gods had temples there; the people would have rioted.

"I had no women friends there," Mother explained. "No young women to visit with. When I went out to shop or sightsee, I was uncomfortable. It was a very unfriendly place. Some merchants were eager to sell me things – at high prices. But some other shopkeepers tried to ignore me, pretending not to see me. I learned that some of them even thought I contaminated their premises. What I touched was made unclean. Sometimes I heard insults hissed at me from alleys or behind curtains; I couldn't see who it was or I could have had him – or her – arrested. That voice outside my home reminded me." She shuddered and pulled her shawl around her.

Mother was going through menopause then, that time when a woman ceases to shed monthly blood and is no longer able to conceive a child. She was sometimes much too warm, sometimes surprisingly chilly, and very easily tired. Bibulus had had no patience with her moods or her frequent weariness.

"I really should have taken you and little Marcus home when you begged me to," said Father regretfully. "We might have had many good years here."

"I shouldn't have given you an ultimatum," she said. "When you refused to take me home, I was too stubborn to back down – so I left you and Marcus. The law says that children belong to their father, so I couldn't take him away with me."

As a four-year-old, I'd been the victim of my parents' stubbornness. However, now things were belatedly getting better. I didn't suppose my mother and father would remarry, but I felt that they would remain friends – especially if, as Mother declared, she was thoroughly tired of marrying. She admitted to me and Sergia that she wanted to go peacefully to sleep without anyone bothering her for sexual satisfaction, let alone afterwards keeping her awake with snoring. Bibulus had a peculiar whining snore that kept penetrating her dreams.

I asked my parents why their first months of marriage had been spent almost exclusively in her new seaside villa rather than in the larger house in Baiae. They said that the Baiae villa had been closed up for the winter months except for a skeleton staff of slaves; my grandfather would open it up for the summer, and Barbatus, a lad of fifteen taking classes in Rome, would come there for his holidays.

Mother frankly liked being in our mansion, which might have become her home. She enjoyed her temporary change of scene. Nevertheless, she regularly took a sweetish potion that was supposed to help her relax. I gathered that it contained an extract of poppies, prescribed for her by a so-called physician who specialized in women's disorders. Mixed with a sweet wine, it would make her lethargic – and from all I've heard about such potions, it's addictive.

It was Sergia who told me about Mother's daily medication; she also felt that Mother had become dependent on it and that it was making her increasingly languid.

"I wish she could be persuaded to do without it," she said.

The doctors had given me a strong poppy syrup to relieve pain after my injuries in the race, but I feared taking it for any longer than absolutely necessary. I didn't want to give up and dream my life away, miserable though it was.

I said to Sergia, "Maybe we can keep her interested and even active so that she won't want the soothing syrup so much. If we had some mild December days, we could go for a sail in my boat."

"I'd love that. I hope we can – for my own sake."

I found Sergia a very candid girl with great enthusiasm for life and for outdoor pursuits. She had her own horse and was a keen rider, unlike so many proper young Roman ladies who were embarrassed to fling a leg over a horse's back. Messalina had been on a horse a few times, but Lepida disapproved.

"It is more proper for a lady to travel in a carriage or in a litter," she insisted.

Having lost a board game to Father, Mother took a nap on the sitting-room couch, accompanied by her faithful dog, while Father retired to his room. It wasn't a good day to get my boat out on the water; indeed I felt we would have to wait a while for that. However, we could go for a ride; the wind was getting colder but the sun was still shining.

Sergia wore a knee-length tunic, and she had ankle boots instead of sandals. She got up on her horse with the help of a mounting block; I rode Sheba. We had a fairly long ride, in the course of which I learned more about her. Lepida had told me some things, which I didn't mention to Sergia.

She was twenty-two years old and she had been briefly married to my old acquaintance Metellus Calvus.

"I was nineteen when Father made the agreement with Calvus, whom I'd met only once. Three years before, I'd been betrothed to Quintus Mallius, a pleasant young man. Just a few days before the wedding, he developed mumps, and so the ceremony was postponed. Then it seemed the sickness had descended to his glands, and the doctor said he could never become a father. He came and released me from my promise. Then he went home so desperately upset that he took his dagger and slashed both his wrists. Nobody found him until it was too late. I didn't really know Quintus Mallius well enough to be broken-hearted, though I thought he was very nice. I didn't find out for quite a while that his mother told people I was ill-omened, a danger to any bridegroom. Such horrible nonsense!"

"It's a ridiculous superstition, Sergia. It reminds me of a Jewish folk-tale about a girl who was successively wed to seven bridegrooms, but on every wedding night a demon came and slew the husband before he could consummate his marriage."

"Poor girl! She must have been desperate. Did she ever find a man able to withstand the demon?"

"Yes, finally the hero came along, and on the advice of an angel – that's a supernatural being that many Jews believe in – he burned a fish's liver in the bridal chamber, and this so revolted the demon that he fled away and never came back."

Sergia burst out laughing – she had a melodious laugh.

"What an anti-climax! Do you know many such stories?"

"A few – some more plausible than that one. If you don't mind, tell me about Calvus. I know him but don't like him very much. Did he seem to you a heroic deliverer – or a demon?"

"Well, I never really thought he was wonderful but he seemed acceptable since my father had chosen him. After the wedding, I don't know – maybe other girls would have appreciated him more. To me he seemed crude and rather vulgar, and he said I was cold. Then he got furious when I pointed out a mistake in his grammar. Actually I quoted *your* grandfather's textbook. I suppose a good wife would have kept her mouth shut."

"Calvus *is* crude. I knew him in my school days and later in the army, though he didn't stay in the East very long. He was proud of being a rough-and-ready soldier, not too refined or over-educated. Certainly some women fancy his type."

I thought of Iras flirting with Calvus when he was on the next couch at a dinner. How far did she go with him? I was so restricted in my movements, and she could easily have gone to him.

Sergia continued her story. "Calvus had a previous attachment to a married woman, Furia Vopisca. Have you ever seen her?"

"Yes. She was a young matron when I was a student of fifteen."

I didn't see fit to tell Sergia that Furia Vopisca had provided me with my first sexual experience. At the time I'd been elated that, despite my youth, I'd attracted such a beautiful mature woman. Then I discovered that she amused herself by enticing young boys to her bed while her spouse was serving on the German frontier.

"She's a lot older than you, Sergia – and older than Calvus too. I should think her charms must be somewhat faded by now."

"She has lines around her eyes and mouth, but she's still quite striking. She tries to look like Cleopatra, with a lot of kohl on her eyelids. Anyway Calvus liked her a lot, and I didn't much enjoy his company. One night her husband – her second or third, I'm not sure – came home and found Calvus in bed with her. They had a fight, and the husband threw them both out of the house, declaring that he would divorce her and keep the two children. So in the middle of the night Calvus came home – with a bloody nose, a black eye – and Furia Vopisca. He immediately raided my clothes chest for her. Early that morning I left Calvus' house for my father's, and divorced Calvus, who soon afterwards married Furia Vopisca.

"Father disputed with Calvus over the return of my dowry, and the stress of it all brought on a heart attack which killed him. His principal heir was my stepbrother, whom he had adopted, which left me at the mercy of Publius and his nasty mother, my father's second wife. Publius argued with Calvus about my dowry, which he wanted to get his own hands on.

"Then he tried to arrange my marriage with a man I found completely repulsive. Do you know Valerius Gratus?"

I pictured Gratus, obese and probably diseased, with a leer on his red vein-streaked face. "I know him. Long ago I respected him; now I loathe him. So, did you refuse him?"

"I refused him to his face. Then my stepbrother tried to beat me into submission, but I ran away. I climbed out of a window and jumped down into a narrow laneway. I prayed to Diana of the swift feet and silver bow to help me escape, and I believe she aided me for I got to my Grandfather Velleius' house. He and Grandmother Lavinia took me in and resisted Publius when he came for me.

"At last Publius gave up, admitting that Gratus had stormed off in fury because I'd humiliated him. He complained to Grandfather, 'I can't get her dowry back from Calvus, and I thought I was in luck that Gratus would have taken her for her beauty and breeding. Now I'm stuck with the stupid vixen. Maybe you'd like the responsibility of trying to marry her off.'

"Grandfather persuaded him to sign over custody, and so I remained with him. Publius sent over my maid and my clothes; he tried to keep the jewellery I'd inherited from Mother, but Grandfather pressured him until he surrendered it. Since then, he has taken Calvus to court and forced him to give back half of my dowry, so now I have ten silver talents – two hundred and fifty thousand sesterces, which isn't a great fortune but is a respectable amount.

"So far Grandfather hasn't tried to find another husband for me, at least I don't think so. I've been happy just living with my grand-parents and lately with Aunt Velleia. Grandfather felt she should have a companion while he and Grandmother were attending to their property in Spain. He's trying to settle a problem about a tin mine that he bought a few years ago."

"I'm glad you got rid of Calvus and refused Gratus. You deserve better than either of them." I thought of an obscene name for them but refrained from using it in front of Sergia, though I imagined Calvus had used it freely enough in her presence.

"Aunt Velleia told me you used to be married – to an Egyptian. Is she still in Italy?"

"I understand she went back to Egypt to claim an inheritance. We're divorced, and I don't expect – or wish – to see her again."

I didn't tell her that the brother of Tirzah, the girl who had so much wanted Mother's house – perhaps more than she wanted her prospective bridegroom – had been the executor of Iras' father's will and after five years had fulfilled his entrusted duty. Sometime Sergia might want to know about Quintus Arrius, alias Ben-Hur, and I would have to tell her something. On the one hand, I didn't want to present myself in an unfavourable light; on the other hand, lies have a way of becoming uncovered and making everything worse. It was really too bad that my enemy lived next door to my mother.

"Aunt Velleia said your Egyptian was very beautiful – but she didn't trust her. I suppose we all distrust foreigners."

"Similarly many foreigners distrust us, and some of them even hate us. Iras wasn't happy here, partly because I couldn't provide well for her. For a while our circumstances were desperate. During the last year Iras certainly wasn't cheerful or healthy, and I must admit I wasn't a loving husband. She may have regained something of her energy and good looks now that she's comfortably situated in her beloved Egypt."

I could see that Sergia was curious about me and that she at least liked me. I was certainly attracted to her, but I kept warning myself. Lollius Velleius was surely looking for a fine successful Roman of high rank to marry his beautiful, intelligent granddaughter; he wouldn't want to give her to someone whose career was mainly distinguished by the burden of dishonour.

Lepida had said things that I wouldn't repeat to Sergia. She would begin, "Of course I don't believe this," and then repeat bits of gossip. Mallius' superstitious mother had blamed Sergia for her son's illness and death, as though Sergia were some kind of witch. Calvus had accused her of cold prudishness and yet hinted that she had secret lovers. And the worst stories could probably be traced to a humiliated Valerius Gratus, who may have preferred his own sex but also wanted a lovely desirable woman at his side, a trophy adorning his rank, a possible bearer of an heir, and a touch of variety when or if homosexuality seemed a little boring.

CHAPTER TWENTY-FOUR

SINCE Quadratus was busy with cases in Rome, we employed a local lawyer who had represented Father before. We set out for the court, wondering what to expect from Judge Rabirius. Father wanted to come with us, but he became out of breath as he tried to get ready, and finally Africanus helped him back to his bed and gave him his medication, a preparation which contained a very small quantity – a mere drop or two – from an extract of foxglove leaves. So it was just Mother, Sergia, and I.

Mother also looked frail enough to stay home. She was too thin and pale, and her black lace veil added to her sickly appearance. She hadn't tried to change her complexion with rouge, and her eyes were already shadowed without kohl on the lids. Sergia, on the other hand, had good natural colour and sparkling eyes. She made me think of Diana of the silver bow, ready to do battle.

Decimus Scaurus, our lawyer, met us outside the courthouse. We had thought we were early but as we came through a corridor we heard voices. The first voice, a rather high-pitched one, sounded like Phineas.

"Do you think we've made a good enough offer? What if the treacherous Roman offered more?"

"Don't worry! A wise head has found the price of Rabirius' favour." This was Sanballat's voice. The words reminded me of something Ben-Hur had said to Iras when explaining how Simonides' judicious gifts of money to Sejanus would probably keep him and his allies safe from arrest for treason.

"Do you think that Messala would try to bribe the judge?" asked Phineas.

"Maybe! But in spite of his father's evident generosity, he won't have a lot of money to throw around. I'm keeping on the safe side, assuming he *has* made some kind of offer. As our good friend often says, 'A Roman in his desire to win cannot keep honour pure.'"

That was one of the numerous platitudes of Simonides, which Iras had found so wearisome. How typical of my adversaries. Stooping to bribery themselves, but commenting that it would be treacherous for me to do the same! Scaurus noted their remarks on his wax tablet. He told me later that he had used the shorthand system invented by Cicero's clever secretary, Tiro. It might not be possible to use the information, but we would see.

Scaurus quietly opened the door to the courtroom, and we followed him in. Sanballat and Phineas looked surprised as Scaurus said politely, "Good morning. Hasn't your lawyer come yet?"

"We're expecting him any moment," said Sanballat, looking somewhat concerned, perhaps wondering what we had overheard. He didn't speak to us and we didn't speak to him. Phineas glowered at us.

Shortly after, their lawyer came in and greeted them. Officers of the court followed. Then the guards allowed six slaves to carry in a man in a litter and to arrange him comfortably in a cushioned seat. A few seats at the back were taken by people we didn't recognize. I don't know if they had cases to come before the judge or if they were just interested in court cases in general.

Judge Rabirius came in and took his high seat, scanning the room curiously as we rose to greet him. The man in the cushioned seat didn't rise and no one appeared to think he should. I was sure he was Simonides, and his lawyer had likely notified the judge to expect him.

Sanballat's lawyer opened. He described his client as an honourable business man claiming his rightful property and pointed out that he had a valid deed given him by Gaius Bibulus in payment of a debt. He talked about the natural right of a husband to dispose of the property his wife had brought him in marriage.

"A husband," he proclaimed, "gives his wife his name, his support and protection, and his guidance in managing money and land. The woman's responsibility is to honour her husband, to give him a pleasant home, and to bear his children. Lollia Velleia failed in all these areas, which is why Gaius Bibulus has divorced her.

"She isn't about to be cast out on the streets with nothing. Bibulus returned some of the money she brought as her dowry, and in addition she has a brother, Lollius Velleius, and a son, Marcus Valerius Messala Secundus, who is here in this courtroom. I understand he is willing to provide for his mother, despite the fact that she has neglected him ever since she left him with his father, the first of her four husbands, when the boy was very young."

I wanted to reply immediately but chose to wait for my proper chance when Scaurus called on me. Instead, I heard Sanballat giving his so-called evidence. He gave his account of his dealings with Bibulus, from whose hand he had received the deed. Scaurus was given the opportunity to question him and asked him exactly when he had got his hands on it.

"It was just after the middle of October – well, actually the fifteenth – but Bibulus had promised the deed to me long before that if he failed to pay off his debt."

"Did you know that the divorce was complete before you received the deed, and that Lollius Velleius had in his possession the divorce agreement stating the amount of dowry which Bibulus returned: one hundred thousand sesterces, which isn't much for a lady of Velleia's family standing, and the villa here in Misenum?"

"I know nothing about the agreement with Lollius Velleius, who isn't here to testify, and I assume his papers aren't here either." Sanballat smirked mockingly at us. Obviously he didn't know about my successful visit to Rome.

Phineas was also called as a witness and he stated that he had been treated most discourteously by the two ladies in question, my mother and cousin.

"They wouldn't let me and my betrothed see the whole house, and the younger lady, that female sitting over there, accused me of trying to pocket paltry little knick-knacks. And then Lollia Velleia's dog bit me; they made no effort to restrain the disgusting little beast."

Scaurus asked him, "Did the dog attack you when you came too close to its mistress? Could it have got the impression that you were threatening her? Did you in fact thrust your finger in her face?"

"I – I don't remember. I don't think I was too close to her, but I was arguing with her and that other – insolent baggage! They were insulting me."

At that point Scaurus objected to the witness's offensive language in speaking of a lady in the courtroom. The judge admonished Phineas to be more careful of his vocabulary.

Scaurus asked, "When were you told that the house might be available? Was it the same day Sanballat took you there to see it, or had he spoken of it before?"

"He told us the previous evening and said he would call on Velleia first to prepare her."

"Then you knew that Lollia Velleia had been given less than one day to find a way to protect her home where she had gone after her divorce thinking to live in a peaceful retreat with her grandniece Sergia Carina, whose name you seem unable to remember. Didn't it seem to you that this was a shameful way to treat a defenceless woman whose brother and protector had left for Spain? Even if the claim to possess the house had been valid, didn't it strike you that he wasn't proceeding in a gentlemanly manner?"

Sanballat's lawyer objected to the question. At the same time, the man who had been brought in by litter whispered something to Phineas, and the judge, though he sustained the plaintiff's objection, cautioned, "No prompting the witness."

Wrapped in a blanket and propped up on cushions, the man

stared back with penetrating black eyes that challenged the judge. Simonides? Was his the wise head that had found the price of Rabirius' favour? He turned his stare on me, perhaps trying to decide if I'd been present in Gratus' torture chamber. I turned my left profile toward him briefly, then looked back at him as if to say, "You can't identify me, can you? Be honest."

Scaurus rephrased his question to Phineas. "Did you really think you and Sanballat were behaving like gentlemen, coming into Velleia's house on such short notice, insisting on an immediate tour, and demanding possession?"

Phineas said angrily, "Many women have had Roman soldiers come into their homes and take possession without warning."

"True enough," said Scaurus, "when the women, or their male heads of the house, have committed crimes. But that isn't the case with Lollia Velleia or any of her family, though Bibulus, her ex-husband, may be guilty of fraud in the matter of the deed."

Sanballat's lawyer objected, and Scaurus said, "We believe we can prove my assertion when our evidence is presented."

Unwisely, Phineas muttered audibly, though I couldn't catch quite every word: "In my homeland – adulteresses – taken out and stoned to death – not left to live in a house they've dishonoured."

Mother shuddered and Sergia looked at me as if hoping I would find a swift way to deal with Phineas, such as knocking out his front teeth and kicking his butt into the Bay – which was what I felt like doing.

Judge Rabirius demanded silence in the court. He gestured to a servant to bring him a drink, whether water or wine I don't know. During that pause the door was opened and Ben-Hur quietly entered and went to the side of Simonides. He was able to whisper a question to him before the proceedings resumed.

Eulalius, Sanballat's lawyer, made a summing-up speech on the rights of honest money-lenders to receive their due and the rights of husbands to control their wives' properties, even insisting that the husband had some property rights in cases of coemptio marriage. A wife retained a claim to her fortune if she spent one night annually away from her husband's roof, but Eulalius used this to support his insinuations that her actions had been immoral – during all four of her marriages. Uncle Velleius, in whose home Mother usually spent the Saturnalia Festival, was unavailable to testify.

Scaurus took over. He began by saying that the aspersions on my mother's character were unjustified. He had been asked by her first husband, Marcus Valerius Messala, and the latter's younger son, Messala Secundus, to take the case. Messala Senior had spoken favourably of his former wife's character as well as her frailness and vulnerability. He had wanted to come to court to testify, but his heart condition had prevented him. He hadn't divorced Velleia for unfaithfulness but had let her go because she was profoundly unhappy in the country of Judaea to which he had been assigned.

Scaurus said, "My client, Lollia Velleia, firmly denies Sanballat's claim to her house and its furniture, especially the items which date from before her marriage to Bibulus: gifts from her family and from her first husband. Some other things – that Bibulus bought and that she now hates to look at – she is still entitled to sell rather than to turn over to Sanballat."

Then he said that I'd taken a recent trip to Rome in search of evidence to support my mother's claim and that I was ready to testify.

So I rose, aware of the hostile stares of Simonides and Phineas – and the surprised expression of Ben-Hur.

"Most excellent Rabirius, I went to Rome and spoke first to Lollius Velleius' secretary, who told me that the divorce documents were in the archives of the Temple of Vesta and that the deed to my mother's property should be with them. Also, he affirmed that the divorce agreement, concluded *early* in October, on the second Kalend*, showed that Bibulus had accepted Mother's right to her house in Misenum. I have here for the court a letter from Vellieus' secretary Aristides stating the terms of the divorce.

"Since, as Sanballat has testified, Bibulus apparently gave him the deed in mid-October, on the Ides†, I concluded that either Bibulus handed over a false deed to Sanballat, or he obtained the

---

*October 2   †October 15

real one by some kind of trickery. Accordingly, I went next to the Temple of Vesta and obtained an interview with the Chief Vestal. When she checked the files, it seemed that the deed, which she had seen not so very long before, was missing. When she questioned the other Vestals, one of them admitted that Bibulus had come to her and asked for the deed. She said he spoke as if he were Lollia Velleia's lawful husband. He misled the inexperienced young woman concerning his rights, and she had handed over the deed without asking her superior.

"The Chief Vestal has given me the following letter, which I would like to read to the court."

Then I unsealed and read the letter which accused Bibulus in the strongest terms of having practised vile deceit in the Temple of Vesta, the most revered shrine guarding Rome's family values. She implied that she would be referring the matter to the Emperor, the Chief Pontiff of our religion; she believed that the Temple would require a solemn cleansing ceremony to avert the wrath of the Goddess. In her opinion, Bibulus' disregard for the sanctity of Vesta was comparable to the scandalous profaning of the Festival of the Bona Dea, when Publius Clodius disguised himself in female attire and penetrated the ceremonies which were only for women honouring our Good Goddess, the Earth Mother. That had taken place long ago in the time of Julius Caesar, and the public furor had been extreme. It had been feared that because of the incident Rome would experience prolonged and terrible bad luck.

When I finished reading the letter, I sensed that our opponents were disturbed. Simonides and Phineas were both whispering questions to their lawyer (that is, officially Sanballat's lawyer) and to Ben-Hur until the judge called for silence in the court, after which I continued with my presentation.

"The letter clearly states that Bibulus had no right to obtain the deed. He was divorced from my mother, Lollia Velleia, and he had no proof of consent from either his former wife or her legal guardian, her brother Lollius Velleius. He committed fraud. I give Sanballat the benefit of the doubt and assume he did not know either that

Bibulus had no legal right to the deed or what the terms were of the divorce contract which confirmed her original marriage agreement and gave her the right to the villa which had been hers since her first marriage, her marriage to my father. This was the seaside house where my parents spent a brief but happy period before he had to take on an assignment to the province of Syria. It seems likely that my early pre-birth existence began in that house.

"Whatever Sanballat and his lawyer allege concerning my mother's character has no relevance at all to her contractual rights in this matter. However, I wish to defend her now. As Scaurus has told you, my father didn't divorce her for infidelity. She requested to go home to Italy because she found life in Jerusalem depressing. She was a very young woman, lacking the stamina and the thick skin of the men we send to serve abroad. She was lonely, with no women friends, and almost no social life except when members of the visiting Herod family included her in a dinner invitation. She was uncomfortable with the unfamiliar language around her and the hostility, mainly silent but sometimes vocal, she met with on the streets. Possibly the Jewish people wish that all Romans shared her overwhelming urge to go home.

"My father, on the other hand, was interested in his work in Jerusalem; moreover, it seemed to him, as it would to most Roman men, unmanly to give in to a woman and abandon a career of foreign service. As a small boy, I was sad – as any child would be in such circumstances. My father hired a well-recommended local woman to be my caregiver. She was a plump widow with enormous breasts and a fat rump, and she kept crushing me to her bosom in a smothering embrace – and pushing at me various foods that I didn't want. She kept hinting that *she*, unlike my mother, truly loved me. One day she took me to a public stoning of a woman allegedly guilty of adultery. As I looked in fascinated shock at the woman with a bleeding face being struck down by a hail of rocks, my nanny whispered to me, 'That should be *your* mother!'

"I broke away from her and found my way home, where I told my father everything. He angrily discharged the nanny and assured me that my mother had done nothing wrong – that I must never think so. After that my physical needs were attended to by slaves, and I was given a well-educated male tutor. The insinuations of Sanballat's lawyer concerning my mother remind me of the most frightening incident in my early childhood."

I heard something like a snort from Simonides. I didn't look at Ben-Hur.

"The counsel for Sanballat has also made incorrect assumptions concerning my mother's later marriages. She wasn't divorced from her second and third husbands; they both died of natural causes, and I know of no gossip or rumour of impropriety concerning those marriages. She had three more children: two boys who died in infancy; and one daughter who lived to be ten years old. I met her only once, but I'm convinced she was a happy child, cherished by our mother."

I was putting my heart into the speech more than I'd expected to. I hoped not to give way to emotion over Cornelia's death, though I'd truly felt it as a loss: a sister a little younger than Tirzah.

"Mother was past forty when she married Gaius Bibulus, and I can't completely understand what she ever saw in him. She shouldn't have tried to bear another child, and he shouldn't have expected it. If he wanted an heir, he should have found another woman – a younger woman. However, Mother had almost a million sesterces, much of which he persuaded her to hand over.

"After going through a lot of her money, he was running up debts, including the debt to Sanballat, which Mother didn't know about. He took her on a cruise to Cyprus, quarrelled with her, and then attempted to drown her. She was protected by servants, and returned to Rome in a different boat. She then sought a divorce. In this letter here from Aristides, Velleius' secretary, it is stated that Velleius has a letter from the governor of Cyprus, confirming my mother's account of the attempt on her life.

"Bibulus agreed to the settlement negotiated with Lollius Velleius, but used trickery to get his hands on the deed. He may have thought he wouldn't be caught, that Velleius would be gone for a long time, and that I would be unable and unwilling to help her even if someone thought of telling me.

"As if this treachery weren't enough, Bibulus has tried to blacken her character by falsehoods, which Sanballat and his associates seem only too happy to believe and to spread. Thus we have the emotional fellow to whom Sanballat was eager to sell the house – muttering audibly during this hearing – references to adulteresses and public stonings. I can picture him back in Judaea, elbowing his way to the front of a line in the hope of casting – maybe not the first but at least the third stone."

Phineas started to scream at me. "Filthy Roman dog! How dare you! Lying evil bastard! Spawn of the devil, to whom your whore of a mother opened her legs!"

The judge banged his gavel and shouted, "Silence!"

Phineas switched to Aramaic obscenities; at least I think that's what they were – my memory of the language has become faulty. Sanballat and Simonides were trying to make him sit down and shut up, and I heard Ben-Hur say, "Phineas, I'm ashamed of you."

Before Ben-Hur and the other two could have any success, Rabirius gestured to a couple of guards who took hold of Phineas and carried him out of the courtroom, screeching curses, including a memorable line, slightly altered, from one of the Jewish psalms Lady Miriam had recited to us, "May your prayers be accounted sin."*

Sanballat said to Simonides, "You should've made the young fool stay home!"

"*You* wanted him to testify! What were you thinking?"

"What were you both thinking?" asked Ben-Hur.

There were dissatisfied comments from some of spectators who had been taking in the hearing from the start. From the way they looked at Sanballat and his companions and from what I could make out of their remarks, I gathered that public sympathy was on the side of my mother. There were a number of uncomplimentary references to the Jews. I was almost sorry for Judah.

I let Scaurus take over the summing up, which he did admirably.

---

* Psalm 109

He concluded, "When we arrived this morning, before entering this room, we heard a short conversation, which I recorded in Tironian shorthand. I don't know if it should be considered evidence, since Sanballat and the fellow who has now left the court would probably assert that I heard incorrectly, particularly regarding a reference to bribery."

Rabirius didn't hesitate. "There is no need to read it, Scaurus. I have made up my mind without a bribe, which I would certainly have found offensive to my integrity. Eulalius, I don't need to hear a rebuttal from your client. However, is there anything you *can* say?"

"No, most honourable Rabirius. Obviously the statement of the Chief Vestal must be accepted. I do wish to assure the court of my client's integrity. Sanballat has acted in good faith and has been basely deceived by his debtor, Gaius Bibulus."

Rabirius then gave his verdict. "Sanballat, you have been in error. I order you to return the deed to Lollia Velleia immediately. You have no claim to her property, not even the furniture purchased by Gaius Bibulus. I'm holding you entirely responsible for the court costs, which you may settle with my clerk. Finally, I order you to pay Lollia Velleia the sum of fifty thousand sesterces as compensation for harassment and for the defamation of her character by your counsel Eulalius and your witness Phineas Ben Zebulon, whom I'm also charging with contempt of court."

We looked at each other in joyful relief.

Eulalius soon came over to us with the deed and a money draft for fifty thousand sesterces – from Sanballat's own account, not from Simonides or Ben-Hur. Sanballat said loudly and grimly, "I will certainly sue Gaius Bibulus."

Ben-Hur looked at us hesitantly. Maybe he felt he should apologize to my mother and explain that he had been away from the community – as Tirzah had said – and had just now learned of the attempt to deprive Mother of her property. It might well be true.

He took a half-step forward, then stopped. Maybe he expected that whatever he said would be met with triumphant derision. Sanballat and Simonides, the latter in his litter once more, came to him and seemed to be trying to explain.

Ben-Hur said audibly, "I wish you had consulted me. Until I arrived home today, I didn't know you were going to court or that my neighbour was Messala's mother. The name Velleia had no significance for me. Sanballat, you handed him the opportunity to be a shining hero defending his mother against the Jews. This affair has brought shame on me. Especially – Phineas shouldn't have been allowed to open his mouth."

At the same time we were talking among ourselves, and perhaps other people could hear parts of our conversation. For example, Mother said, "I hope I never see Sanballat or that horrible young man again. I feel sorry for that poor girl that was supposed to marry him. He has such disgusting manners and a dreadful temper."

Ben-Hur turned his head to look at Mother. He may have felt humiliated that *my* mother could pity Tirzah because *he* had made such an appalling choice for her husband.

He spoke to his friends, but loudly enough for us to hear. "I will never give Tirzah to him. She is wise to refuse him."

Simonides answered, "Clearly I shouldn't have urged her. Now do explain to me about the Vestal Virgins. From their name, I shouldn't think they'd be temple prostitutes."

I imagined Ben-Hur would give him a good explanation. He surely knew quite a lot about our culture.

As we made our way out of the room, Mother wiped her eyes with a lace handkerchief. In a tremulous voice she said, "My dear, you were wonderful. Oh, I do wish that I had never left you and your father."

Sergia said, "I could kiss you."

Looking at her lovely face with the provocative smile, I lowered my head and let my lips meet Sergia's. It was delightful. It had been more than two years since I'd last kissed Iras, and there had been no pleasure in it.

Outside we met Herod Agrippa; somehow he had heard about the case. I introduced Mother and Sergia; then Scaurus joined us, saying, "Rabirius is summoning Phineas back into the courtroom to pass sentence for contempt of court."

Eulalius approached Phineas, who was scowling as he stood under guard. He argued, but consented to accompany the lawyer and a couple of guards as they reentered the courtroom. Simonides evidently chose not to stay. His slaves carried his litter and Ben-Hur, mounted on a fine bay horse, rode near him. Sanballat in his mule-drawn carriage departed toward Baiae.

CHAPTER TWENTY-FIVE

SCAURUS reported to us that Phineas had to stay in jail for a whole market interval – eight days. He was also fined heavily – thirty thousand sesterces – for contempt of court. Was this Rabirius' way of getting his bribe money after all? And then Rabirius said, "In addition, I am fining you another forty thousand – to compensate Lollia Velleia and her son Messala for your offensive and unfounded accusations."

Phineas tried to protest that Mother was already being paid fifty thousand as compensation from Sanballat, but the judge wouldn't permit him to argue.

So Mother gained seventy thousand sesterces, and I received twenty thousand. I helped her and Sergia select new items of furniture to take the place of the ugly couches and tables with the crocodile motif, which we turned over to an auctioneer. He quickly sold them at a reasonable price, naturally less than Bibulus must have paid for them. With Sergia's common sense and good taste, we were able to choose replacements which were attractive, well-made, and not extremely costly. After all, Mother's annual income was still modest; she couldn't afford a showy establishment with a lot of servants.

A letter came from Uncle Velleius expressing great indignation at both Bibulus and Sanballat. He wasn't able to leave Spain yet, but was hoping for the best in the court case. He affirmed that Mother's divorce agreement had clearly left her the house, and he was hoping his letter would reach us before we entered court.

"I hope Bibulus will be arrested and charged with fraud. He had no right to the deed and I think he must have got his dirty hands on it by some foul means. To think that I couldn't go out of the country briefly on business without such an outrageous attempt to rob my sister! And to have her insulted by the likes of Sanballat and his contemptible partners or allies or subordinates, whatever they are."

My uncle evidently didn't know the present Quintus Arrius but had formed a rather low opinion of the young Jew adopted by the late admiral. He assumed that Phineas Ben Zebulon and his host were cut from the same cloth.

He was properly grateful to my father and to me. I don't suppose he had thought well of me in the past. Certainly he had never reached out in friendliness during my difficult days in Rome. Now, however, he congratulated me on my recovered health and wished me well. Still I hesitated to offer for Sergia till I was assured of his good opinion. He would be pleased when I wrote to him about the judge's decision. Yet he would certainly wish to do better for Sergia, and he would hate to have it said that because there had been slanderous tales about her, because of her damaged reputation, he had been reduced to giving her to a disgraced aristocrat best remembered for having lost both a chariot race and a moderate fortune to a Jew.

On the other hand, I was certainly drawn to Sergia. She is beautiful: tall and slender and fine-featured. Her hair appears dark-brown in a dull indoor light but shows golden streaks in the sunshine. She has large dark-blue eyes and a fair complexion. In addition to physical beauty, which is naturally the basis of a first impression, she has a quick mind and a ready laugh. She can hold her own; she is clearly not a weak, passive woman. Whereas some men prefer a very fragile, dependent woman whom they can protect, I admire women of strong character. I have rediscovered my affection for my long-absent mother, but I wish she had been a stronger person, something like the generally revered mother of the Gracchi brothers.

Sergia was making it fairly clear that she found me attractive and interesting. Her eyes lit up whenever I came into the room. We have talked about a lot of things: the furniture which we helped my languid mother select, books we have read and liked, dogs and horses from our past and present. She had a keen wit and she appreciated mine. We have had several rides around the country, and once went for a sail in the Flammifer, which I'd delayed taking out of the water in spite of some cold windy days.

She remarked that evidently I knew Tirzah from long ago. I didn't tell her much, but I did say that her brother and I'd once been friends when we were children.

"When we met again as adults, I'd become very Roman and admittedly rather insensitive about the aspirations of lesser nations. Some of the restrictions the Jews placed on themselves seemed so nonsensical – for example, if they fought a war, they thought they should call a halt every seventh day, their sacred Sabbath. I said what I thought and outraged my old companion who had become an intense nationalist. Our friendship ended; he walked away ignoring my hand."

I hesitated about telling her anything more. But she had heard the words of Sanballat and Phineas implying that I'd done shameful things. Perhaps I ought to give her a partial explanation from my point of view.

"Right after our quarrel, he got into trouble for attacking Valerius Gratus the procurator – which seems like not such a bad idea in retrospect, if it could've been managed better."

"I certainly can't feel sorry for Gratus. The man is quite detestable."

"I think he was always cynical and ruthless, but in those days it was possible to admire him. He wasn't obese or diseased; he seemed in every way a strong man.

"I was a young contubernalis, and I gave Gratus my cooperation in putting down what was almost an insurrection. Judah Ben-Hur said he didn't throw the tile from his roof at Gratus – it just slipped.

To me and to many of his cheering countrymen it looked as if he gave it a push.

"The Hur family were all harshly dealt with. Initially Gratus wanted to crucify all of them. However, instead, the women were incarcerated; it wasn't that they had done anything wrong as far as we knew, but they definitely had potential as agitators. As for Judah, my ex-friend, he was sent to row in our galleys."

"But – don't we use paid rowers in our war ships?"

"Yes, usually, and it's much more practical. They're motivated and they're kept fit by the programs in our off-season facilities. Gymnasia, baths, entertainment. But a few years ago we were short of professional rowers, so we resorted to galley slaves.

"As it happened, Judah Ben-Hur was able to win the favour of Quintus Arrius, the heroic admiral, and was adopted by him. In due course he recovered his family and his property in Judaea."

I saw no need to mention the possibility that on their release from captivity the Hur women were suffering from what looked like leprosy. As Sergia had seen, Tirzah was now a healthy young woman, beautiful in a different style from my lovely cousin.

"In spite of all he'd accepted from Arrius, Judah was still passion- ately anti-Roman. During my time in the East, he worked actively for Judaean independence. He may have finally accepted failure; I'm not sure. I don't quite understand why he has come back here to live.

"Oh, and I might as well mention, he learned chariot racing – he became very good at it!"

"Then he was the one you raced against in Antioch?"

"Yes, and I didn't handle that very well at all. I felt sure he not only wanted me defeated and humiliated – he wanted me dead! Someone who worked for me had heard him and a Jew called Malluch discussing plans for the race; Judah, alias Arrius, spoke of something that would happen on – it was either the second or the sixth turn. His plan was to take my wheel off – which he did. Remembering all this now, I am still angry! However, things have got a lot better lately. One of the philosophers, I don't remember which one, spoke of the assurance that the universe was unfolding as it should – which is the way I've been feeling lately."

I shrugged my shoulders in apparent resignation which I couldn't entirely feel.

Sergia said, "Then that's why you asked Sanballat if Judah – er – whatever – was going for a petty anti-climax by attacking your mother."

"It seemed a natural question. He and Sanballat have long been allies, as is the man in the litter, Simonides, the financial manager and now the father-in-law of Ben-Hur. Actually I'm inclined to believe Tirzah, that her brother wasn't involved. He would have preferred some grand design in which he could cut a heroic figure."

"I don't think I would like him anyway."

"Oh, you might. As you may have noticed, he has a noble countenance and flawless manners. He also has a romantic imagination and likes to quote Hebrew poetry, though I don't know if he's ever written any."

"If he's anything like those others in his circle, I don't believe he *could* write the sort of stories you have written. I didn't like any of those people, even the girl – rather a gentle creature, but oversweet – until the end when she snapped at both Phineas and Sanballat – which they deserved!"

Sergia imitated Tirzah's soft voice, exaggerating a little.

"'Oh, I do like this house! And the garden has possibilities, doesn't it, Phineas? Only of course we couldn't keep that idol of the girl at the fountain! Or any of those other small idols that I see on the shelf.'

"I told her – those are our Lares and Penates*. If worst comes to worst, naturally we'll take them with us."

Sergia's reaction to Tirzah reminded me of Iras' sarcastic comments on Esther, the daughter of Simonides and now the wife of Ben-Hur. Even though Iras said she loved me, she was competitive toward the pretty Jewish girl who evidently adored Judah. She probably continued to be jealous of her during the time she was recovering her health in the Arrius mansion.

A couple of days before the Saturnalia, our winter holiday of jollity

---

* Guardian spirits of a Roman house

and permissive misrule, I received an invitation to the Emperor's Saturnalia banquet. When I called on Mother and Sergia, who had just moved back into their house, it turned out that they were also invited. Probably a lot of other well-born residents of Misenum and Baiae would be there too.

I offered to pick them up and escort them, hoping we would be assigned to the same dinner couch. I didn't relish the prospect of going alone and wondering if anyone would welcome me as a dinner companion. Herod and Cypros would be close to members of Caesar's family, maybe even sharing a couch with Claudius, whom the Emperor was reluctant to place on the dais with himself because he had clumsy table manners.

On the afternoon of the banquet Father wished me a pleasant evening. He was glad the Emperor hadn't invited him; he knew it wasn't a slight but a realistic recognition of his feeble condition and need for rest. I dressed in my long dark red dinner robe and put my two gold armillae on my arms. I could walk fairly well without any sort of aid, but I took my more festive cane, with the gold *M* and a few extra gold flourishes cut into the dark wood. I hoped that, in the circles of our honourable families, word had got out that this time, assisted by the able advocate, Decimus Scaurus, I'd actually won a contest with Sanballat.

I rode in the carriage, letting Nestor drive the matched greys. I was proud of our appearance as we stopped to pick up my two ladies. Sergia was lovely in a white cloak and hood, rather as I imagined immortal Helen arriving on the shores of Ilium. She had a warm smile, and I couldn't help thinking of her as my girl.

Mother was bright and cheerful, her cheeks flushed, and her eyes sparkling like the coloured stones in her necklace. She was too thin but still attractive. I hoped nothing would tempt her to remarry.

After we were under way, she said thoughtfully, "I decided we didn't need the guard dogs anymore. I was afraid of them."

"I really wish you hadn't done that, Mother. I was willing to pay for them. As it is – you've likely given most of the slaves the evening off in honour of the Saturnalia. So your house is unprotected, isn't it?"

Mother looked uncomfortable. "Sergia thought the same as you. I didn't tell her until I'd ordered the dog handlers to go. Anna is staying in the house alone, and Theron is at the stable. I don't have many slaves, but I rather like them all, and I thought they should enjoy some time off too. I'm sorry if I did wrong, but I didn't like the prospect of those growling scary beasts greeting me when I came home. Also, what if little Flora had got outside and those awful animals had eaten her up?"

Sergia and I looked at each other doubtfully. I even thought of going back to the town and arranging for the guard dogs after all – but then we might be late for the banquet.

When we arrived at the palace, we could see many other guests, some entering the vestibule, some strolling on the pebbled paths admiring what was left of the autumn colour of the shrubbery. It doesn't usually snow in the Bay area, though the previous winter we had twice got a dusting of white flakes in Rome.

What a relief to be living in a comfortable home, to be able to walk again, even though I was far from ready for Olympic foot racing. It was such a contrast to the cold and dismal winter we had spent in our squalid Suburan room, from which I could escape only by crawling down dark dingy stairs.

We got out of the carriage and let Nestor take it to the stabling area for guests. The Emperor could hardly have provided parking if all his invitees had come by carriage, but fortunately many of them preferred litters; their slaves could be dispersed to the servants' hall, where there was likely food and entertainment. Saturnalia is supposed to be a time for servants, in particular, to enjoy themselves.

Entering the vestibule, we gave our outer cloaks to a servant. Then we started making our way through the already crowded atrium toward the dining area, where liveried attendants would show us to our designated places. At a smaller dinner the couches would be arranged in a *U* formation, with the Emperor's couch on a low dais and the other couches in parallel lines on either side of an open space. However, with many guests, it was more likely that the couches with their small tables would be arranged in groups for sociability. Most people wouldn't be anywhere close to the Emperor and his family group.

A Saturnalia party is often an occasion for misrule and even orgies where social distinctions between masters and slaves are overturned and where public sexual activities take place without concern for propriety or family values. But Tiberius Caesar would never allow festivities to get out of hand here in Misenum, whatever he allowed to happen on Capri, details of which I knew only by hearsay. He had evidently invited some local people who wouldn't normally be his guests; probably they would feel not only honoured but awestruck. Woe to the revellers who dared show disrespect to their Emperor!

When we all began mingling in the wide atrium, I recognized some people I knew. There were brief greetings – "Nice to see you looking well." There were also some faces that turned deliberately away. I'd long become used to this in the dark days when I felt I was practically hanging by my fingernails to the edge of the class to which I belonged by birth. Then I had lost my accounting job and had to retreat into the oblivion of the Subura.

For a nauseating moment I looked straight into the face of Valerius Gratus. More obese than ever, his face dark purplish red, he looked ready for a stroke, and I hoped it wouldn't be long in coming. At his side was a heavy woman – certainly no beauty. Oh, yes, now I remembered. His wife was Decumia: rich enough but rather low-born. She was known for her interest in both sexes, though she preferred slim young women. So she and Gratus had teamed up!

Gratus recognized me and was clearly surprised and displeased. He didn't greet me but said loudly to Decumia and anyone else within range of his voice, "The Emperor's guest list isn't very exclusive, probably because the Saturnalia reverses class distinctions."

I heard a friendly voice. Herod and Cypros were approaching us, both splendidly dressed. Herod wore a violet robe decorated with bright gems set in silver. As a member of a foreign royal house, he could be magnificent without being suspected of trying to outdo the Emperor, who would probably appear in deeper purple.

"I've arranged for you and your family to be together near us," Herod said after we had all greeted each other warmly.

That was a considerable relief!

Cypros said, "I had to call on the Hurs yesterday. You may know that Phineas is out of jail at last. He's supposed to procure a place to stay in the town, since Ben-Hur refuses to let him marry Tirzah, but for now he's still Judah's guest.

"I caught Ruhamah, my slave girl, dallying with Phineas in the Arrius ravine next to the Emperor's property. She had slipped away to meet him there. They didn't know I could see them from a window. So I talked to Esther, Ben-Hur's wife, and urged her to have Phineas strongly warned to leave my maidservants absolutely alone."

"Good! I hope they succeed in restraining him. At least Tirzah won't be pressured to marry that – semi-demented effete jackass."

Herod smiled. "From what our own servants tell me, Simonides and the Hurs were at first impressed by Phineas' professed devotion to the teachings of Jesus, and Simonides was also pleased that he had a good head for business. And despite all that Jesus may have taught about forgiving others, both Simonides and Phineas like to pour out their disapproval of Romans in general."

He continued, "Ben-Hur asked Cypros about our friendship with you. He said something like 'Do you know if Messala thinks *I* knew about Sanballat's efforts to take his mother's house? Does he think I would be so mean-spirited? If I'd known of Sanballat's plans, I'd have tried to discourage him. And I certainly wouldn't have permitted him to take Tirzah there. I've already told him I can't imagine what he was thinking of.'"

A trumpet sounded to summon us to the dining area. A liveried guide took charge of us; Mother and Sergia were to be with me, just as Herod had said.

I saw Gratus and his bulky Decumia trying to push past someone and being checked by two of the imperial servants. There were also members of the Praetorian Guard at hand; they said something to Gratus, who desisted with a mumbled protest that I couldn't hear.

Then I saw the group Gratus had tried to push ahead of. Wouldn't you know it. The Hurs. Judah was in a rich blue robe with a touch of gold embroidery and with him was a pretty little lady with brown curls partly covered by a thin lacy veil – surely his wife, Esther. And Tirzah in white, with a light veil over her shoulder-length black hair, as – no doubt – she was still a virgin.

Apparently Judah hadn't procured invitations for his mother, Simonides, or Phineas. Perhaps Lady Miriam didn't feel well enough to attend a long imperial banquet, and she could have thought it the wrong place for a respectable Jewish matron. Probably Simonides wouldn't want to be carried in to Caesar's banquet even if he were made welcome. I suspected that Phineas was back at the Hur residence feeling left out. He might have wanted to be included in spite of his freely expressed contempt for Rome. The Hurs would have had to relax a few rules to be present at a gathering of Gentiles, but probably Judah had got used to this during the period he lived as a son with Arrius Senior. For that matter, now that I thought of it, he had sometimes dined with me at my father's table – which was all right since we had a Jewish cook who served kosher food. Now they could abstain from pork and shellfish but perhaps not ask whether Caesar kept separate milk and meat dishes in his kitchen. They would eat politely and hope for the best.

At one end of the dining hall was the dais for the Emperor. There was an ornate couch in the middle of the platform with two other couches, one on either side. All three had purple and gold covers and cushions. Tiberius Caesar was going to have a few favoured people, probably close relatives, near him.

The other couches in the room were spread out in groupings of two or three – each wide enough for three diners. They extended past the dining room proper into the portico of the peristylum, which was protected from the December breeze by a scarlet curtain. There were also a few charcoal braziers in that area. We saw Gratus and Decumia being escorted to the portico section and could hear his voice loudly protesting such unworthy treatment of a man of his rank, a man who had served long and well as procurator of Judaea. Decumia seemed to be urging him to be quiet and not annoy the Emperor.

As we began to move forward with our guide, another not very welcome acquaintance, Metellus Calvus, smirked and said, "What a surprise to see *you* here, Messala Secundus. Any idea which of the Gods helped you back on your feet? Maybe Vulcan, the lame spouse of Venus?"

I controlled my irritation. "To tell the truth, I'm not sure. Maybe it was at one of those celestial meetings described in Homer's poems. The Gods decided they had a quorum present and so they considered my case favourably. Naturally I'm most grateful; it's strengthened my faith."

The Hur party was within earshot. Judah looked at his women-folk as if to deplore my praise of false Gods.

We were brought to a couch on the edge of the space left open for serving and entertainment, about four couches below the impe-rial dais. Herod, Cypros, and Claudius Caesar were nearer the dais but within speaking distance. The Hurs were directly opposite us on the other side of the entertainment space. Slaves came and removed our shoes, bathed our feet with scented water, and dried them with warm towels. They left our sandals beside our couch so that we could slip them on if we wanted to walk around the hall later.

The trumpets sounded again. The imperial party entered, led by the Emperor himself in his special purple robe with elaborate gold embroidery. Then Lady Antonia walked in, stately as ever. Caligula was next in bright green with his fair hair encircled by a gold wreath. He had had his racing laurels gilded.

Completing the imperial group were two of the Emperor's grandnieces, Agrippina, with her husband Ahenobarbus, and Junia Claudilla, Caligula's pregnant bride. Caligula was with the Emperor and Lady Antonia. Junia Claudilla's father, a consul, wasn't on the dais but with his wife among the ordinary guests.

On the far side of the central couch there were two more people: Drusilla, the favourite sister of Caligula, and her husband, Cassius Longinus, who was soon to leave Italy for a governorship. Young Tiberius Gemellus was evidently judged too young to be there; he hadn't yet gone through the ceremony of putting on the toga of manhood.

As Tiberius Caesar stood facing us all, the room became respect-fully silent. Then he spoke words of welcome in his deep growling voice. He had a strong voice that carried well, even across a crowded stadium. Among other courteous things, he said, "We are gathered here not only to celebrate the joyful season of the Saturnalia, the relief from the cold and gloom of winter days, but also to honour those who have expanded and helped preserve our glorious Empire stretching north from Our Sea to the colder lands of pines and sturdy oaks, south to the sands and palm trees of North Africa, and to the rich but frequently troubled East."

He went on about the heroism and stamina of those who defended our frontiers and maintained justice among subject nations, many of which had existed in a state of chaos before our civilizing pres-ence. Also worthy to be praised were those who had made cultural contributions to the honour of Rome; some of these persons were to be recognized this evening.

Finally he called on us all to raise our cups in a toast to the Roman state and the deities who watched over our beloved city and homeland. He poured out a few drops of wine as a libation to the Gods, then raised the cup and drank. So did we all, though the Hurs probably said a silent prayer to the one God they believed in.

CHAPTER TWENTY-SIX

THERE was an abundance of appetizers, some quite simple, others chosen to surprise and titillate because of their rarity or their original presentation. For example, some of the delicacies from the sea looked like what they were, but there were also arrangements of shrimp and scallops that reminded me of enormous strange flowers. Some nicely browned little sausages were obviously sausages, but others had been molded into animal shapes. There were small, curiously shaped pastries stuffed with light spicy meat mixtures, and there were tiny roasted birds – some of them may have been songbirds, which seems rather a waste considering the numerous edible creatures that can't sing a note. Need I mention the obvious, that some items on the trays had been cut, pounded, or rolled – whatever it took – into startling phallic shapes, which are always fashionable? I myself had a stuffed egg, an oyster in batter, and some salad bits: lettuce, olives, and floral-shaped radishes.

There were pitchers of water at each table for mixing with our wine to whatever degree we wished. As usual I added some to mine. In my youth I drank more freely, but after my accident, I realized the danger of wine as a comforter.

During lulls in the music and the bustle of serving, we could hear bursts of immoderate laughter from groups that were probably enjoying bawdy jokes. I thought I could distinguish the raucous laughter of Calvus. Some people got up and moved about, leaving the room briefly, or stopping to talk to friends, or flirt with women.

Mother was soon occupied in conversation with another old friend, a chatty lady on a couch which shared our table. There were two chairs on the serving side, and presently they were taken by friendly women.

I turned my attention to Sergia, who wanted to know more about the new novel I'd recently dispatched to Sosius. She tempted me to tell her the whole plot all the way to an impromptu chariot race along a hazardous mountain road in North Africa; however, I resisted. It was better to tantalize her with details from here and there in the story. Her big dark-blue eyes, shining with interest, her soft bubbling laugh did much to compensate me for the proximity of persons I would have preferred far away from me forever.

The main dishes were brought in and the visiting ladies returned to their places. There were big roasts of venison, pork, and lamb, suckling pigs roasted whole and decorated with fruit and herbs, roasted chickens and ducklings, and peacocks with their feathered tails spread out on the platters. The servers cut off pieces of whatever meats everyone fancied, and made the pieces small enough to be easily picked up with the fingers or fragments of bread, which we always used to soak up juices on the plate.

There were fish dishes, including the rich carp of the Tiber and the excellent sea fish of the Neapolis area. Also, platters of fall vegetables, such as squash, turnips, and marrows. Warm water with lemon slices was brought, along with heated towels, for cleaning sticky hands.

I took some chicken and pork but declined most of the exotic dishes which I have never enjoyed, though in my student days I tried to develop a taste for them. During the summer Lepida had remarked on my refusing a roasted dormouse, stuffed with pork, pine kernels, pepper, and liquamen sauce, which is distilled from the juice and entrails of fish: its flavour suggests that whatever one is eating has been dead for several days too long.

Lepida had said reproachfully, "After eating so poorly while you were away in the slums, Secundus, I'm surprised you can turn down a delicacy."

There were moments when I sympathized with Iras' dislike of Domitia Lepida. I refrained from saying that if I'd gone in for trapping in my Subura apartment, I could have obtained plenty of rodent meat, though probably not dormouse. Of course I couldn't legally have cooked it inside the room.

When the dormice, no doubt expertly prepared by the Emperor's chefs, were brought for our choosing, Mother and I had no appetite for them, and Sergia, looking apologetically at her enthusiastic fellow guests, said, "It looks like the pet rabbit I once had."

Another bond between us, though I never had a pet rabbit; I merely wanted one. I told her a little about my childhood.

"When I was younger, I wanted to try everything. In Judaea, Father and I ate Jewish food, which is usually good but restricted by religious taboos. So in Rome, I had to find out what I'd missed. But now I prefer simpler dishes – the same as Father. That doesn't mean I've reverted to Jewish food rules. By the way, this is excellent roast pork. Mother, might I have the raisin sauce?"

Suddenly everyone, or nearly everyone, stopped talking. Though the servers were still quietly offering second helpings, sometimes setting down a tray on a small table for people to take what they wanted, a group of musicians had come to the centre of the room. They were joined by a eunuch – one could tell by looking at him. He began to sing a sweet plaintive song about wine and the pursuit of happiness and the poignant memory of love long lost. His command of the high vocal ranges was admirable as he kept reminding us that life was sweet but the dark was always waiting.

This wasn't the sort of banquet that people of the East describe self-righteously when they feel like talking about what barbarians Romans are compared to themselves. The eunuch gave place to male and female dancers in filmy robes which they slowly removed in the course of their dance. But they didn't strip completely and they didn't perform lascivious acts or stop to caress the guests and make dates for later. Tiberius was giving a banquet for people he more or less respected. And he hadn't gone and spent a ridiculous amount on the food either.

One of Father's old friends came over to talk. He said, "I believe you once served under Valerius Gratus. Have you noticed what a fool he's making of himself? He really shouldn't have been invited to a dignified function."

"He's outside my line of vision, for which I'm thankful. Isn't Decumia checking him at all?"

"Oh, she's trying a little, when she isn't ogling the female dancers. But he doesn't listen to her, except for shouting at her a while ago, 'Shut up, you overheated bitch!' He keeps making inappropriate remarks to his neighbours and trying to tell scandalous tales about other guests. And now the damned fool seems to be ranting about the private activities of the Emperor."

"Macro will soon find out and deal with him," I said cheerfully.

"Yes, he's here himself and he has agents strategically placed. You know, Gratus used to be very astute, quite a diplomat, but now it appears he's losing his mind. I wonder if Tiberius invited him to see for himself how far gone he is."

"That might be, though I don't think he would expect Gratus to insult *him* in his own palace."

"I wonder if it's true that Gratus experimented with exotic potions – that mix up one's mind."

It was true. He had been interested in curious herbal concoctions, which I'd refused to try. I was adventurous enough, but my mind was my most precious possession.

The friendly senator continued, "His recent speeches to the Senate have made no sense – weird ramblings about Stoicism and Epicureanism and purely practical philosophy as applied to the management of subject nations. He never makes it clear what exactly he's talking about, but just goes on and on."

I recalled that Caprarius had mentioned Gratus' confused and boring Senate speeches. I was embarrassed to think I'd ever admired the fellow. Before he took his posting in Judaea, he had been a guest lecturer in one of my classes. He had outlined his philosophy of life, which was mostly about how to be successful. Combine Stoic self-control with Epicurean appreciation of the finer things. But never let yourself become a slave to emotion, for love was untrustworthy. Power was important – getting to the top and staying there, not letting anyone pull you down either by overt attack or by the subtle deployment of sentiment.

Now it seemed that the great Gratus was destroying himself – from within.

The servants brought in dessert trays to the accompaniment of light music. They were followed by dancers in feathery costumes who confined their acrobatic leaps and twirls to the central area so that they didn't get in the way of the servers. We were offered a generous choice of sweets: fruit pastries and custards, honey cakes, apples, grapes, peaches, and several kinds of cheese with very sweet dessert wine.

Then the Emperor's major domo, who supervised the presentation of the food and the entertainment, came to the steps of the dais. A trumpet was blown to get our attention.

He announced that we were to see a short but very amusing play which had been presented on Capri last summer in the Emperor's private theatre, where it had won the Augustan Prize for Latin Literature – two thousand aurei*, in other words, two hundred thousand sesterces. An impressive reward. We were to relax over our wine and enjoy the dialogue composed by Asellius Sabinus.†

In the dialogue, a mushroom, a fig, an oyster, and a thrush competed for a culinary prize and boasted of their superior taste and the ways in which they could be prepared for true gourmet pleasure. The oyster made much of the fact that it was not only delicious but also an aphrodisiac. Roars of laughter greeted some of the humour on this subject. Similarly the fig, sweet and nourishing,

---

*An aureus was a gold coin equal to one hundred sesterces.
†Asellius Sabinus, his play, and the amount of his award are mentioned by Suetonius.

whether raw or cooked, was also a great laxative – a fact which the audience generally thought hilarious. I noticed that Ben-Hur's wife, Esther, was shielding her face behind a painted fan, probably in embarrassment. If Iras had been there, she wouldn't have sheltered behind her fan; she would have watched everything disdainfully as the performance confirmed her growing opinion that the Roman sense of humour was very coarse.

Each of the competing foods wore a cleverly designed costume appropriate to what it was supposed to be. The mushroom outfit drew the most laughter, perhaps because the actor inside it had a comical bouncing walk and a ridiculous way of bowing.

After the play and the applause there was another fanfare of trumpets, and Tiberius Caesar came forward to a throne-like chair which had been placed on the dais. He began a speech, welcoming us, and thanking us for the pleasure of our company. He said he had some praise and honour to bestow and some admonitions to give.

CHAPTER TWENTY-SEVEN

"I must speak out against gambling. The curse of the nation! It's illegal, except for sporting bets, but the laws are hard to enforce rigidly."

Tiberius made sporting bets himself in his careful, parsimonious way. But gambling with dice had his strong disapproval, though it continued to be popular in every Roman club and tavern. It was known that he had even lectured his nephew Claudius on this. Claudius had written a mildly humourous treatise on the history of dice-playing and the nature of the odds in human experience. Tiberius hadn't laughed or even smiled.

"I hate to see money thrown away carelessly. It certainly doesn't reflect the way I've cared for the finances of our nation, thank the Gods, or Rome would be headed straight for ruin. It is especially a shame when members of great families are irresponsible with their wealth. Men of rank have a duty to set an example."

Without looking at him to confirm it, I felt that Judah was watching me, thinking of our bet on the chariot race and wondering if Tiberius would single me out by name. He would find that amusing.

The Emperor didn't refer to me personally; the Gods looked after me. Instead he lectured youth in general like a stern grandfather, saying that he might have some good years ahead of him yet and that he would never show favour to young aristocrats who embarrassed their families by persistent foolishness which detracted from Roman dignity.

Moving on to a mood of praise, Tiberius summoned an official from Pompeii to commend him for certain worthy building projects and gave him a silver cup with his name and achievements engraved on it. The man went back to his couch looking joyful and dazzled.

Macro, the harsh-faced Prefect of the Praetorian Guard, was praised for his fine work in security and crime detection. He was given a gold neck chain with an inscription.

Tiberius then named other people who deserved commendation, even though he could offer them nothing more tangible at this time. For example, he mentioned major contributors to civic enterprises such as the improvement of parks and the sponsoring of special commemorative games.

Then he summoned Quintus Arrius, who didn't seem very much surprised as he walked proudly to the dais. Here, Tiberius proclaimed, was a Roman citizen adopted into the family of a great naval hero. He had conducted himself with exemplary Roman dignity – would that everyone did as much. Absorbing this praise, Ben-Hur maintained a modest but attentive demeanour.

"I am delighted that, after revisiting the land of your birth, you have loyally returned to make your home here," said the Emperor to Judah. Was he testing him, wondering about his real loyalty?

Tiberius then announced that Arrius had very generously allowed his finest Arabian stallion, a magnificent animal of great speed, to cover the best mares in the imperial stables; moreover, he had refused all compensation for the service.

"Arrius, your fine public spirit deserves our warm applause."

Everyone politely applauded or pretended to. For all we knew, Macro might have posted agents to note who didn't applaud. I moved my hands correctly but soundlessly; so, I noticed, did my mother and Sergia Carina. Taking their cue from me?

Then Tiberius gave Arrius a silver statuette of a chariot and driver with a racing team of four. The Emperor read out the inscription at its base: "With sincere gratitude. Tiberius Caesar, Imperator*."

I remembered that, in my childhood, I wasn't allowed to give my playmate a horse I'd clumsily carved because it was a graven image. Lady Miriam said that, in the Temple long ago, seen only by the High Priest, there had been the famous ark with winged cherubim on top. Lost in the Babylonian invasion, it would some day be revealed to the world, which would then applaud the genius of the Jew. Meanwhile, I thought, centuries of that sort of genius would be forbidden expression.

Caligula asked Arrius for a look at his trophy and then informed everyone, "*I* personally posed for the driver."

With creditable self-control, Ben-Hur replied that he felt truly honoured. I reflected that, if he continued to live in Misenum and have contact with the Emperor and his probable successor, he would feel increasingly like a hypocrite.

Some people congratulated Judah as he passed them, and he responded pleasantly. He didn't look at me at all as he proceeded to his own place, where he was greeted joyfully.

Tiberius made his next proclamation. "Let Marcus Valerius Messala Secundus come forward."

Me! What did he have in mind? I rose from the couch, adjusted my sandals for security, and picked up my initialed cane. I would walk up to the dais slowly, with my head held high, listen to what Tiberius Caesar had to say, and then walk back, my head still unbowed. Thanks for saving Gemellus would be nice – and well-deserved, but I couldn't count on it. In case of reproof, I would show everyone that no one and nothing could break me.

"Messala, you wrote a novel, a long serial in Latin."

"Yes, Caesar, I did."

Was he going to tell me to desist from writing such stuff?

"I started to read it last spring, looking for some light reading to take my mind off a touch of arthritis. It was the most ridiculous piece of utter nonsense I'd ever seen."

I braced myself for a lecture.

---

* Supreme Commander, Emperor

"It was different – same basic format as a trashy Greek novel, but it had more humour. I looked forward to each new absurd episode."

This was better than I could have expected.

"At first you were writing as some modest fellow named Incognitus. When the story appeared under your name, I was astonished."

"Oh?"

To my relief, he didn't elaborate on his previous low opinion of me. Instead he said, "I've looked at your complete military record, including Pontius Pilate's report on your organizing a special security unit, and I've made further inquiries about you. I note that the citizen list committee has justifiably restored you to the equestrian order as befits your father's son."

The Emperor has spoken! My rank is secure.

"And now regarding your novel: it's an entertaining work in good Latin. It doesn't contain any instruction or moral admonition, and it isn't likely to improve anyone's mind – just distract and amuse. When a man reaches my age, believe me, he gets tired of heavy instructive works and second-rate moral musings."

"I can't imagine anyone wanting to read my moral musings."

"You're right. Just keep that in mind when you pick up a pen. But now I've made a decision. In most years, with the exception of last year, I didn't award the Augustan Prize for Latin Literature to anyone because nothing was written that, in my opinion, merited the honour.

"It is my pleasure to present you with this gold statuette of Thalia, the Muse of Comedy, as well as two thousand aurei, the amount of the Augustan Prize."

In the silence, there was the sound of people taking a deep breath. It seemed that no one had thought of me as a candidate for a major literary award.

"One thing more. I'd already decided to reward your writing in some way before you dived into the sea and saved the life of my grandson, Tiberius Gemellus. For that, I'm grateful, but there is no reward which would be sufficient. However, you have my thanks and best wishes."

He gave me the statuette and the money draft for two thousand aurei (two hundred thousand sesterces). I put the money draft in my belt wallet but kept the statuette in my hand.

Before I walked away from the dais, Lady Antonia smiled and said, "I'm truly pleased for you. I enjoyed your book very much."

I felt honoured; she was the greatest lady in Rome of her generation: a model of feminine dignity and intelligence.

Agrippina smiled warmly and said, "Congratulations!" Ahenobarbus grunted. Caligula grinned as if amused.

I said, "Thank you, Caesar, with all my heart!" and prepared to go back, facing the crowd. I was dazed and had some fear that, when everything had sunk in a little more, I might give way to unmanly tears. I could hear applause from my fellow guests. Some of it would be sincere.

I paused beside Herod, Cypros, and Claudius and gladly accepted their felicitations. I also took the opportunity to publicly thank Claudius for the help of his *History of Carthage* in writing my second book. Then I went on to my family, who greeted me happily.

Maybe Father would be awake when we got home. I could imagine his pride. The complete edition of my book was dedicated "To my father, whose encouragement has meant everything." Sosius would bring out another edition now for sure.

Mother was emotional; she had tears in her eyes, and her voice trembled with wavering laughter. "For so long I felt that I'd been a poor mother, not noble and supportive like the famous mothers of history – like Cornelia the mother of the Gracchi brothers. Now I can hold up my head when people speak of you."

How like Mother – to think of my zigzag career mainly in terms of the ways in which it might reflect on her. Yet she did have some affection for me.

Sergia Carina said, "May I look at the statue?" Her beautiful eyes glowed as she told me how happy she was for me. Years ago I would have been more attracted by a pretended coolness that didn't quite conceal a spark of interest and the excitement of a quickened heartbeat. It had attracted me to Iras at the fountain in the grove at Antioch when she apparently ignored my gallant speeches and turned to Ben-Hur. But now the reassurance of undisguised admiration was as welcome as shelter to a traveller after a long journey in the cold rain.

I hadn't looked at the Hurs at all; I didn't want to think about them in my moment of triumph. Yet from the corner of my eyes I saw them all talking to each other with composure.

Just then there was a disturbance from the portico section. A loud female was shouting, "You can't do this! It's a misunderstanding."

We all looked back and saw Praetorian Guards beside Gratus' couch. They were compelling him to get up and he was protesting, "I didn't say one word about the Emperor. Don't touch me, you ignorant dogs!"

Sergia said gleefully, "Oh, I do hope Macro deals with him."

Decumia was shouting; we could hear her protests despite the fact that the musicians were playing a well-known jolly song. The guards led Valerius Gratus past us. He was sputtering furiously.

"An award to an enemy of Rome – whom I should've crucified! Instead of listening to a smart-ass contubernalis! I suppose, Messala, you found a way to flatter the fornicating old he-goat in your second-rate book, which I haven't bothered to read, though I guess I could use it to wipe my backside. Did you entertain Caesar by describing the sexual acts a paralysed man can do?"

I turned away from Gratus to go on admiring Sergia, who said to me, "What a revolting man! Such a mean face on top of all that pink. And my stepbrother wanted so much to marry me off to him."

Macro approached, his face like a hammer.

Gratus snarled, "I demand a proper hearing before Caesar himself. I can explain everything. I've been slandered."

All this in spite of the fact that in the hearing of many guests he had called Tiberius Caesar a fornicating old he-goat! This would be especially offensive to the Emperor because a few years previously there had been a dirty song calling Tiberius an old goat no longer able to pursue the does in the usual way.

Macro said, "You'll be put on the list for a hearing before Caesar. Meantime you're to be kept in custody."

People sometimes remained in custody for years. Asinius Gallus stayed in prison awaiting a promised hearing until he died. I felt no sympathy for Gratus, though I knew he might never be free again.

As he and his guards reached the exit, Gratus collapsed.

The report rippled back through the room. "He's unconscious, his face is all pulled to one side and it's very red. He must have had a stroke. They're getting a litter for him."

Decumia had come to the door to see what she could or should do. We heard later that Macro told her, "No, house arrest isn't possible. I have my orders. You can send a couple of slaves to attend him in prison; you can even get a doctor for him, but everyone allowed near him will have to be searched."

A couple of Decumia's friends were heard advising her, "I hope you kept control of your money."

"Yes, but I wish I had more of it."

"You should divorce Gratus immediately. It's not good for you to be connected with him. The Emperor may confiscate all his possessions, so you shouldn't lose any time making your arrangements."

In other words, clear out of Gratus' villa right away, and take whatever valuables you can before Macro has someone take inventory.

"Poor Decumia," said Mother with insincere sympathy. "She must've hoped to become a well-off widow in short order. Only a little while to put up with Gratus – though even that little while would have seemed too long for me."

"I'm glad," I said. "I would hate to think you could tolerate even a single night."

Again I remembered my revulsion at Iras' surrender to him.

Tiberius Caesar had the trumpet blown to get our attention once more. He said he was bidding us all goodnight; however, we should feel free to linger over our wine and conversation. Those on the dais followed him out.

The slaves came to help us on with our footwear. Herod and Cypros joined us for a few moments to repeat how very pleased they were for me. Herod said he and his family, along with the entourage of Tiberius Gemellus, would be taking up residence in Rome soon, in an apartment in the imperial palace.

"The Emperor will spend the winter in Capri, not here, and he says he'd like Gemellus to learn more about history and government through field trips to the Senate and the principal temples and other buildings," said Herod.

I wondered if Caligula would go to Rome too. In the past he had spent a lot of time in Misenum and on Capri.

We said goodbye and reclaimed our cloaks. I assisted Mother and Sergia, silently admiring the creaminess of the latter's arms and throat. I wondered what her grandfather, Lollius Velleius, would say to me as a suitor. She was beautiful and sweet; I was attracted to her – more than that, I was in love with her. But would Uncle Velleius consider me sufficiently rehabilitated even now that I'd received unmistakable honours?

When we left the building, she was still holding my treasured gold statue of Thalia, a charming second-rank Goddess. It was tempting to indulge my imagination and suppose that Thalia had really come into my dreams and inspired me with ideas for my story. And what if she had also brought me Sergia Carina, as Venus had brought Helen into the life of Trojan Paris?

When we got out in the open air, we could smell smoke. Several guests, waiting for their carriages or litters, were commenting on the direction of the wind and wondering what could be burning.

The Hurs were near us. Judah hesitated, then asked me, "Did I hear Caesar correctly – that you dived into the sea and saved Tiberius Gemellus?"

"Yes, I did. Herod had kindly invited me on a yacht cruise and picnic. On the way back the sea became rough, and a freak wave carried Gemellus off the deck. As I *told* you, I enjoy swimming, so I dived in after Gemellus. I found him quickly enough, but I was relieved when the lifeboat came for us."

"That wasn't the first time –" he began, but then his carriage appeared, drawn by a pair of bay horses. At the same time Nestor came along with the greys.

I knew he was belatedly recalling the time I'd jumped into the Sea of Galilee – which had become rather stormy – to help him back into a sailboat. But I was glad we didn't discuss it. I felt we should get to Mother's house soon.

CHAPTER TWENTY-EIGHT

WE didn't try to catch up with Ben-Hur, who made all possible speed along the curves of the road until he reached his driveway. By the time we reached there ourselves, we were sure *his* house wasn't on fire, but had a very bad feeling about Mother's house. I thought of the guard dogs and their trainers – dismissed by my trusting mother.

From the vantage point of a hill near her property we looked down into the shallow valley and saw our fears confirmed. Flames were shooting up from both the barn and the house.

Sergia exclaimed, "The horses!" and Mother gasped, "My little Flora! And my new birds!" I'd given her a pair of yellow songbirds as a Saturnalia present.

We pulled up in time to see that Theron was leading out Mother's team of silver mares, rearing and screaming. The barn roof collapsed just afterwards, nearly on top of them. Sergia's chestnut horse, Atalanta, was tethered to a gate.

We stopped, and I approached the burning house, telling Mother and Sergia to stay back. Nestor tied up our greys beside Atalanta, then went to the aid of Theron, who was attempting to drag out a light carriage. To our relief, Mother's tiny white dog Flora ran toward us barking. Mother gathered her up in her arms. Then she said, "The little birds! They're trapped in there. And where's Anna?"

The walls of the house were stone, but inside there were wooden panels as well as sections of plaster. I wondered what was insulating the walls. Was it inflammable material, perhaps sawdust?

I pushed open the front door a little, releasing black smoke. I would need some protection to go in there. I turned on the fountain and Sergia and I took carriage blankets and soaked them. By this time Nestor and Theron were free to help us. They had found buckets and begun filling them and dashing water on the walls.

I told Sergia to stay back with Mother, as I went again to enter the vestibule, leaving my cane behind me. She said, "No, I'm coming too." We half-crept into the atrium, draped in the wet blankets. By the impluvium*, we found Anna, the maid, lying half-conscious on the tiles. She'd fallen on her back, her right arm still clutching what appeared to be cloaks or blankets. We couldn't see her very well, and it was hard to breathe in the thick smoke.

Sergia said, while trying to lift her, "Anna, can you hear us? Let us help you out of here!"

Anna croaked, "He hit me – the young man who – wanted this house. I scratched his face. He was – trying to catch – Flora!"

"Flora's safe. Come on, get up."

Sergia and I lifted her, one on each side. I discovered she had the bird cage under the garments and was carrying a box in her left hand.

We dipped our blankets in the water of the impluvium, then guided Anna out the door, almost crawling to keep below the smoke. Our eyes were burning and we were coughing. Behind us we could hear what seemed to be part of the ceiling falling, though we thought it wasn't the roof of the atrium but part of the inner ceiling in one of the other rooms.

Mother had taken her dog to a safe distance and was holding her close. We helped Anna to a stone bench and took the things from her grasp. The little birds seemed not quite dead, but the smoke

*A small open cistern that collected rain water when the roof was opened just above it

obviously hadn't done them any good. Mother quickly rose and came to tend to Anna. She had managed to save Mother's velvet cloak with the ermine trim, and a couple of fine silk robes. The box was Mother's jewel case. There was no use trying to go back and rescue any other valuables.

Sergia took charge of the dog. We could see now that there were bruises on Anna's face and forehead. Mother exclaimed, "How did it happen?" Anna tried to tell her, but while Sergia listened, Mother's attention had wandered to the two birds. She wrapped them in the velvet cloak and talked baby talk to them. I really think she was more concerned about them than about either faithful Anna or the valuable jewels. As it happened, she was wearing her best gems – most of them amethysts.

I felt that Mother and Anna should be taken home to my father's house as quickly as possible. Sergia had gone over to check on her nervous horse, the dog tagging behind her.

I told Nestor to take Mother, Sergia, and Anna away in my carriage with a brief stop in town to inform the fire department. The fire wagon had water barrels, a metal hose, and a pump. While it wouldn't save the house, except for the stone and brick, which wouldn't burn anyway, it should be able to put out the flames.

Sergia decided to ride her horse; it was the best way of getting the animal home. She laid aside her drenched blanket and retrieved her white cloak and hood. She wanted to help me but realized she would be most useful seeing that Mother and Anna reached our mansion safely and were properly taken care of. Father had given most of our slaves a Saturnalia holiday, but there would be at least a couple on hand in case of emergency. Certainly Africanus and Philip would be there.

I watched them leave while helping Theron pour buckets of water on the flames. I thought of our nearest neighbour. Judah knew very well that *something* was burning. It would have been decent of him to offer help, but I didn't expect it. He'd assure himself that I would ungraciously refuse, and he'd probably overlook the fact that the fire could spread through the grass and trees and up the slope to his own property. The wind was from the southeast, blowing the flames in his direction.

Near the slope, not far from the smouldering barn, I stepped on something which wasn't pavement or grass – or dung, thank the Gods! I picked it up: it was a thin leather wallet with a zigzag design in green thread. I opened it and found a compartment of coins and a flat area in which was a bank receipt. In the light of the dying flames I read it – four hundred thousand sesterces deposited with Simonides of Antioch by Phineas Ben Zebulon. Well, well!

Just then the fire department arrived, with two mule-drawn wagons. The men told us that the fire had been noticed in the town and they had been on the way here when they met Sergia, riding slightly ahead of the carriage driven by Nestor. They lost no time in going to work with their equipment. Their captain said they might be able to douse the flames enough to go in and bring out some valuables.

Three servants arrived from the Arrius property, telling us that Quintus Arrius had noticed the fire and had ordered them to offer help. They had buckets and were able to make themselves useful.

"Give Arrius my thanks," I said.

I knew he and his household would be upset over my discovery of Phineas' wallet. And there was the fact that poor Anna had identified him – and had scratched his face, which would be evidence that he had been here.

Now there came riders from the palace. Macro and three mounted Praetorian Guards.

"What happened? How did it start?" Macro demanded.

"Anna, my mother's servant, said she saw an intruder moving around the sitting-room. He was holding one of the candles against a wall hanging and had already ignited the draperies over a door. When he turned, she recognised him as Phineas Ben Zebulon, who had wanted to buy the house from Sanballat. She rushed at him and struggled with him, scratching his face. He hit her back and broke away, but my mother's small dog flew at him and bit his leg. Screaming, the man chased the dog.

"Anna went to my mother's room and picked up certain garments, as well as a bird cage and Mother's jewel box. She was in the atrium when the man came back and struck her down. My cousin Sergia and I found her when we entered the house, covered by wet carriage blankets. We were able to bring her outside and get her to tell us what had happened. She's not young, Macro, and she might not survive this. She has some heart trouble.

"Meantime the dog had escaped outside. I don't know if the arsonist set fire to the barn before or after his invasion of the house. Theron here, who was in the barn, discovered it was on fire and managed to bring the three horses out."

"Were there any other barn animals? Most people have a donkey or two for the slaves to take to the market."

"Fortunately, my mother had given four servants permission to take a cart with the two donkeys into town for the celebrations."

I showed Macro the wallet and its contents. He said, "We'll have to get our hands on the culprit immediately. I've heard about him. He carried on like a madman in Rabirius' court. I'd say there's something definitely wrong with his head."

Macro then declared I must come with him to identify the felon – his choice of terminology. Theron got the silver team ready, and he and I got into the light carriage while Macro mounted his horse. The fire department people could be trusted to deal with what was left of the fire and to salvage what they could. We'd be back to check on them soon. The three Arrius servants went on filling buckets from the fountain. I wondered if they might try to get to their master before us to warn him.

I could imagine the effect of my arrival with Macro. The Hurs would all be reminded of that far-off day in Jerusalem when the tile had fallen on Gratus, and the mob, seeing Judah on the roof with his hands stretched out, had cheered him for his act of insurrection, if it was really that. That time I'd gone with a centurion and his men into the Hur mansion and had identified Judah, his mother, and his sister. I'd left before they were led away, saying, "There is better entertainment in the streets." Judah had begged for my help in vain.

I'd thought, "Now you turn to me; yet you rejected my hand in parting just yesterday."

Judah's memory of the occasion had become rather distorted. He had told Iras, "Messala laughed when they led my mother away." That wasn't true. His suffering had blurred his memories. Now it would seem to him that history was repeating itself.

I realized that my face, hands, and clothing were smeared with black soot, and my cloak and red robe were damp from the wet blanket. I wondered if I looked anything like the Devil, a strange evil being that some Jews believe in.

CHAPTER TWENTY-NINE

SOMEONE found my cane and handed it to me before we left. I hadn't really needed it in the excitement of fighting the fire. Still I might as well carry it into the Arrius mansion.

Macro did the talking to the porter in the vestibule. He demanded to see both Quintus Arrius and his guest, Phineas Ben Zebulon. I had to tell him how to pronounce the latter's name.

The porter left us for a moment, then returned nervously and led us into a sitting-room lit by many lamps, some suspended from the ceiling. Ben-Hur stood to greet us, his expression sternly inquiring. Simonides was there in his chair, the lamplight accentuating his severe gaze. Lady Miriam and Judah's petite wife were both there, the latter clasping two small children in her arms. And Tirzah, her black hair hanging loose, her dark eyes huge.

And there was Phineas Ben Zebulon, trying to slip out a side door with a curtain.

Judah spoke loudly, "No, Phineas. Prefect Macro said he wanted to see you."

Macro nodded at me, and I held up the wallet. "Does anyone claim this?"

A heartbeat's silence before Tirzah exclaimed, "But that looks just like your wallet, Phineas. Except it looks burned."

"Yes, it does, doesn't it?" I couldn't resist the touch of sarcasm.

Phineas glared unlovingly at Tirzah and said, "It must be someone else's wallet."

My voice was hoarse from the smoke I'd taken in. "That's surprising – since it contains a receipt for four hundred thousand sesterces belonging to Phineas Ben Zebulon on deposit with Simonides." I looked at the man in the cushioned chair. "I assume *you* are Simonides."

"I am indeed. May I see this receipt?"

I gave him the wallet and its contents. He opened it and took out the receipt.

"Yes," he said sadly. "Yes, that is my writing and my seal. Look at it, Judah."

He showed it to Ben-Hur, who turned again to Phineas and said, "Don't go. You've some explaining to do. Where were you – that Messala could have found your wallet?"

Macro said harshly, "You have to give it back to me – both the wallet and the receipt. It's all evidence."

Phineas tried to appear surprised. "Evidence? Of what?"

"This evening someone set fire to the house and horse barn belonging to Lollia Velleia, Messala's mother. This wallet was found on the property – which seems very suspicious, doesn't it?"

Judah said, "We saw the fire from our east balcony. I sent three of my men to help, though I suppose I should have done it sooner."

Maybe he really had been wrestling with himself over this. I said politely, "Thank you."

"Was there much damage? I could see flames from both buildings. Was anyone hurt?"

"The barn roof is destroyed, and the hay inside was all burned. Probably the equipment in the barn was either destroyed or damaged. But Mother's coachman got the team of horses and their light carriage out safely. Her maid Anna was the only servant in the house – which must have considerable internal damage. She says she saw Phineas setting fire to the drapes. He struggled with her, and she scratched him."

Everyone turned to look at Phineas' face, which was scratched on one cheek.

"You told us you stumbled against a rose bush in the garden," said Tirzah.

"The little dog bit him, whereupon he ran after the dog. Anna was trying to save some of Mother's belongings when he attacked her again in the atrium. We found her and brought her out. She thinks she can identify her assailant."

Phineas looked desperately at the door.

Simonides wasn't going to give up easily. "Isn't it possible that the servant woman was mistaken and that she mistook a common intruder for our friend Phineas because she'd seen him in the house before – with Sanballat? I can't believe he would set fire to someone's house. Could the fire have started by accident? Maybe some of your slaves were having a pork barbecue in honour of the – Saturnalia, is that the right name?"

Probably he would have liked to think that the fire was some form of divine judgement for our disgusting dietary habits. And maybe he imagined Anna had been bumped into by a drunk and disorderly manservant.

"And how do you explain the matter of the wallet?" said Macro.

"Perhaps it was stolen and deliberately dropped on Messala's mother's property, to incriminate Phineas."

Macro raised his eyebrows. "And why exactly would anyone want to do that?"

"There were separate fires in the barn and house," I said. "That doesn't seem like an accident. Also Mother had given all but two servants permission to go to the town and celebrate. But the coachman and Anna are very quiet, steady people – in fact Anna is probably close to sixty."

"Was she badly injured?" Tirzah was sympathetic, probably remembering her faithful Egyptian nurse Amrah.

"She's bruised about the head where she was struck from behind, and she may have hurt her back when she fell. But she was able to talk to us after we brought her out of the house.

"I sent Mother and Anna on to my father's house in my carriage. My cousin Sergia chose to ride her own horse and help look after them. They may stop at the nearest inn and try to get a litter for Anna."

"You would have been welcome to bring them here. We would have tried to make them comfortable," said Ben-Hur.

"But I couldn't assume that," I answered.

Macro turned to me. "Do you affirm that this young fellow here is Phineas Ben Zebulon? Is he the very same fellow who wanted to purchase your mother's house from Sanballat?"

"Yes, that is certainly Phineas Ben Zebulon. Several other people here have also identified him by name."

Macro beckoned to the guards waiting at the entrance. They came forward and hemmed Phineas in on either side.

"You don't need me any longer, do you, Macro?"

"No, Messala, I have enough evidence to arrest this culprit – though tomorrow I'll try to talk to that maid. I think you said everyone would be at your father's house."

"Yes. Father will welcome them – just as he did when they fled there because they'd been harassed by a voice cursing them and screaming foul names. That was when I was temporarily in Rome collecting evidence for the court case."

The Hurs looked at me and at each other, as if this was a surprise to them.

"The stupid women imagined things," said Phineas defensively.

"I don't think so," I said. "I think the ugly sounds they heard in the night were very much like what we later heard from *you* in the courtroom. You have a coarse vocabulary – in both Greek and Aramaic – and hardly any self-control."

"You – you evil spawn of a Roman harlot!" He tried to lunge at me but the guards held him.

"I'm just wondering," Macro said slowly, "if these other people are quite blameless or if they encouraged this – this cringing felon.

I've heard rumours, after all – that some of them look on *you* as an enemy. And this man here, Simonides, doesn't seem very sympathetic, does he?"

Simonides wasn't capable of faking sympathy for me and mine. He was probably concerned with keeping a fearless face in front of Macro and his men, despite a frightening memory of having been taken into custody and tortured by Gratus.

"It could be just his natural gruff character, I suppose." I sounded as if I was kindly making allowances; I'm sure this annoyed him.

I continued, "These people aren't my friends, Macro, but I don't think any of them – except the accused there – would commit arson. It would definitely be beneath – Quintus Arrius' dignity. As you know, the Emperor thinks well of him.

"But it's too bad they allowed Phineas to remain here so long and to have the freedom to go where he liked, wreaking havoc. He's a danger to the whole community."

Phineas struggled as the guards began leading him out.

"Simonides, Ben-Hur, help me please. I'm innocent. Someone must have stolen my wallet and planted it at the scene of the fire. Stand by me! Don't let me be sentenced unjustly."

His large dark eyes and handsome face with the weak quivering mouth may have reminded Judah of himself at seventeen pleading to me when he was arrested for throwing the tile at Gratus. However, Ben-Hur's common sense prevailed, and perhaps he had spent long enough with his guest to read his character.

"You *were* out of the house this evening, Phineas. My mother mentioned it, and she spoke of the scratch on your face, which we can plainly see. If you had anything to do with the fire, there should be the smell of smoke on your clothes. You aren't wearing the same robe you had on before we left for the banquet."

Phineas stammered and didn't quite manage to come up with anything coherent.

Judah touched a bell and summoned a woman servant. "Go to Phineas' room and examine his clothes and shoes. See if any of his garments smell of smoke."

"Yes, sir," she said, and went out swiftly.

Macro signalled to the men to wait but to maintain hold of their prisoner.

Simonides said to me, "I assume you'll be asking for money to pay for damages. If you and your family submit an itemized list, we will naturally try to do the right thing."

I could picture him haggling over the details of such a list.

"Yes, we'll be seeking proper reparation for destruction of property: buildings, furniture and personal belongings, as well as shock and possible damage to Mother's health through smoke inhalation. Also there are the injuries to Mother's elderly servant."

Esther was still holding her two children. The little boy spoke. "Please – Aunt Tirzah said your mother had a little dog. Is the dog all right? It didn't get burned, did it?"

They were all apparently surprised that the child had spoken to me. I said, "The dog is safe. She ran away from the man who attacked the maid, and was outside to greet my mother when we arrived."

I thought it better not to tell the child that two pretty little birds had probably died.

Another point came to mind, and I said to Simonides, "The repayment should come from the prisoner here if he is convicted. Or from his estate in the event of his death."

"They wouldn't give me the death penalty, would they?" said Phineas pathetically. "Nobody died, and it was only a slave woman that was injured."

Another misstep! Iras thought that Simonides had once been a slave of the Hur family.

"I'm very disappointed in you," said Simonides to Phineas. "I felt like a father to you. For the sake of your family, I hope you'll be proven innocent of this shameful action. Failing that, that the judge has compassion on you. But your lack of self-control in court was a great embarrassment to me, as I've already told you. And what we've now learned concerning your treatment of your late wife has come as a sad shock. Herod's wife accuses you of improper attentions to her maid; I don't know what to believe about that. And now this! It looks bad for you. You aren't among your own people here. You'll be facing a Roman magistrate, and you don't have Roman citizenship – unfortunately."

He turned to Macro. "Could he be sent to the galleys or mines – or tortured?"

"I can't say. I'm not the judge. But the Emperor wouldn't excuse him if he *were* a citizen. He'd say the fellow disgraced the Roman citizenship. He'd get a severe penalty. As he isn't a citizen, I wouldn't rule out crucifixion."

Phineas moaned and tried to twist free of the guards. "Let me go, you Roman dogs!" He lowered his head and bit a guard on the arm. The guard cuffed him twice about the face.

The Hur ladies looked distressed, and Ben-Hur's wife led her children out of the room. No one stopped her.

My unkind side asserted itself. After all, I'd fought hard to save my mother's house. I'd had only a brief hour, as it were, of triumph, including this evening's banquet – and now the house was a blackened ruin, probably including the fine furnishings that Mother had joyfully chosen so recently.

"There are other possibilities. He could be saved for the next Games – and given to a hungry lion."

Phineas shivered and looked almost ready to fall on his knees and plead for mercy. Ben-Hur and Simonides both gave me a glance of disapproval; they must've been thinking, "Typical Roman barbarian!"

Just then the maid returned with a tunic and cloak in her arms. She was also carrying a pair of sandals with mud on the soles. She handed everything to Ben-Hur, but Macro insisted on having a close look as well.

From where I stood, I couldn't tell if the smoky odour came from Phineas' garments or my own. I knew I looked a strange sight, with a black-streaked face and bits of ash in my hair. My fine dark-red dinner robe, now torn and stained, would see no further service.

Ben-Hur spoke regretfully. "His clothes do smell of smoke, and there's mud on these sandals, fresh mud. So you did go down the hill and over to Lollia Velleia's property, Phineas! You did set the fire. You've not only harmed a neighbour, a lady; you've brought disgrace on me, your host. We welcomed you; we showed you friendship and honour. I even considered you a possible husband for my sister until I learned more about your past. Your hysterical performance in court has shamed me before this community. And now you've cast suspicion on me and my household. I'm mortified by your conduct, and I don't see how I can help you."

"We can get him a lawyer," said Simonides. "Everyone is entitled to a court hearing and legal assistance. Phineas, did you not miss that wallet until now?"

"I – I thought it was in the waistband I took off. I didn't look for it. Do you suppose one of the servants stole it – along with my clothes and shoes – and then went down to that woman's property?"

"Frankly, no!" said Ben-Hur.

Phineas glared at him. "You never really wanted me for your sister. It was only because of Simonides that you said you might consider my suit. But she liked me at first. She did!"

He turned bitterly to me. "It was after *you* came to your mother's house to stop Sanballat that Tirzah changed her mind. You fascinated her – in spite of everything! You took her away from me."

Judah and Simonides were looking curiously at Tirzah. Simonides was frowning as if he thought her an unstable girl. She was flushed with obvious embarrassment.

I said firmly, "That is about the silliest piece of nonsense I've ever heard. Tirzah never cared for me in her life, not long ago and not now! She turned from you, Phineas Ben Zebulon, because of your asinine hysterics – and rightly so. Why would she want to spend the rest of her life with a fellow who spits on other people's floors and screeches obscenities like a candidate for a choir of castrati?

"And you were clearly jealous of her brother, who has been her hero – since my earliest memories of them both.

"Now, if you don't mind, Macro, I'd like to go home and see my own family."

"Of course. We'll be leaving too, with the prisoner. Take him out, men."

Lady Miriam put her arms around her daughter as the guards led the sobbing Phineas outside. He was trembling, partly with rage perhaps and also with fear of a man-eating lion.

"Quintus Arrius – or whatever one is supposed to call you – I may be back with further questions," warned Macro.

I didn't say goodbye to the Hurs, nor they to me.

CHAPTER THIRTY

THE two little birds died on the way to our house. Mother cried over them, and the next morning we cremated them and put together a brief religious ceremony with a prayer to whatever Gods took an interest in birds and animals. Venus, we were assured, was very fond of doves and perhaps she would also welcome the tiny spirits of songbirds – if that is possible. Our philosophers generally insist that death is the end for man and beast and that the invisible soul atoms, like the atoms that make up all things, separate and mingle with the myriads of other atoms that are not only part of all living creatures but of all substances on earth. Be that as it may, I helped soothe my grieving mother by reading a couple of Catullus' poems about his mistress' pet bird.

Anna was bruised but seemed likely to recover. We had a physician check her out, and he recommended a few days of bed rest. She was in good spirits and was relieved to know that the arsonist had been caught.

We made an inventory of all that had been lost in the fire: dishes, furniture, rugs and curtains, clothing. Also some paintings and pieces of sculpture. Assisted by our lawyer, Scaurus, we estimated the cost of rebuilding and refurnishing the house, as well as restoring the barn and its contents, including a couple of loads of hay. Some pieces of furniture could be refinished, but that wouldn't be cheap. Several works of art were totally ruined.

Then there was the amount which should be paid to Mother and Sergia simply for the grief and fear they had experienced and compensation for Anna's injuries.

Scaurus met with Eulalius, who would represent Phineas. He was lawyer to the Hur family and Simonides. They were willing enough to compensate us, saying that they could pressure the accused into repaying them; he had money deposited in Antioch in addition to the amount specified in the draft found in his wallet, and he surely had some money and property in Judaea.

Phineas himself objected to paying us anything but gave in when Ben-Hur convinced him that he and Simonides might be able to persuade a judge to be lenient. Ben-Hur hoped that the magistrate, Father's old friend Antistius, would agree to hold Phineas in prison till spring if he paid for the damage, and then allow him to sail away with Simonides to Antioch, with orders never, never to return to Italy or else face the severest consequences.

Simonides had even hoped Phineas could be kept in the Arrius house, strictly confined until April, but Ben-Hur opposed the idea. He said, "He's given us enough trouble without all the family, especially Tirzah, enduring him every day for three more months."

When the case came before Antistius, Father himself came with us to see justice done. We didn't bring Anna, but since Theron was a freedman, we brought him along so that he could testify concerning the barn burning and the difficulties of saving three valuable horses.

Antistius did suggest house arrest with relays of Roman soldiers as guards, but no one in the Hur household liked that thought at all. So it was settled that Phineas would spend nearly four months in a cell with some comforts supplied by his friends; he would even have access to an exercise yard shared with a few other privileged prisoners including a couple of elderly German chiefs. When it came time for Simonides to sail away, Phineas could be escorted to the ship and placed in confinement until the vessel was safely out to sea. Meantime my mother and Sergia received money drafts totalling almost a million sesterces. Most of this was for Mother, but Sergia was recompensed for the loss of her elegant wardrobe and jewellery.

When Antistius handed down his ruling, he warned Phineas that he was being treated very generously and had better stay out of trouble in future. "Especially, young man, I don't want to see you or hear of you in an Italian court. Bear in mind, I could have sent you to a lifetime of service in the mines."

Phineas said nothing; he stood there with tears streaming down his cheeks. Then he was led away.

Ben-Hur avoided approaching my father and mother but spoke briefly to me. "You made no demands for yourself – only for your mother and cousin." This apparently surprised him.

Scaurus had already told me that Simonides had wanted to question the amount of settlement, but Ben-Hur had considered our claims reasonable.

I answered, "None of my possessions were in the house. I couldn't bring myself to ask for compensation for a ruined dinner robe and sandals, which I'd worn when I was fighting the fire. After all, I could afford others."

Which was a not very subtle way of reminding him that I was quite far from the state of poverty over which he had once rejoiced, viewing it as a joint accomplishment of his almighty God and himself.

Back in Father's house, we had a celebratory dinner. We hoped to hear from Uncle Velleius soon. I'd written to him and asked for Sergia's hand in marriage, and we'd reason to hope that the day's success in court would win his approval and consent. We'd embraced and kissed whenever there was opportunity and spoken as if we took Uncle Velleius' consent for granted. We considered which of my new properties would make the most satisfactory home. Or should we build a new villa? And when Mother's house had been rebuilt, we should probably stay with her frequently.

We used to meet in a small sitting-room, once the household

had gone to bed. One night we were on a couch, proceeding with preliminary love-making. I was about to suggest moving to the privacy of my room. Sergia's room was out of the question as it was next to Mother's.

Just then we heard Mother coughing violently. She rang her bedside bell, evidently needing some kind of service. She often had trouble settling to sleep owing to her persistent cough, which was worse since the fire. We went to check on her, as did Anna, though she was still in some pain from her injuries. Sergia and Anna spent some time trying to coax Mother to gargle hot salty water or to drink a warm mixture of wine and honey.

As I waited, I felt apprehensive. I truly desired Sergia, delighting in her lively wit and her enticing body, but I worried how I would appear as a lover. I remembered how much I'd needed Iras' help for sexual intimacies in those dismal years after the race – and then at last I'd been repelled by her and gave it all up. Really, Iras deserved some pity; she had thrown away so much to find herself living in extreme poverty – undesired, rejected by the man for whom she had given up her security as Balthazar's daughter.

I fell asleep in my own cubicle, a little relieved that I could put off proving myself till another time. To my surprise, the next morning there was a message from Macro, asking me to meet him in his office in the palace.

He had also invited Ben-Hur and Simonides, the latter sitting in his cushioned chair litter wrapped in a cloak and a couple of shawls. Herod Agrippa was there too. He hadn't left for Rome with Gemellus yet because the boy had a cold.

Macro explained, "Herod has a letter from the Jewish Sanhedrin to forward to the Emperor; it concerns Phineas Ben Zebulon. It seems he's more than just an arsonist."

"What does that mean?" asked Simonides. "If it's a question of religious differences, I don't see why that would concern the Emperor."

Herod explained, with no attempt to disguise a certain amount of glee: "Phineas has told people that his first wife died naturally in childbirth. Since his marriage was in Galilee, where he owns land, he managed to deceive new acquaintances who weren't close to what really happened. His wife's parents had died together in a fire a week before their daughter, and if *his* parents knew the truth, they certainly kept quiet about it."

"Well, what's the real story?" asked Simonides. "I've heard something recently, but it may be just slander."

Ben-Hur said, "I doubt that it's a case of slander. I was told things by certain Jews I met in Rome – people I respect. But go ahead, Herod."

Herod was enjoying the drama, the unfolding of a shocking tale. "Phineas' young wife miscarried, and in her pain, she blurted out what he took to be an admission of adultery. It may not have been; Phineas himself was apparently the only male witness to her statement. Anyway he accused her of unfaithfulness and had her dragged from her bed and stoned to death."

Ben-Hur said, "That's worse than the story I heard. I thought that at least the poor girl had been found guilty by a court. Though it's illegal to carry out the death penalty without authorization either from Pilate in Judaea or Herod Antipas in Galilee."

Simonides said, "Where were her kin? Wasn't anyone trying to defend her? And why didn't they immediately take their protest to the Sanhedrin? Or to a representative of Rome?"

Herod explained, "Her only brother was in Mauritania when it all happened. This fall he returned and began investigating – and now he's furious, demanding redress.

"In the meantime Phineas had gone through a spell of drinking and riotous living, then settled down and proved himself steady and capable on a long camel trip to Persia. He evidently made a good impression on you, Simonides."

I thought of Phineas' extreme reaction to my remark about pushing his way to the head of the line in order to cast the third stone. So it had been the *first* stone instead!

Simonides glanced at me, obviously recalling what I'd said. Then he commented, "I suppose the brother wants Phineas to be tried by the Sanhedrin. We've no way of knowing what the girl admitted in her confession, unless there was another witness besides Phineas. We should still give him the benefit of the doubt and find him proper legal help in Jerusalem."

I could imagine Ben-Hur's reflections at this point. He had come near to giving Tirzah in marriage to Phineas.

"Macro, I don't understand how this concerns me," I said.

Herod spoke up. "I told the prisoner about the Sanhedrin's message to the Emperor. Macro was with me. Phineas became frantic with dread of the penalty he would face in Jerusalem. Thanks to Rome, the Jews can't impose the death penalty, but the Sanhedrin could compel him to give all his money and land in Judaea and Galilee to his late wife's brother. Accordingly he objects to repaying Quintus Arrius and his partner for the money drafts to Lollia Velleia and Sergia Carina."

"Don't worry! We aren't going to cancel payment of the money drafts," said Ben-Hur. "If necessary, we can take the whole matter to Phineas' uncle. He's a fair man – as well as a rich one. But he'll be deeply pained by all this."

Herod smiled. "I wonder if it will come as a surprise to him."

Ben-Hur had another question. "Herod, how is it that the message from the Sanhedrin to Caesar came through *you* instead of Pontius Pilate?"

"Pilate's been very much occupied. Trouble with the Samaritans! He's being criticized for his handling of the problem. The elders of Jerusalem felt that I might be able to get through to Caesar more quickly."

"I suppose Phineas will be kept here until the sailing weather is more reliable," said Simonides. "I'll help him get the best legal counsel that can speak to the Sanhedrin. But I have to agree that he'd have been a deplorable husband for poor Tirzah. I'm ashamed of having brought him here and recommended him. I used to think I was a good judge of character."

"Doubtless many of us have, at least once, built a mistaken trust in someone," said Ben-Hur. He was probably thinking of Iras and me.

"If I'm not required for anything else, I'd like to take my leave now," I said to Macro.

Just then an officer entered and said something quietly to Macro, who said, "Ye infernal Gods! Well, I suppose it saves everyone some trouble."

He then told the soldier to explain to everyone present.

"That fool, the Jew Phineas, tried to escape from the yard. He actually got part way up the wall before he was spotted. Then as he scrambled faster to get to the top, he caught a foot in a twisted ivy vine. While trying to free himself, he lost his grip on the stones and fell, hanging upside down for a moment until the vine gave way. He landed on his head; his skull broke on the stones. It seems to me he got what he deserved."

Macro agreed to release the corpse to Quintus Arrius for an immediate Jewish burial.

"I presume," said Simonides with a severe gaze at Herod and me, "neither of you particularly wants to view the remains to satisfy yourselves that the man is indeed dead."

"I'll gladly accept your word – in addition to Macro's," I said with somewhat overdone graciousness.

"I too, of course," said Herod. "I do hope he hasn't left our servant Ruhamah pregnant. However, what will be, will be."

CHAPTER THIRTY-ONE

O
UT in the palace yard, I walked toward my carriage, saying goodbye to Herod. Simonides was in his chair litter, with Ben-Hur walking at his side. The wind was cold; Ben-Hur took an extra cloak from the litter and wrapped it around his father-in-law before drawing the curtains on three sides, leaving one open so they could converse.

Herod remarked to me, "Phineas may have had money deposited elsewhere than with Simonides. Doubtless he hoped he could get over the wall and get to it – and then head for a far-off place. Perhaps he could have got word to his slaves. Well, it was a desperate effort, and it failed."

Ben-Hur and Simonides looked at each other. They may have reflected that, by going with Macro to Phineas in prison and telling him about the Sanhedrin's letter, Herod had precipitated Phineas' grim end.

Ben-Hur said, "Herod, do you regularly pass on messages to Rome from the Sanhedrin?"

"Not often. As you must know, the Sanhedrin sends dispatches through Pontius Pilate or sometimes through the governor of Syria province. In this instance, they considered that I might get their request to the Emperor's attention a little sooner because of my position here."

He smiled – a very pleasant smile which did justice to his well-shaped white teeth. He enjoyed emphasizing his influence with both Caesar and the Sanhedrin to Ben-Hur.

I parted from Herod, wishing him a safe journey to Rome with his pupil. At home I told the story to my family.

"Curiously enough," said Father, "Philip has just brought us news that a few days ago Valerius Gratus died in his dungeon. He'd shown some signs of recovery from his stroke, but his wife Decumia didn't bother sending any comforts to him, not even a slave with good food or blankets. Instead she cleared out everything she could from their villa and headed for some place in the countryside."

Ben-Hur probably would have been interested, remembering the imprisonment of his mother and sister. However, I wasn't going to tell him. In time he would hear about it.

"Another bit of interesting information," said Father. "Bibulus is under house arrest in Rome, awaiting trial for his deception in the Temple of Vesta. Much easier than being in a dungeon, but he won't like being under guard, perhaps for a long time until the Emperor sees fit to look at his case."

We were feeling elated about the future except for some concern over Mother's persistent cold. But then the Fates showed their capricious hands. A carriage drove up, followed at a distance by a heavier vehicle drawn by mules. It was Uncle Velleius.

He came in and greeted my father very respectfully and me cordially. He was glad we had reached a financial settlement for my mother, but thought *he* could have squeezed several hundred thousand more out of the Jews. We didn't argue with him much, but I did say that the process of recompense would have taken longer if Quintus Arrius had disclaimed any responsibility and left us to sue Phineas' estate.

"Well, you didn't do badly, though I must say I was horrified when I read your last two letters, which came to me on my way back from Spain. The house should have been better protected. There should have been guard dogs. Why weren't there?"

Mother struggled to speak despite an attack of coughing.

"My son – had arranged for – the dogs. But I sent them away. I – I was afraid of them."

Uncle Valleius frowned. "Foolish of you, Velleia! You need someone to make decisions for you. Now listen, I left Lavinia at my villa in Capua. We can get there tonight."

"Mother shouldn't be travelling. She has a bad cold. Can't you wait awhile?"

Father said much the same thing. It was clear that he was truly worried about Mother.

Uncle Velleius wasn't prepared to listen at all because he had a definite plan.

"While I was in Spain I got to know Sextus Antonius, who was serving as a legate in Corduba. You may remember him, Sergia."

"Yes, I do remember him." Was I imagining that her large blue eyes brightened?

"He's just been appointed to the office of praetor in the corruption court of Rome. He's there now. Sergia, he's offered for you in marriage, and I've accepted for you. I understand he once wished to wed you before, but your father chose Calvus as the better prospect."

"Yes. At the time I didn't know either of them well enough to care which one would become my husband."

This time there was definite excitement in her expression. Cautious interest mixed with ambition.

"Antonius has done well since then. His service in Spain has been distinguished, and he's shown himself accomplished not only in fighting rebels but in government administration at the provincial town level. He's become a local hero. He took part in a chariot race against a British prince – and won! He's added to our national prestige. That's the husband I want for my girl."

So much for my proposal! He hadn't come right out and said that my own honours were purely literary, not at all on the same level as Antonius' laurels. But that remark about the chariot race – that was a low blow.

"He's also made nearly ten million sesterces by various business deals in Spain; naturally I don't know the details."

I remembered Antonius well. He had attended the lectures of Gratus just as I had. Had he enriched himself at the expense of unfortunate Spanish citizens? Maybe not, but I wondered.

Sergia said, "Grandfather, I appreciate all that you've tried to do for me. But I've already formed a serious attachment to Messala. I was hoping you'd agree to his offer. He has a lot of property, and he's recently been given an award by the Emperor."

She would have said more, but Velleius interrupted. He addressed my father. "I'd like to speak alone with my sister and granddaughter. I've made a firm decision, and I want to make the girl understand what's best for her."

Father and I withdrew politely and left Velleius to make his case, which he did with increasing loudness. We couldn't hear everything, but it sounded at first as if Sergia was trying to persuade him in my favour. Mother also seemed to be speaking on my behalf.

Velleius thundered, "I will not agree to your foolish choice. I don't care if he is your son, Velleia. He simply doesn't compare with Sextus Antonius in fortune or achievements.

"Sergia, if you persist in your ungrateful attitude, I'll hand back your guardianship to your stepbrother. I'm sure you won't like that. I'll wash my hands of you. You've disappointed me."

We couldn't hear much more, but soon they all came into the second sitting-room, where we were waiting. I had too much pride to argue over my unwelcome suit. I let Father try to convince Velleius that he shouldn't drag Mother away in her frail state of health. But Velleius said the drive to Capua wasn't far and that Mother could be wrapped up warmly. He'd brought extra furs. He and Sergia and Mother would ride together in his light carriage, while the luggage and servants could travel in a wagon drawn by mules. Theron would bring along Mother's white mares and their carriage; Anna would ride with him. It was all settled.

I said with my best haughty composure, "Sergia, if this is what you want, naturally I wish you happiness."

I was glad that she had returned my gold statuette of Thalia; otherwise I'd have had to ask for it back. Tiberius would have been offended if he thought I'd given it away. Not only that, Velleius would probably have accused me of presumption in giving his granddaughter such a gift.

She answered formally, "I'm most grateful for everything, Messala. You saved Aunt Velleia from a very distressing situation, and it certainly wasn't your fault that a crazy fellow burned down her house."

"Yes, I must say you did quite well for your mother," said Velleius. "But now I'm the proper person to take charge of my sister and granddaughter. From Capua we'll go on to Rome, weather permitting. The astrologer has already given us a propitious wedding date in February. I trust my sister will be recovered enough to enjoy the festivities."

He looked doubtfully at Father and me, as if wishing to say the polite thing but not to mislead us by feigned enthusiasm.

"I don't suppose either of you would find it convenient to come to Rome for the wedding?"

"No," said Father. "I'm not well enough to travel in winter. The cold wind wouldn't do my old heart any good."

"I have things to do here," I said, thinking of my exercise program. I planned to ride my horse and sail my boat whenever I could. Anything but let my thoughts dwell on Sergia.

"I can be useful to Father, and that's important to me."

Sergia looked at me as if she wanted to say she was sorry but didn't really want to get into the subject.

Mother said, "Later you must come to see me in Rome, Marcus. And maybe I can visit you here in the summer – and you can help me rebuild my house by the sea."

"Hummph!" said Uncle Velleius equivocally. "We'll see what the future holds."

So while Uncle Velleius consumed a seafood salad with wine and new bread, Sergia organized their packing and Mother hugged her dog and tried not to cough too much. Indeed, every time she tried to say anything, she either sneezed or coughed.

Again I advised her not to leave. I said she should be in bed with a warm poultice on her chest. Sergia agreed with me. But Mother replied that she mustn't miss Sergia's wedding, and Uncle Velleius was insistent that she travel with him at once.

In about an hour they were ready to start. I embraced Mother and said, "I'll miss you. At least keep warm."

Sergia spoke to me haltingly, "I've truly enjoyed your friendship. You're a very interesting man – and I really wish you the best."

"Thank you." That was all I could say to her. I watched her join Mother and Uncle Velleius in the carriage; she took charge of the dog. Then I turned back and reentered the villa, not indulging in the mingled sadness and anger of watching them drive away.

CHAPTER THIRTY-TWO

UNDERSTANDABLY I was depressed. I'd worked hard to help my mother and Sergia. I'd believed them when they professed to be grateful and admiring. Indeed I think Mother *was* grateful and had some affection for me, but she was used to being guided by her brother, Velleius. Father had told me that before he and Mother separated, Velleius had written to her informing her of their father's death and assuring her that, if she were a free woman, he could arrange a fine marriage for her which would enable her to live in Italy and enjoy the benefits of civilization. She hadn't yielded immediately. She tried first to induce Father to give up Jerusalem and take her home. But when that failed, she'd made her choice to leave Father and me in an alien land without very much inner struggle. And now history was repeating itself except that she was going only from Baiae to Rome this time, and perhaps she wouldn't remarry this time – she surely wasn't well enough.

Maybe Sergia Carina had been attracted to me when she had no more exciting marital prospect – considering how she'd been viciously bad-mouthed by Mallius' battleaxe of a mother and then by Calvus and his new wife, Furia Vopisca, and finally by an angry

Gratus. She may have reasoned that I might be her best hope. I'd a respectable income and some property; I could walk upright without stooping; I'd won the Augustan Prize for Literature and received words of commendation from the Emperor. And I'd come effectively to Mother's rescue.

Perhaps she'd liked Sextus Antonius years ago, when her father chose Calvus for her. I remembered Antonius – about my own age, well-built, dark-haired, strong-featured. He wasn't brilliant, but he was shrewd and practical. And now he'd risen to an enviable position: praetor of the corruption court for the year. He hadn't been in Rome for the election; he'd been serving in Spain. Elections aren't what they were during the Republic. Usually the Emperor chooses the candidates – any competition is more apparent than real. The Senate votes to confirm the Emperor's choice. I've never heard of them opposing his wishes. Now, as Antonius' wife, Sergia Carina will be honoured – and also envied. All that will add to Lollius Velleius' prestige.

Two days after our guests departed, two of Velleius' grooms came for Sergia's brown mare, Atalanta. She and Mother both sent notes to us expressing thanks. Mother also hoped we wouldn't mind pasturing her two donkeys for a while; she had bought them for the convenience of her servants when she was living in the country, but they weren't needed in Rome. She hoped we could make use of them, and when she had rebuilt her house by the sea, she might reclaim them.

During the rest of January and part of February I worked on my physical fitness, going frequently to the local baths, practising my swimming and archery, and boxing with a stuffed leather bag suspended from the ceiling. The last activity was an outlet for my anger, and was better than risking a drastic physical setback by wrestling or boxing with a human adversary.

One day Father said, "I persuaded your mother to make a will. It was after the court case but before that fool Phineas burned down the house. I told Velleia plainly that she owed you a decent legacy and that she should will the property to you and also leave you whatever money she could. She agreed, and we had Scaurus help her prepare it. She didn't have much money at the time, but she left you what she had, aside from legacies to servants. She willed the property to you and made you executor of the will. Certain works of art from the house were to go to her brother, also her white horses and the slaves she didn't choose to free. Sergia has been left all of Velleia's jewellery and her dog."

"Was the will sent to the Temple of Vesta?"

"No, it's here in my safe. Of course, if she's mentioned it to Velleius, he's probably convinced her to make a new will. He certainly wouldn't be pleased that *you* would get all the money she received from Arrius, in addition to the land itself."

"So I'd better not get my hopes up! For that matter, I certainly don't desire Mother's death – whether I ever inherit from her or not."

I felt somewhat cheered that she was willing to reward my filial devotion, though I couldn't be sure she would've thought much about it if Father hadn't talked bluntly to her.

Then early in February I got a letter from Lollius Velleius informing me that Mother had just died. It happened the very day after Sergia's splendid wedding, which she had managed to attend despite a persistent fever and cough. The funeral would take place on the twelfth day of February, leaving me barely time to get there if I started immediately.

Uncle Velleius' letter went on. "At the last she said something about a new will. Do you know anything about this?"

"Just to be on the safe side," said Father, "I think you and the will should travel by boat – one that clings to the coast in case of storms."

"You think Uncle Velleius would actually have me intercepted on the road to Rome?"

"Well – like so many of us, he has a strong sense of entitlement, especially regarding money and land. He would think that most of his departed sister's possessions should come to him since she was divorced. He's – I would call him *reasonably* honest, but I'm not sure he wouldn't arrange a robbery. Scaurus is in Rome right now; you should get hold of him before you go to see Velleius – even if it means missing the funeral ceremony. It will likely be brief and simple anyway. He certainly won't go for a parade or athletic games in her honour."

I located a boat about to sail that evening. It would skirt the west coast of Italy as far as Ostia, though it might be delayed by storms. Actually the boat belonged to Ben-Hur, but I didn't let that deter me. I willingly paid the fare, and said nothing to the owner. I spent most of the time on deck, retiring to a small cubicle to sleep. I shared it with one of Father's servants who carried my bag and was generally useful.

We had a favourable wind at our back; it was a strong wind but not a stormy one. We felt quite safe and made excellent time, reaching Ostia on an early morning tide after three days at sea. Hastily I rented mounts for us; we got to Rome about the third hour* and went to my brother's house. I changed to the proper black tunic and toga, and sent a note to the house of Decimus Scaurus, asking him to meet me at the mansion of Lollius Velleius. My brother kindly offered to accompany me; he said, "You may need support; Velleius has been giving himself as much credit as possible for saving his sister's estate. He's probably afraid she's left you a decent amount.

"By the way, I heard that the funeral is on for today. Originally it was to be tomorrow, but Velleius' astrologer has determined that today is more auspicious."

Riding in my brother's chair litter, we arrived at Velleius' marble-faced residence with its pillared porch. Scaurus came just behind me. Uncle Velleius greeted us politely enough.

"It's all over except for the funeral feast, such as it is. We didn't feel like heavy refreshment. It was a cold, sad journey to the Temple of Venus Libitina for the cremation. Poor Velleia's ashes are now in the family vault."

So I was not to look on her pale, thin face with coins on her lids and a gold coin between her lips for Charon the ferryman. Nor would I see the death mask and the effigy that might have covered her coffin on the way to the final ceremonies. No chance to speak a

---

*About nine a.m.

last tribute; I'd rather dreaded the task, yet was annoyed that I was being denied my right.

"Naturally I gave the eulogy, as was proper," said Velleius. "I praised her beauty and sweetness of character and lamented that the Gods had given her so little enduring happiness. And I clearly blamed Bibulus and Sanballat for hastening her death. Not to mention that crazy Jew with the odd name."

In the atrium we greeted his wife Lavinia, a plump woman who wiped her eyes from time to time. Sergia Carina, was there also, tall and beautiful, gowned in black. We spoke to her with formal correctness and moved on to her new spouse, Sextus Antonius. Being now a praetor, he was entitled to the senatorial toga with the purple band at the edge, worn over a tunic with a wide vertical stripe, also purple. He was civil, not ostentatiously condescending. After him there were several Velleian cousins whom I didn't know but Barbatus did.

Uncle Velleius said, "Before we proceed to the triclinium, I must ask you, Messala Secundus, if you know anything about a will. Before she breathed her last, Velleia seemed to be trying to say that she'd made a will which was in the care of your father – and that she'd made *you* the executor. That's really ridiculous; she'd made a will right after the divorce, and left most of her money and all of her land to me. Obviously *I* would be the one to take charge if she'd made a further decision. Do you know anything about it? Or was she just wandering in her mind?"

"I have the will here," I said. "Scaurus and my father and three senators who were his close friends witnessed it, along with two freedmen secretaries. It's still sealed, as you can see. I don't know its exact terms."

Father had managed all that while I was out riding with Sergia, not long before the imperial banquet.

"Humph!" Velleius said. "My sister was easily led; she had poor judgement throughout her unfortunate life. Well, let's get the reading over with before we try to eat."

Scaurus opened the will and read it. As he went on, Uncle

Velleius' frown deepened and his cheeks turned somewhat more purple than usual.

Mother had made her choices while she had a modest sum of money to live on and still owned some works of art in a fine well-furnished house with a good view of the sea.

She'd freed her slave Anna. The groom Theron was already free. She'd given them each ten thousand sesterces and had recommended that they look to her brother Lollius Velleius as their patron. She left all her jewellery to her beloved grandniece, Sergia Carina, who was also to have her precious little Maltese dog, Flora.

Uncle Velleius was to have certain works of art from the house, but only two had been salvaged from the fire with minor damage: a bronze wall plate with a scene of military combat, and a marble bust of my maternal grandmother, the mother of Lollius Velleius and my own mother. Both of these were in the hands of experts who were trying to restore them. Uncle Velleius stopped the reading of the will to ask just how much of his newly inherited art work was fit to look at, and I told him.

"A pity you and the fire department couldn't have moved a little faster," he said, glancing at my cane. "Well, Scaurus, get on with the reading, would you?"

He then learned that Mother had left him her white horses and carriage, which had originally been a gift from him. He was also to have all the slaves who hadn't been given their liberty. Four of them! Not a bad legacy.

But then the will went on to state that she was leaving her house and land and all the money not designated for other persons – to her only and well-loved son Marcus Valerius Messala Secundus, who had so splendidly protected her and her property from the perfidy and connivance of her ex-husband Bibulus and the wily Sanballat. She hoped that her last gift to me would make some amends for many years of maternal neglect. She concluded, "I leave him my warmest love."

I felt touched almost to tears but controlled myself. The will also proclaimed me executor of my mother's final testament.

Uncle Velleius exploded. "A fine thing! This is utterly disgusting. It was up to your father to provide for you. He held back some of Velleia's dowry at the time of their divorce so that he could invest it for you. And it certainly wasn't Velleia's fault that you lost your first fortune on a stupid chariot race against some conniving Jew! Velleia's money and land should come to her own people. I'm tempted to take this to court."

Scaurus said, "This will is perfectly in order."

Barbatus said firmly, "It's well-known, probably even to the Emperor himself, that my brother ably defended his mother before Judge Rabirius and proved that Bibulus had only obtained the deed by deceiving the Vestal Virgins. Surely you don't wish all Rome to see you as petty and grasping! Besides, wasn't it up to you to make better arrangements to protect Velleia and her property before you went to Spain?"

"How dare you presume to criticize me? Everyone knows you don't look after your own wife very well. She's become rather notorious for her extravagance and licence. Everyone knows about her fondness for Appius Silanus." Uncle Velleius glared at my brother, who glared back.

"That's all a lie! Nothing but slanderous gossip! And some of it was probably started and circulated by that slimy Sanballat. My wife is blameless."

"You two brothers can't leave this house soon enough for me. I suppose it isn't worth the time and expense to fight this absurd will in court. However, frankly I don't feel like sharing a funeral luncheon with you – or Scaurus either. It will be better for all our digestions if you take your departure now."

Aunt Lavinia tried to say something about manners, but he told her to be silent. "You know nothing about this, Lavinia."

"First – if I might have the deed to my property?" I said politely but resolutely.

"Oh, very well." Uncle Velleius went to his office and quickly came back with the deed. Scowling he held it out to me.

"Here's the damned thing! And here are her bank papers. Bank of Granius – the branch in Rome. Oh, and I suppose those donkeys your father is so kindly boarding go with the estate. I certainly don't want a couple of asses. They're all yours.

"As executor it's up to you to write two drafts for ten thousand sesterces for the maid Anna and the groom Theron."

"Certainly. I'll do that immediately."

I prepared the money drafts for the two ex-slaves, and Velleius' steward handed me the cap of liberty to present to Anna, who still walked stiffly from her fall. Theron was happy to drive for Velleius as a paid employee, and Sergia offered Anna a place.

Velleius was calmer now. He was hungry for the funeral feast and although he didn't want to prolong our stay in his house, he wanted to end the incident with some dignity.

Sergia spoke sadly. "I will certainly miss my aunt. I was happy with her. She valued you, Messala Secundus; she spoke about you with love – and hoped you would marry the right woman some day."

I said thank you, and then we left. I told Barbatus how much I appreciated his coming to my aid. I didn't say that I hadn't expected much of him. I'd thought him over-inclined to take the easy way, giving in to Lepida most of the time and avoiding conflicts with his peers except when very greatly offended. There was more to my brother than I'd once assumed.

We went to the bank of Granius and had Mother's legacy transferred to my own account. I now had more than nine hundred thousand sesterces from her in addition to the large vacant lot with the ruined walls of her villa. I wasn't yet sure what to do with it.

I thought briefly about Sergia. So very beautiful – and she was trying to be gracious. Maybe she was embarrassed by her grandfather's explosion of frustration.

Antonius, her new husband, had barely spoken to me. He looked handsome and important in his senatorial toga – except for his deepening scowl when his wife spoke to me about my mother. Also, just before we left, he seemed displeased because the little dog came into the room and Sergia picked it up and petted it. I don't believe good nature is his strongest characteristic. Or did he suspect that Sergia cared more for the dog than for him?

CHAPTER THIRTY-THREE

WHILE I was in Rome, I saw Sosius and received a few copies of my new book, now ready for the market. Sosius was very pleased with it. He especially liked the dramatic ending in which the rabid revolutionary falls over a high cliff into a raging torrent which carries him away into a rocky gorge full of rough water. While fighting the current, he loses his grip on two heavy bags of gold and rubies, including the royal regalia of Queen Dido. Possibly the great Carthaginian warrior, the anti-hero, survives but without either the riches or the royal talismans that would have inspired others to adopt his cause.

Barbatus, Lepida, and I were invited to dine with a cousin who was interested in buying the property I'd inherited from Mother. He said he'd like to build a large villa by the sea. I said I'd discuss the matter with my father.

I wasn't sure what I wanted to do with Mother's land. If I built on it and tried to live there, Judah Ben-Hur and I would probably keep on glaring across the valley at each other's residence, each of us wishing the other would give up and go away. On the other hand, if I sold it, I must make sure I got enough for it; it was a prime location for a grand villa, something more spacious than the pretty but modest house where Mother had lived for a short time.

I wouldn't consider selling it to Ben-Hur or Sanballat. They would get it over my dead body. I could imagine the Hurs and Simonides enjoying a triumphant conversation, praising their God who had enabled them to possess the land of their enemy. Judging from Iras' reports, as well as my own early memories, that was the way they'd talk.

Father had already given me the deeds to several good houses in Pompeii and Baiae. They were rented to tenants, but I could have chosen one to live in. Yet I dreamed of a well-built villa by the sea, with stables, pasture, a garden, some orange trees, and a grape arbour behind the house, sheltered from the sea spray. And I'd have a boathouse.

Barbatus and I both had some land in Sicily, and I'd been promised some farmland in Italy. In Sicily I'd have large vineyards and considerable pasture, with flocks of sheep feeding on the hills. Unlike some slave owners, my father has thought it best not to keep his workers shackled, whether at work or at rest. Our people have decent quarters and can move around on the property; they have adequate clothing, including coats for the brief times of cold up in the hills at night. Since our working conditions are tolerable and prospects for escapees aren't encouraging, our servants rarely run off. In the hills there are wild men, fugitive slaves, and bands of robbers living mainly in caves. Most farm slaves, if accustomed to a fairly comfortable situation, are willing to stay in their places.

Nevertheless, I'd been wondering if it wouldn't be a good idea for me to go and look at our property in Sicily. But not yet.

In Italy, my brother had a lot of grazing land, which was very profitable. He also had several fields for market gardening, owned a couple of stone quarries and had three blocks of medium-sized rental houses. Father was preparing to sign over to me a farm north of Pompeii, near Nola. I'd have a good vineyard and an orange orchard. It was certainly time I took a look at my possessions.

Father had been depressed thinking of his briefly renewed

friendship with my mother, now gone from us forever. We have tales of the afterlife: the underworld with its sections for the noble and heroic persons that have lived virtuous lives and the dismal place of torment for outstanding evil-doers. People who fall somewhere between those categories don't figure much in the stories at all; maybe they have some kind of existence like wisps of smoke, incapable of understanding or communicating unless, as in the *Odyssey*, they hover close by when black sheep are sacrificed, hoping for a gulp of blood which will give them back a few moments of humanity.

Many of our learned thinkers, including Julius Caesar, believed that death is the absolute end and that we survive only in the memories of our fellow men. Cicero, however, in his essay *On Old Age*, speculated that there might be an afterlife, especially for those who have lived honourably. He said he looked forward to meeting Cato Uticensis in the spirit world. But most wise teachers of my youth smiled indulgently at any mention of Cicero and encouraged us to think realistically.

Barbatus, who'd accompanied me back to Baiae, went with me to look at Mother's land. Already we had had the ruins of the house cleared away. Some salvaged material had been sold: chunks of scrap metal, partly charred wood panels that might be turned to kindling, and pieces of damaged furniture. We'd been willing to send the proceeds of the sale to Mother or to her estate – but now that wasn't necessary. As Uncle Velleius' two works of art had been repaired, I had them sent to him. He sent back no message of thanks, but I know he received them.

Mother's land contained enough space for a large villa and extensive grounds. I'd be able to keep a few horses.

Father said that Quintus Arrius, through an agent, had been making inquiries. He'd even mentioned a million sesterces as a possible offer.

"A starting offer, I assume," said Father. "You could get him to go higher. But do you want to sell to him?"

"No, never! And certainly I don't want Sanballat to have anything to do with the property he tried to take from Mother."

Our cousin wrote that he and his family had purchased a summer home in Antium, nearer to Rome but close to the sea.

Lepida wrote to Barbatus that Antonius had bought a very splendid marble palace near the Tiber and that he and Sergia had given a banquet. Sergia outshone most of the ladies; she was beautiful and proud in a gown of filmy black, relieved by gold and amethyst jewellery. "I wonder if her jewels had belonged to Secundus' mother," Lepida commented.

"There are plenty of fine young women who'd be happy to marry you, brother," said Barbatus. "I could start making discreet inquiries."

He named a young lady of excellent ancestors; she was a ward of the Emperor and had a good dowry. "Not bad looking either," said Barbatus. "But Tiberius might have someone else in mind for her. Indeed he could even be thinking of her for Caligula – if anything went wrong with Junia Claudilla."

There were rumours that Caligula's bride of last summer was undergoing a difficult pregnancy.

Father and Barbatus brought up some other names. There was Terentia, of the Varro family. She was a widow of thirty, with two children, both boys. She was said to be fairly attractive and good-natured, but her boys were spoiled brats who might make a stepfather's life hell.

Rabiria, the widowed daughter of the judge, was well-off and not unattractive, though getting thickset like her sire. She had no children.

Or there was a Sulpicia, whose most favourable attribute was her ancient noble name. My father and brother both had to admit that she was more than ordinarily plain and dull; as a result she was still single though in her late twenties. Though she had a respectable dowry, it wasn't enough to allure any man who had a chance of doing better.

"Let's not think of my marriage right now," I said. "I'm still wearing mourning for Mother. And it's less than a year since I became liberated from Iras."

Barbatus lingered with us in Baiae because he perceived that

Father was failing – too soon out of breath, his fingers shriveled and blue, his voice even weaker and more rasping than it had been last summer when I first came to him. The cold wind which crept into corners of the house wasn't good for him. But most of all, he felt let down after the brief excitement of my mother's visit – just as I did myself. I'd lost Mother after such a short time in the winter sunshine of her affection, and I'd been a fool to dream of Sergia Carina with all her beauty and high spirits. After years of cynicism, I'd been ridiculously susceptible to her flattery, her encouraging smiles, and her increasingly physical demonstrativeness. That final night – if she hadn't been kept busy trying to soothe Mother's cough with hot poultices and warm spiced wine – we probably would have wound up sharing a passionate couch somewhere private. I wondered if she and Antonius were compatible.

One morning early in March began fair with sunshine and bird-song, but was followed by a chilling change in the wind blowing from the sea. Father complained of chest pains, and we summoned a doctor – to no avail. That evening he drew his last painful breath, with Barbatus and me at his bedside. We knew how ill he was, yet had hopes he would be with us longer. I felt alone, despite my brother's efforts to be consoling. The old dog Tarquin howled several times, as if he knew, but finally came to my room and lay down near the door.

We had Father's body prepared by a local undertaker, and then travelled to Rome slowly, escorting the litter bearing our father. Barbatus arranged a suitable funeral. A procession with actors wearing the funeral masks of various ancestors, many of them consuls and victorious generals, including our grandfather, who had been a young supporter of the conspirators Brutus and Cassius, but had later become a loyal friend to Augustus Caesar in his rivalry with Mark Antony. The litter carrying Father was ornate; he was dressed in his senatorial toga but also wore the military ornaments he'd earned. His face was covered with a death mask. In the funeral procession there were professional mourners, some of them trained singers and acrobats.

Barbatus delivered his eulogy in the Forum, reminding Rome of Father's long and honourable service. I was also permitted to speak briefly. I took care to control my tears as I spoke of my great respect for my father and my regret that I'd ever displeased him by unwise choices. In conclusion, I testified to how much my father's wisdom and kindly concern had meant to me in the months I'd been reunited with him. Then we went on to the Campus Martius for the cremation and at last along the Appian Way to the large tomb where most of my family's ashes rest in honour.

The will was brought from the Temple of Vesta, and Barbatus read it before the funeral feast. A large sum had been bequeathed to Tiberius Caesar, our revered Emperor; that was expected. Of course, Barbatus, the eldest son got the greatest share of the estate, but I was given two million sesterces, some additional farmland in southern Italy and in Sicily, several excellent works of art, and many of Father's books. I already had two million sesterces – one from Father while he was alive, a second million composed of my literary award and the money Mother left me. And I had land which would give me a regular income.

Africanus was given his freedom and a substantial sum of money and recommended to my service. I was also to have Nestor, the groom, along with the pair of grey carriage horses and Sheba the black mare, now in foal by one of the Emperor's stallions. Father had purchased her from Barbatus so that he could give her to me. And now Tarquin became officially my dog.

Barbatus said to me, "Now that I'm back in Rome, I hope you'll be occupying the Baiae house for a while. At least keep an eye on it. And if you don't mind, it would be helpful to me if you supervised the agent who looks after the rural property. Philip will stay in Baiae as well, and you can depend on him. I'll come back in the summer, maybe sooner."

CHAPTER THIRTY-FOUR

I T was lonely in the big house. There were the servants, of course, most of them really the property of my brother. And Philip continued to help me with the management of the rental and farm property, even though there was also an agent with specific duties. I talked to Philip frequently. Africanus stayed with me, and we often shared memories of my father. And there was the chief non-human mourner, Tarquin the big old dog. Africanus said that Tarquin had seemed depressed, and uninterested in his food, even when the cook gave him fresh bones. However, he came to me eagerly when I returned from Rome, and followed me about the house and grounds as if afraid of losing me too. I thought inevitably of my early childhood when I wandered around Jerusalem with Argus at my side.

Some of Father's friends called on me to express their sympathy. I served them wine and had conversations with them, glad of the company. Some of them asked what I intended to do about the property I'd inherited from Mother.

One man said casually, "I've heard that Quintus Arrius – you know, that Jew on the hill – might like to buy it."

"I'm not planning to sell at this time. He'll have to find some other place."

A few days later I was walking around the foundations of Mother's villa when two chair litters approached me. One was carrying Eulalius, Sanballat's lawyer, and the other contained Simonides himself. They stopped in front of me, and Eulalius said, "My client Simonides wishes to speak with you – on business."

I could imagine what this confrontation was about. Simonides said, "Some weeks ago I sent a message to your esteemed father. I was acting for Ben-Hur, who was willing to offer you a million sesterces for this property. Did your father inform you of this?"

"Oh, yes, but I don't want to sell, so I don't see any point in discussing it."

"Surely you don't want to live here, right across the valley from a childhood friend who became your enemy – whom you wronged?"

"And naturally he doesn't want me to live here. I suppose I'll spend a lot of my time at my other properties. But Mother left this piece of land to me – as she should, for I worked hard to save it from the clutches of your ally Sanballat. It's my birthright – and I'm not Esau. Thank you all the same."

He looked surprised that I'd heard of Esau. "So you value your birthright! But what if we increased the offer? Say one million, two hundred thousand sesterces? Granted this is a prime location, a very desirable place to build. But it'll be hard for you to find a buyer to better that offer. These days Antium is the preferred area for vacation homes, isn't it?"

I kept my speech slow, my tone ironic. "One million, two hundred thousand sesterces. Coming quite close to what I foolishly lost. But I still refuse your money – or Ben-Hur's money. Tell him there's nothing he can offer that would give me as much satisfaction as the refusing of it.

"I want to build a fine villa here, worthy of my parents' memory. As for the proximity of my old adversary, I imagine I can improve my view in that direction by planting more trees and hedges and building a wall along the ridge which is my property line. And very likely Ben-Hur will adopt somewhat similar measures.

"Now I presume that's all. I don't wish to waste your time."

Simonides and his lawyer didn't linger to argue. They signalled to their litter bearers to take them away. They left me determined to make the new villa as splendid as I could.

Conveniently Barbatus owns a limestone quarry and a small factory for turning out both rough stones and finely finished marble. He willingly supplied my needs – giving me a lot of well-cut stones free of charge, in addition to large blocks of smooth grey marble at a bargain price. He also helped me engage a band of competent workmen. I wondered if he told Lepida how generously he was treating me. She'd always been very practical concerning property, though extravagant in matters of dress and jewellery.

I didn't plan a mansion as large as my brother's but I did enlarge the original foundations. I wanted it to be well-constructed and elegant, attractive from every direction. On the outside it would have dark grey limestone carefully put together by skilled masons. The pillared porches would be of the lighter grey marble; more of this material would be used in the vestibule and the atrium and dining-room – maybe even in some of the sleeping quarters. Common brick would do for the kitchen and service areas.

I'd enlarge the bath, using bright tiles painted with floral designs and pictures of voluptuous sea nymphs rising from foamy waves. With the shutters open, the bathroom windows would provide a view of shining blue water below the cliff.

After conferring with Philip, I bought four of the house servants that Barbatus had found superfluous and had urged Philip to sell. As I'd promised, I'd watch over my brother's house until he came for the summer, but I'd move into the new place when it was finished. Meantime I took a few days off and stayed at the farm north of Pompeii. I enjoyed it; it had a small comfortable villa and fields already green with fruit trees in blossom. A great place for riding.

When I returned I had a landscape expert help me plan the gardens and fountains for my new place. There was already a very small grape arbour; there were even a few orange trees back of the medium-sized hills that faced the sea. I planned to enlarge the grove.

I thought about having a small outdoor pool with a miniature waterfall. Should I hire a sculptor to create a statue of a beautiful girl resembling Thalia, my Goddess of comedy? I kept her statuette on the table by my bed. I decided against putting goldfish and water lilies in the pool.

I took my boat out a lot, sometimes catching a few fish for dinner. Africanus and I often ate at the same table, and sometimes our catch was enough to feed all the servants.

Being sufficiently busy, I was mainly happy. Sometimes I thought about Sergia. She'd seemed to genuinely care for me. My old cynicism concerning love revived. Probably all women – or nearly all – were fickle.

Word came from Rome that Caligula's young wife, Junia Claudilla, had died in premature labour. The baby was born dead. Caligula's display of grief was dramatic; apparently he tore his hair, what there was of it, and made speeches on the cruelty of Fate. Yet it seemed he'd given his bride very little attention while she was alive.

At the end of April I received a message to go and see Cypros at the palace. She'd returned there with her children. Herod was still in Rome.

She greeted me warmly and brought the children in for me to admire. They were all healthy and beautiful, especially the oldest girl, Berenice, who had golden curls.

"I know you're busy creating a lovely house; Agrippina saw it as she drove past. I do hope you will give me a tour."

"Gladly! Any time you're free."

"There's something else I'd very much like you to do if you can – for Herod and me. You see, Tiberius Gemellus and his entourage (servants and tutors) came back with me. Herod's being paid to mentor him and supervise his education, but right now Caligula needs him. He pleaded with Herod to stay and console him: to go to the races with him, go driving with him in the country, and lift his spirits with witty conversation. Meanwhile, could you, would you, work with Gemellus until Herod returns to Misenum? The boy really likes you; he sometimes speaks about the picnic on the island – how you were so interesting to talk to – and how you saved his life."

She looked at me hopefully. "We would pay you, you understand. Herod suggested three thousand sesterces a month for May and June after which he should be here himself. You wouldn't be teaching exactly; Gemellus already has tutors, one for mathematics, and one for history, literature, and rhetoric. Also he has an instructor for manly sports. The trouble is – the boy is terribly nervous and not very good at anything. Frankly, Herod finds it boring to be with him so much.

"If you move soon to your new house, which is nearer the palace, do you think you could come here almost every day and be with him for a little while, checking his homework and trying to stimulate and encourage him all you can? I think you'd be very good at it. I remember when we were children; you were so interesting when you told Judah and me stories from Roman history.

"Oh, that reminds me! Your former wife, the Egyptian, has written to Ben-Hur. She's married again. A merchant named Aeolus, who was her lover when she was about fifteen. He was rejected by Balthazar, so he sailed away in a merchant vessel. Now he's made his fortune – I hope he wasn't a pirate.

"I suppose you won't like this very much, but I've learned that Aeolus wants to acquire a fine house in this area. At least an impressive residential property near enough to Puteoli for business purposes, but something better than a plain tradesman's dwelling. So be warned! They may be here by summer."

"Damn! At least there's nothing they can buy or rent near my new villa, which should be complete enough for me to move in by June. Till then if I wish to stay on site, I'll put up a tent or shack.

"I wonder if they'll be guests of Ben-Hur until they find their own house."

"According to servants' gossip, the Hurs aren't overjoyed at the prospect of Iras' return. It seems that last summer, when she was delirious, she said some things which Lady Miriam has seen fit to tell Judah – for example, Iras raved about deceiving you and prostituting herself to various men, mainly after you'd become extremely poor but a few times before that. Even Caligula was mentioned. She also talked about intercepting letters between you and your father, so that you'd think your whole family had abandoned you.

"Judah was shocked. He'd imagined that she'd played the whore to support you and that you encouraged her in it. Now he's still sorry for Iras, but uncomfortable about the prospect of having her and her new husband as his house guests – maybe for months if they don't find a satisfactory house."

"If I'd ever allowed myself to be supported by her prostitution, I'd have lost forever my right to any rank beyond the lowest order of citizenship. People who sell their bodies or their family members' bodies are removed from the noble and honourable ranks if they're found out. This decree was brought in by Augustus, who condemned his own lusty daughter Julia, and that law has never been changed. Not that it's turned us into a society with impeccable sexual morals!"

"As I recall, you divorced Iras for infidelity."

"Yes. I didn't make public mention of her attempt on my life."

I felt that I shouldn't place all the blame on Iras.

"She was bored and desperate. She was never the housekeeper type and, besides, I really didn't like having her around all the time. She misled me for a while, though I should have been suspicious sooner. I think most of her adultery took place during that last year when we lived in the slums."

She'd told me that she was employed selling jewellery and clothing – positions that never seemed to last, if they'd ever existed at all.

"I hope Ben-Hur finds a place for Iras and Aeolus to live respectably not too near me.

"Now about your proposal that I give some attention to Gemellus – does the Emperor know of this plan?"

"I believe Herod has written him a letter – or will soon do so. The Emperor should understand that Herod needs some free time and that he's performing a valuable service by cheering Caligula up at this crucial point."

Would Herod actually get around to informing the Emperor that I was going to be a substitute mentor to his grandson?

"Herod isn't the only person who needs free time. I want to go on supervising the building of my house, besides sailing my boat and riding Sheba regularly. I wonder if I could take Gemellus for a sail sometimes. I know I could take care of him."

"Of course! And could you go riding with him? He often asks Herod to accompany him on a ride, but Caligula keeps making demands on Herod's time. He really should tactfully explain that he has an obligation to put Gemellus first."

Herod's offer to me was very good, as it should be, since the Emperor was paying him a liberal salary.

I wondered what would come of this new project. I liked Gemellus; I felt sorry for him, a lonely orphan with no one to stand in for a parent. On the one hand, I didn't want to elbow Herod out of his paid position, even though he wasn't giving it his best. On the other hand, everything might fall into place as it should. Herod's Uncle Philip was said to be at death's door; hence a tetrarchy might be opening up for Herod. And if I proved really helpful to the Emperor's grandson, who could say what further opportunities might fall my way?

"All right, Cypros, I can't promise to work wonders, but I'll certainly do all I can. When would you like me to start?"

CHAPTER THIRTY-FIVE

TIBERIUS Gemellus was happy to have me visit him and review his assignments. Nervous at first, he began to relax and express opinions of his own concerning events of history and modern times. His tutor had taught him some rhetoric so that he could deliver artificial little speeches on topics such as 'Should Hannibal Have Attacked Rome?' In a regular Roman class, this could have been a question for a debate. Instead I asked Gemellus questions to bring out his more spontaneous ideas. Incidentally I've always been relieved that Hannibal didn't attack Rome, as I don't think we were ready for him. It was a good thing Quintus Fabius Cunctator (the delayer) kept leading him here and there, tiring and confusing the Carthaginians and their war elephants and frustrating them by never quite joining battle when he was expected to. Fabius bore patiently with criticism from the Senate for his apparently cowardly tactics until Hannibal actually departed with what was left of his weary army. Later, under the brilliant leadership of Scipio Africanus, we embarked with a strong army for Africa and defeated the Carthaginians thoroughly.

I helped Gemellus with geometry problems and was pleased as

the boy relaxed more and more and showed that he could reason logically. It seemed that his regular teachers either bored or intimidated him. He'd lost both his parents when very young, and I learned that he knew of his mother Livilla's execution (carried out privately) for her secret affair with Sejanus, with whom she'd conspired to overthrow and probably kill the Emperor, her uncle, the father of her late husband, Drusus. Gemellus also knew that some of his close relatives, perhaps falsely accused by Sejanus, had been put to death after first being imprisoned on local islands. He realized that he was surrounded by a web of intrigue and that his cousin Caligula, the only surviving male descendant of Augustus Caesar, despised him and would, if he could, wipe him out as readily as he would crush a housefly. He was alone, except for sporadic notice from his grandfather and occasional grandmotherly kindnesses from Lady Antonia, his mother's mother. Lady Antonia had put Rome's welfare first and had exposed Livilla and Sejanus' plot to the Emperor. Gemellus admired her – he knew he was supposed to – yet he also feared her.

I took him for several sails in the Flammifer and joked with him lightheartedly. In addition, I listened to him as he gave me his ideas, and I tried to expand the scope of his mind. It was a responsibility, building up a young lad's confidence and courage, helping him to grow up in a dangerous world in which he might become Emperor – or instead meet an early demise. It would be good for him to laugh more easily, to sharpen his mind with the exercise of wit. I believe we made some progress.

When I wanted to take a good look at my rural property with the orange orchards and the vineyards, I actually – with Cypros' consent – took Gemellus and his entourage of instructors and personal servants with me. We spent five days there, enjoying the country atmosphere and doing a lot of horseback riding. Gemellus was excited and very happy.

Soon I began living in my own house, though the workmen still had some things to do. To give my gardens more privacy, I had some small trees and bushes planted. They were very pretty: Persian lilacs, peach, and plum trees. They all took the transplanting very well, though it would be a few years before they grew big enough for shade and fruit.

At the palace Cypros observed some of our lessons, and a couple of times the two imperial ladies in residence, Antonia and Agrippina, came and watched us. Agrippina even participated. She raised questions about ethics – for example, was it acceptable now and then to break a law for the greater good of the state or for one's own greater good? Some of my own brilliant instructors, famous for their lectures on philosophy, had demonstrated admirable adroitness combined with cool wit as they made us imagine situations in which it was really hard to say what action was the right one. It was evident from their arguments that they favoured whatever was most practical, even if it involved creative lying – or cruelty and injustice.

For example, Julius Caesar, though known for his clemency, had been harsh in subduing the Gauls after he found that reasoning with them didn't work well enough. He enslaved thousands of them, men, women, and children, thereby making a lot of money, which – he could argue – was really for the good of Rome, not so much for his personal indulgences. As an example to discourage further rebellion, he cut off the hands of numerous Gallic warriors, whom he turned loose to beg from their horrified compatriots. This did help bring an end to the fighting in Gaul, which was good for Rome. Interestingly Gemellus declared that Julius Caesar should have found a less cruel solution, though he couldn't say what it would've been.

I gathered there were persons Gemellus would've liked to treat harshly if he ever had the power, and I'm afraid Agrippina recognized that Caligula, her own brother, was at the top of Gemellus' hit list. However, in general the boy had compassion for innocent people and harmless animals, and although I'd been schooled to be somewhat ruthless and ashamed of sentiment, I now thought it best to avoid pushing Gemellus in that direction. On the contrary, he needed to experience real friendships; he needed to feel that, at least with some people, expressions of liking, sympathy, and even love were not necessarily false and self-serving.

I thought of his grandfather, a lonely old man who was rumoured to solace himself with disgusting amusements and who trusted no one in the world. Tiberius had really loved his late wife, Vipsania, whom Augustus Caesar had forced him to divorce, although he loathed and despised the Emperor's widowed daughter, Julia, who was to become his second wife. He did respect Antonia, his brother's widow; she had shown real loyalty by exposing Sejanus and her own daughter, Livilla.

In late May I found two more people sometimes joining my conversations with Gemellus. There was his older sister, Julia Helena, blonde, blue-eyed, with a very pretty face and a very plump figure even, I was told, when she wasn't, as then, pregnant. After her mother's execution, she'd been married off to a knight named Rubellius Blandus, a good-natured fellow of undistinguished background. This was to make sure no one with high ambitions tried to use her to climb to power. Tiberius thought that one Sejanus was enough for a lifetime. Most of the time Julia Helena lived in a country villa with her bucolic husband but, because of her pregnancy, she was allowed to live with Grandmother Antonia where she would have better care from doctors and midwives.

Besides Julia Helena, there was another young lady, Lutatia Catula, a distant cousin of Caligula and Agrippina. About a hundred years ago the Caesar family had needed money and so had given a son to be adopted by the rich Lutatius Catulus. The young man had been a credit to both the Catuli and the Caesares; he had become consul and had written some history. However, he had been eclipsed by two conflicting great men, Gaius Marius and Lucius Cornelius Sulla, and is now chiefly remembered as an aristocratic supporter of the latter.

Young Lutatia had as much blood of the Caesares as Caligula and his sisters. Gemellus was the great-grandson of Augustus' sister Octavia. Tiberius himself was the stepson of the Emperor Augustus, but his mother connived to see that he became Augustus' successor. Lutatia had lived quietly in the country with her father, sharing his love of books and peaceful surroundings, in which respect he was evidently like his noted ancestor. After he died, her mother being already dead, she became a ward of the Emperor.

Naturally I was attracted to her. She was beautiful: tall and rather slender, but very shapely. Her hair was dark golden, tied back simply. Her eyes were a soft brown, nearly hazel, and her cheeks had a healthy rosy colour.

The girls sometimes joined our discussions, though neither of them was aggressive about it. Julia Helena would make laughing or complimentary remarks as she lounged in a hammock set up between the trees in the Emperor's gardens. Lutatia had more ideas about the things we discussed. She loved all tales of the past and sometimes became as absorbed as if Horatius' defence of the Tiber bridge had just happened. She had caught up Gemellus in her enthusiasm, and I'd found myself with two young people who cared very much about Rome's story and spoke of Coriolanus and Cincinnatus as if they were personal acquaintances.

I've seldom been able to resist the temptation to make flippant comments. Even as a boy, I enjoyed word play and absurdities. Although Judah at that time was a cherished comrade whom I would've hated to lose, he was sometimes a disappointment to me when he failed to appreciate my humour and appeared instead worried by my lack of gravity. I was definitely more in my element discussing history with Gemellus and the girls.

Lutatia, in particular, had a quick wit and, though she looked demure, could come up with lightning flashes of repartee. I hadn't enjoyed myself so much since Sergia went out of my life. I had to remind myself not to fall in love with her. She could never become my lover or future wife. I knew that before long, Tiberius Caesar, just like Sergia's practical grandfather, would find her a husband of fortune and distinction, unshadowed by scandal. He wouldn't choose a suitor on the rise, either in politics or the military; he was wary of ambitious men. But he'll choose a fellow with breeding and finesse, someone with a more admirable record than Blandus – or me.

One day we'd been engaged in a combined history class and board game in the peristylum of the Emperor's villa. Julia Helena observed that a man had been watching us for a few moments, then had gone away. She took her lyre and began to play a lively country tune. Lutatia got up from the table, took Gemellus by the hand, and danced off with him, leaping and whirling to the music.

Suddenly Julia Helena put down her lyre and said, "There's that man again!"

Gemellus and Lutatia stopped and everyone looked at the man, standing by a portal. Ye Gods! Judah Ben-Hur! Why?

"Messala, I'd like to speak with you."

I turned to my three young friends. "Carry on. I'll be back to you soon."

We walked a short distance away. He said, "Are you replacing Herod Agrippa as mentor to the Emperor's grandson?"

"It's supposed to be temporary. Herod asked me to take his place until he comes back from Rome. It seems he has special responsibilities right now."

"I know. I've seen him with Caligula in Rome, riding around in Caligula's chariot. While you are here, apparently doing his work."

"Herod's paying me quite well. And I'd rather spend the time with Gemellus and his companions than ride around in Caligula's chariot. Really – wouldn't you?"

He answered carefully, "Unlike Herod, I don't think I could please Caligula by finding the right words. Maybe the Emperor will give you Herod's position, since Herod obviously isn't making the lad his first priority."

"I'm not trying to push Herod out of his place. However, I enjoy what I'm doing."

I knew that I was doing well as Gemellus' mentor and that Herod was too bored with Gemellus to put any enthusiasm into their sessions.

Ben-Hur said, "I wanted to tell you that Iras has returned – with a new husband. At the moment they're occupying the east wing of my villa."

"So who is the fortunate bridegroom, and why have they come here, of all places?"

"His name is Aeolus. He wanted to marry Iras when she was a young girl, but Balthazar refused him, so he went away to sea. Perhaps she told you about him."

"Yes, she did mention him. Aeolus, the God of the Winds. Does his name suit him?"

Ben-Hur looked almost amused. "He talks a lot about his successful rise as a businessman and ship owner. His activities, up to now, have been mainly along the coast of Africa. However, he wants to expand his trade. He's acquired a warehouse in Puteoli, but he's looking for a local residence."

"I hope he finds something soon – and not too near here."

There was now an eight-foot stone wall along the ridge that marked the west boundary of my property. It gave me a better sense of privacy, but my buildings would still be somewhat visible from the elevation of the Arrius villa.

He shrugged his shoulders in apparent resignation. "I may as well warn you. They were immediately attracted to *your* place – what they could see of it. Iras was astonished to hear that it belonged to you and that things had improved so much for you."

"I'm not going to give them a tour. I don't want to see Iras at all. In fact, I might contact the agency that rents out guard patrol dogs along with their handlers."

He looked concerned. "I hope things won't come to a confrontation between my guests and your guard dogs. Iras likes animals but I think she's afraid of dogs."

"She is. She prefers cats."

"I've been trying to make it clear that you don't want to sell – I assume you still don't. You emphatically refused a good offer for the land before you started building a villa. Are you still continuing with it?"

"Yes, definitely!"

"Aeolus, like many newly rich, thinks he can purchase *anything* if he offers enough. So he's gone to your house, determined to see you and – if the house pleases him – to make you a *very* large offer. He can't believe you might refuse it."

"Then he'll be amazed at what I can refuse. I *want* my house and gardens; they aren't completely finished, but it gives me a lot of pleasure to work on them. This is *my* project, and I won't let him spoil it.

"Moreover, he'll have to wait a long time to see me – because right now I'm going fishing. I have all my gear in my boat, and I'm looking forward to a sunny afternoon on the deep blue sea."

"I'll send a messenger to tell him. Otherwise he may waste hours waiting for you. And Iras may be with him. Maybe I can find another place to interest them. A house in Baiae with frontage on the Bay, for example."

He paused, then added, "I don't think Aeolus gives up easily. Especially as Iras has her heart set on the place. She's attracted to the location, and the fine marble walls, and the garden you've started. Only she says she can improve it, given the chance."

"That sounds just like her. And she probably wants to improve Aeolus too."

"They talked of how you might change your mind for several million sesterces – which would enable you to rise politically – as perhaps you would like. Ambition fulfilled after all."

Was he mocking me?

"Listen, Judah, I don't care if they offer me enough to put on spectacular bloody games and bribe the whole Senate into voting me the consulship. Not that they would. But I care about my house; it's *my* land, *my* life – the way I'm putting it back together. I'm enjoying myself for the first time in years, and no one, especially not that infernal slut and her windy spouse, is going to blight my joy. Tell them that. Tell them to leave me alone."

"All right! I'll quote you. Frankly I hope they'll soon find a home some distance away. I wish them well, especially Iras, but I'd rather not have them permanently on my doorstep."

Was he implying that he could think of worse neighbours than me? At least we had no social contact and he could safely trust that I wouldn't come around asking to borrow his gardening equipment or plumbing tools.

We ended our conversation, and I walked back to my little class. We didn't resume any academic studies. I told them we'd get together the following afternoon.

CHAPTER THIRTY-SIX

WHEN I got home, very late in the afternoon, with a fair catch of fish, my steward Achates informed me that Aeolus and Iras had waited three hours in my atrium – which they rather admired – before going back to Ben-Hur's for dinner. He must have explained my feelings clearly enough, for they didn't accost me afterwards. He must have persuaded them to look for another house.

My short conversation with Judah was the first in many years to be unmarked by open bitterness. Yet I didn't delude myself that he wanted friendship. I knew from Cypros that he felt deep anger whenever he remembered his time in the galleys; even more was he outraged at the thought of what his mother and sister had suffered. For that I really can't blame him. I didn't intend them to contract leprosy – if they did. But I did work with my commander, Valerius Gratus, in arranging their imprisonment, and I did receive a reward from my ex-friend's confiscated estate. So he'd exulted at my sufferings in the years after the race, and naturally it must have irked him that I was now doing so much better than anyone had expected.

Cypros' servants had contacts with Ben-Hur's staff. They reported that the Hurs prayed in the names of the Father and the Son who was Jesus of Nazareth. They considered him the Messiah, but they didn't think he was going to return with legions of angels and conquer the world very soon. Apparently the Nazarene, having reappeared after his death, had instructed his followers to take his teachings to all the world. Obviously it might take quite a while to carry out such a command. Indeed, I supposed the task might be even harder if there were no Roman Empire, no well-constructed roads, and no law enforcement to make travel comparatively safe. Maybe Rome won't last forever (nothing ever does), but I think we might endure quite a few years, or even centuries, and if we fail, we won't be replaced by a ruling class of pious Jews but by barbarians – likely hundreds of years of barbarians.

Cypros said Ben-Hur was troubled by the Nazarene's teaching about forgiving others as one hoped to be forgiven by God at the final judgement. To him I was a stumbling block, an impediment to keeping the commandment about loving one's neighbour. His mother and Tirzah had told him that I'd left the scene before they were led away instead of staying there laughing as Judah had recreated the scene in his mind. But this correction hadn't made a significant difference in his feelings. Not very long before I talked to him at the palace, he had commented – as Cypros reported – on my exasperating pride, my cool air of superiority, and my mocking wit. I wasn't inclined to replace these characteristics with humility to make him feel better. So there we were.

Recently Cypros gave me a strange piece of news – that one Saul of Tarsus, a learned Pharisee with Pilate's consent to track down heretics who were a danger to traditional Jewish customs and beliefs, had had a drastic change of mind. After arresting and imprisoning followers of the Nazarene Way, maybe even making use of the cell block once holding the Hur women, he had set out for Damascus to go after heretics there. Yet on the road he'd had a strange vision which had temporarily blinded him, and he had heard Jesus speaking to him and reproaching him. After he'd regained his sight, he began to teach that Jesus was indeed a Divine Being. He infuriated the very

Jews who had looked to him as a potent leader against heresy. Now they hated him as a traitor.

Herod had mentioned Saul back in September. His intense pursuit of Jesus' followers had been Ben-Hur's reason for leaving Jerusalem. I couldn't find a rational explanation for the change in Saul, and I had to admit that Jesus must have been an extraordinary person, gifted with eloquence and perhaps with unusual powers of healing. I'd been in disguise, riding a mule near the entrance of Jerusalem, when Jesus entered and spoke words full of sadness for the city's future. For a moment I could even imagine that his gaze of pity included me and that he saw through my disguise of false beard and Jewish headgear. But that was surely impossible. He couldn't have known that my legs were useless and that a companion was quietly watching over me.

I couldn't think of him as Israel's promised Messiah, whatever that concept might involve, nor could I believe that he was a God, the Son of the unseen God of the Jews. Indeed the whole idea of the Jewish God – the creator of everything, the only real God, yet with an inexplicable preference for the Jews – seemed unfair. If only one God existed, why in the world would he like those people best?

Before Aeolus and Iras could move out of the Arrius mansion, the Hurs had another guest, a young man named Barak Ben Samuel, a new suitor for Tirzah. Cypros' talkative contacts said he was handsome and very nice, and, of course, a follower of Jesus. He and his parents had come to Puteoli from Caesarea and had known Ben-Hur and his family somewhat but not been close to them. Now he was indignant that the person who had caused them so much trouble was daring to live next door. He had to be told very emphatically that it wouldn't be a good idea to approach me and inform me of his low opinion.

The Hur family all liked him; he was welcome to be their guest as long as he remained in the area. He was involved in some kind of trade; Cypros didn't know the details.

Their other guests were rather wearisome; everyone was getting tired of Aeolus' lengthy boasts about his mercantile successes. Iras could be a fascinating conversationalist but she had a tendency to make herself the centre of everything, especially once Aeolus began applying himself to his food and wine and started getting sleepy. She showed some impatience with him, and I imagined that could get worse.

My brother and his family came early to Baiae, and I moved completely into my new place. I invited them to dinner and took pride in showing them around. The new gardens were in vivid bloom, and the view of the waves below the cliff – and the small lagoon formed by the rocky breakwater – gave me particular pleasure since my family were with me to admire it all. Wherever the house was finished, it was nicely furnished. Some of the works of art had been contributed by my brother, who had kept them in storage because Lepida wanted to replace them with the productions of fashionable new artists. Barbatus said he was proud of my taste. "Now what you really need is a suitable wife."

Hopelessly I thought of Lutatia. Had it not been for that damned chariot race, I might have been considered an acceptable candidate for her hand, even though she was descended from a Caesar adopted by a Lutatius Catulus. She was under twenty but not a child. A very intelligent golden beauty – gentle and idealistic, unlike most of the young women, Roman and otherwise, that I'd known. Maybe a little like Tirzah, though physically different and probably more intelligent. Granted that Tirzah's opportunities to develop her mind had been restricted by her situation. Anyway, I could never have married Tirzah even if I'd become a circumcised convert – what a grim thought! But with Lutatia I could share the traditions of our own people; we would revere the same ancient Gods and burn incense to our Lares and Penates.

Then one day I had a visitor – Sergia, carrying her dog Flora. I greeted her and welcomed her to my peristylum. My housekeeper brought us wine and honey cakes while another serving woman willingly took Flora for a walk.

"You have a beautiful home here. I hope you have time to give me a tour."

"I'll be happy to." I passed the cakes to her and poured her wine. "Now tell me about yourself. Are you planning to stay in this area for the summer?"

She hesitated. She was still very beautiful but was evidently quite troubled.

"Antonius has rented a villa close to the town. He'll be going back to Rome part of the time because of his duties as the praetor of the corruption court, but like everyone else in Rome, he wants to relax by the sea during the hot season. Already it's very warm for the beginning of June."

"Well, it's courteous of you to call."

"Messala, it's more than that. I – I think I made a serious mistake, and now I have a problem. I need your help."

"What is it? What can I do for you?" I was tempted to say, "Leave Antonius! Come live with me!" I still felt her attraction. I'd almost forgotten the loveliness of her face, and her figure was certainly enticing. Was her bosom somewhat fuller?

Yet if she was actually offering to leave her husband for me, the scandal, just as I was beginning to be respected by my peers, would be unfortunate. Ten years ago I'd have been arrogant enough to take another man's wife openly. In my grandfather's time Augustus Caesar himself had taken Livia, who was pregnant with her second son by her husband. Augustus and Livia had a long life together; Augustus' final words to her were "Livia, remember our marriage!"

"Last winter I had mixed feelings. I truly cared for you, I knew I would miss you, yet Grandfather was so pleased about arranging the marriage with Antonius. And I thought he was quite attractive. As well as rich and important."

"And now you aren't satisfied? Are you really unhappy with him? Or just bored?" I remembered Antonius as very ambitious and aggressive – but dull.

"He's terribly jealous – especially of you! Someone told him we'd been close, both of us living under one roof for a while. Oh, he's generous with gifts; he's bought me jewels and silks. We have a fine mansion in Rome, and the house here in Misenum is lavishly furnished. In fact he bought up some of Valerius Gratus' household treasures, souvenirs of the East.

"But he has a bad temper, and now he hates my dog because Flora belonged to your mother. Today he got angry and kicked Flora; naturally she turned and bit him. Then he tried to kill her – only I fought him."

She showed me her arm, bruised above the elbow. Then as she pushed back the white scarf from her neck, it was obvious that he'd had his hands on her throat.

"Sergia, don't go back to him! Divorce him!" I was ready to offer her a refuge and risk the scandal.

"The trouble is – I'm carrying his child, though I don't think I show yet. I reminded him of my condition, but I had to scream and strike at him before it got through to him that he was endangering his heir. Then I said I'd find a good home for Flora, but if he killed her, I would definitely leave him. So he let me go and said, 'I'm going out. See that the damned bitch is gone when I return.'"

She hesitated and then added, "He even said he might hand Flora over to the centre for dogs kept to be crucified at the September festival of the Sacred Geese."

This gruesome event commemorates the time, centuries ago, when the Sacred Geese made a horrible noise to warn Rome of the attacking Gauls. The dogs had failed to bark, so thereafter a number of stray dogs were crucified annually at the aforementioned festival. It may sound strange, but the suffering of those pathetic dogs troubles me even though I've been present calmly watching several crucifixions of men, some of them criminals deserving death – and some of them possibly innocent.

"I assume you at least want me to take the dog."

"Yes, please! Aunt Velleia would wish it, I know she would. Please keep her. She's a sweet dog, even if she did bite Antonius."

I was glad she bit him. "Yes, I'll take Flora. As I remember, she got on well with Tarquin. Though I suppose I'll have to keep them apart when Flora's in heat. A little Maltese certainly can't have the puppies of a huge mastiff."

"Of course not. But she can't have any more puppies, anyway. About a year ago Aunt Velleia let her mate, and she had a terrible time birthing her litter. All the little puppies died, and Flora was injured. So the veterinarian reached inside her and did something so that she won't have any more puppies."

She thanked me for agreeing to take Flora. "I brought her dish and basket; they're outside in my litter."

"One thing, Sergia. Flora is used to being a woman's dog. She'll miss you, though I should be able to find a slave woman to fuss over her and groom her like the one who took her out just now. But if I could find her a really good home with a lady, maybe one of Caesar's family, would you mind? Would you feel betrayed?"

She looked not quite pleased, but said, "I'll leave it to your judgement. I've heard that you fill in for Herod Agrippa as mentor for Tiberius Gemellus. I suppose that you meet various female relatives of the Emperor. It's just that Aunt Velleia would want Flora's mistress to love her, and not be someone who might get tired of her and neglect her."

Her voice trembled a little, and she seemed to blink back tears.

"I promise I'll keep that in mind." Already I was thinking of Lutatia's comments on her early pets, all of them evidently cherished until death did them part.

"Sergia, you shouldn't stay with an abusive man." I was strongly tempted to urge her to move in with me and damn the consequences. On the other hand, maybe she didn't care for me so very much. Maybe she just wished to be away from Antonius, safe from his jealous rages. So I advised her in a practical way.

"You could lose your dowry and your good reputation if you went to a lover before getting a divorce, but if you're unhappy and in danger, you could go first to your grandfather or to a female friend."

"I've thought about it. But it's a serious step to take. Antonius may be more reasonable now that I've given Flora away. He's glad about the baby. He's determined it will be a son."

"That's surely in the hands of the Gods – but maybe Antonius has influence in the highest places."

She wanted a tour of my home and gardens; gladly I obliged her and enjoyed her praise of the way I'd enhanced the natural beauty of the ground with the inspired assistance of a landscape gardener.

She said sadly, "I could have been very happy here with you."

"Then stay, darling! To Hades with Antonius!"

She kissed me quickly – at least she may have meant it to be just a quick kiss, but it turned out to be rather lingering. Her perfume had a scent of spice; her warm curves were exciting to hold.

I felt a strong urge to lead her to a couch in the colonnade and satisfy my manhood. But we both hesitated, and then we heard a wailing cry like a woman's voice in the direction of my west boundary wall. We were startled; I don't know which of us made the first move to break away. I knew that although she desired my love-making, she was mindful of her position and reluctant to throw away a grand marriage to the rich and successful man who was the father of her unborn child. A son – maybe.

I wondered about that voice. We couldn't see anyone on the wall, much less on this side of it. Could it have been Iras? She had a husband; she had no right to care if I made love to another woman. The very thought encouraged me to kiss Sergia again.

And then once more we parted.

CHAPTER THIRTY-SEVEN

THE next day Herod Agrippa came back to the palace at Misenum. He called on me and asked if I would please continue to see Gemellus every day.

"I've a lot of special problems and obligations. I trust I'll have more time for the lad when the Emperor leaves Capri to spend time here. Gemellus has been making real progress with you. It's obvious that he likes you."

"I like him and feel sorry for him. He lost both his parents and it seems there's been no male adult to take the place of his father."

"I hear that his sister and distant cousin like to join your classes. You have a reputation as a very interesting teacher."

"They aren't exactly formal classes, but we discuss a lot of useful subjects in addition to going for rides and sailing in my boat."

Herod smiled. "Julia Helena isn't able to go riding these days; it's close to her time. But Lutatia – a real female equestrian! I imagine both you and Gemellus enjoy her company."

I assured him that I admired the young lady. "I presume," I said as casually as I could, "the Emperor will marry her off to either Caligula or Gemellus."

"Caligula doesn't want to marry her," said Herod. "He prefers mature women. Actually he's having an affair with Ennia, Macro's wife – with his tacit consent. He's told Caesar he doesn't want another naïve young creature like Junia Claudilla."

I thought, "Lutatia doesn't like him either, but perhaps I shouldn't tell Herod that. Maybe Cypros will."

Lutatia had said, "Caligula is boring. He keeps talking about how many races he's won – as well as the races he would've won if only he'd had the chance to compete against Achilles or Alexander the Great. He's full of himself – except when he's being obsequious to the Emperor."

Herod said thoughtfully, "Caesar might choose Lutatia for his grandson even though she's four or five years older. Or he might give her to someone with excellent credentials but not too much ambition. Even as he gave his own granddaughter to Blandus."

I didn't let myself hope that Tiberius would think me eligible. However, I joined Gemellus and Lutatia in the early afternoon after the boy had finished his lessons with his other instructors. We had a lively conversation about the problems of an Empire with far-flung restless territories to control.

Afterwards we went for a boat ride then stopped for a while at my new house. When I showed them the little dog, they were both interested, especially Lutatia.

"When I was small, Mother bought me a little Maltese dog. I really loved him. Unfortunately he ran out into a courtyard and was run over by a wagon. I cried a lot; indeed I still feel like crying when I picture it in my mind."

"Little Flora has always belonged to a lady; first my mother, then my cousin Sergia. She seems bewildered in my house, and she isn't much interested in her food so far."

"Messala, I want her – please! I'll take good care of her. She can sleep in my room, and I'll take her for lots of walks."

I asked some questions before giving consent. I learned that she and Julia Helena were living with Lady Antonia and her little granddaughter; I had to be assured that Lady Antonia wouldn't object.

It was also important that the dog not be allowed to run loose around the palace compound. Bad things could happen to a small dog on its own: poisoning, being attacked by a large fierce dog, or being ill-treated by someone with a cruel streak – Caligula, for example. He was kind enough to horses, but he might find it amusing to hurt Lutatia's small pet, especially if she showed her aversion to him. He was known to make advances to women of all ranks when the mood took hold of him.

I told her I thought I should write a brief letter to Lady Antonia asking her approval. But before I could begin to write, there was a loud noise: an angry voice in the vestibule. It was Sextus Antonius, demanding to see me at once.

He barged into my reception room. Lutatia held the dog firmly in her arms, and Gemellus bravely put himself in front of her.

"Give me that damned dog; I'm going to drown it," he snarled.

"No, you aren't, Antonius! Sergia brought the dog to me because it belonged to my mother. Now I've promised to give it to Lutatia Catula, if her guardians are willing. So it isn't your concern."

He glared at us all. "I told Sergia to get rid of the cursed animal; it bit me! But I never supposed she would come to *you* with it. Just an excuse to be with you again! The faithless whore!"

"You stupid imbecile! I should've urged her to leave you. Sergia isn't a whore; on the contrary she's much too good for you."

"She's a slut! She married me for my money and position but never stopped lusting after you – the infernal Gods know why! Mallius' mother is right – Sergia is an ill-omened witch. Mallius died because he thought he couldn't father a child; his male parts were cursed."

"That's superstitious nonsense!"

"Her marriage to Calvus didn't last, did it? He was lucky to get free of her. Then old Gratus wanted her – and now he's dead."

"Sextus Antonius, you're a fool!"

"I hit her as she deserved. I gave her a black eye and some bruises. I'd have done more – but I was afraid she'd lose our son. Surely it will be a son! I deserve a son.

"But now she's threatening to pack up and go to a friend – or to her grandfather again. Or to *you*, though she denies it. You slick bastard! I'm going to knock you back into your cripple's chair, and this time for good!"

He charged at me, his bull-like head lowered, his large hands clenched. Lutatia screamed, "Tarquin, come!"

My past training must have merged with my instincts of self-preservation. I ducked my head sideways just in time, brought up my right knee and quickly kicked out. My sandaled foot connected with the tender area of his crotch; he backed up screaming and clutching his most treasured part. My exercise program for the past year had included kicking a stuffed leather sack suspended from the ceiling. The effort had certainly paid off.

Just then Tarquin rushed in, growling fiercely. Africanus was right behind him.

"I'll kill you, you son of a whore!" shouted Antonius, lunging toward me despite the fact that one of his hands still grasped his reproductive equipment.

"Africanus, show this fellow out while I hold Tarquin!"

Part of me wanted to let Tarquin rip his throat out, thereby making Sergia a widow, but I didn't want a magistrate to order me to have my dog put down.

At that moment a dog handler with his leashed mastiff came to the door. "Are we needed, sir?"

Antonius saw them. At the same time Africanus was approaching him, gesturing toward another door. Antonius backed out of the room, muttering, "You're going to pay for this, Messala!"

Keeping my hold on Tarquin's collar, I watched as Africanus firmly escorted Antonius along a corridor and out of the building. He made sure Antonius got on his horse and left the property.

I'd ordered the servants to prepare light refreshment for Gemellus and Lutatia; now I directed that a substantial afternoon snack should be offered to Africanus and the dog handler. We all relaxed and enjoyed fruit drinks and honey cakes. Lutatia cuddled the little dog as Gemellus asked me questions about the defensive training he was beginning to receive from his physical instructor. He was much impressed by my practical demonstration. But something else troubled him, possibly because, as his substitute mentor, I was supposed to set a good moral example.

"I don't know if it's proper for me to ask you this, sir," he began, blushing. "Did you – did you?"

"If you're wondering – did I lie with the wife of Sextus Antonius, the answer is no. She and I were friends last winter when she was a companion to my mother. Then her grandfather, my maternal uncle, Lollius Velleius, appeared and announced that he'd promised her to Antonius. She seemed willing, so I wished her well and said goodbye. When she called on me recently, we talked, and she felt she might have made a mistake in marrying Antonius. However, we showed proper restraint. I promised to take care of her dog, and she went home to Antonius because he's the father of her unborn child."

Lutatia asked, "Do you love her?"

I answered, "No, not now, though I'm angry at Antonius for abusing her. Last winter I thought I was in love with her. I was disappointed that she went so easily to Antonius, without much of a protest. But now – even if she were free, I don't think I would offer to marry her."

I'm not sure I told her the exact truth. I still hadn't quite sorted out my feelings.

Was I lying?

"For her own sake I hope she gets herself legally released from Antonius!"

CHAPTER THIRTY-EIGHT

I was invited to dinner at my brother's house. I took the grey team and followed the road that goes around the edge of Misenum and then on to Baiae. I avoided the main part of the town because of the daytime restriction on wheeled vehicles. An earth and gravel laneway took me to the back of Barbatus' villa.

I was standing to drive – enjoying it – when I spotted a litter escorted by two horsemen. They were turning off the lane to another residence about two lots away from Barbatus' house. Well, well! It was Ben-Hur on a fine bay horse, a heavy bearded man on a bulkier animal, and Iras in the litter. Ben-Hur obviously saw me; he spoke to the others and they turned to look before proceeding on their way.

Was Ben-Hur taking them to a new house? Were they going to move in there or just look at it and agree to think about it?

I came to Barbatus' residence. My brother welcomed me graciously and led me to the peristylum. Lepida was waiting, eager to talk.

"So your former wife and her husband – or whatever he is – are going to rent the house that belonged to the Balbi family. Their luggage was delivered early this morning, so our steward tells us. They've got a lot of foreign-looking slaves running around making a noise. I suppose you're glad they aren't near you anymore."

"At least they aren't right next to you. I can't imagine that there'll be any occasion to socialize."

"In my opinion this neighbourhood is going downhill. It's really too bad."

Lepida had another topic on her mind. She had heard some exciting gossip – that Antonius had beaten Sergia because she had visited me.

"Whatever have you been up to now, Secundus?"

"Sergia's visit was just to offer me her dog to protect it from Antonius. We didn't have sexual intercourse."

Maybe we should have made love. It seemed that everyone was assuming we that had.

"Antonius didn't believe her. They say he went to see you, and the two of you got into a fight – and you – *damaged* him – at least temporarily – by kicking him in the groin. Everyone is remarking on how well you've recovered the use of your legs."

"What about Sergia? Is she still with Antonius, putting up with his rotten temper?"

"No, she's left him. Serves him right! When he got back to his villa – a very elegant rented place where Valerius Gratus had planned to live – he found Sergia and her maid gone. The two women, and Sergia's favourite horse, had all got on a boat going round the peninsula to Capua, where her grandfather has a place. Then, when she got there, she miscarried."

"I hope she isn't injured."

"I think she's all right. But she wouldn't have liked to hand her baby over to Antonius. It's the law, you know. I hear she wrote Antonius a short letter saying, 'I lost the baby, and it's all your fault! I'm divorcing you and I never want to see you again. Don't try to find me; I'm going to stay with some friends but I'm not telling you where. Only that I'm not moving in with Messala, so don't waste your time bothering him.'

"Antonius went to Capua and talked to Velleius and his wife, but they wouldn't tell him how to find her. Velleius had witnessed her signing the divorce paper, and he badgered Antonius about returning her dowry. Antonius raged that he wouldn't give back *anything*, not a damned denarius! He's gone back to Rome because of his duties, but he's kept the vacation house in Misenum, so you might run into him again. In other words, be careful!"

I often thought about Sergia, but I reminded myself that she wasn't trying to communicate with me. Perhaps she was hoping for an entirely new life.

Then in late June I was astonished to read a public notice of the boat races to take place in July. What shocked me was the sight of my own name as one of the contestants in the last of the small sailboat races. There were seven other names, two of which I recognized. One was my old fellow soldier Metellus Calvus. Well, I knew he'd raced boats in the summer long ago, though never against me. At the time I was obsessed with chariot-racing.

The other familiar name was Sextus Antonius. I'd heard that he'd raced a sailboat at least once. He was supposed to be in Rome most of the time because he was a praetor, but he evidently planned to be here with his boat whenever he could. Why was *my* name on that list? I certainly hadn't submitted it.

Long ago Father had taken Judah and me with him to the Galilee area, and there I'd learned a little about sailing a boat with my friend as crew. We'd almost been overturned during a sudden gale on the Sea of Galilee. Since that summer I hadn't sailed a boat until a year ago when Africanus began giving me lessons. I'd enjoyed taking the Flammifer out over the waves whenever the winds permitted. I'd fished frequently and had my catch served at the dinner table. However, I'd never attempted to prepare for a race, though I practised turns where markers had been placed for shipping in the bay.

The Ludi Apollinares* would take place soon, and here in Misenum the games included boat races, probably to be judged by Tiberius Caesar. I went to see Herod, hoping for information.

He was evasive. "How strange! I thought *you* had entered your name. Are you sure you didn't tell a servant to take your name to the office for the entries?"

---

* Games in honour of Apollo

"My memory isn't faulty, Herod! I know I didn't intend to be in the race. I assumed *all* my racing days were over."

Just then, to Herod's apparent irritation, Gemellus spoke up.

"Caligula did it, two days ago. Lutatia and I saw him. He and Antonius were laughing as he put your name up on the wall. They thought it was a big joke."

Very funny!

"Are you going to withdraw your name?" said Herod. "You can, of course. But Antonius will say you're afraid of him. He probably regards the boat race as his chance for vengeance. Everyone has heard that his wife left him after less than six months of marriage – because of you."

"Hades and Tartarus! I didn't steal his wife! I never went to bed with Sergia. She left him because he struck her – more than once, I understand. I take it, Herod, that you *knew* what Caligula and Antonius were doing. You should've warned me. I need all the time I can get to make ready for this contest."

"Don't you have *any* professional training? Then you should back out. Boat races aren't as dangerous as chariot races, but there have been accidents – and *apparent* accidents. A few contestants have been seriously injured – and Caligula said someone drowned last year."

"I won't back out. Not even my bitterest enemy can call me a coward. No, Herod, I'll practise and do my best – and if I don't win, I'll be prepared to congratulate the winner graciously. You believe I can do that at least?"

"On the contrary! I feel sure you can give a magnificent display of sportsmanship – if it proves necessary. I say, wouldn't it be amusing if Sanballat bet against you and lost?"

"It won't matter much to me because I'm not hazarding any money on this race. I do learn from experience. However, I'll try to win. And now, if you'll excuse me, I'm going to sail my boat for a while."

"Can't I come?" asked Gemellus. Herod didn't like to spend time with the boy; he was glad to have me relieve him even though he was perhaps displeased that I'd done so well with Gemellus. He may have feared that the Emperor would give his position to me and not compensate him with any other high office.

As we were approaching my boat, Lutatia appeared.

"Won't you take me too?" she asked.

She was lovely – a young Venus before Jupiter bestowed her on his lame son, Vulcan. Naturally I welcomed her.

Gemellus lost no time in telling her that I'd been trapped into racing my boat against an angry enemy. Lutatia joined Gemellus in indignation at Caligula's love of mischief. They both wondered how good my competitors were. I said I thought Calvus was very good and possibly Antonius also but that I knew nothing about the other contestants.

"I'll just keep practising till the great day and then go ahead and amuse Caligula – or not, the Gods willing!"

They enjoyed sailing with me around the various markers in the harbour. As I concentrated on completing every tricky turn without loss of speed, I couldn't help remembering the days when the great challenge was guiding my team around the sharp turns of the spina* in the circus. At least a boat doesn't have wheels to come off!

Another thought came to me. I'd better see that my boat was always well-guarded in case someone had the idea of drilling a hole in it and filling it with a substance that would dissolve in water. Caligula might think that was a truly hilarious joke.

I asked Lutatia about her dog. She said, "Flora definitely likes me, and Lady Antonia says she's glad I have a pet. Flora and I had a long walk just now."

They wanted to see how my place was coming along, so we went there, entered the gate into the garden, and strolled around. By this time the pool and waterfall had been completed. Near them were huge yellow lilies and beds of smaller flowers in a variety of warm colours. Sometime I might have rosebushes, but they weren't among my priorities, perhaps because Judah's rose gardens were famous.

We all remarked that, for some reason, we felt we were being watched. The guard dogs patrolled at night, but rested during the

---

*The wedge-shaped divider in the centre of the circus

day. Their handlers were probably taking a break at the nearest tavern. My servants would be available if I rang for them. But neither they nor the dog handlers impressed me as the prying sort.

I saw a shadow, as if someone were up on the west wall, with the sun lowering in the background. But surely it couldn't be Iras – could it?

"I should take you back home in time for dinner," I said to Gemellus and Lutatia.

We sailed cheerfully in the Flammifer, singing a song proposed by Gemellus – a boat song slightly rowdy but still decent enough for Lutatia's maiden ears and voice. In no time we landed at the Emperor's dock. I said goodbye to them and watched as they hurried to the palace.

Soon I'd be skimming home across the water, sped by the late afternoon breeze. I was just turning to go when I heard Macro's voice calling my name. Ben-Hur was by his side. Whatever did they want with me?

CHAPTER THIRTY-NINE

MACRO began, "Were you married to an Egyptian woman named Iras?"

"I was, but I divorced her over a year ago. She went back to Egypt. I've been told that she's remarried and returned here. Why are you asking me about her?"

Ben-Hur attempted to explain. "Iras' husband, Aeolus, has been accused of piracy, and Macro is wondering if Iras is involved in his criminal activities. I've been explaining that I don't believe she's done anything wrong and that if Aeolus has been a pirate, Iras herself is a victim, deceived into trusting a man she hadn't seen since they were very young."

Macro said gruffly, "Arrius here is the executor of her father's estate; he's trying to protect the woman and her inherited property. Naturally, if Aeolus is convicted, all his wealth is forfeited to the Emperor. Now what can *you* tell me about the woman's character? You divorced her for infidelity, didn't you?"

I could have condemned Iras as a creature capable of anything. For all I knew she had willingly taken up with a pirate. But did I really want to be so vindictive?

I said, "She wasn't a faithful wife to me. For a number of reasons, we were both miserable. Then, after her father's death, she inherited a very good dowry, which was in the care of Arrius until she could be located. Back home in Alexandria she would have had opportunities to marry a decent citizen and enjoy an honourable life. I can't believe she'd be so foolish as to knowingly take up with a criminal."

Macro commented, "Then you don't think we're making a mistake in allowing the woman to stay in the house of Quintus Arrius instead of in prison? Naturally she'll have to be available to appear in court once we catch Aeolus."

"You haven't caught him yet?"

"We had him in custody, but some of his crew helped him break free. They didn't leave in his own ship, which we are holding. But they may have stolen another vessel. Or set out across country toward another port. Maybe Brundisium.

"In any case I think the woman should be kept in a secure place where she'll be unable to contact Aeolus and his thugs."

Macro was assuming the fellow was guilty, but maybe he had enough evidence.

"How did you find out about his piracy?"

"A couple of men from Puteoli declared they recognized him from a few years back when their ship was attacked off the African coast. But more than that – the woman Iras came to us and accused her husband and his mistress. She'd caught them together, and she'd heard them talking about his activities. Laodice, a well-known prostitute in Puteoli, had originally come from New Carthage. When Aeolus met her again in Italy, they picked up their old relationship."

"So Iras turned them in?" That did seem like her.

"Aeolus' mistress escaped along with him and his men," Ben-Hur said. "For the present Iras is back in my house."

He didn't look pleased about it.

Macro said, "Maybe you'd like to take charge of her, Messala. You live alone now, don't you?"

My face may have revealed the shiver of horror I felt at the prospect of cohabiting with Iras.

"No, Macro, absolutely no! I was just thinking how pleasant it is to have my own quiet house with a small efficient staff – and my dog and horses. Sometime I should marry for the sake of my line – a lady acceptable to my family. As for Iras, I hope she gets free of all charges and can return to her ancestral property in Alexandria. But I don't want to see her at all."

Judah knew better than to urge me to change my mind. He'd do his best for her.

A couple of days later I heard that Julia Helena had had her baby: a girl whom they named Rubellia Blandina, the feminine forms of her father's name. Blandus took them back to his rural retreat, once his wife was able to travel. Julia seemed contented with her spouse, who was a good-natured country fellow. As a very young girl she'd been briefly married to Caligula's older brother, Nero, whom the Emperor had imprisoned and finally killed because he was suspected of disloyal ambition aimed at the throne of power. She preferred her present position: safe and comfortable if not prestigious.

Soon after that, I had a surprise visitor: the Emperor himself! He said he'd heard about my new villa and wanted to see it. The building of picturesque villas was one of his hobbies. He'd built twelve villas on Capri in honour of the twelve major Gods.

Of course I took him on a tour with his Praetorian Guard escorts following at a discreet distance. I valued his comments and suggestions as he was an expert builder and possessed undeniable taste. After he'd viewed everything, I offered him some light refreshments: wine and cakes. I was glad that my cook had baked them fresh that very morning.

After I'd congratulated Tiberius Caesar on his new great-grand-child, he said, "I want to talk about Gemellus. I've learned that you've been filling in for Herod and doing very well. I've questioned the boy about his studies, and it seems to me he's learning to express himself with more confidence. I know Herod may deserve some credit too, yet the improvement in Gemellus is more apparent now than it was when I saw him in the winter. It appears you've been a good influence."

I thanked him for his favourable opinion. Then he said thought-fully, "I may give Herod authority in his homeland some day soon; he seems loyal to Rome. And now his Uncle Philip is dead, leaving his tetrarchy vacant. Herod owes us a lot, including a Roman educa-tion. But I'd like to be surer of him before sending him back to rule as a little king.

"I'd like him to prove himself by paying attention to what I've paid him for – which is *not* sucking up to my nephew, who might succeed me if the Gods don't choose to let me hang on till my grandson grows up.

"I'm being frank with you; I don't care if you discuss it with Herod. I don't want to humiliate him but I do want to observe his work closely while I'm staying in Misenum for the rest of the summer. Accordingly *your* arrangement with him is terminated."

This came as a shock, but I think I responded calmly.

"Caesar, it's been a pleasure to work with Tiberius Gemellus. However I can find plenty to occupy me: checking up on my farm property, putting some finishing touches on my house and grounds, and sailing my boat."

"Yes, I hear that you're participating in a sailing race, like some of the Trojans in the Aeneid – except that they were working in pairs and I believe you are making the attempt solo."

I said yes, remembering that Tiberius Caesar was known for his fondness for referring to the classics.

"Gemellus and Lutatia tell me that you didn't choose to enter the race, that Caligula posted your name as a joke. Some joke! You'd be called a coward if you backed out now, particularly since one of your rivals is a jealous husband. I advise you to be very careful."

I felt he meant not only that I should be wary of foul play from Antonius but also that I should avoid any self-protective action that might reflect on my Roman honour. He knew about the chariot race and might even have guessed that his neighbour, Quintus Arrius, an ex-galley slave adopted by a Roman hero, was also the Jewish chario-teer Ben-Hur. Maybe in his shrewd way he was watching both of us.

"I've been reviewing your past career – as well as reading your second book with amusement. It's possible that I may find appropriate duties for you. I'm not ready to make a statement right now."

I thanked him for his interest in my future and assured him that I'd be willing to serve anywhere he chose.

He said, "Your brother tells me you have some Sicilian land which I suppose you'll want to take a look at sometime. Don't rush into any commitments; I may be in touch with you again."

So he'd been discussing me with Barbatus! There might be cause to hope for an honourable assignment, but with Tiberius Caesar one could never be sure. His mind could change quickly.

The next morning I woke thinking that Sheba might have her foal soon. She'd been bred to one of the Emperor's stallions. I was starting toward the barn when I heard my name called from the direction of the gate facing the beach below. A chillingly familiar voice: Iras!

I walked toward the gate, glad it was locked. This woman had tried to kill me just a little more than a year ago.

"Please come and open this gate! Let me in!"

I stopped and stayed still, about two paces from the locked gate.

"Messala, I don't want to harm you. I want you to take a good look at me and try to forgive the past."

She certainly looked better than when I'd last seen her at close range. Her black hair was trimmed to her shoulders and was neatly arranged with a straight bang on the forehead. I wondered if she'd used a hair dye to get rid of the grey. She wore a thin white gown and her bosom was emphasized by a gold and jade pendant, probably one of the ancestral treasures I'd returned to her.

"Listen, I was wrong to trust Aeolus. He promised my jewels to a whore. I followed him and heard him. So I accused him to Macro. And now they're pursuing him."

I wondered if she knew about his piratical career before she discovered him with his lover.

She continued, "I hope they catch him and send him to the lions in the arena. I'd enjoy watching a lion tear his guts out. Meanwhile I borrowed the gardener's donkey early this morning and rode down the beach to see you."

She was standing on the stairs leading down to the beach, where a donkey was patiently waiting for her.

"If they catch him, you'll soon be a widow. In time you may make a better marriage."

No doubt the tolerant patronage I was expressing was irritating to her.

"You're thinking I might take up with some mediocre tradesman who might marry me for what's left of my money – but *you* don't want me. And none of Judah's associates – mostly followers of the Nazarene Way – would approach me with an honourable offer. I believe Tirzah's new fiancé considers me a fallen woman.

"When I left Father to be with you, I had high hopes – which were cruelly dashed by circumstances – and the dishonesty of Sanballat. If I'd received my inheritance then, our marriage might have been saved. Just think about it!"

"I don't want to think about it, Iras. Every day when I wake, I feel a great wave of thankfulness to whatever higher power has brought me to my current situation."

As I spoke, I could see Tarquin coming across the lawn to my side. He didn't bark at Iras but sat down without being told. Yet he'd come, ready to defend me. The guard dogs were probably resting after their night patrol.

"But you aren't doing without women, are you? They say you've been running around with another man's wife. In fact I saw you with her – the shameless creature! You two were *kissing*. And now you're getting involved with a blonde doll whose guardian is Caesar himself."

I was taken aback by her accusations.

"I haven't been running around with a married woman. I presume you're speaking of my cousin Sergia, whom I might have married last winter if she hadn't chosen Sextus Antonius. There's been no affair, but she's left Antonius because he's a jealous, abusive brute!

"And I'm not *involved* with Caesar's ward either."

"I got on a ladder and observed you from that wall over there. I saw the way the silly girl looks at you, as if you were the man of her dreams. As for the married whore, Sanballat told Simonides about her, going on gleefully about how jealous the woman's husband is – boasting of how he's going to humiliate you in that boat race. Whatever were you thinking?"

"I didn't submit my name for the boat race. I'm told Antonius and Caligula planned that together. But I can't back out without appearing a coward. So I'm just going to do my best – and you and your friends can cheer if I lose."

"I don't want you to lose. But I wish you'd think about giving us another chance. You must realize that you don't have a reasonable hope with that foolish blonde girl. It's obvious the little bitch is leading you on. But believe me, she's beyond your reach – at least where marriage is concerned. And you could be ruined; you *would* be ruined if you were caught in bed with her."

"Do you suppose I don't know that? I'm fond of Lutatia; I admire her and I could easily fall in love with her. But I'm not going to be carried away by reckless passion – for her or for Sergia Carina. I'm being very careful, very restrained. And sometime I'll probably marry a pleasant lady from an honourable family. Barbatus has been thinking of a few possibilities."

"You and I had good times at first. I could still be a good wife to you. We could live in this beautiful villa – that even the Emperor seems to admire. With my taste, we could make our home a show-place the Hurs would envy. And I do believe Ben-Hur could become your friend again if you wished."

"But we *don't* wish it; he doesn't and I don't."

"Well, anyway, we could keep expanding those gardens of yours; we could make them spectacular. Oh, just think of it! It would be the life I used to dream of – at last!"

"No, Iras! Find something else to dream of. Because your dream is my nightmare. I don't want to live with you and I don't want to lie with you. I have horrible memories of our life together. Now please just go."

She glared at me. "You ought to take me back. After all I did for you – when you were a disgraced, impoverished cripple! I could've found a man of wealth and position to keep me and maybe even marry me. Did you know that Calvus once offered? But I stayed with you! Fool that I was!"

"So don't be a fool again! Try for some dignity!"

"I could give you pleasure as I used to – unless you've become permanently impotent. Maybe that's why you're able to use restraint. All right, I won't throw myself at you. In fact I despise you. I don't know why I let myself indulge a delusion about you and your manly potential, supposedly restored along with your legs.

"It's a real pity I ever let go of Judah Ben-Hur. His wife is sickeningly sweet and pretty. She's also dull and domestic, but he dotes on her. His mother, and his stupid, insipid sister love her too. They pity me; I can't stand much more of it."

"Then go back to Egypt as soon as you can. You've money, don't you? Ben-Hur might even give you a generous present to get rid of you. Enlarge your rose garden in Egypt. Start a new life. Without Ben-Hur and without me! Think about what your father would wish for you."

"My father! He wouldn't understand me. He never did. And now he'd be ashamed of me."

I turned partly away from her, looking toward the horse barn.

"I don't have time to discuss your problems further, Iras. Get on your ass down there and ride back to the Hurs for breakfast. I expect my favourite mare to foal today, and I want to be there for her. Vale!"

As I walked away from the gate where she was still standing, she shouted at me, "You cold, heartless bastard!"

CHAPTER FORTY

I sent a messenger for the veterinarian. It would be Sheba's first foal, so naturally I was anxious. She'd been bred for the first time just before I came to Baiae.

I couldn't help thinking of Iras' troubled outburst. As she spoke about Ben-Hur's wife, her face hardened and her mouth twisted. The effect was to erase the moderate good looks she'd regained over the past year. Her dark green eyes had blazed with bitterness, even as they had filled with tears. She really needed to get away from the Hurs – and of course from me.

When the veterinarian came, Nestor and I assisted him. My principal task was to hold Sheba's head and speak comforting words to her, such as 'Good girl.'

Without very much trouble, she produced her colt, a little black male with a small white star on its forehead. Nestor and the veterinarian both remarked on it, mentioning that the Arabian horses of Quintus Arrius had star names. That I knew well. His winning team were all named for stars. The swiftest, Aldebaran, had been a reward from the Sheik. I certainly wouldn't want to duplicate the names of his horses. I turned my thoughts to Roman and Greek legends, but nothing seemed right.

Then in the evening we looked at the sky and observed a star that, although usually obscured or even invisible, was just then shining brightly. Algol, the demon star, the ill-omened, according to eastern legend. It's said that the demons amuse themselves by turning its light on and off, however that may be done. I don't really believe it. If there are demons, as most eastern people believe, they surely have enough mischief to do here on earth without playing silly games with a star.

But what if I defiantly named my new horse after the demon star? No easterner would risk such bad luck; I'd probably never see another horse named Algol. But how appropriate the name was – a star that disappeared into darkness, then came back bright and triumphant. Yes, little horse, Algol it will be!

A few days later I noticed that there were decorations, including a canopy, on the platform in the Arrius garden. No doubt they'd chosen the elevated area because it gave a wide and splendid view of the sea and mountains as well as of their own garden, which I'd heard many people praise, though I'd not seen it myself. I could see the canopy and what might be ornaments, so I took my boat in a little closer than usual to try out the turn around a marker.

Impelled by curiosity, I sailed to the palace dock and made a morning call on the Herods. They were both present; they offered me wine and told me that Ben-Hur was about to have a party, a wedding or maybe just a betrothal uniting Tirzah and Barak Ben Samuel. They said he was handsome, affluent – and a new convert to the Way of Jesus the Nazarene. Barak was of Jewish origin, of course. But to the Herods, and probably to the majority of Jews in Judaea, the young man was another brother gone wrong.

I pictured Tirzah in a white gown and light veil. Her black curls would hang to her waist, as was proper for a maiden. I didn't stay on Herod's balcony even for a distant glimpse of her, but I wished her happiness and was glad she'd recovered from whatever dreadful sickness had appeared to be leprosy.

I returned to the Flammifer and practised taking it around the markers in the harbour, then sailed out quite a long distance, keeping far enough from shore to shut out the joyful music from the Hur family celebrations. Returning home, I went to the barn and admired my horses, especially the new foal.

The same day I received a message from my brother. He urged me to join him next day at the Games in honour of Apollo; he'd arranged for me to be admitted to the senatorial section as a member of his family. The boat races were still two days away. With Barbatus, Lepida, and an eager Messalina, I watched the gladiatorial contests and animal shows, including several executions of felons by wild beasts. There was a rough fellow I recognized from my Subura days. He was torn by attack dogs, very large mastiffs. Remembering him as a bully who habitually extorted money from his neighbours, I didn't feel sorry for him, though I turned my eyes aside as the dogs mangled him.

We heard a rumour that Aeolus and several companions had been captured and would probably be put to death, but not today.

"What a pity!" said Lepida. "I would've enjoyed seeing his execution. And I suppose that Iras creature will get off completely."

"She turned him in to Macro," I said. "That would certainly count in her favour."

To my surprise, at the end of the Games, Barbatus and I were summoned before the Emperor himself. The ladies had just left the imperial box.

"Messala Secundus," Tiberius began, "are you attracted to my ward Lutatia Catula?"

I was startled, wondering what could be coming next.

"Of course I'm attracted to her, Caesar. She's intelligent as well as beautiful. And she's very gentle in her behaviour to Tiberius Gemellus. I could certainly be in love with her, but I'm aware that you surely have great plans for her."

He smiled wryly. "I believe she's all you say. It's really a pity she and Gemellus aren't of an age. If he were three or four years older, I might marry them to each other."

"She has several possible suitors," he continued. "I'm trying to make up my mind. She doesn't like Caligula, and he says she isn't his type either."

"I've had another offer for her – which upset her as soon as I mentioned it. It was from Sextus Antonius, now divorced from your cousin Sergia Carina."

My horror must have been apparent, though I was silent. Tiberius was watching me curiously.

"Lutatia complained to me that Antonius had beaten Sergia and that she'd heard him tell you about it. She witnessed the fight between you. Apparently it was all about his hatred of Sergia's dog, which you gave Lutatia after Sergia brought it to you. Lutatia declared, 'I wouldn't be able to keep the dog if I had to have Antonius as a husband. I'd much rather have the dog!'"

I commented, "Dog or no dog, he'd find some reason to abuse his wife. Of course if Lutatia *must* be married to Antonius, I'll take Mother's dog back. But I despise the man and pity any woman he marries."

Barbatus spoke hesitantly. "Caesar, my brother has a good income from his property and over three million sesterces. Granted, his early career got off to a deplorable start, but he has considerable promise now that he's back on his feet."

Barbatus is a good brother. It helps that he is related to the Emperor through his mother.

Tiberius asked, "Messala Secundus, do I understand that you are making an honourable offer of marriage for Lutatia?"

"Yes, Caesar, I am," I said firmly. "It may well be that you could do better for her, finding her a husband who has led armies with distinction and served in high public office. But this I promise – she'd have my loyal devotion as well as my love and admiration. If she wished to be my wife, I'd go to great lengths to make her happy."

How I wished *I* could say that I'd led legions to victory and had risen through the traditional course of honour to the consulship! The Emperor's three grandnieces had husbands of senatorial rank; Ahenobarbus was now a glum drunk, but he'd once been consul; Cassius and Vinicius all had honourable positions.

"I admit the girl likes you. She wasn't compelled to share Gemellus' classes, yet she insisted on joining him for your Socratic discussions.

I understand that you were never alone with her. Gemellus or his sister or Princess Cypros was always present."

"And occasionally the ladies Antonia and Agrippina."

"So your words and actions have never crossed the line. But you think you're in love with her. And she admires you, more than any other man who has approached me. You may as well know that she has said this to me."

"I'm greatly honoured." Was it possible that Lutatia had dared attempt to persuade the Emperor? Yes, she didn't lack audacity.

"All this was brought to my attention recently. You should know that yesterday afternoon your former wife, Iras, the Egyptian, managed to enter the palace complex; she slipped away from a party in Arrius' garden and followed some servants through my gates. The guards never should have admitted her, but they say she disguised herself convincingly. Then she unveiled herself and confronted Lutatia in a rose garden. Her language was offensive; Princess Cypros heard her and summoned guards to remove the stupid woman. She'd insulted and belittled Lutatia, who evidently held her own very well. According to the Egyptian, my ward lacks the maturity and intellect to hold your affections – unlike herself, I suppose. She tried to tell Lutatia that all you could want from her was a roll or two in bed."

Was I never to be rid of Iras?

Tiberius went on, "I gather the woman is still staying with Quntius Arrius, to whom I've written, telling him how thoroughly offended I am by that bold creature's invasion of my property and her insults to my ward. I've warned Arrius to control the miserable female and to get her far away from you to some place where perhaps she can regain her sanity. Either Pandateria or Rhegium would be suitable."

The grim island Pandateria and later the southern town of Rhegium had been prisons for Julia, Tiberius' licentious wife, the daughter of Augustus Caesar. Her father had ordered her imprisonment. When Tiberius succeeded his father-in-law, he didn't let her go free. She died in Rhegium.

"I take for granted you don't want to take the Egyptian back. Arrius might be grateful if you did."

"I doubt it! But even if he were, it wouldn't be an inducement for me to trap myself once more in a wretched alliance which nearly cost me my life."

"Of course not. One more thing. The pirate Aeolus and some of his comrades have been captured. They're to be executed in public view – by crucifixion along the road just above the town: the road where both you and Arrius live. I've mentioned this in my letter to Arrius.

"I'll consider your offer – and your future. I'll be speaking to you again soon, Messala Secundus. Meanwhile – may good luck attend your sails!"

CHAPTER FORTY-ONE

I went to my brother's place for dinner after the Games. I was angry at Iras for calling attention to herself – actually trespassing on the Emperor's estate and insulting his ward. How long was she going to make trouble for me and for others? Ben-Hur would be embarrassed by the Emperor's letter warning him to do something about Iras. Next day I awoke still troubled.

I considered talking to Ben-Hur, much as I didn't like to. Accordingly, I summoned my courage and drove my grey team to his house. It was the first time I'd approached it in the daytime. It was a large and well-built villa of rose-coloured brick festooned with climbing vines. The vestibule and atrium were lined with gleaming white marble tiles.

I could hear sounds of music and laughter. Of course! It was Tirzah's betrothal or maybe wedding celebration. Guests who had come from a distance would expect several days of festivities, as is usual in Judaea and other eastern countries.

I was shown into Ben-Hur's office. He greeted me and invited me to be seated.

"I presume you're here about Iras' recent behaviour. The Emperor has written to me; has he contacted you too?"

"Yes, he summoned me in person after the Games yesterday. He wanted to know about my conduct and my intentions toward his ward Lutatia Catula. Iras had accused me of wanting to seduce the young lady. I think he's now assured that I was completely honourable. But is there anything – short of murder or incarceration – that can be done with Iras?"

"Caesar has urged me to find a safe place for her where she won't cause any more trouble. He even offered to let me use the prison facilities on Pandateria. I don't want to do that, but I've warned her that it's been suggested. I think I should make her return to Egypt – as soon as the execution of Aeolus is over. As you may have noticed, right now they're marching the condemned men with their crosses to their assigned stations along the road."

"I saw them on my way here. They'll probably be left on the crosses until after the boat races."

"I haven't told Iras that the executions will take place within sight of our villa. And I don't want the women and children of my household to see the crosses. Iras must be bitter at Aeolus, but I'm not sure how she'd react if he were dying on a cross right before her eyes."

I thought of her expressed wish that she could watch a lion tear at his intestines. I don't like watching crucifixions, though I've been trained to oversee such events. I haven't had to do it for a long time.

Judah continued, "She's been building up bitterness for years. In his letter, Caesar saw fit to tell me things that I'd only recently learned from my mother, who watched over Iras when she was delirious last summer. Mother hesitated to speak of it at first; she didn't want to shame Iras in our house.

"Caesar said that Caligula had told him of meeting Iras in the Gardens of Lucullus more than two years ago. She offered herself to him freely, and he gave her a small gold brooch with what looks like an emerald. When she came to us she had nothing, but later she said she had some money and a small piece of jewellery in an account in Rome. She'd fled without getting them because she thought she'd killed you. I had Sanballat retrieve them. Until Mother enlightened me, I supposed the brooch was a gift from happier days with you.

She often wears it along with her jade ornaments. I guessed that her money – about five hundred sesterces – had been obtained through prostitution, and I took for granted that you encouraged her actions. Yet Mother heard her muttering about deceiving you."

"I never consented for my wife to prostitute herself. To profit from her whoring would have been to destroy any chance of regaining the status to which I was born as the son of a patrician senator. I supported our household, not very lavishly, but we were surviving. Then – I might as well speak of this – Gratus came along and lied to her – told her I wanted her to – oblige him. Instead of checking with me, she gave him what he asked for.

"After that, I wanted to reconcile with my family and send Iras back to Egypt with a financial settlement. However, she intercepted several letters I wrote to my father. I imagine it was about that time she offered herself to Caligula."

"She may have been desperate and felt that trying to be faithful wouldn't win back your love or trust."

"She could've been right about that. Anyway, she certainly didn't try to be a chaste wife, though she attempted to deceive me."

Ben-Hur said seriously, "Caligula's told Tiberius Caesar about his frolic with her and has probably enjoyed telling other people too. When I break the news that she's become much talked about, maybe she'll realize she should go home to Alexandria.

"I'm going to put her on one of our ships with an escort of Simonides' employees, including a kindly married couple. The ship isn't going directly to Alexandria; it'll go to Greece first and then to Antioch, Caesarea, and finally Egypt.

"We've managed to protect her property from being confiscated along with whatever belonged to Aeolus. She still has her jewels and the money on deposit with Simonides. She has a letter from a magistrate here, affirming her claim."

"You are doing your best, then. She should appreciate it."

"I suppose I should mention Simonides' alternative suggestion, though I believe you'll refuse it, as you refused our offer for the property. Would *anything* be enough for you to take Iras back?"

It was Simonides' fixed opinion that Romans would do anything for money.

"You might advise your father-in-law to widen his concept of the Roman character. Take back a woman who repeatedly cuckolded me and finally tried to murder me? No, not for twenty million! Not even if I believed I could kill her the next morning and get away with it."

Just then we heard a sound of voices in disagreement – Lady Miriam saying severely, "No, Iras, you can't barge in there."

Iras was replying angrily, "I tell you I *will* confront him. Get out of my way!"

Iras yanked the door open and came in. Her white cotton gown looked soiled, and she appeared to be perspiring, as if she'd been in the July sun. Her dark green eyes blazed anger at me.

"Aeolus is dying now. They've nailed him up on a cross near the driveway. If you go outside, you'll hear him moaning and screaming. But I don't care. He betrayed me with that whore Laodice, who's probably servicing the men who arrested her.

"I'm a widow – or virtually so! Messala, you should do the right thing – take me back! Simonides even says so. I don't want to go back to Alexandria where everyone knows I made a fool of myself twice – once over a crippled bankrupt Roman and then over a conniving Greek pirate because he'd been my girlhood lover.

"I know you'll never command an army or be elevated to a high office. But you've some favour with Caesar. He likes your writing, and you've been tutoring his grandson. I'd be a good wife to you. I understand you."

"Iras, you're wasting everyone's time. Can't you aim for some self-respect?"

Judah spoke then. "Iras, in his letter to me the Emperor said that Caligula had described an intimate encounter with you in the Gardens of Lucullus. You were very troubled then, and I feel pity for you. But I don't see how you can live in this area after Caligula has been talking so much about you. In fact, I think you've made it impossible for Messala to take you back, even if he were so inclined. And obviously he isn't."

I said, "Ben-Hur wants to help you return to Egypt. Slowly – on a sightseeing trip. His intentions are kind, and you should be grateful and cooperative. You wouldn't like to be imprisoned on Pandateria – like Caesar's late wife, Julia."

"So, the two of you are as much in league as that! You're actually commending him for offering to get rid of me."

She turned furiously to Ben-Hur. "Judah, you're doing a favour to Messala. You should remember that he tried to have you killed by Thord the Norseman. Even last year he would've taken his set of notes to Macro if I hadn't destroyed them. And this is the thanks I get for saving you and your whole family. You trust him now – and I am the criminal!"

I wasn't going to grovel, explaining a change in my feelings. I said to Ben-Hur, "I may have some good news for you: the Emperor may give me a foreign assignment for a while, in which case my brother will take care of my property. I'm sure you'll find my absence restful."

"I'll reserve comment," he said.

Would he discover he was slightly bored?

Iras' face was less haggard than it was a year ago, and she was looking her best in front of the window with the morning light behind her. Unfortunately, distress and shame dominated her expression.

"It'll be so hard to live as a woman alone. In Egypt people remember Balthazar's daughter and gossip about how I've come down in the world. I had hopes of a better life with Aeolus but he was a cheat. A despicable cheat!

"My father wanted me to be more spiritual; he would've liked me to be a follower of his hero, his Divine Son of the Supreme God – Jesus, whom my father and the other Magi worshipped in his cradle. But I can't. I don't fit in here in your pious household, Judah. I don't have the same religious feelings – there's no use pretending. Even if I asked for baptism and followed the Nazarene Way, no man of your sect would marry a divorced woman whose husband is still alive. I heard Tirzah's handsome young fiancé, Barak, say that. I'd be trapped into a life of celibacy as long as you lived, Messala – and I'd be wishing you dead!"

"And if – the Gods forbid! – you were with me, you'd try – again – to make your wish come true!

"Surely the leaders of the Nazarene sect – Christians, or whatever you call them – must recognize that eggs can't be unscrambled and some relationships can't be repaired. And are all the members of this group so righteous, so morally pure? From my own fragmentary knowledge of the life of Jesus, it seems to me that he sometimes incurred criticism for his friendliness toward pariahs such as tax collectors and prostitutes."

"I didn't realize you knew very much about Jesus," remarked Ben-Hur.

"I don't really. Just bits that were reported to me. I've never put together a clear picture of his character."

Ben-Hur spoke thoughtfully. "I can't believe God would condemn Iras to a lifetime – actually your lifetime, Messala – of loveless bondage. For one thing, I don't suppose you took your vows before the God of Israel."

I refrained from laughing. "We were married in Caesarea in the coemptio ceremony which allows for divorce at the will of either party. Roman confarreatio marriage is for life, and it's very formal and ceremonious. Only anciently noble families bother with it and even then only if they want sons eligible for the higher priest-hoods such as the flamen dialis* – or daughters who may become vestal virgins. If I remarry, it won't necessarily be confarreatio, but I've promised to consider my family and choose a Roman lady of honourable status."

Iras had been pitiable when she talked about her situation. But now she raised her voice to somewhere between a hiss and a screech.

"If you marry that – blue-blooded tramp with her innocent airs, I curse you both. I curse your bed – and your manly parts (such as they are). I curse her womb. I curse –"

"Shut up, Iras!"

Surprisingly this came from Judah. He took Iras' arm and said firmly, "Let's hear no more cursing. It's revolting."

---

*The special priest of Jupiter

He opened the door. "Go to your room. We'll have a lunch tray sent up. Get your maid to help you prepare for a voyage – a journey into new happiness. Mother and Esther and I will all pray for you."

Lady Miriam was in the atrium, but not near the door. She looked concerned. Listening at a keyhole wasn't her style, though she probably heard some of the louder speeches made in the office. Judah said to her, "Don't go to her and try to soothe her, Mother. She'll be rude, and it'll just upset you. If only she could calm down."

Here she was pitied – but less so with every crisis. She didn't love me, but was attracted to my new home, my increased income, and my newly favourable reputation, so much better than we'd dared hope for in the difficult years.

I thanked Ben-Hur briefly; I was genuinely grateful. From the staircase Iras looked back once more – in hate.

CHAPTER FORTY-TWO

THE boat races and other marine displays were scheduled for two hours before noon, which meant they would be attended mainly by early risers who had a sincere interest in boats. People who partied late and then slept late would wait for the chariot races in the afternoon. The seating arrangements for the boat races weren't as capacious as those in the stadium, where rows of seats accommodated viewers on every side of the action. All the seats at the boat races faced the sea. The section for the Emperor and his family and associates was covered with a purple and gold awning, which would be taken down afterwards so that the sun wouldn't fade it too quickly.

I dressed in a red tunic with a gold edge at the neck. Scarlet and gold had been my colours long ago, and I refused to regard them as bad luck. When I was last in her company, Lutatia had remarked that a mirror in my boat would help me to keep an eye on my competitors, if only it wouldn't get in the way of the sails. Immediately I thought of a solution: my gold armillae! If I looked at my arms from time to time, I might see the reflection of a boat coming up behind me.

I hadn't seen either Gemellus or Lutatia since my position was terminated, but Gemellus had sent me a letter. He said he hoped to see my new colt soon; the Emperor hadn't forbidden him to visit me. He'd heard that I was on the list of applicants for Lutatia's hand, and he wanted me to know that both he and Lutatia hoped that I would be chosen. Lutatia had talked about how much she liked and admired me. I felt encouraged but still cautious. The Emperor might well look at my failures as well as the difference in our ages and the possibility that an old back injury might appear again in the form of debilitating arthritis.

There were several events in the program ahead of my race, so I waited with the red-sailed Flammifer along with my competitors and their boats. I'd brought Africanus with me, though he'd stay on shore during the race. Meanwhile I was glad he was with me as I greeted scowling Antonius and sneering Calvus.

Calvus said mockingly, "I hear your Egyptian wife is living somewhere around here. I'd like to renew our acquaintance, but perhaps Furia Vopisca wouldn't like it."

"It doesn't concern me. However, I'm told she's leaving the area. I trust you aren't particularly disappointed."

Antonius growled, "You can have your sluttish cousin, Sergia, now. I've offered for Lutatia Catula. Maybe she'll give your mother's vicious little dog back to you – if you live through this contest, that is. It would be poetic justice if your boat capsized and you drowned like a rat."

I turned away from him rather than exchange insults, though I reflected that rats have been seen swimming. But not pigs!

When it was time, we all brought our boats to the starting place where a cord stretched a little above the water. It would be removed immediately after the Emperor dropped a scarf. Then a trumpeter would blast out a loud signal. Years ago I correctly counted on the consul Maxentius to give the signal just as I anticipated it by an unsportsmanlike premature start. Then I'd thought, "I have to win – for myself and for Rome. Rules be damned!" This time there was no question of breaking a rule. Win or lose, I'd aim at an impeccable display of skill with honour.

I won't describe the boat race turn by turn around the markers but quickly get to the crucial part. I'd been keeping up with the leaders, who were – as one might expect – Antonius and Calvus. Then turning to the left-hand marker, slipping around it very closely, I moved into the lead position just as Antonius was on my right, swearing and advancing toward me. Ye Gods! In my armilla mirror I saw that he was actually aiming to ram me. There wasn't time to breathe a petition to the Gods of the wind and the waves. I can't really say what it was that I did to avoid Antonius but the next moment I knew I'd passed the left-hand marker and was clearly in the lead. I could hear the crowd shouting, some of them for me but likely just as many for my competitors. A high feminine voice – Furia Vopisca? – screeched, "Come on, Calvus! Come on!"

Meanwhile Antonius had turned his boat so that it was not only behind mine but at right angles to it. And then – Calvus struck him broadside. I could hear the sound of the collision as well as loud profane outpourings from both Calvus and Antonius, but I didn't try to look at them, I just kept my beautiful Flammifer gliding with the helpful wind as we approached the next marker. I did distinctly hear Calvus screaming at Antonius, "You stupid *culus!*"

The five remaining contestants made their way around Calvus and Antonius, but they didn't catch up with me, though they were coming along very well when I reached the final turn. Then I was safely around it. Just a short distance to the finish. And next moment – I was there! I'd won.

As I docked my boat and handed it over to Africanus, I heard about the disaster. Calvus had loudly blamed Antonius for getting in his way and denying his chance of victory. While their boats were still close enough for them to exchange obscene epithets, Antonius reached across and hit Calvus, whose sneering face was tantalizingly just within reach. Calvus retaliated by jumping into Antonius' boat and aiming his fist at Antonius' nose. Then they proceeded to pound each other.

Calvus' unmanned boat struck the marker and rebounded against Antonius' emerald-sailed Ariadne. Antonius, delivering a powerful punch, knocked Calvus back into his own boat, against his orange sails, one of which came partly loose and billowed around him. Freeing himself from his entanglement, Calvus leaped back at Antonius, who was laughing heartily. The spectators were shouting warnings at them, but they paid no attention until the Ariadne heeled over, dumping both men into the water.

Professional sailors in a dinghy came to the rescue. They dragged a spitting and swearing Calvus into their boat. Antonius was less fortunate; he'd struck his head against one of the boats and lost consciousness. He was dead when they pulled him into the rescue boat. Calvus protested, "I didn't kill the crazy jackass. I didn't even knock him out. And he started it!"

On shore, Calvus, dripping wet, grinned sarcastically. "Congratulations, Messala! All the same, I should've won. Antonius wanted to wipe you out; instead he ruined everyone's chance but yours. Are you always so lucky in your enemies?"

"Far from it! I hope you didn't hazard too much."

"Not as much as Antonius, the reckless fool. One of the benefits of marriage is a wife nagging one to be cautious with money. The fact is, Furia thinks she's psychic – and she had a premonition that you might be lucky. She said you've been having a run of good fortune."

"Indeed! Give her my best wishes!"

I walked on up toward the enclosure where the Emperor would acknowledge my victory. I could hear comments from the stands.

"Would you believe it? What a comeback! A few years ago – ruined, disgraced, crippled! Now look at him going to receive his laurel crown! He doesn't appear to need that fancy cane, does he?"

"Mark my words, you'll see other men sporting gold-initialed canes as a fashion statement."

Trying to seem as if I hadn't heard the flattering conversation, I glanced higher into the stands and saw Sergia. She was dressed in black and white, looking beautiful but rather pale. Her dark-blue eyes met mine. There were no apparent tears, yet she didn't look really happy, though she gave me a little smile. Impulsively I waved to her.

Had she been in Misenum very long? Did she grieve for Antonius' death, despite his vicious behaviour to her? Or did she have feelings for me? Too late!

I presented myself to Tiberius Caesar, regal in his purple toga. With him were members of his family: Lady Antonia; Gemellus, beaming with joy; beautiful Lutatia, who wasn't quite smiling. There was a newcomer to the imperial box – a man I knew slightly, Sergius Paulus, Sergia's distant cousin. He was older than I, but still in his prime.

Sleek Agrippina was also there, graciously amused, though her spouse, Ahenobarbus, looked bored. Caligula too. Why did he seem mischievously elated? And there was Claudius with Herod and Cypros.

Tiberius beckoned me in front of him, reached down, and placed the victor's crown on my head. In a loud voice, he made the requisite speech to the effect that I'd won my race honourably and that I'd receive the proper reward: a money draft for ten thousand sesterces. He then handed the draft to me, and I thanked him.

He continued in a quieter conversational tone, "I'm assigning you to the staff of the governor of Sicily. You should leave before the end of this month. You'll have the rank of quaestor; the Senate will confirm the appointment. The man you'll be replacing has died of a fever. You'll serve until the New Year, and you'll be mainly in Messana, which is close to your own property. This should give you the chance to oversee your estate."

"Caesar, I appreciate the appointment and will do my best to serve Rome." I was thrilled at being called back to service.

Then came the shock. Caesar said, "I've reached a definite decision concerning the disposal of my ward, Lutatia, in marriage. There've been several offers for her hand, including your own. I've chosen the worthy Sergius Paulus to be her husband; she is already acquainted with him as he was her father's old friend. I've appointed him to be governor of Cyprus, and he'll take his bride with him. They'll travel a few days after the ceremony.

"I intend to announce this tonight at my banquet. I believe you've already been sent an invitation."

"Yes, Caesar." I was trying to be calm and stoical; I avoided looking at Lutatia, though I saw sympathy in the eyes of Gemellus.

"Feel free to bring a suitable companion. I know you're looking for a good wife, and if you find the right lady, you may take her with you to Messana. But for the love of all the Gods, don't take back that hysterical Egyptian."

"Indeed I shall not."

Had Iras already left for Egypt? I hoped so. I cringed at the idea that she might gloat over my disappointment.

Determined to show perfect composure, I said, "Caesar, I'm truly grateful for your generosity, and I wish Lutatia Catula every happiness. And I congratulate Sergius Paulus on his great good fortune."

Then I retreated from my position in front of the imperial box. For the closing ceremonies I went quickly to the row where Barbatus and his wife and daughter were. They wanted to know what the Emperor had said to me. Was it all good news?

Messalina even said, "Has he told you that you can marry Lutatia? Because I'd love to be a bridal attendant."

"Lutatia is to marry Sergius Paulus."

I told them about my new assignment and about the Emperor's suggestion that I come to the banquet with a companion. They offered to find someone for me, but I said, "No, give me some time. I need to think, and if I must, I'll come alone."

My pride was hurt, but I was determined not to show it, not to admit that I cared. I'd developed strong feelings for Lutatia, but there had lingered in my mind a few misgivings. She was very young and rather unworldly, unused to high society. Books and rural living had been her world until her father died and she'd come to Misenum as Tiberius' ward. Although she clearly idealized me, that wouldn't have lasted. I'd been resolved not to let her down, though. I still remembered the look of hurt and shock on the face of my child-hood friend as I went on talking as a sophisticated Roman to a naïve provincial Jew.

So if Lutatia and I weren't meant to become a couple, what now? What of tonight's banquet? I had a thought, but it might well come to nothing. Sergia's face came to mind, but perhaps she was already encouraging an admirer. Had she come to the Games alone?

As the crowd began to disperse, I started walking toward my boat. Africanus was waiting there. As I passed Sanballat in his usual pristine toga, he appeared to be paying coins to – Ben-Hur!

Sanballat looked up and smirked sourly at me. "Well, well, Messala! Fortune has smiled on you at last. Are you planning to have your laurel wreath gilded?"

Ben-Hur and his wife had backed off a little but were within earshot. It was well known that Caligula has had several of his symbols of victory covered with gold.

I answered modestly, "Oh, no, I don't wish to be ostentatious. Waxed, maybe."

I wondered what Judah had done with his laurels. He appeared amused, perhaps at the idea that, despite my scarlet-sailed Flammifer, my gold-trimmed red tunic, and my decorated cane, I denied seeking to be ostentatious. Instinctively I smiled back, a little surprised at myself.

Then, near the exit, I saw a familiar feminine altercation. Two black-clad hags screaming at – Sergia!

I said, "I believe I'm needed!" and moved quickly.

One old creature was shouting, "It was because of your witchery that my son Mallius took his own life. And now you've driven another good man to his death."

Her friend snarled, "You killed my Antonius, my only son! And I'm sure you did something to lose his child too."

"No, I didn't abort the baby, though I'm glad I'm not carrying Antonius' child anymore. But *he* was to blame for my miscarriage! It was because of his beating me that I left him. I was trying to save the baby – but it's for the best that the poor little thing is gone."

"You killed my grandchild! You selfish whore!" She tried to strike Sergia, who was backing away from her ugly accusers.

Fortunately I was able to grab the old woman's arm and twist it back as she screeched in pain and surprise. I interposed my own body between Sergia and the two women.

"Both of you, go away – now! Leave Sergia alone. Mourn Antonius with proper decorum." My tone was severe, and my grip on the arm of Antonius' old mother was relentless.

I swung both of the yowling harpies around and said, "Go! Get away from us before I summon Macro!" I gave them a shove.

Seeing a couple of Praetorian Guards watching – as were the Hurs – the two old women scuttled away, muttering what sounded like curses.

"Sergia, come with me in my boat. Let's talk. Can I help you?"

"You've helped me already. But you're committed to the Emperor's ward, aren't you? You shouldn't be spending time with me."

"No, I'm not betrothed to Lutatia Catula. In fact, Caesar has chosen another husband for her – and I think I'm relieved. I was attracted to her and felt great affection for her, but I never quite put you out of my mind – and heart. When I saw you as I walked up to the Emperor's box, I asked myself, 'What am I really doing?'"

Maybe I was exaggerating my feelings, but the more I spoke, the more I believed what I was saying.

I took her hand in mine and we walked down to where Africanus waited with the Flammifer.

CHAPTER FORTY-THREE

I let Africanus handle the boat while Sergia and I talked.

She said, "What are your plans, now that you've won the race? Are you going to stay here?"

"Not very long. Caesar's giving me a quaestorship in Sicily. I'm to leave before the end of the month. My office will be in Messana, which is close to some land that Father left me. My brother and the family steward will keep an eye on my property here."

"So you'll be getting away from everything! I wish I could leave Rome and Misenum – get away from all the gossip."

"You could come with me. I mean it; I need a gracious lady at my side. A wife. Think about it."

"You can't be serious. I'm to run off with you, just like that? Sailing with you to a new life?"

"Maybe my offer is presumptuous. Your grandfather may have a high-ranking candidate for your hand. Whereas I'm getting a late start on the cursus honorum*."

"I've never stopped thinking about you. I wasn't unfaithful to Antonius with my body but was with my mind. He had reason to be jealous, though I tried to hide my thoughts from him.

*The course of honour; the succession of magisterial offices all the way up to the consulship

"As for Grandfather, he's going back to Spain with Grandmother. He said he's disgusted that I couldn't make a success of my marriage to Antonius. He admitted I couldn't help Mallius' getting the mumps that descended on him. But I also failed to keep Calvus contented and then I provoked Antonius to violence. He's angry at Antonius too, of course, for his lack of control."

"So then Velleius would probably accept it if you chose your own man this time. Sergia, I know it's sudden, but, believe me, I do love you and want you. I tried to fall in love with someone else – and partly I did. Lutatia is sweet and very desirable – but I couldn't escape the feeling that she was too young for me – and that we'd both come to realize it."

"Yes, yes, I love you and I'll go away with you – in fact the idea is very exciting. But all my clothes are with my maid at the Peacock Inn. And those miserable witches said they know where I've been staying. Will you come back with me?"

"Of course. We'll get your possessions and then sail to my house. Actually there's a small shrine to Juno north of the road that goes by my place, so we could have a simple marriage ceremony today. And then, this evening, we can go as husband and wife to Caesar's dinner. Would you like that?"

She laughed. "That would really shock people. They'll say that Antonius' toes aren't cold yet. They'll assume we were carrying on during my marriage. But I don't care what they say if you don't."

So we turned the boat back to shore and walked into the town of Misenum. The Peacock Inn wasn't too far from the waterfront. It was a respectable establishment – but it's never good for an unattached lady of quality to live in an inn with only her maid. Sergia said she had stayed with a cousin in Rome for a while but had come to Misenum because she had to see what would happen in the boat race.

"I was praying that you'd win – or at least come through it safely, though I supposed that you didn't care for me anymore. By the way, do you think Lutatia Catula would let me have my dog back now?"

"We can ask. She's marrying Sergius Paulus and going with him to Cyprus. Perhaps they'd prefer not to take a little dog."

"And my mare is at Grandfather's place at Capua, but we could send for her before we sail."

"Of course. I'm sure my brother will lend us his yacht, the Nereid, which has some spaces for horses."

We did see the two old fugitives from a midnight coven – that's what they looked like – hovering near the inn. Conveniently we had Africanus with us to help with the luggage, having paid a local fellow to watch the boat. Soon we were all back with the maid who had the bags beside her. She was a very proper sort of servant – my mother's Anna – but she seemed excited at being part of a romantic adventure. Probably she hadn't liked staying at the inn; now she was going to a nice villa by the sea in the same location she'd lived with her former mistress, Lollia Velleia.

However, before Africanus could untie our boat, Sergia remarked, "There's a shrine to Juno right over there on the western edge of the town. What if we had our marriage ceremony first? Then no one could stop us, could they?"

Remembering how Uncle Velleius had spoiled everything back in January, bullying and coaxing Sergia into a union which proved distasteful to her, I agreed that we should get married right away. It would show greater respect for Sergia. I would have waited for the ceremony if the virgin Lutatia had been my bride; the Emperor would have demanded it.

So we returned to land and walked to the shrine of the Goddess of Marriage. Seeing a small jewellery shop, we bought a gold ring with a blue stone that the man assured us was a real sapphire. I told Sergia I'd buy her a more elaborate ring later if she wished and that I also had some jewellery that had belonged to some of my ancestors – pieces that Lepida considered too old-fashioned for herself.

At the shrine the priest was ready and willing. I paid him his usual fee. The ceremony was short: I presented Sergia with a gold coin and her ring; we promised to be faithful as long as we remained together. Coemptio marriage isn't a life commitment, though one may hope the union lasts that long – and I had great hopes this time. Confarreatio marriage gives all the wife's money to the husband

– which is why most women prefer the simpler form of marriage. It was all we had time for anyway. For the stricter form, we would have needed many witnesses and an animal sacrifice, commonly a pig, with omens being taken on examination of its entrails. I wondered if Lutatia's marriage would be of that kind.

The priest offered up some incense to Juno's statue and kindly gave us some extra for our Lares and Penates, as well as some wolf fat for Sergia to use in anointing our threshold when we got home. We shared a cup of wine, and the priest gave us a certificate attesting to our union.

We were soon docking at our home. I said, "The gardens aren't bad but you may think of some improvements. And you could select some new furniture."

"I've been in your house. It's already very pleasant."

As we approached the house, a fluffy white body galloped toward us and leaped into Sergia's arms. It was little Flora, the Maltese dog.

Achates, my butler, said, "An imperial servant brought the dog this morning. He left this note for you, sir."

It was a farewell letter from Lutatia, which I read to myself while Sergia was hugging her dog.

Lutatia began, "Caesar has said I must marry Sergius Paulus. He's a good man, an old friend of my father. We're to go very soon to Cyprus, where my future husband will be governor. Caesar says I should return little Flora to you.

"I'll try to be a good wife to the man I'm to marry. I know him from his visits to my father, and I esteem him. But you've been my first love, and I'll never forget you, though perhaps in time you'll forget me. May all the Gods bless you and give you happiness!"

I handed the note to Achates and instructed him to burn it. I didn't want Sergia to see it.

We had a light lunch with fruit, bread, and wine. Then we bathed – not in the lagoon but in the modest but adequate bathing pools inside the house. From the solarium we could look at a very private garden. Finally we went to my room and made love on my large bed.

Even in an imaginary journal I don't choose to describe our

love-making in detail. However, we both enjoyed every moment together. Sergia has a lovely body, and her previous husbands were wrong to label her the ice-queen. She has a capacity for passion that Calvus and Antonius were simply unable to arouse. In Antonius' case it appears she was thinking of her desire for me, which she'd repressed to please her ambitious grandfather and – to be honest – her own ambition. Marriage to an acclaimed hero who'd just attained high office was attractive.

Afterward she regretted her choice and was very happy that suddenly, in the middle of her despair, she had received a second chance. She had healed from her miscarriage. I had resolved to be careful but it wasn't necessary. She welcomed me into herself for prolonged delight.

During the previous year I'd thought of obtaining a mistress: either a willing slave or a professional courtesan, but I'd always talked myself out of it. I was ready to imagine embarrassing failure, and the memory of Iras' last advances repelled me.

But with my Sergia it was all natural and easy. She was truly my woman.

Afterwards we bathed again, then dressed. Sergia's maid had unpacked her clothes and pressed a rose-coloured linen gown for her.

"I don't have any of the garments that Antonius paid for," she explained. "I left most of them in his house and then gave three more robes to charity after I got away. I just couldn't bear to wear them again. This gown is one of several I bought with my own money."

"It suits you," I said admiringly. The rosy material was thin and clinging, doing justice to the luscious curves of her breast and hips.

I had the small casket of ancestral jewellery brought to her, telling her, "It's all yours, darling, I hope you like some of them at least."

She took a look at the gold rings, necklaces, and earrings. Selecting a ring with sapphires and tiny diamonds embedded in a fine gold band, she tested it on her hand and announced, "I really like this one." It looked as if it had been made for her long slim fingers. Lepida's hands were somewhat pudgy; I was glad she hadn't fancied these pieces.

Sergia kept on the wedding ring I'd bought her but put the finer ring on her other hand and picked out a set of earrings and a necklace that matched it. I finished dressing myself in my new dark crimson dinner robe, brushed my hair, and put my gold armillae back on. I hesitated about wearing my new laurel wreath to dinner, but Sergia said, "This once you should. Today was your victory – and it still is!"

Nestor brought the carriage with the greys. He drove us so that we could concentrate on other matters. As we approached the Emperor's palace, we could see the crosses and bodies being taken down. Would Iras relent and claim Aeolus' remains for burial? Or – more likely – would she be exultant at the prospect of his corpse being burned like common garbage?

CHAPTER FORTY-FOUR

ARRIVING at the imperial villa, we left our carriage and walked across the courtyard to the entrance. Since parking for carriages was limited, and we lived so near, Nestor would drive home and return for us at about the right time.

The imperial gardens were bright with summer flowers. Flaming poppies and orange lilies with black spots seemed to dominate. We didn't linger to admire them but went straight to the vestibule.

There were already many guests strolling around the crowded atrium, waiting until we all would be admitted to the triclinium. I remembered the banquet Sergia, Mother, and I had attended last winter. Then I'd been fascinated by Sergia and had let myself build up hopes that had been dashed when Velleius came back from Spain with his grand plans for her. And now, after all the disappointments and losses of last spring, things had turned around. I had an honourable position ahead of me, and I was with the love of my life.

Herod and Cypros greeted us, friendly but hesitant, probably wondering if I needed tact and silent sympathy over the loss of Lutatia. It was a pleasure to surprise them with the news that Sergia and I were married.

"You got married? When?" asked Cypros in a voice that carried. People turned and looked at us – among them Ben-Hur and his wife, evidently still in the Emperor's good graces.

"This afternoon! I'm assigned as quaestor on the staff of the governor of Sicily – as you already know – and I'm to leave as soon as I can, so we didn't want to waste time. Sergia is coming with me."

They congratulated us, and some other people approached and added their good wishes. Sergia looked radiant; her cheeks glowed and her long-lashed blue eyes shone.

We did hear some murmurs of negativity – gossipy voices exclaiming, "Poor Antonius, she didn't even wait for his funeral," and "Is this her second or her third marriage?"

There were other comments, "Antonius was a fool; I'm sorry I ever bet on him. All the same, I was hoping – anyone but Messala!"

I said quietly to Sergia, "It sounds as if we aren't universally popular. But it doesn't matter; we're going away from them all – for some time."

"I'm glad – and I'm so happy to be travelling with you. Have you ever been to Sicily before?"

"No, though I've a country estate near Messana, the place my family is named for. We should find time to do some sight-seeing. We might take a look at the famous volcano, only not too close."

We talked a little about the historic sights, and other people made suggestions, especially that we should go to the theatre at Taorminium, the favourite centre for classical drama.

Then we were ushered into the dining-room. Our escort led us to a couch next to my brother, his wife, and their daughter. I announced to them, "Sergia and I were married this afternoon in a quiet ceremony at a small temple of Juno."

They were surprised, but wished us the best and were perfectly friendly to Sergia. Barbatus noticed that she was wearing our great-grandmother's sapphires.

The Emperor and his party entered and the banquet began. Caesar greeted the guests and made an announcement.

"Tonight I'm giving in marriage my ward, Lutatia Catula, the daughter of Quintus Lutatius Catulus, to my esteemed friend Sergius Paulus. He's to go to Cyprus as governor, and Lutatia will accompany him."

Everyone politely applauded.

"The auspices have been taken from a sacrificed pig. Clearly the Gods are favourable to this marriage. Therefore you will all have the pleasure of being witnesses to the rest of the marriage ceremony, and afterwards this will be their wedding feast."

The couple appeared on the dais and sat together on a bench with a sheepskin on it. They repeated their vows of fidelity before Tiberius Caesar, Emperor and Chief Pontiff. The Emperor intoned a very long traditional prayer to all the Gods concerned with marriage.

Lutatia wore the traditional orange veil over a golden gown.

Messalina whispered, "I don't see much of her hair."

Lepida replied, "Hush! They've arranged it in the customary manner for virgin brides – divided into seven locks, each of them looped up under her veil. And, on top of the veil, she has a wreath of verbena, as you can see."

"I can't properly see her face," complained Messalina, "to tell if she looks happy."

"She should be happy enough," said Lepida. "It's a very good marriage. They're going to Cyprus, and she'll be the principal lady there."

"I think," began Messalina, "I'd rather be married with my hair more visible, like Sergia's – or even loose to my waist so that everyone can see it."

Messalina is proud of her girlish beauty: her thick black curls, large eyes, and clear complexion.

I looked at Sergia, who was smiling at the implied praise. Her dark brown hair with golden highlights was caught up at the back with a gold circlet, but curls framed her face at the sides.

I said enthusiastically, "I prefer Sergia's hair too."

The bridal pair shared a cup of wine and a piece of cake made with spelt flour. I've heard that such cakes taste dry and salty. All this is formal tradition in a confarreatio marriage. The vows had now been spoken, including the words that committed all Lutatia's money and land into the care of Sergius Paulus. He'd have absolute authority over her, second only to the Emperor himself.

The couple were escorted to a proper dinner couch and table near the Emperor and his party: Gemellus, Julia Helena, and her husband, Rubelius Blandus. Also with Tiberius was his grandnephew, Gaius Caligula, and his dignified sister-in-law, Lady Antonia, grandmother to both Caligula and Gemellus.

Herod, Cypros, and Claudius Caesar were close to the dais but on the same level as the rest of us. Equally close to the dais, but farther from our party, were Agrippina and Ahenobarbus.

The Hurs weren't far away. I wondered if Iras was already on her way to Egypt.

The courses were served and the entertainment went on. A choral group sang the nuptial hymn composed long ago by the poet Catullus. Dancers floated around the centre of the floor in gauzy costumes, and a couple of clowns strolled from table to table telling bawdy stories to any guests who looked even halfway interested.

Once dessert trays had been passed, the Emperor stepped forward and announced some new postings he had assigned to guests at the banquet. Most postings, ratified by the Senate, began in the New Year, but occasionally vacancies had to be filled. Tiberius called up two men before me and congratulated them. Then he spoke my name and asked me and my wife to come to the steps of the dais.

"Messala, as I've told you, I'm giving you the rank of quaestor, since the staff in Sicily has lost a man. You'll be the acting prefect of Messana until someone is appointed for the beginning of next year. When you come home, you'll be eligible for a Senate seat if you meet the financial qualifications. At that time, if you've done well, I'll find another assignment for you.

"Now I'm told that you and Lady Sergia were married just this afternoon, within hours of Antonius' death. I suppose you both know that a widow isn't permitted to remarry for nine months after the death of her husband, to prevent the question of paternity if she should bear a child during that period. Sergia Carina, were you and Antonius divorced before his violent demise today?"

He knew perfectly well that she and Antonius were divorced; indeed, he himself had told me so. Maybe he wanted to clarify matters in public to discourage gossip.

She answered boldly. "Caesar, I divorced Sextus Antonius more than a month ago, after I lost my baby because of his abuse. So there is no question of me carrying his child – and I thank the Gods for that! I did grieve for the baby, but truly I don't mourn Antonius at all – and I'd be a hypocrite to pretend I do."

I said, "Sergia and I weren't lovers during her marriage to Antonius, though she called on me to ask me to take her dog. We didn't cuckold him – but I thought of her often though I certainly tried to forget her. Today we met again, both of us free from commitments – so we seized the day and hastened to the shrine of Juno!"

Tiberius Caesar smiled wryly. "It sounds like something from one of your novels, Messala. I should warn you that Antonius' grieving mother has lodged a complaint; however, she fails to show sufficient grounds. Antonius clearly caused his own death. I believe it will be a good thing for Sergia Carina to accompany you to Sicily, Messala. She should get away from the malice of an angry old battleaxe. And the citizens of Messana should find you an attractive couple."

We thanked the Emperor and returned to our places. First, however, we spoke to the bridal couple very briefly, wishing them all happiness.

Sergius Paulus said civilly, "Thank you, and we wish you both the best. It seems our wedding feast is also, in a manner, yours."

Lutatia looked at us and managed to smile a little. Or was she making an effort not to cry? Her eyes seemed to be saying, "Did you have to be consoled so quickly?"

I didn't want her to be hurt and I hoped she would get over any feeling of pain at my defection. At the same time, I was glad to be with Sergia; in my eyes she was more beautiful than ever.

The time came for the bridal couple to be escorted to the palace chamber where their marriage would be consummated. Sergius Paulus would go with a few friends and have a final drink; meanwhile, Lutatia would be attended by a party of noble matrons, including Cypros and Julia Helena, who would help her disrobe and offer advice and encouragement. Soon Paulus would join her. If they'd gone to his house in Rome, she'd have rubbed wolf fat on the doorstep, and they'd have burned incense before their household Gods. But Lutatia might wait to do that when they reached their residence in Cyprus.

It was time for all of us to leave. We went outside to wait for our transportation. Several families had litters ready at the door. Barbatus' carriage came very quickly, and we said goodbye.

The Hurs were waiting near us. Judah evidently made a resolve and then spoke to me. "My congratulations, Messala. You've had a remarkable day!"

"Thank you!" I almost left it at that, but decided to ask, "Has Iras left for Egypt yet?"

"She's supposed to sail tomorrow evening. Meanwhile she's being watched closely."

Then he added, "She says she's willing to go. She broke down and wept when she knew that Aeolus had died. She seems eager to get away from everything.

"She took the news of your victory quite well. She declares she's embarrassed that she asked you for a reconciliation. She doesn't know yet that you've already remarried."

"I hope she'll continue to be sensible and have a good life."

I could imagine her relaxing as she sat on deck enjoying the sunshine and the movement of the waves and interesting herself in new sights as the vessel came to various Grecian ports. Surely she'd begin to feel better.

At that point our carriages arrived. Judah and his wife got into a carriage drawn by a pair of bays. Nestor pulled up with my grey team. We didn't attempt to race; we let them go ahead. I sat with my arm around Sergia. When we got home, I lifted her over the threshold, and Nestor took the carriage to the stables.

CHAPTER FORTY-FIVE

WE shared a joyous wedding night, even though at times we could hear distant thunder from out over the sea. I was glad Iras hadn't sailed yet; I didn't wish her dead. Then I put her out of my mind and gave my full attention to the delight of making love to my Sergia.

The next morning was leisurely. The sun sparkled on the waves below the cliffs, birds sang in our garden, and the flowers themselves seemed to be participating in our jubilation. The dogs romped together for a while and then lay down in the shade as the July sun became hotter.

We'd just finished a light lunch in the garden when my butler, Achates, announced a visitor: Quintus Arrius. I told him to bring the guest to the peristylum. Sergia had gone to direct our servants about packing.

I had a feeling Ben-Hur might be bringing unpleasant news of Iras. From the look on his sober face I knew my guess was correct. Was he going to tell me of her death? He had once dreamed that the blue waves could tell of her fate – as he expressed it.

He said simply, "Iras is dead."

"What happened? She didn't find a way to take her own life, did she? Her situation really wasn't that bad."

I wondered if it was possible she committed suicide to make me feel guilty and to cast a shadow over my happiness as a bridegroom.

"We aren't sure whether what she did was intentional. Let me explain."

He spoke with care. "This morning she rose late and then said she wanted to sit out in the sunshine. She appeared cheerful. We didn't want to spoil her mood, so we didn't tell her about your remarriage. She went to the stone steps that go down a long way to the beach, and she stopped halfway and sat down on a large sunny rock. For a little while Esther could hear her singing a favourite song about Egypt, the storied land to which she'd said farewell."

"I remember that song. Perhaps you do too."

"Yes, she once sang it on the lake at the Orchard of Palms."

That had been at the Sheik's camp. I asked, "What happened next?"

"She stopped singing, and we heard her cry out. Esther and I ran to see what was the matter. Iras had a gold-coloured snake in her hand; she let it go just as we came down to her. She said, 'The snake bit me – here.' And she pointed to a mark on her breast."

"Like Cleopatra! Did she touch the snake before it bit her, did she hold it against herself? Or did she grab it in self-defence *after* it attacked her? Did she manage to tell you?"

"She didn't say. She let us take her indoors; she mumbled something like 'God forgive me everything.' My mother prepared a poultice for her breast to draw out the venom. We gave her some wine, but I don't know if it helped at all."

"I don't know whether wine would do any good. The flesh of a newly killed animal might absorb some of the venom – or so I've heard anyway."

"She soon began having convulsions and then at last lost consciousness. It didn't take her long to die – about an hour – but it was a painful death.

"We'll bury her this afternoon before sundown. As you know, it's our custom. You probably won't wish to attend the burial service, but if you do, I promise that everyone will be courteous – even Simonides and Barak, Tirzah's betrothed."

"Neither of them would feel like being courteous but would try anyway. I don't think I should put them to the trouble. My absence will allow greater freedom of expression in the eulogies."

Also, I thought, it would be awkward to appear at my first wife's interment when I've just married my second wife. And Sergia would certainly not be attending Sextus Antonius' funeral.

I knew a little about Jewish funerals, though I'd never been part of the graveside ceremony. If I understand it correctly, mourners placed a handful of earth on the grave and spoke words of dismissal in Hebrew or Aramaic. Being unable to recall any appropriate words in either of those languages, I might have adapted the concluding line of Catullus' ode to his dead brother. *In aeternum, ave atque vale.** "Would it be proper for me to send flowers?"

"Yes, of course. Have you time to answer another question which has been on my mind for some time – in fact since last winter at the Emperor's banquet? Gratus said something that puzzled me."

I had a suspicion of what was coming next, but I tried to be very cool about it.

"You realize he was losing his mind. I hope you aren't thinking of his crude attempt at literary criticism. I'd have been disappointed if he *had* admired my novel."

"I wasn't thinking about your novels, though I've now read them. They're very cleverly written. You certainly have a gift for tearing strips off your enemies with your pen. You went after both Sanballat and Gratus, and I suppose I appear as Adherbal the Carthaginian. At least you didn't make a caricature of me."

"I couldn't – because you aren't comical. So Adherbal had to be a serious character; accordingly I looked for humour elsewhere, as in Cato's endless haranguing the Senate – 'Delenda est Carthago!*†'* At the end I even left Adherbal alive."

I hoped Judah would forget about another remark by Gratus.

---

* Forever, hail and farewell!   † Carthage must be destroyed.

He said, "Gratus said he wished he'd had me crucified. He implied that *you* talked him out of it. Is that true? Yet you accused me, not reluctantly but gladly!"

Rather wearily I said, "If you insist on getting into this subject, I suppose I must explain as well as I can. Except for some details, I acted as you have assumed I did – and yes, I was willing enough.

"I concede that the tile on your roof could have slipped. It looked to others than me, in fact to your near neighbours, as if you'd pushed it. They cheered you as if you were a divinely inspired blend of King David and Judas Maccabaeus. To me, on the previous day, you'd expressed a strong dislike of Rome. You may feel that I provoked that. But I could remember occasions years before – especially the day before I left for Rome – when I heard words from your mother that I wasn't meant to hear. About striking a blow for the Messiah. Still I admit – the tile may have slipped."

He looked shocked. Did he remember the speech his mother had made to her children?

"Gratus wanted to execute all of you – on crosses – as a public example. The legate replacing my father didn't mind crucifying *you* – but he didn't like to crucify women. Nor did my father approve, but he was about to leave and so really had no say in it. And I – I thought you were guilty – still I didn't like the prospect of crucifying three people I'd once been close to. And then I thought of something I believed I should mention.

"As a young contubernalis, just out of my advanced educational training, I had a natural urge to show off my historical knowledge, my acquaintance with a relevant precedent. I told Gratus about Cicero's execution of the Catilinarian conspirators without trial. There was clear evidence against them, and at the time Catilina and his rebel army were mustering at Praeneste. Most of the Senate voted with the consul – Cicero – for immediate execution by strangling in the Tullianum. One of the very few exceptions was Julius Caesar, who declared that life imprisonment under severe conditions would be a more correct sentence.

"The executions took place. Catilina and his army were destroyed soon after. But a little later, when Cicero was no longer consul, his adversaries ganged up on him. Caesar was one of them. For having executed Roman citizens without due process, Cicero was sent into exile – though he got back to Italy after a while.

"Gratus knew that, once he'd left office, he'd be vulnerable. His enemies would pick over his record to find something he'd done wrong. He was rather lucky they didn't dig a little more. Of course he could have decided to give you a full trial, probably a noisy disorderly affair – but then he might not have got his hands on the sort of compensation to which he felt entitled. Instead he took Julius Caesar's advice – about some form of life imprisonment. And you know the rest of the story.

"I still deny torturing anyone or planning for your mother and sister to get leprosy – if indeed they did. However the other facts are grim enough.

"Obviously, if I'd kept my mouth closed about the Catilinarian conspirators, you might not be here now. But you've no cause to be grateful. Not to me. I've never denied accepting an informer's reward. Moreover, I willingly assisted Gratus with some administrative details, though not everything. Some things he preferred to take care of personally. Be grateful – if you like – to your ever-watchful God."

"I *am* grateful to the Lord. But as for that speech by my mother years ago, which I suppose you and Cypros both overheard, I wish you'd talked to me about it. Though even then I'd have admitted that I dreamed of liberating my country – fighting as a soldier if necessary. But I'd no notion – ever – of pushing a roof tile down on a Roman. Tell me, do you wish you'd kept your mouth closed and that I and my mother and sister had been nailed to crosses?"

"No, Never! Last year when I was living in the Subura, I might have sent Macro my portfolio on your Judaean revolution. But Iras destroyed it – so you do owe her something. Maybe a marble marker on her grave.

"I'll tell you what I've often wished. That, for my first military assignment, I'd signed up for service along the Rhine. Then whatever happened in Jerusalem, whether the damned tile fell at the same time or the day before or after, as Fate determined, I'd have been completely uninvolved.

"When we were young, just before I left for my education, if we'd spoken frankly about your dream of freeing your country, I think I'd have faced the fact that our national dreams were on collision courses – and I'd never have returned.

"This last year has made a difference. Life's turned around for me, and I have had successes I never dreamed of just a short time ago. I'd have enjoyed it all somewhat less had you not been alive and present to witness them.

"The night of the fire – when your little lad was concerned about Mother's dog – I realized I could never want harm to come to him or his sister. Even before that, when Macro offered me the opportunity of accusing everyone, I chose not to."

He half-smiled. "You enjoyed saying that you didn't believe I'd commit arson, that it was beneath my dignity. I'd only erred in letting a raving lunatic run around loose to endanger the community. You must've got some satisfaction out of my embarrassment.

"Simonides and I were both taken in at first by Phineas' combination of religious fervour and business ability. I found him slightly pompous and boring, but I tried not to be over-critical. However, by the night of the fire, my opinion of him had changed. I appreciated your defending Tirzah – as I should have done myself – when Phineas accused her of infatuation with you – and Simonides was ready to think it might be true."

"Tirzah didn't deserve to be humiliated. When she spoke to me in Mother's house, it was to defend *you*. I hope she'll be happy in her marriage."

He said, "She's been more cheerful since meeting Barak. I believe he truly loves her."

Thoughtfully he said, "When we were children, you liked us, didn't you? But did you also resent the Jewish people though you kept silent? You never told me about your loathsome nanny – or the prying questions of the High Priest's wife. Did those things prey on your mind?"

"Yes, sometimes. And, while you were plainly horrified if you heard of Roman cruelty, I occasionally reacted the same way to militant street prophets – like the one who declared that some day all nations would have to make yearly trips to Jerusalem or experience drought and plagues. I wanted to walk up to the bearded blatherer and tell him to go to hell."

"He was quoting from the prophet Zechariah. I suppose most non-Jews would resent that prediction. Did you ever speak back to a street orator?"

"Yes, once. And I never regretted it. I said his prophecy was silly and that rather than crawling to pay homage to his God, I'd prefer to find a lonely far-out Atlantic island and stay there, maybe with no God at all."

Judah looked shocked and rather sad.

"You had all that resentment bottled up inside you? And you still feel it?"

"Yes, I suppose I do. Anyway, In a few days Sergia and I will be far away. My brother's agent will take care of the property. You won't have to think about me at all."

He left soon after that, but wished me well, and I gave the proper courteous response.

CHAPTER FORTY-SIX

I didn't send flowers to Iras' funeral. Though Judah was being gracious, I could imagine the sarcastic reaction of certain other people, especially Simonides, who apparently thought I should have atoned for my misdeeds by enduring further years with a woman for whom I had no desire. A violent woman who'd already tried to murder me! I pitied her, but I was extremely glad to be with Sergia.

Also, I recognized that, in his heart, Judah didn't really want reconciliation; he couldn't erase from his mind the misery of his service in the galleys and the suffering of his mother and sister. He wanted to be fair and to obey the teachings of Jesus about forgiveness. But enough was enough.

We stayed for another day in our villa overlooking the sea. I engaged some extra workmen to check out the rock piles beside my stairs going down to the beach. I've been told that Ben-Hur had also removed most of the rocks on his side of the beach. He was probably thinking that his children could come to harm climbing around large rocks even if they weren't sheltering poisonous snakes.

Then we travelled to the farm north of Pompeii. Velleius sent Sergia her beloved horse and included the groom who brought it as a wedding gift. He sent me no message but grudgingly wished his granddaughter well. He was relieved that she was going away for a while. Perhaps by the time he saw her again the talk about Antonius' death and her immediate marriage to me would be replaced by some other scandal.

For a few days we rode our horses around the property, enjoying the country air full of the scent of ripening grapes and orange orchards mingled with the fragrance of hay fields. The dogs played and rested under the trees.

Then it was time to go to my brother's place and board the Nereid. We'd engaged a cargo boat for the horses. We took the grey team, Sheba, and her foal, Algol, and Sergia's mare, Atalanta. We had to leave the Flammifer, and I felt rather sad. But I could rent a sailboat if I had time to sail around the harbour of Messana. Since I'd be busy with my official duties and would also need to visit my estate with its vineyards and flocks of sheep, I might have to content myself with looking at my waxed laurel wreath, which I planned to hang in the household shrine.

Cypros and Herod sent us a gift of silver cups. In his accompanying letter, Herod told us that his regular driver, Eutychus, proudly bearing the name of a famous charioteer, had apparently tired of his station in life. Perhaps it was the gulf he felt between his life as Herod's servant and that of his celebrated namesake. Accordingly, he quietly took off for an unknown destination taking with him several of Herod's most gorgeous robes.

"The fellow was always rather arrogant," Herod wrote. "But I must say I rather enjoyed the showy way he handled my carriage. However, he's gone too far this time. I won't be merciful when they catch him. How dare he help himself to my finest robes, the ones encrusted with gold, silver, and precious gems?"

Tiberius Gemellus sent me a brief letter, wishing I weren't going away. He'd have liked me to marry Lutatia and to continue living nearby. He was trying to do well in his studies and sports – making the best of things.

I remembered a recent speech by Herod. "I take a proper interest in my own boy, who is very bright and a credit to the house of Herod. But it's a penance to spend time stimulating Gemellus' mind. You evidently have the knack of it, but I'd rather not be bothered – except that I'm paid to do it."

His uncle Herod Philip was dead, and it seemed high time for Tiberius Caesar to decide to award the vacant tetrarchy to a deserving person, preferably Herod Agrippa. But he'd made no promises.

We boarded the Nereid after saying goodbye to Barbatus and Lepida. The dogs came with us to our large cabin. There was still a lot of room for the staff we were taking with us. As darkness settled down over the great bay, our boat went smoothly with the night tide. When we awoke the next morning we were well out to sea. Two days later we docked at Messana.

I had an office in the chief government building where the governor had quarters when he visited the city. However, Sergia and I took possession of a large villa that really belonged to my brother. It had been cared for by a small staff of servants; everything was clean and comfortable but not particularly showy or new. It had good marble tile throughout and several wall frescoes that needed a little brightening up. There was an attractive garden inside the peristylum with an abundance of colourful flowers, especially scarlet poppies that flourished in the hot sunshine. There was also a small fountain with a slightly weathered marble statue of Venus. We could let the horses graze in the field behind the house and take our dogs there for walks. Sergia liked the place, and she bought some hangings and small pieces of art to make it more alive and homelike.

We drove out to my rural villa, which wasn't in bad condition but needed some painting and redecorating. Sergia enjoyed taking charge of this project, giving the villa her personal touch. I was pleased that the vineyards were in good shape but was concerned at the shepherds' complaints about robberies by a band of scruffy marauders who lived in caves in the hills. I gathered they were a problem for all the local sheep farmers.

I didn't have to travel to the capital, Syracuse, to see the governor, as he came to Messana to interview me and discuss local needs.

Sicily isn't under military rule, but we have law-keeping cohorts and urban vigiles on the watch for fires, the same as in Rome. There are magistrates who take care of most disputes and infractions of the law, though a serious matter could be referred to me, or even to the governor. I also had to supervise port administration and see that duties were paid where required.

Sergia and I entertained the governor in our town villa during the three days he was in Messana. I felt extremely proud of my wife as she organized the household perfectly, planning menus and decorations and welcoming the governor and his lady with grace and charm. The servants all respected her, yet she never screamed or snapped at them; she just had natural authority, as if she was born to be a queen.

In September we celebrated the grape harvest, watching the workers tramp out the grapes. It was an occasion for singing, dancing, and feasting. Wine bottles from previous seasons were opened and enjoyed. Sergia and I were restrained as befitted our position; we didn't expose ourselves in scanty attire or take part in wild Bacchinalian dances, but we did have garlands of grape leaves in our hair, and Sergia had a grape leaf necklace. We walked around the vineyards and the courtyard greeting everyone with friendliness.

It was also the time for the Ludi Romani, the mid-September Games. Since the governor was officiating in Syracuse, it became my obligation to occupy the place of honour in Messana: to represent the head of state during the gladiatorial contests, the animal shows – and, of course, the chariot races.

With Sergia at my side, I presided, enforcing rules, and awarding prizes. I think I was scrupulously fair; during the races I disqualified one driver for striking a rival's team (hoping no one there would know that I'd ever done such a thing myself). I also disqualified a contestant for taking a competitor's wheel off resulting in the unfortunate man's death as he failed to cut himself loose from his frantic team and so was dragged along and finally trampled by the team following. Remembering my own experience, it took fortitude to watch that with apparent indifference.

At the end of September I received letters from Barbatus and Cypros, both of them telling me that Herod Agrippa had been arrested. His runaway driver, Eutychus, had been caught in Brundisium, where he was trying to arrange a passage to Greece. He didn't have Herod's robes in his possession but had likely sold them for ready cash. He insisted that he was an innocent man and had left Herod's service so abruptly only because he'd heard treasonous conversations between Herod and his good friend Caligula. He said that, while he was driving the two of them in a carriage, they'd talked audibly about their hopes. Especially Caligula's hopes! Herod allegedly said that it was about time the aged Emperor passed on, one way or another, and left the rule of the Roman Empire to his worthy young grandnephew, Gaius Caligula.

Herod denied these accusations, but Tiberius Caesar ordered his imprisonment to await trial, which would take place sometime or other, once he'd had time to think about the case. Cypros would be allowed to furnish him with clothing and extra food, and he could spend time each day in an exercise yard, the same yard where Phineas Ben Zebulon had climbed a wall and fallen to his death.

Cypros wrote, "Please write to the Emperor and put in a word for Herod. I'm desperate; I don't want to lose my dear husband, the father of my four children. The disgrace is horrible. I know Herod cultivated Caligula's friendship, but he wouldn't scheme against Caesar, I'm sure.

"I'm angry at Gemellus. I admit Herod neglected him, and the boy preferred you as a mentor and instructor. Still I wish he hadn't told his grandfather that Herod was *always* ignoring him, not wanting to be bothered with him, and constantly preferring to go places with Caligula."

Unfortunately, everything Gemellus said about Herod was quite true. Gemellus had good reason to hold a grudge against both Herod and Caligula. However, I'd write to the Emperor and do my best for Herod. I could point out that Herod wasn't a stupid man. If he'd had such disloyal sentiments, he surely wouldn't have been foolish enough to utter them in the hearing of a servant.

Cypros also said, "The children and I can no longer live in our quarters at the palace. Ben-Hur has kindly found us a nice house and is charging us just a nominal rent. I believe he's wrong in his notions about the Nazarene as the Messiah – and even the Son of Almighty God, but he's been kindness itself in my terrifying situation."

Replying to my letter, Tiberius Caesar sent me a brief note saying that Herod's case was under consideration. The implication was that, unless I had real evidence to offer, I would be wise to shut up.

CHAPTER FORTY-SEVEN

LIKE other landowners in this part of Sicily, I was increasingly annoyed by the outlaw bands that kept raiding our flocks. They were expanding their operations now, attacking farms and even invading houses. I decided to organize attacks on them where they lived – in a system of caves in the hills.

I used a law-enforcement team unit from the town and also recruited local volunteers from the farming community. Having found a couple of helpful informers, I was finally ready to lead a surprise raid – one of several planned for about the same time, targeting different caves. Fittingly, we had chosen the last day of October which, according to the Celts, is when evil spirits and deceased ancestors revisit the earth: a proper day for darkness and fear. I knew the outlaws weren't Celts, but I'd noticed that sensational superstition tends to travel across intercultural boundaries.

As I suspected, the planned raids didn't completely surprise the outlaws. They'd made some preparations; however, we outmanoeuvred them effectively and killed or captured many of them, taking control of their caves. I could make a longer story of all this, but I've already done so in my report to the Emperor, which Sosius published.

While my men were collecting the loot they found in the caves, I was questioning prisoners, trying to find our where their leader had gone. One of them let slip that the Wolf, the chief of the robbers, had led a small band into the valley where my own estate was located, rich and tempting. Quickly I divided my forces, sending the necessary men to Messana with bound prisoners, but taking my best cohorts and volunteers with me to the valley as fast as we could ride or run.

I'd given instructions to my servants to be prepared for raids, so the robbers had met some opposition before we arrived. Riding in, we immediately got into a battle with thieves trying to carry off wine casks and drive off the best animals. I was on Sheba when I saw someone trying to put a rope on Algol, my colt. In addition to regular military equipment, I had a slingshot and a few smooth stones. As a child, remembering tales I'd been told of David, the shepherd king of Israel, I'd often practised my skill. This proved advantageous. I got the horse thief right in the middle of his sloping forehead, and he fell back senseless.

We slashed and stabbed our way to the house. In fact I rode Sheba right into the vestibule. I dismounted and ran into the atrium, followed by a number of my men. The servants were fighting or just struggling and screaming, depending on what they could do. I saw Sergia at the top of the stairs, looking over the wide balustrade. My dog Tarquin was fighting for us; he'd pulled one outlaw down and was tearing out his throat. For Father, he'd always been a big, gentle dog who simply *looked* fierce. Here his inbred killer instinct was emerging as if he'd been created to tear to pieces the criminals in the arena.

A fellow with a curved sword was about to slash Tarquin. I thrust him through the belly with my own Roman sword, and he fell backward. "Attack my dog, will you?" I snarled at him and swiftly cut his bearded throat.

A tall man with a yellowish wildcat fur over his cuirass was gazing up at Sergia, laughing and showing his yellow teeth. Before I could get at him, she had pushed a large, heavy painted vase containing a houseplant down onto his head. He bent forward and fell over with his head and knees close together. Pottery pieces, leaves, flowers, and earth were all over and around him.

Meanwhile my men were getting the better of the raiders, inside and outside. One man swung his axe at me, but his aim was put off when little Flora, who'd escaped from Sergia's protection, nipped him in the leg with her sharp teeth. While he was recovering from the surprise, I took advantage and ran him through. It came to my mind that not even in the skirmishes with Parthians on the Syrian border had I done so much personal skewering of my foes.

Tarquin, huge and powerful, showed himself a worthy descendant of his ancestors from the Fortunate Isles* and chased several outlaws out of the house and into the clutches of my men, who were mopping up the remaining combatants in the gardens and farmyards. We now had things under control. The enemies who weren't lying dead in their gore were being roped together. After being taken to Messana, they'd either be crucified or sent to the mines. I'd made up my mind not to send anyone to the galleys, where paid professional rowers were preferred anyway.

It wasn't all joy and relief. After sinking his teeth into several outlaws, killing one and seriously injuring at least a couple of others, Tarquin was exhausted. He sank down breathing very heavily making sounds as if in pain. I feared he was having a heart attack. I examined him, talking to him gently, while Sergia pushed a spoonful of wine into his mouth. There were no marks on him from sword or knife and no apparent bruises, though later I concluded that some vicious bastard had likely kicked him in the ribs. He was an old dog, and he'd been giving the last of his strength in defence of his people and home. He licked my hand, his big head lowered against his paws, and his chest heaved several times. I feared losing him the way I did Argus, long ago.

We made Tarquin as comfortable as we could and gave him a little more wine. He rested for the remainder of the day and gradually regained some of his energy. I was glad we didn't have to say goodbye to him just yet.

---

*The Canary Islands, noted for large, fierce dogs

Back in Messana, I wrote reports to the governor and to Tiberius. I also sent an account to Sosius containing the same information with a few more descriptive flourishes. I suggested that, if it were published, a suitable title would be *Lupus in Fabula**. For the Wolf, the outlaw leader, was the very man with the yellow teeth and matching fur piece that Sergia had bashed so effectively with the heavy flowerpot. He never woke up. An ignominious conclusion to the career of a much-feared robber chief.

---

* *The Wolf in the Tale*; or one might say, "Speak of the Wolf"

CHAPTER FORTY-EIGHT

A FTER the battle with the hill bandits, we enjoyed our days in Sicily. I had four of the bandit leaders crucified; I chose the fittest and best trained in arms from the remainder to go to Rome to be prepared for the arena, where they'd most likely die in combat but had at least a chance of becoming successful gladiators who might even obtain freedom and fortune. Those who would've been dismal failures as public combatants were sent to mines in the south of Sicily, where they would labour hard and die in a few years.

With this band of miscreants out of the way, life was pleasant. Sergia and I found time to go to the famous classical theatre at Taorminium, where we saw productions of *Oedipus Rex* and *Iphigenia at Tauris*. My only regret was that in classical Greek theatre the men and women of the audience must sit separately; the performances are considered religious ceremonies. I'd have preferred to have Sergia at my side, sharing the experience. However, we talked a lot afterwards about the plots of Greek tragedies.

We celebrated part of the Saturnalia in our town house, entertaining local government staff and also had holiday festivities at the farm. We didn't go in for all the traditions of Saturnalia; for instance, we didn't give our slaves permission to order us around or act like masters. We had too much regard for our dignity. But we did give them time off and, both in the town and the country, we put on special banquets for everyone who worked for us. I politely refused the suggestion of one of the maids in our town residence that I share my bed with her; similarly, Sergia informed one of our footmen that his Saturnalia privileges didn't include sexual games with the lady of the house, whatever might take place in households with lower standards.

Soon after the New Year, the quaestor appointed by Tiberius and the Senate arrived, and it was time for us to pack up and leave. The Nereid was at Ostia for the winter, so we found ourselves another ship, the Cassiopeia, as well as a cargo boat for the horses.

Though it was January, we didn't encounter any storms, and when we entered the harbour of Puteoli the sun was shining brightly on the blue waves. As we knew the Emperor to be on Capri, I didn't report to him in person but sent word of my return and readiness for new service. He replied in a brief letter that he'd like me to resume some tutoring of Gemellus. I was glad to do so, and the boy was very happy to see me again, though he missed his sister and Lutatia.

It was a good feeling to set foot in our own atrium and to burn a little incense in the shrine of our Lares and Penates. It was cooler than in Messana, but we had warm covers and portable stoves for the evenings, and in the daytime the sun was bright.

Sergia was now in the third month of pregnancy, though no longer suffering from the occasional nausea that had sometimes annoyed her in the morning. Her body was still slender, except that her breasts were fuller and her belly a little more rounded. In my opinion, she was lovelier than ever.

We called on Cypros at the house she was renting in Misenum. She was woebegone, thinking of Herod Agrippa still languishing in Caesar's prison. Tiberius refused to be hurried in dealing with the case. I remembered Asinius Gallus who'd awaited a hearing for years until he died in prison.

Cypros had just read my short book *Lupus in Fabula*. We

conversed a little about conditions in Sicily: the grape harvest, the bandits, the fascination of a large but currently inactive volcano, and the experience of attending a world-famous Greek classical theatre.

Soon the topic was the dismal situation of Herod.

She said, "Poor Herod is so unhappy! I do wish the Emperor would have some fairness, some compassion – and let Herod appear before him to explain the truth of the matter. Messala, could you try again to ask the Emperor?"

"In his reply to me, Caesar indicated that he didn't want to be bothered about it – that he would see about Herod when he was good and ready."

"I was afraid of that. I've even asked Judah to intercede, but I think he doesn't trust Herod and may even feel safer because he's in jail. Maybe he thinks Herod was gossiping to Caligula about some of his former activities."

I didn't tell her that I thought it very likely and that Herod had probably talked about me too – in which case neither Judah nor I would be secure if Caligula replaced Tiberius as Emperor.

Cypros went on. "It's too bad. My children need their father. I need my husband. We had some more news recently about that strange fellow, Saul of Tarsus, and it's upset Herod more than ever. We told you about Saul, didn't we?

"Most of the leaders in Jerusalem had counted on Saul to energetically track down the Nazarene's followers and crush the whole movement. But Saul completely changed his mind about the sect: the Christians, as they call themselves in Antioch. Of course, Judah and his family are pleased about that – and they've said so to me. They've tried to convert me – as well as being very kind and generous with anything my household might need. As if they thought gratitude might win me.

"Meanwhile Saul's kept proclaiming his new beliefs regarding Jesus, winning new Christians but also angering many people. At last he had to make an escape from Damascus in a basket lowered over the city wall. Now they say he's gone to a place in the desert to meditate, and no one is clear about what he might do later on."

The thought of Saul, free to direct his passionate spirit and energy to the Christian cause, depressed Herod. He'd complained to Cypros, "That turncoat is in the clean desert air, likely enjoying sunsets and bird songs on a local oasis. And I'm in this chilly Roman prison!"

Remembering my life in the Subura, I felt sympathy for Herod.

She asked me what I thought about the Christians.

I replied, "They don't greatly concern me. If they were a band of Jewish rebels planning a war, I wouldn't cheer them on; but, if they're non-violent, I see no reason to get involved."

Was she trying to influence me as she and Herod had done when they wined and dined me and tried to draw me into a scheme against Ben-Hur, in spite of the consideration he and his family had shown her? Of course! Herod always came first with Cypros.

She said thoughtfully, "You talked to Judah a few times last summer, didn't you? I trust you didn't tell him about Herod's asking you to work with a special organization."

"No, we never got into that subject." Now I wondered if I should warn him about Herod. Tiberius favoured Judah and was displeased with Herod for good reason, even supposing Eutychus' story to be an exaggeration. But if Caligula gained power, not only would Gemellus be unsafe, I'd certainly feel the weight of his dislike, and Ben-Hur might be in serious trouble. Herod would have no scruples about accusing him of disloyalty and rebellion.

CHAPTER FORTY-NINE

WHEN the Emperor returned to Misenum, I went to the palace and presented myself. Tiberius was planning to travel north as far as Rome. He said it was time to reacquaint himself with his country and to show everyone that even in his late seventies he was remarkably fit, both physically and mentally. I sensed that he had been irked by the story about Herod and Caligula commenting on his approaching senility and hoped-for demise.

He was friendly to me and sent his best wishes to Sergia, congratulating both of us when I told him we were expecting a child. He'd enjoyed reading about our victory over the Wolf and his bandit gang.

"You've done well. In the fall you should be able to enter the Senate. Meantime I'm glad you're giving attention to Tiberius Gemellus. Herod Agrippa let me down; he was most ungrateful in carrying out his responsibilities to my grandson."

Gemellus enjoyed visiting me at my villa, and he admired Sergia, although he still regretted that Lutatia was so far away in Cyprus.

He said, "If I'd been a little older, ready to put on the toga virilis*, I might have been the one to marry her. Many boys of my age have had the manhood ceremony, but I don't look old enough."

---

*The plain white toga worn for the first time in the ceremony of manhood

I told him, "Some fellows wait until they're seventeen – when one can become a contubernalis in military service. Who knows? By that time Lutatia herself could be available. Her husband is past forty, after all."

I wasn't wishing for Sergius Paulus' death. From what I knew of him, I rather liked him. I just wanted to cheer Gemellus up.

We went fishing sometimes, and I supplemented his riding teacher's instruction. I even taught him how to use the reins of a carriage or chariot and sometimes took him for practice in a long laneway.

Sergia accompanied us on a lot of local excursions, visiting places of interest. As the warm weather increased, we occasionally made a fire on the beach and fried fresh fish. Sometimes we saw members of the Hur household at a distance, but we never got together.

Cypros had mentioned that Simonides had gone back to Antioch, but Tirzah had still not actually married Barak, and their enthusiasm seemed to be cooling.

The Emperor's journey to coastal towns ended before he actually reached Rome. Attending some local games of welcome in a town along his route, he attempted to demonstrate his fitness by taking a javelin and hurling it at a wild boar in the arena. He hit the beast but complained of a chest pain afterwards. He had exerted himself too much. Urged by his doctors, he consented to turn back to his home in Misenum. He talked of going all the way to Rome later in the spring.

Back in Misenum, he invited some local residents, including Sergia and me, to a banquet. He appeared well and cheerful, though his face was a little red. He was affable to the comparatively small company of guests.

Ben-Hur and his wife Esther were there. We exchanged brief greetings. Sergia had met Esther and her two children on the beach, where there is no fence to divide our property. The children wanted to get acquainted with little Flora – Tarquin was out in the boat with me – and Sergia admired their sand castle. Sergia told me that Lady Miriam watched everything from the garden above the beach, but she didn't come down because ascending the steps again would be bad for her heart.

At the banquet, Caligula approached Ben-Hur and urged him to part with his prize stallion, Aldebaran. Understandably, he wasn't successful. Judah said that his favourite horse was no longer a racer, though able to serve as a stud.

"That horse is an old friend. I'd never sell him; he's mine for life."

Caligula walked away looking displeased. He said audibly to Ahenobarbus, "I don't care. Even when Arrius' old horse was in its prime, it couldn't have beaten my Incitatus."

He went on, rather wearisomely, to inform everyone near him of the perfections of Incitatus. Then he impudently asked me, "Messala, do *you* think Incitatus could have outrun Arrius' Arab nag? You used to live in the East. Maybe you had the chance to see it run."

Obviously Herod had told him all about it. I controlled myself and said as casually as I could, "I didn't really get a good look." Softly to Sergia I added, "Not having eyes in the back of my head." I'd been leading during most of the race. I think Judah heard what I said, but he didn't respond.

I added, "I've never seen your magnificent Incitatus in action either. Some day I should go to the local races – when I've nothing much else to do – and watch you coast to victory."

To myself I admitted that my apparent lack of interest in chariot races was reminiscent of Aesop's fox that decided the unreachable grapes must be sour.

Caligula said, "Didn't you inherit a black mare that had been bred to one of Caesar's best stallions? How did the foal turn out?"

"Very well. The colt will be a yearling around the end of June. Inspired by the night sky, I named him Algol. Whether or not he proves fast, I've no intention of parting with him. Like Arrius, I can form a strong attachment to an animal."

"Like the dog you wrote about," said the Emperor, suddenly appearing behind Caligula. He was known to be sentimental about a large pet lizard.

"Why, of all the stars, did you name the colt 'Algol'?" he asked. "Isn't that supposed to be an unlucky star?"

"I did so for that very reason. Algol probably won't have to share his name with any other horse. And who knows – for me he may be good luck."

We went to the triclinium and the evening continued. Tiberius Caesar looked increasingly flushed, and his private physician, Charicles, slipped to his side and checked his pulse, receiving an angry response from the Emperor. But before the banquet was over, while we were helping ourselves to cream-filled pastries, he fell over on his couch. The doctor once more rushed to his side and revived him with smelling salts. When the banquet ended, Tiberius Caesar stood with a lictor at the door to say goodnight to each of his guests. It was the last time I saw him alive.

CHAPTER FIFTY

TO the best of my information, Tiberius Caesar died on March sixteenth, the very day after the anniversary of the assassination of Julius Caesar. There's some confusion about this. It's been reported by servants' gossip that Tiberius died in his bed and that Caligula and his friends were rejoicing noisily when a slave informed them that the Emperor had come out of an apparent coma and was demanding food and wine. Caligula and Macro rushed to his bedside, and we don't know for sure what happened there. They said they found the old Emperor dead and suggested that perhaps he'd revived briefly but then collapsed again. In any case, they insisted he was definitely dead when they got to him. Of course there's been speculation that they smothered him with one of his own pillows. Whatever the truth, Caligula was the new Emperor.

Tiberius' will left the rule of the Empire to his grandnephew, Gaius Caligula, and his grandson, Tiberius Gemellus, jointly, with the assumption that until Gemellus reached maturity, the responsibility would rest on Caligula. There was a rumour that the old man had misgivings about this, but he saw no way of protecting the boy other than living as long as he could. Maybe he thought of eliminating Caligula as he'd already done with some other family members; however, Caligula was always submissive to the point of servility in all his audiences with the old Emperor. Perhaps Tiberius wanted to believe that this one young kinsman wasn't an ambitious enemy like the others.

Tiberius had a splendid funeral in Rome, and Caligula delivered a fine eulogy in which he praised the deceased fulsomely. Having got that over with, he made several quite different speeches before informal gatherings. He even had a tear-jerking tale of how he once entered the Emperor's chamber, thinking to avenge his mother and brothers. However, Jupiter himself spoke to him and told him not to attempt vengeance: the Furies were already taking care of the matter, tormenting Tiberius in his dreams. This was a fiction as good as any tale I ever wrote.

Most of the peninsula's gentry travelled to Rome for the funeral. Sergia and I went by ship; it was very calm sailing. If we'd gone by carriage, the jolting might have been bad for her.

In Rome we stayed at my brother's mansion.

After placing Tiberius' ashes in the family monument, Caligula sailed out to the two islands where his mother and eldest brother had died. He'd also had a second brother who'd been imprisoned in an attic, where he apparently died of starvation after attempting to eat the stuffing of his mattress. Caligula gave all his family members a respectful public internment. Then he appeared before the Senate, which proclaimed him Emperor. Nothing was said about the claims of Gemellus; however, Caligula graciously gave him the title Youth Leader. It's never been clear what that appointment involved – if anything.

We went back to Misenum. There was an understanding that, since I'd served as quaestor, a Senate committee would look at my financial position and admit me to the Senate in the fall. At that time we'd have to acquire a town residence; we couldn't keep on imposing on my brother. Besides, Sergia ought to be mistress of a house of her own.

For a little while things went quite smoothly. Right after Tiberius' death, Caligula had released Herod to house arrest in the villa with Cypros and the children. When he returned after being proclaimed Emperor, he declared Herod not guilty of anything and bestowed the tetrarchy of the late Herod Philip on him. Thus Herod could count on a princely income from the revenue of his country. He wasn't free to go there and take possession yet because Caligula felt the need of his friendship and wise counsel. So he remained in Italy, sometimes in Rome, sometimes in Antium or Misenum, but always at an imperial palace, and he made a point of telling Caligula that he believed his other uncle, Herod Antipas, the tetrarch of Galilee, was a secret nationalist conspirator who was collecting weapons. He had rooms full of hoarded swords, spears, catapults, battering rams, and other military equipment. Herod Agrippa said that, of course, his uncle would explain all this away to Romans as intended for defence against rebels.

Herod Agrippa's accusations were no secret; they'd become common gossip. He had great ambition and now saw a golden road of opportunity. It made no difference to him that his own sister, Herodias, was married to Herod Antipas and was attached to him, having left another uncle-husband for him.

One day I had a conversation with Ben-Hur. We were both in the area where our beach properties joined, so we spoke politely, each of us acting as if all was well. However, he did seem a bit downcast.

He said, "I'm thinking seriously of going back to my old home, at least for a while."

"Is something wrong?"

"Tirzah's fiancé has rejected his betrothal contract. Sanballat induced him to do it with support from his family. They're opposed to his Christian faith, though they leaned toward it once. I'm glad she isn't marrying him, though I think a change of scene would be good for her."

He seemed rather surprised at himself for confiding all this to me. He must have sensed that I truly wished Tirzah only good.

"You are friends with Herod Agrippa. How much do you trust him?" he asked.

"Actually I *don't* trust him, though I find him very likable. He and Cypros came to me my first autumn in Baiae and offered me friendship. I appreciated that. But I realized he was prepared to sacrifice me or anyone else – except Cypros and his children – to his ambition. He has Caligula's favour and has gained a tetrarchy, but he's willing to badmouth his uncle, the husband of his sister, to obtain another tetrarchy. And in due course he'd like to get Judaea too; then he'd have all the territory that was once ruled by Herod the Great.

"It's not just power in his homeland he craves. He also wants very much to be liked – and honoured – by the leaders in Jerusalem. If they see the sect of the Nazarene, the Christians, as a threat, then Herod is willing to be the champion of the traditional faith and the enemy of heresy. He may have blabbed freely to Caligula about – your patriotic past. He got some information from Caiaphas and asked me for further details – but didn't get them, thanks to Iras."

"I was wondering about that. And what about you? I gather that Caligula doesn't like you. That was apparent at the last imperial banquet. I'm sure you had some hopes of advancement. But what about now – with Caligula as Emperor?"

"I don't think I can advance very far while Caligula reigns. Becoming Emperor hasn't made him more tolerant of whatever he resents in my personality. He makes snide remarks about my friendship with Gemellus, though he hasn't forbidden it – yet. I think while he's in Misenum, Sergia and I might spend some time at our farm near Pompeii."

"I take it you really like rural life – and sailing your boat."

"Oh, yes, and it's a good thing I can content myself with outdoor activities because I don't think I'll be offered any further magisterial positions under Caligula. I feel sorry for Gemellus, but it may be impossible to help him."

He was unable to hide a degree of wonderment that I could calmly face a major block to my ambition and that I was sincerely concerned about Gemellus.

He said, "If my Esther weren't expecting a child in June, I think we'd sail for the East immediately. I just hope I don't regret the delay."

He was clearly uneasy about his decision and might very well change his mind and sail away without waiting another month for the birth of his third child. The weather was quite pleasant, and there were many places where he could dock his boat if it seemed advisable.

Despite all the enmity in our past and the uncertain cordiality of the present, I would miss him when he departed.

We went to the farm and stayed there three market intervals, pleased with the condition of the orchards and vineyards. Blandus had a farm nearby, close to the town of Nola, and Gemellus had been invited there to visit his sister. Caligula was busy, partly in Rome, partly in the comparatively new resort of Antium.

The spring weather was bright and sunny, and we all hoped this might help restore the boy's health. He'd had a severe cold in the winter, and the resultant cough had not only lingered but worsened. He kept taking a medicine which smelled of all the usual ingredients presumed to defeat a cough. I'd taken something similar for my bad chest cold that miserable spring in the Subura.

In May we returned to our house overlooking the sea.

Gemellus was back in the local palace, supervised by tutors. Caligula sent me a note to the effect that he didn't wish me to call on the boy, much less counsel him any more; he felt that I would make Gemellus discontented with the instructors he had.

One day, on a street in Misenum, I met Agrippina, the cleverest of Caligula's sisters. She was finally pregnant after several years of marriage to hard-drinking Ahenobarbus. She was happy and eager to tell people about her hopes. So far her sisters Drusilla and Julilla were childless, as was Caligula himself.

She's a fine-looking woman, with keen black eyes and thick black hair pulled back into a large bun. She openly scorns the very fussy hairstyles of her sister-in-law Domitia Lepida. Though attractive, she lacks Sergia's special beauty: her glowing complexion and the sun-touched dark curls which frame her exquisite face.

She said to me, "Obviously you're happy in your marriage, Sergia must have given you more satisfaction that she ever gave Calvus or Antonius. And maybe you gave *her* more satisfaction."

She was probing.

I answered, "We've been fortunate in each other."

"But now that she's showing her condition, soon you might have difficulty taking your full pleasure. I'm not so far along yet. My son – I hope for a son – should emerge into the world in December. But it doesn't matter to Ahenobarbus. He prefers his wine."

Clearly she was hinting that she was open to a passionate encounter with me. She was pregnant, bored, and openly lustful. I had to be careful not to anger her, but I didn't want to do anything that would hurt Sergia and damage our relationship. I wondered if the early moral guidance of Lady Miriam had belatedly taken hold of me.

"Sergia and I have found no impediment to our mutual pleasure. And there'll still be things we can do even close to her time."

Later Sergia told me she had noticed that Agrippina kept watching me on the street. "Darling, I'm telling you – I don't want to share you at all."

We made love for about an hour before bathing and then had dinner.

My brother and his family came to Baiae. We entertained them and they invited us back. We also socialized with my cousins and with my old friend Caprarius and his wife, who had taken a summer villa near us.

Gemellus and one of his servants rode over to our place a couple of times – without Caligula's permission. His education was being taken care of, though not by Herod. He said that he was kept indoors a lot, working at his lesson books. Caligula had said this was important for him. His cough persisted, and he carried his bottle of medicine with him.

Caligula was still very popular. The common people called him pet names such as Chicken and Star. He cut taxes and embarked on expensive building projects. He also recalled all exiles and dismissed criminal charges that had been pending since Tiberius' reign. He appeared to have burned the written evidence that had been brought forward against his mother and brothers, which must have relieved those who'd given the evidence if they could have been sure that Caligula had really destroyed their recorded testimonies. He published a regular budget and revived the electoral system for magistrates. He also paid all the bequests in Tiberius' will and compensated many people whose houses had been damaged in the great Aventine fire. He gave presents of money to the common citizens and staged frequent games and public spectacles.

He'd tired of his affair with Macro's wife Ennia and was exploring other women. The husband of Drusilla, his favourite sister, had gone to Greece as a governor, but Caligula insisted that she stay in Italy, as near him as possible. He bragged that he had been intimate with all three of his sisters, and he made open advances to married women. At one banquet, he looked over several married women, then invited one of them to leave the table with him. In a little while he came back and boasted of what the two had done together, publicly describing the lady's good and bad physical features (for example, fat backside and skinny legs) and rating her sexual performance, much to her humiliation. I wasn't at that banquet; Caligula didn't invite me then or any other time. After hearing of this conduct I thought I'd prefer to miss future banquets too, particularly once Sergia had given birth and had her normal figure back. I could imagine Caligula inspecting her and deciding to try her out. And then I'd try to kill him!

Cypros approached me, wanting to talk seriously.

"You've always been my friend. When I was thirteen, I was in love with you – but I knew it was no use. And now I truly love my husband, though sometimes he exasperates me.

"Ben-Hur and Esther were good to us when Herod was in jail. Am I right in thinking that you and Judah sometimes talk quite civilly to each other – without declarations of eternal hate?"

"Yes, you could say that."

She went on. "I can't go along with their religious ideas – about Jesus rising from the dead and after forty days going up to join his Heavenly Father. Herod and I try to think like real Jews, even if our blood is a bit mixed. But I don't want to be ungrateful. They've already suffered greatly. Do you agree?"

"Yes, I agree. In spite of their present civility, they must still hate me when they think of Miriam and Tirzah's imprisonment and – whatever illness they had."

"It could have been real leprosy. Esther described it to me. There was an ulcer on Tirzah's face making her partly blind. Her mother had more typical symptoms: numb white spots, hair white as snow. But they might not have contracted leprosy from their cell. Lady Miriam had a sick slave woman once and sent her to the High Priest. He judged that her skin affliction was leprosy, so she was sent out to the cave tombs where the lepers are permitted to live. But the Hur women didn't find the girl there when they went themselves.

"The miracle itself sounds too fantastic to be true. Everything apparently cleared up immediately when Jesus spoke a word of healing. That's what Esther told me."

I was astonished. "He must have had a supernatural gift then, like Aesculapius. Among Greeks and Romans it's natural to think that such an unusually gifted person must be a God, or at least the son of a God. But to a Jew, there's only one God. I know the Hurs have deviated drastically from the main body of Judaism."

"Ben-Hur thinks most of his fellow Jews are blind to the truth. Now my dear Herod wants to be a popular ruler, and it annoys him to think of the influence a Hur prince could have among his own people. It would make them more hostile to the idea of Herod on the throne – instead of a blood descendant of David, as they say Jesus was."

"Does Judah preach to crowds or just tell his story to some individuals?"

"Just the latter, I believe. And I should assure you that he avoids using the names of those who've injured him, though a lot of people have heard that the chariot race was for vengeance."

"So I assumed."

"Since Jesus stressed the importance of forgiving one's enemies as one hopes to be forgiven, Judah probably doesn't boast of winning revenge. He talks more about the healing. And he donates a lot of his wealth to the Jerusalem Christian community. This is very helpful as many of them have suffered losses in business. Some of their old neighbours shun them and won't deal with them at all.

"Now he's really planning to leave here. Did you know?"

"He said he was thinking about it. Tirzah may be feeling disappointed over her silly fiancé's change of mind."

Cypros knew all about that. "Barak wants to please his parents, and he's become a friend of Sanballat's older son, so he listens to his disparaging comments about Tirzah and all her family. Since they live near Puteoli, I can see why Judah might prefer to go far away from them."

"You imply that Barak's people have decided not to follow Jesus' teachings or to regard him as the Son of God. Judah also said that about them. So it wouldn't be a good union for the two families. I hope Tirzah doesn't mind too much."

"Frankly, Messala, I think she's relieved. Especially considering that when Barak had a stomach problem in the winter, his mother remarked that, if – the Lord forbid – he should die, Tirzah should obey the ancient custom and be wed to his next brother in order to raise up seed to the deceased. Tirzah got angry and told her it was out of the question. And I certainly don't blame her."

I remembered my conversation with Judah long ago. He had been determined at that time to hold to the ways of his fathers, to the Laws of Moses.

"I don't think he'd force Tirzah – he'd be ashamed to after what she's already endured," said Cypros. "But they're fanatics, so who knows? Herod worries about them. He doesn't want the Hurs to go back to being a religious nuisance in Judaea. He's beginning to wish Caligula would – deal with him."

"Cypros, it may seem a strange reversal on my part, but I don't want Tirzah to be hurt any more. And I don't like the idea of Caligula pouncing on the Hur family."

"Good! You'll be relieved to know that I sent a message to Judah, advising him of danger – maybe coming soon. I strongly suggested that he and his family take ship for other parts. I haven't told Herod what I've done. Please don't say anything to him."

I told her that that I'd say nothing whatever to Herod.

Cypros asked me to warn Judah myself next time we spoke. I wondered what to do. Could I ever risk asking about the miraculous healing of his mother and sister?

The next day I received a brief letter from Caligula, informing me that I wasn't eligible to enter the Senate in September as my quaestorship hadn't lasted a complete year and my record was flawed in other ways. Tiberius had told me otherwise, but obviously this would carry no weight with Caligula.

I discussed our situation with Sergia. I'd looked forward to becoming a senator, but already I'd noticed that some senators were treated with blatant disrespect by the new Emperor, and I had the feeling that things would get worse. Gaius Caesar, popularly called Caligula, didn't look up to any fellow Romans, although he admired Herod and welcomed his unfailing praise.

Sergia said, "We could revisit our property in Sicily, couldn't we? I'll miss this place; I love our garden and the view of the sea. But I never liked the way Caligula looks at me. Even when we were in Rome for the funeral, he managed to leer at me. I really don't want to be a guest at any of his banquets."

"I don't want him to touch you, love. If you don't mind leaving Italy, I think I'd like to pack up and sail away to see how our farm is doing."

Africanus had married a local freedwoman, and I'd offered him the overseership of the farm north of Pompeii. He and his wife were running things well. Now I was thinking about the Sicilian estate.

"We needn't wait for our baby to arrive. We could go to Sicily very soon and be in time for the vintage gathering."

Practically every time I've encountered Caligula, he's referred to the chariot race I didn't win. He's convinced he'd have won it himself. And once he's aware of someone's most sensitive spot, he delights in rubbing it raw. It amuses him to humiliate men of good reputation, airing their weaknesses, and making them look like fools. He particularly enjoys making fun of his uncle Claudius, with his limp, his stammer, and his general clumsiness.

Barbatus said he'd be willing to look after all my Italian property with Philip's help. Since I wasn't going to buy a house in Rome, I spent a fair sum of money on a large second-hand yacht called the Andromeda. It had room for the Flammifer on the deck, and there were enclosed stalls for several horses. We'd take our best pieces of furniture and works of art as we might be away from Italy for some time. Caligula might not want us back.

We were sorry about Gemellus. His cough should've improved with so much warm weather, but it was getting worse. He looked sick. Was Caligula poisoning the boy? It seemed in character. I thought it quite likely that Caligula had pushed the boy off the yacht nearly two years ago. But perhaps it was simply a bad lung infection which the physicians didn't know how to treat. I felt I should say goodbye to Gemellus, though I could do nothing for him. It would be no use asking permission to take the boy with us in the hope the hot Sicilian sun would cure his cough. Indeed, if Caligula did allow him to come with us and Gemellus died, I'd probably be accused of causing his death.

CHAPTER FIFTY-ONE

THE Hur baby, a girl they named Susanna, was born slightly premature in late May. They didn't notify us, but one of the maids mentioned it to Sergia. It was inevitable that our staff would become acquainted with those who worked at the Arrius villa.

Remembering my last conversation with Judah, I imagined they would set out for the East as soon as Esther and the baby were able to travel. We were making travel plans ourselves.

Sergia and I decided to take in a horse fair outside Misenum. We went in a light gig driven by Nestor, who was there to assist us if we decided to buy another horse or two. A mounted groom escorted us. He might be able to lead home an extra horse also. I didn't really need more horses. I just liked to look at them, and so did Sergia.

As we drove slowly through the fairgrounds, commenting on the horses on display, we noticed Ben-Hur with a bay team. There was mutual recognition but we didn't stop to talk.

After a bit I saw an ivory mare that interested me because she reminded me strongly of a horse I'd been very fond of once.

When we came closer, I said, "Gemma!" She turned toward me and whinnied softly. She remembered me. Sergia said, "She's beautiful! How do you know her?"

Then I saw the horse dealer leading forward her old mate. What fantastic luck! Victoria! Rather inappropriately named, as things had turned out. Still – she was a fine mare and had helped win races for me until that last disaster.

I'd brought a few apples, just in case I felt like offering some to a horse I admired, so I spoke to Nestor. He drove the gig near the mares and handed me a couple of apples. I got down and fed them to my old friends and petted their noses while the dealer proceeded to tell me their history and merits. Sergia got out of the carriage and stroked them.

"Sir, they used to be good racehorses. Part of a team that won three times in Syria! They got in an accident when some miserable bastard took the wheel off their chariot. The owner sold them for breeding and light carriage work. Today a gentleman made an offer for them; he'd like to breed them.

"They're not young fillies any more but they're not old nags either. They could still race as a pair. Just look at their teeth."

He took hold of each mare, one at a time, and displayed their healthy-looking mouths and teeth. While he continued to tell anecdotes of their speed and intelligence, I walked around them, touched them and examined them. Nestor got out of the gig and did his own assessment of their condition.

Again I observed Ben-Hur approaching in his chariot. I wondered if he was the interested bidder, the prospective breeder. He seemed to be watching us. I resolved to outbid him if I could.

The dealer said, "That man over there made a decent offer, but I hope I can get him higher." He told me the amount and I raised it without argument. Judah had stopped to talk to someone, so I didn't lose time by long bargaining. I just wanted my horses.

The dealer and I reached an agreement; I paid in full and he threw in a light copper-walled chariot which the mares had pulled for their deceased owner, an elderly Roman businessman who'd purchased them in Antioch a few years ago. I wanted to drive my new horses, so Sergia joined me, saying, "Let me ride with you please!"

Judah drove closer to us, looking curiously at the mares. They were still elegant and obviously bred from partly Arabian stock worthy of Caesar's stables.

He said to me, "I take it you just bought those mares?"

"Yes, I did. Why?"

"I was looking at them earlier, wondering if I should buy them and breed them to Aldebaran."

Breed my mares to his Arabian champion, Sheik Ilderim's delight!

"You really wouldn't want to do that."

I decided to tell him. "They were my horses a few years back. In fact you could say we are fellow survivors."

"Those two were *your* racehorses?" Now he seemed a little embarrassed.

"Yes. I sold them for breeding. I suspected they wouldn't be very willing to race for a new owner. They had minor cuts and had become quite nervous. But now that I've found them again, naturally I want them."

"What happened to your two black stallions? Did you sell them too?"

"Xanthus and Balius, named after the horses of Achilles, were badly injured – so much so that they had to be put down. They became horsemeat to feed the lions."

It was difficult for me to say this.

He looked as if he was thinking of saying "I'm sorry!" but in the end he said nothing.

Sergia spoke up. "In another year maybe Algol would be ready to cover these mares. What if he gave us a pair of black colts?"

I smiled at her. "We'll see." I was picturing a new pair of stallions named Xanthus and Balius.

"It's ironic," I remarked. "For years I tried to obliterate a sentimental streak in myself. I didn't want people to think I was soft. Only now I sometimes find certain emotions catching up with me. And it doesn't seem so regrettable after all. Finding Gemma and Victoria again, I just knew I couldn't let anyone else have them."

"Especially not me," said Judah in a low but audible voice.

I thought of Sheik Ilderim gushing over his Arabians, showering them with endearments, and calling them his children. Nevertheless – he was willing to put them very much at risk in a chariot race for the sake of his pride. He'd have looked to Allah for protection, and if harm had come to his equine children, he'd have wondered what Allah could have been thinking.

As a Roman, I refrained from a public display of feeling for my team, but in private I enjoyed petting all four of my chariot horses.

With some concern, Judah said, "Don't keep trying to suppress all your sensitivity. During the past two years I've been getting used to the fact that it still exists."

"Are you saying it matters to you?"

"Yes, it certainly matters. Perhaps this isn't the best moment to discuss it, but before I leave for Judaea, which will be this month, I'd really like to talk to you – and try to understand the sort of person you are now."

I somewhat dreaded the prospect, but I said agreeably, "Let me know whenever you want to talk."

I asked myself, "What good can come of further discussion? We can't change the past, and I can't become the boy who said goodbye when I was fourteen. I've changed somewhat from the way I was a few years ago, but it's certainly not a total reversal. And I probably wouldn't understand him very well either."

CHAPTER FIFTY-TWO

W E'D completed our travel arrangements; and so had our
neighbours. All my horses except the new pair had been
taken to the Puteoli docks by the grooms. The Andromeda's size and
depth meant that she needed to be anchored in the harbour, not
drawn up to the dock at Barbatus' own place. Sergia had just gone
to Baiae, taking the dogs with her. Tarquin had sat up proudly on
the seat beside her. I'd meet them there later.

I'd been attending to some business matters during the last few
days. There was the need to move my money to several safe places
not easily within Caligula's reach, in case he became more annoyed
with me than usual.

Also we'd written brief letters to some friends and relatives,
including Sergia's grandfather, to let them know we were going
away. We mentioned that we might, in addition to checking on our
property, just enjoy a period of exploring the Mediterranean by sea.

I would leave a message for the Emperor stating that I had to go
to Sicily immediately – trusting that he didn't require my services.
Also I would try to say goodbye to poor Gemellus. Unfortunately,
distracted by my ongoing preparations, including trips to Baiae and

to the Puteoli docks, I hadn't kept up with what was happening at the palace.

I left my chariot and cream-coloured pair in the care of a palace servant who agreed to walk them a little. During the past few days I'd enjoyed giving them short workouts on minor roads. It seemed to be what they craved. They surpassed my expectations in their eagerness to run, and they'd preserved their memory of how to do quick but accurate turns on sharp corners. I thought, "By Jove, they could still race as a pair. But I should resist the temptation."

Inside the palace grounds I quickly sensed a quiet sadness emanating from both guards and servants. Then I saw a throng of people, some in dark mourning togas, in the garden near the wing where Claudius lived.

Someone explained, "It's the funeral of Lady Antonia. A quiet ceremony because the poor woman committed suicide yesterday. They say she intentionally took an overdose of pain medicine."

"Why did she do it? Was she in great pain?"

"Because yesterday morning Caligula had Macro execute Gemellus! Macro ran the boy through with a sword. A slave was killed trying to protect Gemellus."

Gemellus dead! Executed without pretence of a trial! I'd wondered about poison, but this?

"Why did Caesar have him killed? What had the boy done?"

"Caligula says Gemellus' cough medicine must've contained an antidote against poison and that he was trying to poison the food at Caligula's table."

"Indeed! Did anyone show signs of poisoning? Anyone who ate at Caesar's table? Was Caesar himself affected?"

Several people said, "Don't look at me! I really know nothing about it."

I suspected Caligula had tried to poison Gemellus, but it wasn't working fast enough to suit him.

Another man spoke up. "Lady Antonia went to see Caligula, but they say he wasn't very polite to her – insulted her in front of Macro, calling her a silly old woman. Then she went back to her quarters and took a very strong dose of her medicine. Her maid said she spoke of dying because she didn't want to go on living. And now we're gathering for her funeral."

The crowd of mourners in the garden were mostly elderly friends of Lady Antonia. Gemellus' sister, Julia Helena, was there with Blandus, her husband.

They greeted me, and Julia Helena gave way to tears.

"Last year we were so happy for a while, you, and Gemellus, and Lutatia, and me. You made classes so interesting, and my young brother had become so alive, so excited! And now he's gone, and Grandmother's taken her own life, and Lutatia is in Cyprus. She writes that she's pregnant, and she hopes Gaius Caligula will never summon her back here because she detests him."

I remembered that Lutatia dreaded Caligula's occasional advances and his playful touches to her breasts or buttocks. Once she slapped his hand hard and threatened to slap his face if he molested her again. He'd been angry that she'd dared to reject him. If she were nearer now, he'd probably try to get even, to conquer and break her. I noticed Macro watching us, maybe managing to listen.

Blandus answered while his wife sobbed. "There won't be any funeral for Gemellus. This morning Caesar had the corpse burned without any ceremony. He made a brief announcement to those who were present to hear him. He said the boy was an ungrateful brat who'd tried to poison him and had kept taking cough medicine with an antidote against the poison. Then he laughed and shouted triumphantly, 'There's no antidote against Caesar!'"

"Blandus, I tasted that cough medicine recently. It tasted exactly the same as the stuff I took for my chest cold when I lived in the Subura two years ago. A mixture of cheap wine, honey, horehound, and the usual drowsifying extract derived from poppies. A common cough syrup – but not even an antidote against the congestion which seemed to be worsening every time I met Gemellus. I feared Gemellus was dying. But I thought he'd die naturally."

Julia Helena spoke up, despite Blandus' efforts to restrain her. "I don't believe Gemellus tried to poison Caligula. He didn't like his cousin, who made fun of him and generally treated him like the family idiot. But how could he have given poison to Caligula? And if he was caught in the act, why hasn't Caligula said so? Why haven't we been told more of the facts? If there are any facts?"

"Hush, darling!" said Blandus anxiously. He had spotted Macro.

Then he said quietly to me, "I'm telling you, my wife and I aren't going to linger here after this funeral is over. We'll go straight back to the farm. We've plenty of money and a beautiful little girl; we don't need the attention of great people, do we, *meum mel*?"*

"Not at all!" she said as she tried to dry her eyes.

"Messala, you should see little Rubellia Blandina. She's started to walk."

I noticed Ben-Hur approaching Claudius. So he hadn't left yet. He was carrying a large bouquet of red roses. He handed it to Claudius who gave it to an attendant for placement on the funeral bier. I waited until Ben-Hur had finished his condolences before speaking to Claudius myself.

Little Antonia, Claudius' daughter, stood with Herod's two oldest, Agrippa Junior and Berenice. Cypros had evidently been trying to comfort young Antonia for the loss of her grandmother. She was telling her about the beauty of the Elysian Fields, though they aren't part of the Jewish religion.

My brother and Lepida arrived and joined me. Barbatus said, "Your boat's been loaded, even to the Flammifer tied down on deck. Sergia and the two dogs have gone on board."

"I'll go there as soon as this is over. I've left a few people at our villa to take care of things. They'll be responsible to you. And take this paper. I had Scaurus prepare it; it gives you legal control of my new villa and other properties in Italy, to be kept in trust for my lawful heir."

This might discourage Caligula from appropriating them – or it might not.

The priests of death, of Proserpina and Venus Libitina, arrived in ceremonial robes. The bier was carried in and placed on the pyre,

---

* My honey

which wasn't yet lighted. Lady Antonia was propped up in a sitting position; they hadn't had time to make an effigy or even a face mask of her. Her hair was carefully styled, and her violet stola was neatly arranged to cover her with dignity. Coins had been attached to her closed eyelids, and one could assume that in her mouth was the special coin for Charon the ferryman of the dismal river.

Several attendants laid wreaths and flowers, including Ben-Hur's, on the bier.

Someone said, "Where's Caligula? Where's Gaius Caesar?"

Herod Agrippa appeared, robed in black. He raised his voice and explained that the Emperor was too grief-stricken to attend in person, though he could observe everything from a palace window.

A priest spoke a few traditional words of introduction, and then Claudius, the chief mourner, took over to the best of his stumbling ability. He was weeping as he spoke of his mother's noble and courageous life, in which she had suffered many bereavements, the first being her husband Drusus, a much admired general, the younger brother of Tiberius. Then there was her first son, Claudius' brother, Germanicus, a military hero, who passed away suddenly in his prime, leaving behind a widow and six children, including the present Emperor.

At this point Claudius broke down; his last words of eulogy were unintelligible. He gestured to Herod to take his place, and Herod began eloquently, praising Lady Antonia for her impeccable character, her strength in adversity, and her sympathy and generosity to others, particularly to him and his wife and children.

He then said, "Alas, she felt the limitations of increasing old age, with its general weakness and arthritic pains. She became chronically depressed and frustrated; she dreaded the onset of forgetfulness and incontinence, the humiliation of helplessness."

I thought, "He's smoothing over the facts to please Caligula."

Herod continued, "She was horrified when the Emperor discovered that his cousin Tiberius Gemellus, grandson of the late Emperor, had ungratefully attempted to poison our new Caesar, the glorious hope of our nation, whom we've joyfully hailed as if he were Germanicus returned to life, as if he were the great deliverer prophesied by the Sibyl to lead Rome into the golden age. The grief of having a treacherous grandchild surely contributed to her death. Now all of us present here must sorrow as we are about to watch her body consumed by flames. May the Gods of the Underworld welcome her honourably to the Elysian Fields."

The officiating priest took over while a small choir of assistants sang a burial hymn. The torch was now laid to the pyre under the bier. We watched as the flames rose and burned the corpse. The children looked on in scared fascination; little Antonia began to sob, and a nursemaid led her away. Cypros also removed her children, whispering to me as she passed me, "Don't say anything reckless, no matter what you think!"

I was disgusted that Herod would not only whitewash Caligula's actions but actually pretend that Gemellus was a would-be murderer, though I ought to have expected it. I knew that the boy detested Caligula. So did I! But Caligula'd offered no evidence that Gemellus had tried to poison anyone. His assertion that the cough medicine contained an antidote was absurd.

I'm sure Gratus and some of my other early instructors would have advised me to follow Herod's example, praising Caligula and blaming Gemellus. But I wasn't in the mood. If, like Mark Antony, I'd had a forum full of emotional Roman plebeians as an audience, I might have tried to stir them to indignation and even rebellion. As it was, there seemed to be nothing I could do for the memory of the unfortunate lad who had been my pupil.

Herod was looking at me, with a half shake of his head as if to warn me. Several other people gazed at me as if they expected some kind of comment.

Ben-Hur spoke up. "I came here because Claudius asked me to attend his mother's funeral. Otherwise I'd now be putting out to sea. Till today I didn't know that Gemellus had been executed. I'm puzzled that the public hasn't been given more detail. And it's strange that there's been no trial or any other formal proceedings."

I couldn't show less courage, so I also spoke my mind.

"Today I came here completely ignorant of what had happened. I didn't know of Lady Antonia's death; I was surprised to find myself at her funeral. I came to say goodbye to my former pupil before leaving for a distant rural property. Actually I feared that Gemellus would soon die a natural death. His cough medicine didn't seem to be doing him any good.

"Usually Roman citizens are given a trial – at least this has been a respected principle since the beginning of the Republic. In fact, if Gemellus had been tried before Caesar, I would willingly have testified as a character witness for the defence – for I'm astonished at the charge. Gemellus seemed to me an increasingly sickly boy, without the cunning or the energy to attempt a devious plot."

Ben-Hur boldly asked the next question of the company in general. "Did the Lady Antonia really believe that Gemellus tried to poison the Emperor?"

"No, she didn't believe it," said Julia Helena, despite her husband's warning frown. "I heard from her freedwoman that, when she asked for an explanation, she was treated with a complete absence of courtesy and respect. Caligula and Macro sneered at her."

Blandus took her arm and firmly led her out of the garden. No one interfered with them, but at the same time two of the guards came to Ben-Hur and escorted him inside. Herod shrugged and smirked as if he were about to get his way. Was Caligula ready to go after Ben-Hur because of accusations from Herod? Should I make a run for it? I decided to stay.

Someone said, "Messala, were you and Arrius accusing Caesar? We should overlook the comments of Gemellus' sister – she's naturally hysterical."

"Of course I don't presume to blame Caesar – perish the thought! One must suppose that his own sadness and the weight of his many responsibilities prevented him from offering comfort to his grandmother."

I couldn't have suppressed the irony in my voice if I'd tried. My brother looked at me as if to say, "Shut up before it's too late."

Agrippina spoke to me softly. "You don't have any chance of advancement through my brother's favour. I don't believe you ever made the least effort to flatter him. Now you ought to plan a swift exit, you and your pregnant wife. Unless you really want to join Grandmother and Gemellus!"

"Thank you, Agrippina. I was already planning to go. There's no future for me in Rome now. I wish you the safe delivery of your baby."

"I do hope for a son, in which case I'd like to give him one of my own family names, Nero."

My brother and Lepida both thought I shouldn't have said anything. Lepida said, "I just hope Caligula doesn't take it out on all of us. You should have thought of that."

Then they left. I'd have followed them and made haste with my precious team, but a guard officer named Cassius Chaerea beckoned me aside. He was a very senior centurion who'd served under Caligula's father.

"I have to tell you something. You're a friend of Arrius, aren't you? Even though he's a Jew! I noticed you two talking together at the horse fair."

"Yes, I might call him my friend. Why do you ask?"

"He's in serious trouble. Caesar and Herod have a plan. Caesar's ordering him to leave the country, but they don't intend to give him the chance. He came here today with his chariot and pair, and they think he'll try to drive from here to Puteoli, where his family are waiting for him – to sail away east.

"But before he gets there, he's supposed to have an accident with his chariot. Caesar has his own team of four and he's going driving. He wants to prove his team can beat Arrius – or whatever his real name is – and his beautiful Arabian horses."

"Caligula wants to race his *four* against Arrius' pair?"

"I heard Caesar and Herod discussing it. There's a place on the shore road to Baiae where there are very steep sides."

"Yes, I know. Is Caligula thinking he can push Arrius' team over the edge and down the slope?"

"That's the idea. Herod thinks it's rather risky, but Caligula is sure it will be fun – to kill or at least injure the Jew. Herod seems to think the fellow could cause him problems in his tetrarchy, and Caligula would like to get his hands on Arrius' riches. He especially wants his horses. The ones not destroyed by the *accident* they're planning! Oh, and he'd also like to try out Arrius' women in his bed. There's a sister as well as a wife, isn't there? And a mother with grey hair. Caligula thought she might be a little too elderly for his pleasure."

What was my Roman world coming to?

"Thanks for telling me, Cassius. I don't know what we can do, but maybe we can think of something. Where is Caesar's team right now? Is it ready to go?"

"Over there where the visitors' horses are. See, the groom is bringing the four out. Caligula intends to go after Arrius as soon as he's allowed to leave."

"Perhaps if someone could delay Caligula and give Arrius a running start?"

The funeral guests were clearing out. Ben-Hur now emerged, looking troubled. He was being escorted by guards. Behind him came Caligula and his faithful friend Herod.

Caligula was shouting at Ben-Hur. "I'm being lenient with you. Go to your property in the East and don't return. And stop calling yourself Arrius. You don't deserve a Roman name. You have no respect for our national religion, and Herod and Sanballat say you aren't even a good Jew."

Sanballat, eh? He must have turned against his former ally. He'd also persuaded Barak Ben Samuel not to marry Tirzah.

"You worship a dead carpenter who was crucified for treason, and you're in a cult that teaches people to expect the carpenter's magic return from the skies to rule the world."

Judah had turned back and started to speak, but Caligula snapped, "Don't interrupt me! I've heard that your Jewish people speak of a Messiah – Herod said that's the word – who'll transform the world. Who wants it transformed, tell me that! And you think – you stupid idiot – that the Messiah is a dead carpenter!

"Well, I tell you that you're wrong. I, Gaius Caesar, am the prophesied one! The one the Cumaean Sibyl foresaw."

He was referring to Virgil's Fourth Eclogue. The poet may have hoped Augustus would have a son.

Ben-Hur said, "Caesar, as I said before, I'm not disloyal to Rome; I'm not in a subversive organization. As a Jew, I believe in the God of my people, the Creator of all things, and I honour and worship Jesus of Nazareth as his Son, risen from the grave and living in Heaven on his Father's right hand. It may be God's will that Rome should continue to rule for a very long time, until distant lands have heard Jesus' message of God's love for all men."

Judah was good at maintaining his dignity under stress. He didn't cringe and whimper; nor did he shout hysterically in defence of his beliefs.

Caligula snarled, "How very condescending of your God to let Rome continue! Take your crazy message to those distant unknown lands you speak of. And don't come back. I warn you, if I hear from Herod that you're causing trouble in Judaea and the adjacent territories, bribing and persuading people to join your asinine cult, fomenting hostility to Rome, be assured of this – I will wipe you out – and all those close to you, including your women and three squalling brats. Now get out!"

Judah began to walk away from the Emperor, followed by the guard Cassius Chaerea. Herod, who'd remained on the edge of the Emperor's tirade, looked at me rather sadly.

Resolutely I advanced toward Caligula, who was staring at me with distaste.

"Caesar, I came here thinking to say goodbye to Gemellus before leaving for my rural property. I was surprised to learn of his death and that of his grandmother. Herod's given his account of Lady Antonia's sad decision to take her own life. What I don't understand is why you haven't shared with the public the evidence which has led you to – exterminate without trial – a child who appeared too sick to concoct and carry out a poison plot. Why haven't the Roman people been given some details?"

I could see Judah and Cassius going out of the gate. Caligula's back was turned to them as he barked at me, "Messala Secundus, I don't know why you should take the brat's death to heart so much.

One might wonder if you liked to fondle him – if he were your child catamite – except that he was never very pretty. A sickly, puking little pest."

I wondered if Caligula visualized poor young Gemellus as he spoke. His nostrils became pinched and his mouth twisted in apparent revulsion.

Caligula liked to taunt other men with accusations of effeminacy. He would humiliate old senators and respected centurions of good military reputation. And soon after becoming Emperor, he'd rounded up the band of girlish-looking male entertainers Tiberius had kept on Capri. I believe he sold them all as slaves in the mines. Yet despite his own boasted prowess with women, there were rumours that he romped with certain male actors and dancers.

I refrained from asking if Gemellus' looks had discouraged Caligula's sexual appetite. I could see teams of horses leaving the courtyard outside the gate, but I wasn't sure about Judah and his Arabian pair. Perhaps Cassius would warn him to go quickly.

Caligula continued with his public rage. "Maybe you dreamed of grooming him to be Emperor one day – and you wanted to be the influence behind the throne. Well, that dream is never going to come true. I could have you beheaded for disloyalty, but I feel some compassion for your brother. But, as of now, I'm banning you from Rome and from all the popular resort areas: Misenum, Baiae, Antium, and Circei. I don't want you delivering treasonous orations to any gatherings of your fellow citizens. How dare you criticize, how dare you demand an explanation of my executive decisions? Has it crossed your limited mind that I'm more than an Emperor? I'm a God, a descendant of the Gods Julius and Augustus."

"Of course I'm aware of your honourable descent. But it has never entered my thoughts that you yourself might be a God. I've always thought a real God would have supernatural power. Do you?"

He became red in the face, his eyes bulged, and I hoped – just for a moment – that he was about to have some kind of seizure.

Pushing the risk a little further, I said, "I recall your saying that you couldn't swim. This surprised me, as I was able to swim even when I couldn't walk. It was a source of comfort. Would you care to explain why your powers are restricted in this area?"

I wondered if I'd driven him beyond speech. He appeared to be gargling. Then our resourceful Emperor rallied.

"It's Neptune – he's my enemy, as he was to Odysseus. But some day I'll deal with him. Then I'll *walk* on the waves. Herod says those crazy Jewish cultists think their carpenter God could do that.

"As for you, I demand that you leave this area completely before sunset tomorrow. In fact, leave Italy. Go to your sheep farm in Sicily and never come back. It amuses me to think of the pride of a Messala reduced to herding sheep. Helping shear the smelly creatures, shovelling their manure! Go to the infamy you've deserved ever since that chariot-racing episode."

He evidently assumed I had few farm slaves.

"And one more command. I don't like poetry and fanciful writing. Plato was against such stuff. So I'm ordering you to refrain from scribbling trash. I'm forbidding Sosius and other publishers to make copies of your nonsensical writing. And don't write any more tales about your own heroism and that of your wretched dog! Do you understand me?"

"Oh, yes, I understand you, Caesar."

"One more thing before you go! That fellow called Quintus Arrius, though Herod says his real name is Hur something or other. Herod says you used to keep track of his activities. Depending on your answer, I might reconsider your sentence."

"Thank you for your kind offer, but I really can't oblige you, I know nothing that could be of use to you. But don't let that trouble you. Truly I'm looking forward to managing my Sicilian farm with its sheep and cattle – and pigs. However, I'll sometimes think of you – when I'm mucking out the piggery."

Had I gone too far? Just then Herod came up to Caligula and said, "Caesar, we're wasting your valuable time over Messala. Remember, we were going to take the four for a good run. I think Incitatus especially must be champing at the bit. They've missed their exercise lately."

Caligula nodded. He said to Cassius Chaerea, who had just come back, "Take Messala out of my sight."

Cassius started to accompany me. We heard Caligula scream something about arresting the insolent champion of Jews and pigs. I suspect he was referring to me.

Then I heard Herod's voice, softer, as if reasoning with him. I expect he was urging him to concentrate on the horses first and deal with his ill-mannered and ignorant subjects later. I was moderately grateful to Herod.

While Cassius and I walked toward my tethered team, Caligula and Herod made haste to his restless four. The outside trace horse on Caesar's right was the much-praised Incitatus.

Driving my newly regained cream-coloured racing mares, I followed Caligula and Herod out the gate. Had Cassius and I given Judah enough time? And would I just follow and watch? Could I, should I, try to do more? What if I could turn this into one more chariot race – and win?

CHAPTER FIFTY-THREE

WE proceeded to the road which would take us around the edge of Misenum and then on to Baiae, where I'd switch to a coastal road that would bring me to Puteoli. Barbatus had said Sergia was already aboard our ship, so I wouldn't have to stop in Baiae.

I could see Caligula on the road, but not Judah and his team. Caligula must have spotted him, though. He gave a gleeful shout and encouraged his team to put on some real speed. Herod was with him, no doubt sharing his enthusiasm.

It crossed my mind that Herod's companionship might be to Caligula's disadvantage and interfere with Caligula's concentration on his driving. I'd never watched him race, and I wanted to think that he might not be as skilled as popular report loudly proclaimed.

The road wasn't empty. There were groups of people standing on the sides watching and cheering their Emperor. "Come on, Caesar! Come on, Incitatus!" A carter with a couple of mules wasn't so pleased after Caligula's right trace horse edged him off the road halfway into a ditch. Part of his load tipped over, whereupon he swore loudly at his Emperor, who turned and shouted an obscene epithet or two. Had Caligula brought along a military escort, he'd probably have ordered the carter arrested. I observed that, when he paid attention to the angry carter, he briefly neglected his team. They swerved unnecessarily to the left, almost hitting a donkey cart going the other way.

My two mares, Gemma and Victoria, seemed to think they were back in a race of some kind. They kept trying to increase their speed from a moderate canter to a near-gallop. At first I tried to slow them down, but my own natural feelings were prompting me to let them go faster and faster. Of course they weren't fit to run seven long laps around the Circus track; they weren't young fillies these days. Still, as I became convinced that Caligula wasn't the world's best chari-oteer, I was really tempted to avenge myself for his tiresome jabs concerning my most publicized failure.

I spoke softly but clearly to my two mares. "Do you think you can catch Incitatus? Is that what you want – to pass Incitatus? Well, I guess we can try."

And I flicked the reins against their backs and called out to them, "Gemma! Victoria! Come on, let's go! Go!'"

They responded with a speed that would have done them credit in the Circus. In the old days they'd been steadied and slightly restrained when the stallions, Xanthus and Balius, were placed as yoke horses. I tried the four in different positions, to see what they would do best. Now my girls were having fun, showing what they could do once again; yet it was easy enough to guide them – straight on down the road, past Misenum and onward to Baiae, We were closing quickly on Caligula's team and I saw Herod glance back and then say something to him.

I could see Caligula laughing. Then he shouted to his team and used his lash. Looking to his left, I could make out Judah's team, still well ahead. Soon we were close to Caligula – about four lengths behind. He knew we were back there. Meanwhile, he was gaining on Judah Ben-Hur. He began shouting out insults, referring to Jewish inferiority (as he presumed) and repeating a coarse term used for female genitals. "I'll show you how a true Roman can win against the scum of the East."

I thought, "Poor Judah! I did strike his team once (a mistake) but I never attacked him with gutter language. But he'll put on speed now. Likely quite effectively!"

Judah's Arabian stallion, Aldebaran, was close to the age of my own horses; his yoke mate was probably younger and perhaps related. They wouldn't be getting tired yet. I saw that they were going faster, increasing the gap between themselves and Caligula's team.

Three pedestrians appeared in front of Caligula, and he used his whip to drive them to the shoulder, shouting, "How dare you slow me down? Stupid trash!"

Now we were coming to the place on the road where the sides were very steep. I remembered that, according to Cassius, the plan was to overtake Ben-Hur and drive him off the road and down the slope. Caligula was still talking to Herod, who looked nervous.

They saw a black dog on the right-hand side of the road. Black dogs are considered bad luck; Caligula began screaming at it. He pulled the team farther to the right and struck at the dog.

That was my chance, my open window. Really I've always liked dogs, whatever their colour. I gave the signal with the reins and shouted, "Go! Go!" Gemma and Victoria practically leaped ahead into the space on the left of Caligula's four. Herod shouted, "Caesar, pay attention!"

Caligula saw us and tried to turn his team toward us. At the same time he lashed at me, just missing me. I caught the end of his whip with my hand and gripped it for just a moment until we were all – horses and chariot – ahead of Caligula and his four winners of public races. Caligula lost hold of the whip and, as I passed him, I dropped it. Caligula could pick it up if he wanted to take the time to stop. Naturally he didn't.

Likely no one had ever presumed to pass Caligula before. His victories had been sweet and easy. Now he was more than shocked; he was outraged. He screamed several obscenities related to parts of the human body. Instead of giving all his attention to trying to catch me again, he used up valuable energy shouting his opinion of me. He accused me of carnal relations with my mother – only he used gutter terminology. He even suggested that I must have Jewish ancestry, and that my father must have been a dirty Hebrew slave. Herod was probably displeased, being part Jewish himself. Their great plan was failing.

Ben-Hur had made good use of all this distraction; he was crossing the section with the steepest sides – the area where Caligula was supposed to crowd him and his team off the road. But it was too late for Caligula to do that. He could try it with me, though. I encouraged my pair to break into a gallop.

Caligula yelled, "I'll drive my team right over you. I'll crush you and your cheap chariot and sickly nags – into bloody pieces – scattered all over!"

I visualized Caligula wriggling in the jaws of Cerberus, the three-headed guard dog of Hades, but I didn't shout at him. I kept on driving with the steep side on my right.

I felt I could keep my lead if Caligula continued to be as incompetent as he had been so far. However, I shouted to Judah, "Keep on! Don't slow down now!"

Normally I would have liked to catch up to him and pass him. But then there'd be no one between Caligula and Ben-Hur. As long as I had a long open space to let my mares run all out, showing the world their speed, I'd be all right. I didn't want anything close in front of me to slow me down. If I actually came up to Judah, I'd attempt to pull up beside him and get ahead if I could, provided Caligula was safely out of the way. If I could at least keep up with him, it would make me feel better about all the years I'd brooded over my lost race and crippled legs.

Ahead of me, at some distance on the left, a rather narrow laneway met the road. I knew it ran through the populated countryside for over a mile and then came back to the north side of Baiae, Judah obviously wanted to avoid a contest with Caligula, though he might have been tempted if he had been driving a young four-horse team. To defeat the Emperor of Rome would add to his reputation among people who knew that Quintus Arrius and Ben-Hur were the same person. However, it was more important for him to make his way to Puteoli and sail away with his family – and his horses. Therefore he swung his team to the left and crossed over into the lane, where he'd soon be out of sight.

I don't think Caligula saw this. He kept on screaming at me – that I was a filthy traitor and that he was going to catch me and my scruffy nags – my pale ghost horses – and trample us to mere mud. Just wait! Bastard! Bastard!

Then something must have happened to him, for his screeching ended, and Herod cried out, "Someone – quickly! Help Caesar!"

I didn't stop, and I didn't want to take my eyes off my team and the road to look back. Remembering how useful my armillae had been as mirrors during the boat race, I'd equipped myself with a small metal mirror tucked inside my belt. I drew it out and looked into it to see what was happening behind me. Amazing! Caligula was slumped forward against the front of his chariot, while Herod was trying to control the team. Had Caligula become the victim of an epileptic attack – like his ancestor Julius Caesar?

A couple of mounted soldiers came up from behind and helped stop the team. Probably they had been following at a distance in case something happened. Maybe Cassius had given the order.

It was too much to hope that Caligula would expire. Julius Caesar always recovered – except when the assassins surrounded him with their knives.

I continued on the main road, slowing my team a little so that they would arrive rested. I couldn't help feeling elated. Quite a few people had seen our race. It would be reported that with my team I'd come up from behind and passed the Emperor and his four champion racehorses, including Incitatus.

The road from Baiae turns northwest toward Cumae, but there's another road following the shore through a built-up community until one reaches the port of Puteoli. There I found Sergia and the two dogs waiting joyfully as they saw my chariot approaching.

I kissed Sergia and petted Tarquin and Flora. Then, after I'd praised my horses as they deserved, Nestor and another groom took them to the ship. I told Sergia the whole story, beginning with my discovery that Gemellus had been murdered at Caligula's orders. She assured me that she was extremely proud of me and was eager to sail away to Sicily where, if left alone by Caligula, we could resume the very agreeable life we'd enjoyed the previous fall.

I wondered if Judah had arrived safely. It might take him longer because of his detour in the laneway. Next to our Andromeda there was a ship with a yellow flag and the painted name – Esther. That had to be his ship.

Now two women approached us: Esther and Lady Miriam, the latter with grey hair showing under her veil. She looked a little frail but very dignified – as Lady Antonia had been. Behind them at a distance we could see Tirzah with the Hur children. A maid was holding an infant.

Lady Miriam took the lead, approaching me directly, "Messala, do you know where Judah is? What's become of him?"

Was she suspicious of me? Recalling that wolf cubs grow up to be wolves?

"Ma'am, I believe he's all right. The last time I saw him, he was turning off into a laneway that would take him around part of Baiae. I suppose he'll be here soon."

"Why didn't he take the direct road all the way – as I imagine you did? You didn't race him on the public road, did you?"

"No, Lady Miriam, we didn't race each other. It wouldn't have been like competing on a proper track. Judah left the palace some-what before I did, and I intended to drive here quite casually, giving my horses a little enjoyable exercise.

"However, Caligula and his team of four – accompanied by Herod Agrippa – had started out ahead of me. When Caligula showed that he wanted to drive at full racing speed, Judah, out of characteristic courtesy and respect for the Emperor, turned off to let Caligula spread out over the whole road – if he wished."

I knew she had always deplored my tendency to mockery, and maybe out of consideration for her past sufferings and weak heart, I should have aimed for solemn accuracy without sarcasm. But that isn't my natural style.

She asked, "What did you do? Follow behind your Emperor – out of respect?"

"Ma'am, I have no respect for Caligula. He has just murdered my young pupil, Tiberius Gemellus."

She and Esther looked shocked. "Murdered? Really murdered?"

"Yes, with no credible reason given. I questioned Caesar, and accordingly I'm now exiled to my estate in Sicily. I'm glad to go, though I'll miss my place here.

"I was following Caligula as he galloped his team along the road to Baiae, chatting to his friend Herod and yelling insults at Judah, who was still ahead of him.

"Caligula probably drives better on a race track. One must hope so. Whatever the hazards of a regular race, one doesn't expect to meet oncoming traffic. Caligula was reacting furiously to every dog, donkey, and pedestrian he saw anywhere on the road, and I simply couldn't resist the opportunity to pull left and pass him."

Sergia visibly repressed a giggle as Lady Miriam said in astonishment, "*You* came up on the *Emperor* and passed him? How did he react?"

"He kept screeching hysterically – in language unfit for your ears. We went on, and soon Judah turned off into the laneway. I was encouraging my team to keep ahead when Caesar had some kind of fit. Herod and some soldiers controlled his team. I didn't stop, so I don't know if Caligula recovered,"

"This is fantastic," said Lady Miriam. "And you didn't follow Judah into the laneway?"

"It wasn't wide enough to pass him there."

"To pass him too – as well as the Emperor?" She sounded incredulous.

"Assuming I could! But as I said, the lane was obviously too narrow. However, I thought it would be very nice, very gratifying if I could outrun Caligula all the way to Baiae."

Sergia spoke up. "My husband hasn't told you that he took a risk by delaying the Emperor with questions about Gemellus – to give your son a good head start. You're speaking as if he'd done something wrong."

Lady Miriam seemed taken aback that Sergia would speak to her in that way. Esther broke the tension by exclaiming, "There's Judah now!"

He drove up to us. "Mother, are you all right? Esther? What about the children?"

The two Hur ladies, speaking together, said the children were all fine. He kissed his wife and his mother. Tirzah now joined them; the young boy and girl came with her.

Lady Miriam was sobbing with joy. "I feared the worst for you. I imagined there was a scheme to harm you."

"There was a scheme, planned by Caligula and Herod Agrippa. To run me off the road down a steep embankment and make it look like an accident. They were foiled by Messala – and a centurion named Cassius Chaerea."

He described what had happened, beginning with his interview with Caligula at the funeral.

"Messala, I know Cassius told you what Caligula had in mind. So when you confronted him about the execution of Gemellus, you were giving me time to get a head start on Caligula."

"That was part of it. I also felt I should ask for a better explanation for his decision to kill Gemellus. However, just as I thought, Caligula sees no need to explain or justify his actions – because he thinks he has a divine right to kill anyone who gets in his way."

"And then you demonstrated that you and your ivory team could catch him and pass him. Placing yourself between me and Caligula! I suppose he kept chasing you after I turned off. I could hear him swearing."

"He had a seizure – I think. He's probably alive or someone would've brought word here. Such news would travel like the wind.

"It's true that I didn't want Caligula and Herod to harm you – but that wasn't my only motive in passing Caligula. I did it for *me* – I felt I could do it – it was the perfect moment, thanks to his essential instability. I enjoyed the whole episode – except for the murder of a lonely child who never had a fair chance."

He offered his hand, and I took it briefly.

"At times," he said, "I've almost reached out to you, but hesitated. I've wondered about your feelings. The past cast a dark shadow, yet there were times when I had to admire you. And now – you actually risked your own life to save mine!"

"You might have kept ahead of Caligula anyway. He was carrying the extra weight of Herod, and he was easily distracted. But I couldn't persuade myself to stay behind him and do nothing. Part of my motivation was simple pride. Anyway, I'm glad you came through safely."

We didn't have much time for speeches of reconciliation. Caligula might send soldiers after us, though neither of us had broken any law. The Hurs planned to go to Antioch. I was exiled to my estate in Sicily where I hoped to enjoy a quiet life with an adequate income from orchards and sheep.

Sergia said she was happy about it. Some women might have reproached me for taking risks that could affect them, but I believe her support was heartfelt.

"Would you ever travel to the East? Syria perhaps?" That was Judah's question.

"I'd like to see something of Greece. Or take a westward journey. If Caligula pursues me – as he might – the East could be a last resort."

Though I had, to a degree, regained my old friend, the lands where he was most praised as a hero didn't appeal to me.

We wished each other a safe voyage and a good life wherever we wound up living. The horses had been taken along the wharf to the gangplank. Sergia and I followed them.

The sun was low in the sky by the time we settled ourselves on deck, our dogs resting at our feet. The anchor was lifted, and we felt ourselves moving away from the shore.

Looking ahead toward the blinding sunlight on the waves, we could see the Hur ship already heading toward the wide sea outside the Bay. They might remain in sight for a little while.

CHAPTER FIFTY-FOUR

W E'VE lived in Sicily more than three years, except for a couple of trips to the Greek islands in our yacht, Andromeda. On the whole we've been fairly prosperous.

I'd wondered if Caligula would pursue us. In a way it was fortunate that all this hostility from him came at the beginning of his reign, while he was still interested in enjoying the good opinion of the public, or at least those members of the public who didn't know him well. Although Caligula had the means of indulging his rages to the full, for a while he tried to preserve his public image: Caesar the generous, the friend of the people, the forgiving monarch who destroyed all the papers incriminating those who'd cooperated with Sejanus and Tiberius to destroy his mother and brothers. As far as I know, Gemellus is Caligula's first murder victim. I doubt he'll be the last. The willingness to kill grows on a person.

I think of our entry to the port of Messana. The late afternoon sun shone down on us as we stood under the shelter of our scarlet awning and enjoyed the sea breeze. Sergia's dark sunlit curls framed her face with its large dark-blue eyes and pink-flushed cheeks. I thought how much more beautiful she was than Agrippina and the other palace ladies.

We reached the harbour and proceeded to the town house for a late meal hastily prepared by the surprised housekeeper. Next day we finished unloading our boat. We then sent many of our belongings to the farm by cart.

I'd taken away my money, some in a very large money draft, some in gold. I decided to distribute my wealth among several unconnected banks, one of which belonged to Simonides. I thought about the beautiful house we'd left behind with its gardens and fountains. Ever since we'd come back to it in the winter after my brief appointment as quaestor, it had been a work of art in joyous progress which Sergia and I had shared. Just as Augustus Caesar had found his true mate in Livia Drusilla, I felt a growing bond of understanding allied to passion for this lovely, intelligent woman, who was strong and spirited yet sensitive.

We remained in the town house until after Sergia gave birth, three market intervals after our arrival. I spent an anxious night fearing the worst and remembering Iras' painful abortion in our miserable Subura apartment. How revolted I had been by the sounds, the smells, and the sight of blood and dung. I had cleared out as best I could and left her to get through the gruesome business alone. Here I'd offered to stay by Sergia, but she told me she would be uncomfortable with me there. The maids – old Anna and a new woman called Penelope – were knowledgeable enough to help her. So I paced around the peristylum, stopping to ask for news every so often, and wondering if the Gods would be cruel enough to deprive me of my wife and child.

It was still just dark enough to see the last stars in the pre-dawn sky when Anna came and told me I had a healthy son.

"What about Sergia?"

"She's all right, just tired. You can come and see them both."

First Anna brought my son to me and placed him at my feet. Picking him up, I acknowledged paternity. Then I kissed Sergia and told her how relieved I was. I'd been truly worried.

We agreed that our baby would bear the name Marcus, like all the eldest sons of my family. He thrived and Sergia was soon energetic and happy. She didn't look for a wet nurse but said, "I have plenty of milk, and I enjoy holding him to my heart."

We went out to the farm in time to enjoy the vintage festival. Sergia sat beside me while I drove the greys. Our saddle horses and my two racing mares had been sent on ahead to pasture. Marcus travelled in a little basket or in his mother's arms while the dogs found places at our feet. We travelled early in the morning because the noon sun in Sicily is very hot, dominating the cloudless blazing blue sky above the yellow-brown fields.

We made ourselves comfortable in the farm villa and were rather glad to be away from the urban sounds of Messana, even though our house there was located on a rise with trees and had a garden and a pasture field. I found plenty to do supervising the property: the management of the vineyards, the flocks of sheep distributed in several locations, and the piggery to the left of the main barns. How revolted my Jewish friends and acquaintances would have been at the sight and smell of that. Even Herod Agrippa, who ate pork with his Roman friends, was disgusted by pigs. Once I'd warned him that there was a risk of worms and disease in insufficiently cooked pork.

A letter came from Barbatus. He wrote that Herod had left for his tetrarchy. Would he keep trying to bring down his uncle Herod Antipas and take from him his territories of Galilee and Perea?

Barbatus said that, after our departure, Caligula had gone to bed and rested for a few days. They said he'd had a touch of sunstroke and didn't remember some things very clearly. Now, back in action, he'd had Macro executed. Macro, his ally! Caligula informed the public that Macro had tried to manipulate him and that he'd used his wife to seduce him when he was young and inexperienced. This sounded about as plausible as the story that Gemellus' cough medicine had contained an antidote to poison. I suspected that Macro might have known too much. If he assisted Caligula in finishing off Tiberius, we'll never find out.

Caligula is extremely restless and has a serious sleep problem. He wakes in the night after about three hours of sleep. In his fury at both Ben-Hur and me, he seemed deranged. What if this state of affairs becomes permanent? Reading my brother's letter, I wondered – could he be deposed and confined as a lunatic? On Pandateria or somewhere like it?

Meanwhile my Sicilian home wasn't a bad place to be. When I remembered being in a wheelchair in a slum apartment at the dubious mercy of Iras, I had to be thankful for my present blessings.

When we parted at the Puteoli docks, Judah and I agreed to inform each other of our safe arrival at our destinations. We wouldn't correspond very frequently; there was a risk of our letters being intercepted by agents of Caligula or Herod. I didn't mention the fate of a letter I'd once written to Gratus when I discovered that my former friend, now a resolute enemy, was in Antioch. I hoped that Judah had burned it long ago. I certainly didn't want him to reread it. I'd come across as callous and flippant.

In a brief letter I announced our son's birth and our so-far safe and pleasant life on our Sicilian property. I also mentioned that Herod had left for his tetrarchy and that Macro had been executed. Not being sure where the Hurs would go first, I sent it in care of Simonides in Antioch.

I invested some of my money in local land but kept enough for improvements to my residence such as an ornamental pool in the garden. I decided to enlarge and redecorate the indoor bath. I might even try building some houses. I'd become interested in planning attractive villas such as the one I'd sadly had to leave behind, and it would be a shame to waste my new knowledge.

Even if Caligula didn't fully remember our last encounter, he wouldn't like to think that I could be enjoying my exile. I suggested to my brother that the public, including the Emperor, if he inquired, might be encouraged to imagine my struggle with agricultural squalor. Perhaps Barbatus could make a few allusions to animal husbandry, with its somewhat disagreeable responsibilities – and the tendency of some of my fields to become muddy after a good fall rainstorm.

In his reply, Barbatus warned me that the local volcano could be a real setback. He thought I should make offerings to Vulcan, the lame smith, or to his spouse, Venus. Though we sometimes offer Venus a little incense in appreciation, we didn't sacrifice any animals to Vulcan. We sold pigs and sheep, but we didn't feel like offering their lives to the Gods. We don't really believe the stories about them in the same way the Jews believe their accounts of Moses parting the Red Sea and Elijah summoning fire from Heaven. But we do consider that there are forces in the universe associated with the functions we assign to our Gods, and we try to keep these forces working for us, or at least not against us.

In October we heard that Caligula was desperately ill and that the doctors thought he would die. My own thought was, "What a blessing! Now if only the Republic could be restored!"

The general response was disappointing to me and to those who shared my feeling concerning the old Republic with its values, and its opportunities for distinction, especially for men of good birth and ability. Both in Messana and in Italy, there were demonstrations of mourning, as if we were about to lose a great treasure. They mourned for a fair-haired, eloquent, imperial charioteer who cared for the common people and showered them with largesse as well as constant entertainment. As his private life was not yet made public, he was considered a better and more interesting Emperor than Rome had been used to.

Frantic adoration of Caligula was carried to the point of hysteria; some people even proclaimed that they would sacrifice their own lives if only the Gods would spare their beloved Gaius Caesar Caligula. One emotional man, who believed he was dying in any case, asked me if I was willing to lay down my life for Caesar. Surprised, I said bluntly, "Not at all! I've been close to dying twice; I'm glad I survived, and I want to live comfortably with my wife and child, the Gods willing!"

About that time I heard from Judah. They had gone on to Jerusalem briefly. It was now a comparatively quiet place. Pilate had some time ago been replaced by another procurator. Saul had gone home to his native Tarsus.

The Hurs moved to Antioch because of Simonides, though they

kept their residence in Jerusalem. In Antioch they purchased a spacious house with a high protective wall around a garden. Judah's horses were stabled and pastured within easy reach and had servants watching over them.

They were glad to hear that we had a son and that Caligula had so far not troubled us.

Judah didn't say much about his involvement in the Christian religion, though he knew I was somewhat familiar with his beliefs. I'd heard him declare his faith before Caligula and I believed he was being honest when he said that he and his fellow believers had no scheme for rebellion against Rome. However, he'd evidently decided not to push, or to preach at me to convert me from the religion of my ancestors. He may have hoped I'd ask questions and thus open the way.

I also heard from time to time about the developing cult of the Christians. A centurion named Cornelius, whom I'd known in Caesarea, surprised me by becoming a convert. He'd already been a believer in one God – the Jews would call him a God-fearer – but he'd never submitted to the full Jewish conversion process which includes circumcision. Nevertheless, the Christian leaders admitted Cornelius and his family to their circle without requiring him to give up his foreskin.

I respected Cornelius. He was the primus pilus* of his legion, a man known for his valour and honour. I gathered that he saw some good in me, but feared I was being guided the wrong way by Gratus. He didn't seem to me to be a man who would go in for undignified religious practices.

Herod had once told me that Christians sometimes spoke in a strange language. Was it a language of heaven? Or something like the babble that comes from the priestess of the Delphic Oracle, babble that the priests interpret into whatever words seem to fit the situation. I thought of asking Judah if he himself had ever spoken in a supernatural language.

I didn't want to lose my old friend again by mocking his beliefs,

*The top-ranking centurion of a legion

and I had a good opinion of Cornelius. Still, I looked for rational explanations of the signs and wonders that were associated with Jesus. I thought of the one time I'd seen him. Had I just imagined the look of perception and strange compassion when it seemed that our eyes had met? Could I have been the recipient of a delayed but real healing?

Letters from Rome brought disturbing news. Caligula had physically recovered, but something had definitely happened to his already precarious mental stability. He was demanding to be hailed as a God who had risen from the edge of death through his divine powers. He was arranging to have his own image placed in all religious shrines and temples beside the Gods who were already there. He required everyone to take an oath of loyalty. To my relief, the governor and his aides never approached me about taking this oath, perhaps because I was usually out of town, either at the farm or at a new building project.

In December Agrippina gave birth to a son whom she wanted to name Nero, but the infant was given the name Lucius Domitius Ahenobarbus. My brother wrote that she was, very uncharacteristically, in tears when Caligula urged her to call the baby Claudius, after awkward Uncle Claudius. Ahenobarbus, swollen with dropsy and very near his end, commented that any child of his by Agrippina was likely to have a rotten disposition and be a menace to society. He could, in his glumly sober moments, see his own glaring faults.

During the winter Caligula's favourite sister, Drusilla, died, perhaps of pneumonia. Winter in Rome can be very damp and chilly. Caligula's mourning was extreme. He drove south, took ship to Sicily, stormed around the governor's residence in Messana (the governor was absent) and apparently paid no attention to his personal hygiene. After a few days of wild grief, he sailed back to Italy, without having shaved or cut his hair. I can't say whether he washed during his stay in Messana, but they tell me he looked as if he hadn't bothered.

Afterwards he made a couple of erratic attempts at marriage. Twice he appropriated another man's wife but kept the woman only a short time. Then he became attracted to an older woman who was neither beautiful nor well-born: Caesonia, a baker's wife with three daughters! She may have projected a mixture of motherliness and sensuality. In any case, she became his favourite and was soon pregnant with his child.

I designed a couple of houses and built them on land I'd bought south of the city. Each time I planned the layout and structure myself and worked with a builder to erect them. It was an outlet for my craving to achieve something. Sergia made good suggestions: she provided a woman's insight into what was practical and desirable in a modern house.

I enjoyed all my horses. The greys were a good steady carriage team. Riding Atalanta and Sheba, Sergia and I joined a few mounted hunts for wolves and foxes. Algol liked to jump ditches and hedges, and he was growing large enough to carry a man easily for a long ride. Gemma and Victoria often pulled my chariot for exciting local drives, though I didn't hazard them or myself in a race. Still, they had a reputation, though not of my doing. I never told anyone of my race with Caligula. Nevertheless, word got around.

Of course we kept hearing about Caligula. My brother soon regretted purchasing a villa in Antium, though it was very attractive. Unfortunately Caligula had also become fond of Antium and even spoke of making it his capital instead of Rome. A ridiculous idea!

He continued arranging expensive spectacles. In the Misenum area, for example, he collected merchant vessels, anchored them in two lines about three miles long, all the way from Baiae to Puteoli, boarded them over, and covered them with earth. For three days he drove back and forth on his new bridge, elaborately costumed, followed by a procession of his choosing. He invited a number of spectators to try out the bridge but then mischievously had them pushed into the water, where many of them drowned. He thought this was very funny.

When I heard of this, I could imagine Caligula's glee had he succeeded in his plan to push Judah and his horses off the road and down the steep embankment. He'd have laughed himself sick, congratulating himself on his victory, even though it would be hard to determine what he imagined he'd won.

It wasn't enough to be recognized as a God while still walking the earth; he had to overshadow the other deities. He had the heads removed from many famous statues of deities, then had his own sculptured head attached to the marble trunks. Surprisingly, none of the Gods retaliated. Instead of being struck down by lightning, he was left to prosper.

CHAPTER FIFTY-FIVE

CALIGULA established a shrine containing his life-sized golden image, which priests dressed each day in clothes identical to whatever he was wearing. He had one-sided conversations with the other Gods, whispering romantic suggestions to the Moon Goddess or threatening Jupiter, his rival for the chief place in the heavenly hierarchy. Cautious lest his letters to me should be intercepted, Barbatus never came right out and said he thought Caligula was crazy. Romans were afraid to speak out and criticize the Emperor. Remembering the old stories of our ancestors who repeatedly resisted dictatorships that had outlasted the emergencies for which they were permitted, and recalling dictators like Cincinnatus, who'd considered it a point of honour not to cling to power a day longer than it took him to deal with a great problem, I felt embarrassed. Where was our pride? Why were none of us prepared to stand up to Caligula and firmly remove him?

He freely insulted both senators and knights. He ordered some high officials to dress in short linen tunics like servants and run for miles beside his chariot, then wait on him at his dining couch. He had persons killed, for reasons best known to himself, and later announced that they'd committed suicide. During gladiatorial shows on a hot day he sometimes ordered the canopies removed from the public stands and prohibited everyone from leaving. He also had respectable but somewhat disabled citizens of the lowest class arrested and compelled to fight duels in the arena. It amused him now and then to close the public granaries and let people go hungry. Several times he compelled parents to attend their sons' executions, even providing a litter for one invalid father. His love of torturing seemed to increase day by day.

Caesonia bore his daughter, whom he named Julia Drusilla. He displayed the baby to all the Goddesses before entrusting her to Minerva, whom he called on to watch over the child's education. He now took Caesonia as his legal wife.

Caligula decided to revisit Sicily. We were glad he chose to go to Syracuse rather than Messana. He busied himself rebuilding Syracuse's old walls and decrepit temples, which took him some time. He held a festival of Athenian Games, and avoided displaying his well-known love of cruelty. He seemed to be showing respect for Greek culture.

We didn't go to Syracuse. We made sure the Andromeda was seaworthy and sailed to Greece, where we saw the site of the Olympics and the shrine of the Delphic Oracle. When we came back, Mount Aetna was rumbling and smoking. I even said to Sergia, "We'd better move the animals to whatever feed lots we can procure near the town, closer to the sea."

We worried about the effect on our vineyards even if the lava didn't come all the way to our farmlands. However, after sending our animals, along with the shepherds and agricultural workers, to places of shelter – as we hoped – we decided it would be best to go to the town house even though it might mean running into Caligula if he left Syracuse to pay a visit to Messana.

We were scarcely settled in the town house with our staff when word came that Caligula and his retinue were approaching Messana where they would stay in the governor's residence. I hoped we wouldn't be asked to furnish billets for some of the imperial party.

At the same time the volcano was rumbling and flames were shooting up amidst a cloud of dark smoke. Soon lava would start rolling down the slope. I thought of the work we had put into the farm projects. Would it all be destroyed and the villa and barns buried under a burning river? Barbatus had told me to pray to Vulcan to avert a crisis. Pray to Vulcan – really? Vulcan was imaginary; he wouldn't do a damned thing!

I was with Sergia on the east patio, keeping an eye on our toddler while observing the flames rising from the smoky crater. A servant came to us anxiously and said, "Sir, the news is that lava is coming down the mountain; it may reach the farms and small towns nearby."

Would we have to get the Andromeda to take us somewhere? Would the captain and crew be available at short notice? Where would we go? And what about our horses, at present pastured back of the house?

Achates, our butler, came to us. He said, "The Emperor has arrived at the governor's residence. He's worried about the eruption, so much so that he's considering taking ship right away, and not staying for a banquet."

"Indeed!" I kept my joy under reasonable control, but couldn't repress my tendency to sarcastic irony.

"What a grievous loss to Messana! After so much preparation!"

The quaestor and his assistants had gone to a nearby feedlot and bought several of my young pigs for the imperial dinner.

As it happened, Caligula was persuaded to dine first. As the triclinium of the palace opened on a courtyard garden with an eastern exposure, he was able to eat his lavish meal while watching tongues of flame against a black sky – which would normally have been the sunlit blue of late afternoon. He was fascinated, but uneasy, and dispensed with most of the planned entertainment. He'd already announced that he wouldn't stay for the games and chariot races scheduled for the next day. Most people were saying that these events might have to be cancelled anyway.

His departure may have pleased the Gods – if they care! The volcano settled down without much more damage to property in its vicinity. We soon had reports from our rural villa and surrounding land. Our house and barns were unharmed, and our grass wasn't scorched except for some slopes close to the mountain. Our animals were all safe with their guardians in feedlots and shelters near the town, but they'd been temporarily forced into crowded conditions.

We imagined Caligula's ship carrying him and his entourage back to Italy, probably to Antium, his new pleasure resort. It would be like him to tell his servile courtiers that he'd personally stopped the volcanic eruption with his words of divine command.

The villagers who had remained on and around my land were, as far as I could find out, all alive and well, as were those of my slaves who wanted to stay on the property. However, the smoke caused some people to suffer from lingering sore throats and coughs. Our dogs had some breathing problems which soon cleared up.

Sergia agreed with me that we didn't owe Vulcan's temple anything, either money or sacrificial animals. Indeed, despite our customs, we suspected that most animal sacrifices were simply wasteful and useless. She asked me about the customs of the Jews, and I said they sacrificed many animals to their one God. Their viewpoint is rather different from ours: we give, expecting something in return, usually something specific; the Jews are principally concerned with the idea of sin and atonement through shed blood. I've never understood this.

I've heard that Jewish followers of Jesus may be denied certain privileges of the Jerusalem Temple. And maybe Judah can't take a seat in their Sanhedrin, which would otherwise have been given to him as the Prince of Hur, holding high rank among his people. Even his sacrifices might not be accepted – I don't know about that. However, as he believes that Jesus himself was the blood atonement for all his sins, he may see no further need to keep offering lambs, doves, and other creatures from the acceptable kosher list. Perhaps he's never done anything that would be counted as sin. Probably taking my wheel off wouldn't be considered a sin at all. I'm never going to ask.

We decided that, if there was a benevolent God – or a family of

Gods – who out of concern for men and other living creatures had checked the course of the overflowing lava, it might be well for us to use some money helping those who had actually suffered sickness and loss before the volcano stopped erupting. So we were – within our means – rather generous.

CHAPTER FIFTY-SIX

CALIGULA went on being cruel. One day he ordered a senator stabbed in the House, then dragged through the streets and torn to pieces. Finally his severed limbs and entrails were dumped at the feet of the gleeful Emperor. He likes to kill by torture, and his favourite order, "Make him feel that he's dying," has become famous.

His temper is frequently out of control. At one race, at which the people cheered for the wrong team, he screamed, "I wish you Romans had only one neck!" At a public dinner he had the executioners bring in a slave condemned for stealing some silver. The punishment ordered by Caligula was that they were to cut off the man's hands, tie them around his neck so that they hung down before him, and then take him for a tour of the dining tables. I haven't been told if any of the guests dared become sick to the stomach.

I still feel fortunate to be here and not there. In good marine weather I sail my Flammifer. Often Sergia comes with me, sharing my excitement in catching a large fish difficult to land.

The production and marketing of agricultural items are safely within the list of activities permitted by law to persons of senatorial rank – to which I still feel entitled. Building on the land also counts as a respectable senatorial occupation; accordingly I've designed and supervised the construction of several modest villas. Local people have begun to recognize my skill, and some families from Rome, owning land in Sicily, have chosen to settle here in view of present conditions back in Italy. Among them is my old friend Quadratus; he complains that Caligula is openly hostile to lawyers and that it is very difficult for a person to get a fair hearing if his case goes as far as the Emperor.

Herod Agrippa has now gained the territories of his uncle Herod Antipas. Antipas' wife Herodias urged her husband to go to Rome and win favour as her clever brother Agrippa had done. Little did they know what awaited them. Antipas found himself grilled concerning his collection of military equipment. Caligula decided he was plotting rebellion and took his land and titles away from him, giving them instead to his loyal friend, Herod Agrippa.

Rome tends to be lenient with the Herods they depose – in case we might need them again, I suppose. Therefore Herod Antipas wasn't imprisoned or executed, just exiled to Lugdunum* in Gaul. The winters there will be chilly and damp, very different from what he's been used to in Galilee and Perea. Caligula tried to be nice to Herodias, the angry sister of his dearest friend; he told her she needn't forfeit her dowry although he was taking her husband's money, as much as he could find of it. He said she could stay in Rome.

However, Herodias stood by her man; she declared she'd married Antipas for both good times and bad, and now she'd go with him to Lugdunum. Thank you very much, Caesar! So now the two are living in a villa in a Gallic town by a major river. They don't have any local authority. For social life they must cultivate the more prosperous natives and the retired Roman army veterans who have chosen to settle there.

Caligula is running short of money, and it isn't surprising that men of wealth are often accused and convicted of a serious offence, leading to the confiscating of their fortunes and property. He has

* Now Lyon on the Rhone

already seized all my Italian property that he found out about. He has taken the farm north of Pompeii. Warned by Barbatus, our freedman Africanus, his wife Maria, and several of my rural slaves have arrived here. Africanus and Maria can go where they like, but they didn't trust Caligula to respect their liberty, and they brought with them the good workers they thought I'd be sorry to lose.

He has also taken my villa by the sea, and sold it to my Uncle Velleius, who always thought the land should be his. Velleius has written to Sergia to say how much he likes the place, and he has conceded that I have good taste. He even hinted that Sergia might get it back in his will. Yet Caligula could go after everything and everybody. I have stocked the Andromeda in case we need to get away in a hurry. We've taken several trips just to get the use of it.

Suspecting that exiled Romans might be praying for his death, Caligula sent agents to their places of exile to assassinate them. Yes, he tried to get me; it just happened that at the time Sergia and I, with little Marcus, were sailing around some of the Greek islands. We shivered when, on returning, we learned that Caligula's agents had been looking for us at the farm. Fortunately he hadn't given them instructions to apprehend any slaves or confiscate our property. Africanus told me that – quite by accident – a large bull broke free and ran loose as Caligula's small band of killers tried to ride up to the front door. They left in nervous haste. I wonder if Caligula will try again.

He's raised a lot of money by conducting auctions, sometimes of used theatrical props, sometimes of items belonging to the Caesar family. For example, he auctioned off the furniture, jewellery, and slaves of his two sisters, Agrippina and Julilla, after he had charged them with adultery and conspiracy to have him killed. He sentenced them to be imprisoned on small islands. The charge could've been true, as I don't believe Agrippina loved her crazy brother. On the other hand, Caligula now saw enemies everywhere.

Agrippina is not one to give up. I can imagine her, angry and resolute to survive, somehow managing to come back in triumph. I wonder if she will win against the odds.

Her baby son, Lucius Domitius Ahenobarbus, is in the care of his aunt, Domitia Lepida, my sister-in-law. My brother wrote that Messalina wasn't pleased at the presence of a baby for her mother to fuss over. Especially as Messalina doesn't like Agrippina.

The accusation of adultery was ludicrous in view of another of Caligula's fund-raising projects: he'd compelled his sisters and a number of ladies from noble families to participate in a temporary brothel held in the Rome palace for several special nights. He laughed at the suggestion that any wife was pure. To him sexual excesses were natural for everyone.

There are high income taxes even for humble citizens. I pay a large tax on the income I report to the local quaestor. All goods and services are taxed. Caligula had begun with a full treasury and had run through it all.

He neglected his administrative obligations, letting favourite freedmen take care of boring details. Instead, he loved to parade around in costumes – especially that of Venus, complete with an elaborate wig. Sometimes he gave private concerts and theatrical recitations. It was considered an honour to be invited to these performances.

Caligula decided to try a German expedition, to show his military genius. He led troops a short distance into Germany, but it wasn't a real war. He retreated as soon as someone suggested that German snipers and warriors might be hidden in the forest waiting to pounce on him. Years ago, Quintilius Varus lost three legions and his life that way. A truly embarrassing excursion for Rome! We still haven't recovered the last of the three looted regimental eagles.

At the River Rhone, in Gaul, Caligula became impatient because certain supply wagons hadn't caught up with him. He threw his uncle Claudius into the river; however, Claudius, though awkward on land, was very well able to swim and to float, so he reached shore. Sanballat, being praefectus fabrum, as he had once been for Consul Maxentius' troops in Syria, was not so fortunate this time. Caligula impulsively had him beheaded. I really can't say I'm saddened.

Caesar went to the edge of the channel between the mainland

and Britain and appeared to be planning an invasion. Adminius, the son of one of the British kings, came to him and surrendered, having been banished by his father. Caligula accepted him, and sent word to Rome that the island of Britain had surrendered to him. Then, instead of actually going to Britain – which might have given him a disagreeable surprise – he ordered his troops to gather seashells. He promised each soldier four gold pieces and began the erection of a lighthouse on the edge of the channel.

By this time our daughter, Valeria Miranda, was born. She has blue eyes like Sergia, and her hair is somewhat lighter than that of Marcus. They are only about eighteen months apart in age, so they'll be able to play together.

After Caligula returned to Rome he staged a triumph in which, to supplement the shortage of genuine captives, he used tall Gallic men with their hair dyed red or yellow. They were supposed to pretend to be German prisoners.

Though attached to Caesonia, the mother of his little daughter, he seldom misses an opportunity to have conspicuous sexual activity with an attractive woman, particularly when it's a matter of imposing his power on a reluctant married couple afraid to refuse him. Yet he also engages in some homosexual pleasures, especially with the famous actor Mnestor, on whom he bestows slobbering public kisses. My brother didn't tell me these things – he's careful in his letters – but other people frequently bring news to Messana.

He still adores his horse Incitatus. The stallion continues to win races and has been rewarded by a life of luxury: a marble stable, an ivory stall, purple blankets, and a jewelled collar. He also has a house, furniture, and slaves to attend to guests invited in his name. Although it seems someone may have invented the story that Caligula was giving Incitatus the consulship.

Actually, Caligula's excessive affection for his horse is the only one of his eccentricities I have any sympathy with. I'm very much attached to my own dogs and horses. Algol, my young stallion, is tall, strong, and very fast. He canters and gallops magnificently in a hunting field, and he has his mother's pacing gait when he isn't galloping. I haven't tried very hard to train him as a chariot horse, but I like to think he could outrun Incitatus in a cross-country race, maybe jumping a few fences and ditches on the way.

Maybe he could even have surpassed Aldebaran in his prime – but that I'll never know.

CHAPTER FIFTY-SEVEN

I received a letter full of distress from my brother. He said that Caligula had demanded that Messalina, now just fifteen, be delivered to him. Barbatus could not think of a way to refuse him. He thought of declaring that she was confined to bed with a heavy menstrual period. However Lepida said, "Don't be a fool. He has spies who'll soon tell him there's nothing wrong with her. On the other hand, if he really takes a liking to her, he might dump Caesonia and marry her. She has both beauty and noble birth. It could be a chance for us."

Barbatus wrote, "I was ready to divorce the stupid woman. I should have done it years ago – she has no morals. She was quite willing to prostitute our child to a dragon. It would have been best if we'd all got in the Nereid and sailed away. But I lacked the strength of will to deal with matters as a Roman father should. To my shame, Messalina was escorted to Caligula."

He was remembering the story of the father of Virginia in the days of the Republic. The powerful Appius Claudius had ordered the girl to be handed over to him. Instead, Virginius stabbed his daughter in the heart and then led a successful revolt against the lecherous Claudius.

Whether or not Caligula deflowered Valeria Messalina, he decided not to keep her youthful charms for himself. Instead he offered her in marriage to his uncle Claudius, nearly fifty years old, and a frequent figure of fun because of his awkwardness, and his general repulsiveness, as well as his unattractive gobbling at the table, followed by severe gastrointestinal cramps. What a husband for a nubile young girl who dreamt of a handsome virile lover!

Barbatus admitted feeling ill as he wrote. He could not help thinking that Messalina would inevitably cuckold Claudius and bring shame to the family name. He was feeling chest pains which extended to his left arm and his jaw. Even more than a divorce, he needed a doctor.

A market interval later Scaurus the lawyer sent me a letter informing me that Barbatus had died of heart failure. There'd been a funeral, the body had been cremated, and his will had been read. Naturally there was a large bequest to Caligula and a generous dowry for Messalina. As the next male of our family line, I should have come into considerable money and property; however, the will ignored me because I was an exile. My inheritance would likely be claimed by the Emperor.

It's lucky that Caligula didn't go further. He could have made a grab for my Sicilian possessions including Barbatus' house in Messana, which had been made over to me much earlier.

Scaurus did have some good news for me, though. Barbatus had written a money draft – one million sesterces – and given it to Scaurus before he died. As instructed, Scaurus had put it into his own account and then written another draft for me. Furthermore, Scaurus transferred to me the deed to a good farm with a decent villa in the area of Nola, farther north than my former property. Barbatus wanted me to have some part of his estate since I am his true male heir.

My annual income is about four hundred thousand sesterces now, which makes me eligible to remain in the equestrian order if I should ever be permitted to return to Italy. This won't happen during Caligula's lifetime.

I composed a letter to Claudius and Messalina combining congratulations on their marriage and condolences on the death of her father, my brother. Naturally I regretted that I'd been unable to attend either the marriage or the funeral.

The months passed quickly. Sergia and I were comfortable and happy with our two children. There was some sadness when my old dog, Tarquin, passed away in his sleep. We buried him in a corner of the garden, and I gave him a marble marker with his name and the words Semper Fidelis, as I had with Argus, the dog of my childhood. Little Flora didn't live much longer; she seemed to miss him. She also has a gravestone.

Fortunately, Tarquin had sired several puppies during his time in Sicily, and we have raised two of them as special pets for the children.

Less than a year after Messalina's marriage, she gave birth to a daughter named Octavia and a little while later we heard that she was pregnant again.

One fall day, to my astonishment, Herod Agrippa stopped in Messana. After sending an ingratiating message, he came to my house with Cypros and the children. We put our large guest suite at their disposal. During my questorship it had been used by the visiting governor before his own residence was renovated.

Over dinner, Herod said, "I'm going to do my very best to dissuade Caesar from putting his statue in our Temple in Jerusalem, the last place in the world for it. The Jews in Judaea, as well as my own tetrarchies, have contributed money for my project, and I'm hoping you will too. But I wasn't able to get anything from Ben-Hur. He doesn't trust me an inch."

"Can you wonder? You and Caligula were going to run him off the road and down a sharp incline. As if the two of you wanted him killed."

"Aren't you exaggerating a bit? Caligula really just wanted to see if he could defeat Ben-Hur and his team. That was all."

"A team of four, winners in several public contests, running on a highway in competition with a mere pair? Granted one of them,

Aldebaran, had been a very good stallion in his day. And Caligula thought that would reflect well on him?"

"He thought he owed it to Rome – to take back a victory from a Jew. That contest in Antioch was remembered as a national humiliation. Which reminds me – why in Hell did *you* get involved?"

"You have to ask? Listen! If any honour was retrieved for Rome in that ridiculous road race, *I* did it! Caligula killed Gemellus, my pupil. A sad sick child! Furthermore, I was very tired of Caligula's continual comments on the inglorious end of my racing career. I'd been lucky enough to regain two of my original team, and they were eager to win one more race. And we did!"

"I won't say that to Caligula. I'm still your friend. I suppose part of your reward is that your childhood friend has become your friend again. David and Jonathan once more! You saved his life."

"Our last parting was as friends. I take it you've seen him recently. How are he and his family?"

"Lady Miriam died about a month ago in Jerusalem. She was buried there. It's a pity Prince Ithamar perished at sea, or she could have been buried with him.

"The family went back to Antioch, since they have a house there. Tirzah is finally married, quite happily. Of course, Cypros always thought she had her eye secretly on you for a while. The husband she eventually chose will surprise you. She's married to a Roman centurion, a Christian convert. Did you ever meet Cornelius, the primus pilus of the all-Italian legion stationed in Caesarea?"

"I know him and I heard that he became a Christian without having to undergo circumcision. I truly hope his marriage to Tirzah will work out well."

We returned to the topic of his project. "Are you planning to hand Caligula a bribe? I understand he needs money. I'm not very willing to contribute; he's taken my Italian property, and, in addition, I pay high taxes."

I didn't like the idea of giving Caligula more money to waste.

"What I have in mind is subtler. I'm planning the most gorgeous costly banquet in Caesar's honour. The finest wines, the rarest delicacies, prepared by expert chefs. Serving plates and cups of gold. Soft music and showers of rose petals. Songs and dances by famous performers, including Caesar's favourite, Mnestor. And, at the proper moment, may the Lord God of Israel help me, Caesar will be telling me, with sentimental tears in his eyes, how touched he is by my lavish expression of true love and loyalty. That's when I'll try to convince him that I have his good at heart when I implore him not to waste his beautiful statue in a Jewish temple for people to sneer at – people whose culture has made them constitutionally unable to appreciate either his manifest greatness or the artistic skill which produced a noble work of art. Now do wish me the best!"

"I sincerely wish you success, Herod."

"Would you care to make a donation?"

I thought it unwise to tell him that I'd rather pay to keep Caligula's statue out of *all* places of worship. Instead I said, "If you like this wine from my vineyards, I could let you take some to Italy with you."

Having tasted our potent unwatered wine, Herod was pleased to carry away six amphorae*. He said he thought it could be served with the dessert.

Recently Sempronius, the local quaestor, informed me that Herod's banquet achieved its purpose. Caligula agreed not to waste his statue on such a mean setting as the Temple in Jerusalem. He wrote to the governor Petronius that if the statue was already in the Temple, it might as well be left there, but if not, it would be better to keep it in storage until he decided what to do with it. Good work, Herod Agrippa! Now the Judaean leaders should be well-disposed toward him.

Herod's still in Italy, befriending Caligula, who doesn't want him to leave. Eventually he'll return to his territories, and maybe he'll be handed the rule of Judaea as well. Understandably he will consider himself the saviour of his country – a national hero – and he'll expect to be welcomed accordingly. But he won't be any more sympathetic toward the Christians, who call Jesus the Christ and believe him to

---

*An amphora is a large container used for wine or grain.

be the Saviour not only of Israel but of humanity. I've heard from several sources that they've been accepting Gentile converts without expecting them to be circumcised or to keep the extensive body of Jewish law. At present there's some disagreement among them about this change in the rules.

I thought of my old acquaintance, Cornelius, a kindly man of unquestionable rectitude, who sometimes gave me worried looks, though he never failed to be courteous. He's some years older than Tirzah, indeed about ten years older than I am, but hardly past his prime. He's a fine healthy soldier who has children by his late wife. I can believe that he'll be very kind to Tirzah and that she will be fond of his son and daughter, now about ten or twelve.

I still don't want to give up my Roman Gods, even though they are either completely imaginary or quite different from the stories about them. In his writings, Lucretius didn't deny the existence of the Gods, but he declared they were remote supernatural beings unconcerned with mankind and its numerous problems. I'm also reluctant to discard our Lares and Penates, our family guardians.

Yet I found myself defending the Christians to Herod.

He said, "Messala, they're widely feared as a weird cult. It's said they practise secret orgies called love feasts. There are rumours of all kinds of sexual couplings – and cannibal ceremonies in which human flesh and blood are consumed in memory of the death of their leader. I'm just telling you what many people say."

"Herod, I can't believe the Hurs would ever be caught up in things like that. Even when I hated Judah and wanted to wipe him out, I could never have imagined him abandoning his refinement and dignity to such a degree as that. I know the kind of upbringing he had. It even affected me. Partly because of it, there are things I won't do."

"Really? Will I soon hear of your becoming one of them? You seem averse to worshipping the Emperor."

"I can't and won't worship Caligula. Tiberius didn't ask for deification, and though Romans burn incense to Augustus' genius, we didn't call him a God during his mortal life. And it's Roman custom that, in our triumphs, the victorious general is reminded – by a slave – that he's only a man."

"Dear me – how that must dampen his spirits!"

He asked me, "What do you think the Christians do at their love feasts? Do they make love?"

"In public? No, they wouldn't – at least the people I know certainly wouldn't. As for what they eat, I have an idea. You know that at your Jewish seders everything on the table is a symbol of something. Could it be that, in the Christian feasts, certain foods on the table are symbols of something they believe in? Even – the wounded body and shed blood of their Christ could be represented by bread and wine. Does that seem possible?"

The next time I get around to writing to Judah, I might ask.

Certain leaders in Jerusalem will encourage Herod to take strong measures against the Christians. And he will if he gets a chance.

Near the end of January, I received news of a shocking event that I'd hoped would take place much sooner. Ever since Caligula had Gemellus murdered, I've been thinking, "Brutus, Cassius, where are you now that Rome needs you?" In fact, another Cassius, my old friend Cassius Chaerea, a senior centurion of the Emperor's guard, had a leading role in what happened.

Caligula had habitually belittled Cassius Chaerea, often accusing him of effeminacy. Finally Cassius had had enough and conspired with several Praetorian Guards. They waited for their opportunity. Caligula had been enjoying a theatrical show: a very bloody play about the robber Laureolus. Suddenly the conspirators attacked, slashing at him with their swords. He fell, shouting, "I'm still alive," so they stabbed him to death as he lay on the ground, even thrusting a sword into his genitals. After that they rampaged through the palace, killing without much discrimination. They found Caesonia and her little Drusilla and slaughtered them both, swinging the child through the air and dashing her head against a wall.

Claudius hid behind a curtain, where he was found by a soldier. By this time the main body of the Praetorian Guards, including Caligula's special German guards, was in control of the palace.

While Romans of noble birth would have liked the chance to meet together and proclaim the restored Republic, the soldiers simply wanted a new Emperor in charge. They hoisted Claudius up on their shoulders, evidently believing he would do. Meanwhile Herod Agrippa managed to talk to the right people among the guards and senators and assisted in establishing order with Claudius as the figurehead. He also arranged for a quiet, but decent, funeral for Caligula. Claudius later had the leading assassins, including Cassius Chaerea, beheaded. I'm sorry about that part and the sad fates of Caesonia and Drusilla.

I wonder what will happen next. Can Claudius Caesar remain long in power even with Herod Agrippa guiding him and my niece, Messalina, as his beautiful imperial consort? She is expecting another baby very soon. Presumably Claudius, not Caligula, is the father.

Unless we're officially invited to return to Italy, we'll continue to regard this as our home. Sergia says she has no yearning for Rome's high society, and we've become very fond of our Sicilian property. Although sometime I'd really like to see Rome again!

CHAPTER FIFTY-EIGHT

I T is late May, and we're going back to Italy. Claudius has sent for us. We have our own yacht, Andromeda, and I've rented an additional boat for our horses. Carrying out my late brother's written wishes, which Caligula never knew about, Claudius and Messalina are giving me the family mansion in Rome as well as some more farmland in which Barbatus never took an interest. That means some hilly land near Rome as well as the farm near Nola, for which I have regularly been receiving rent since my brother died. Like the place near Pompeii which Caligula sold, it has orange trees and a vineyard. Barbatus' villa at Baiae was left to an elderly cousin who has already moved in. Messalina is keeping considerable property, administered by stewards, and she owns the villa Barbatus had at Antium. She's letting her mother live there, though that will change if Lepida ever remarries. Lepida also has a house of her own in Rome.

And there has been more good news. Caligula had sold my house by the sea to Uncle Velleius, who always thought it should belong to him. But now he has died of chest congestion and, at the last, he chose to will the house and land to Sergia on condition that his wife, Sergia's grandmother, Lavinia, may continue to live there, sharing the house with us when we wish to live there too. That seems a fair enough arrangement. Sergia is fond of her grandmother, who is a good-natured lady. She wrote to Sergia that she is relieved not to have to live in the same house as her son's bossy wife.

Claudius wrote that my experience as a quaestor should qualify me for a Senate seat if I meet the financial standard. Evaluating all my property and income, I think I'm entitled to a back-bench seat for a start. If I thought I could afford the expense of campaigning – paying for public games, distributing largesse in the right quarters, and so on, I might go for a higher magistracy which would give me more clout as a senator. But for the present, I can just be glad about the advancement that has come to me.

We're taking all our favourite horses. Sheba and Atalanta are still good mares for riding. Algol, now a mature stallion, is coming too. He's been bred a couple of times and has sired healthy colts, one of them by Gemma, my racehorse. She and her stall mate, Victoria, are still a delight to drive. We are also taking the grey team. Today I've been getting most of the animals on the cargo boat which will sail this evening and should reach Ostia before we do. The grooms accompanying the horses will unload them and take them to the capacious stable near our family mansion. The grey pair will go with us on the Andromeda, so that they can be hitched to our carriage when we drive to Rome.

The children are excited but concerned about the things they have to leave behind. The farm here has been their main home, more than the town house. They are sad that we can't take with us all the farm animals, especially two cats and their new litters, and a mother dog with four puppies. We are taking two dogs, both descended from Tarquin. Rex, Tarquin's son, is a mature sober dog, just now lying beside me as I work at my desk. Felix, from a different litter, still almost a puppy, is the children's playmate.

Africanus and Maria aren't coming with us; they want to stay on the Sicilian farm which Africanus manages very well. He's used his savings to buy some land of his own. We'll miss them. Philip will be on hand in Rome. He's a free man and has chosen to work for me.

Sergia and I have discussed the changes in Rome under the new government. Claudius is doing better than most people expected, and he has the support of the troops. Herod Agrippa stood by him until he got fairly well established, then he left for his territory, which now includes Judaea. Claudius agreed with him that he was the best person to deal with the unrest among the Jews who had felt greatly threatened by the plan to put Caligula's statue in the Temple. So it seems we won't be seeing Herod.

Though Herod appears to Romans as a Jew of liberal ideas, that doesn't mean he will allow the Prince of Hur to practise and promote a radical variant of the Jewish religion, which is reaching out to non-Jews with unprecedented permissiveness regarding departure from the Law of Moses. Judaism already has some divisions: the Pharisees and Sadducees disagree about the resurrection of the dead and the existence of spirits, for example. But the Christian religion is a more shocking deviation, a threat to its own Jewish roots. Judah certainly won't be able to stay comfortably in Jerusalem if Herod goes there. Of course, there is Antioch; they'd be near Simonides. I also know that his Italian property, apparently sold when he left, is mainly in the possession of surrogate owners who pay him rent. This arrangement was to keep Caligula from grabbing his property. He could decide to come back to it; Claudius has nothing against him.

Messalina gave birth to a son soon after Claudius assumed power. The infant has been given a lot of names from the Julio-Claudian family, but is especially called Germanicus, after Claudius' heroic brother. It has been remarked that, if Claudius ever sent an army to Britain, he could call his son Britannicus.

Is it possible that Claudius, who has always been unfit for military service, secretly dreams of conquest? He accompanied Caligula on his ridiculous expedition to Germany and his journey to the coast facing Britain; perhaps he thinks of restoring Rome's honour by defeating enemies and winning new territories. He has read a lot of military history and probably has some practical ideas. If he has the sense to work with capable generals, he might accomplish something. Rome's prestige needs a boost.

The bureaucracy of Rome is, more than ever before, being managed by very competent freedmen who have won Claudius' confidence: men who treat Claudius with respect and sympathy, not like the well-born Romans who were accustomed to look down on him as a clumsy failure and a disappointment to his class. They really shouldn't expect Claudius to shower favours on them.

We aren't sure how our return to our homeland will turn out. Everything could go wrong for Claudius, and Messalina is nothing like Livia, the wife Augustus Caesar called the partner of his labours. Messalina is impertinent enough to claim such a role but, even though she is very clever, she could plunge herself and all those who are close to her into a spectacular disaster. As I remember her, she believes she can and should have everything she wants.

We said goodbye to the farm yesterday and travelled to the town house. We hope to get back here from time to time. Now Miranda and Marcus are romping in the garden with Felix, their enthusiastic bouncing dog. I can hear Sergia giving final instructions to the gardener, who will remain here along with some other staff members.

Tomorrow evening we'll board the Andromeda. There will be days at sea, peaceful days, we hope. And at last, arrival in Rome, to which I'll be returning with honour.

CPSIA information can be obtained at www.ICGtesting.com
Printed in the USA
LVOW011156110112

263248LV00004B/7/P